THE
COVEN
TENDENCY

Also by Zoe Hana Mikuta

Off With Their Heads

THE
COVEN
TENDENCY

ZOE HANA MIKUTA

HYPERION

Los Angeles   New York

All rights reserved. Published by Hyperion, an imprint of Buena Vista
Books, Inc. No part of this book may be reproduced or transmitted
in any form or by any means, electronic or mechanical, including
photocopying, recording, or by any information storage and retrieval
system, without written permission from the publisher. For information
address Hyperion, 7 Hudson Square, New York, New York 10013.

First Edition, April 2025
1 3 5 7 9 10 8 6 4 2
FAC-004510-25016
Printed in the United States of America

This book is set in Minister Std/Adobe Systems
Designed by Zareen H. Johnson
Stock images: rabbits with star 2253614783/Shutterstock,
rabbits with flowers 2242164729/Shutterstock

Library of Congress Cataloging-in-Publication Data
Names: Mikuta, Zoe Hana, 2000– author.
Title: The coven tendency / Zoe Hana Mikuta.
Description: First edition. • Los Angeles ; New York : Hyperion, 2025. •
    Audience term: Teenagers • Audience: Ages 12–18. • Audience:
    Grades 7–9. • Summary: A coven of lovesick teen witches, whose
    magic causes mental erosion and apocalyptic destruction, searches
    for a cure to their violent and addictive tendencies.
Identifiers: LCCN 2024026563 • ISBN 9781368099196 (hardcover)
    • ISBN 9781368099202 (ebook)
Subjects: CYAC: Witches—Fiction. • Magic—Fiction. • Horror stories. •
    LCGFT: Witch fiction. • Horror fiction. • Novels.
Classification: LCC PZ7.1.M5554 Co 2025 • DDC [Fic]—dc23
LC record available at https://lccn.loc.gov/2024026563

Reinforced binding

Visit www.HyperionTeens.com

I am going to put death in all their food and watch them die.

—SHIRLEY JACKSON, *We Have Always Lived in the Castle*

For the lovesick ones.
Get well soon.

THERE WAS A LETTER. Not the first one, Ellis believes. Yes, they'd already been older. Limbs spilling longer down longer sleeves. Baby fat lifting, pushing the lines of their skin past the threshold of being adorable into the great grand cold room of being gorgeous. By then—already in the habit of passing prohibited letters between them, since Ellis had known to find this one, someplace. Perhaps behind an oil painting in the Museum mansion, or under a rock beside the electric fence, or buried off one of the paths stamped to dust under hundreds of dirty tourists' shoes. Retrieved, so then the lines of Clover's handwriting sprawled in his palm, ink and strokes bold, pretending to be unafraid.

You need to be careful, because Vanity is in love with you.

Ellis knew this already, of course. He'd been finding the creatures, small and dead, she'd slipped into his coat pockets, because she cared about him so.

He thinks often of brushing their delicate bodies with his hands, the initial jump in his chest, gracing that absence. The first one he'd crushed. He'd felt so bad about it that he had what Clover might call an "episode" and snapped the neck of the gardener's dog. But the dog was mean, anyway—was what he would've said if Clover asked—he'd prepared such explanation, since she would probably smell its death on him.

Ah, so, then—was this at the point all three of them had ventured to be physically around each other? Must be. Yes, because how else could Vanity have her hands in his pockets, leaving the little bodies? How else could he know her hair smelled like the soft sweet rot of flowers melded with the sharper edge of formaldehyde?

So Vanity must've already been killing him at that point. How many times? Well, obviously, about as many times as she brought him back.

The details were all fuzzy, but dying had that effect. Sometimes.

Either way, really and truly—what a horrible idea it'd all been.

PROLOGUE

"WHAT IS IT, THEN? A girl in a cage?"

Monroe looked away from her. This wasn't right. The room was dirty and cramped. The walls whitewashed, streaked. Fuzzy yellow light stained the crowd—common people in common clothes. Monroe pulled his shoulders inward; he was sweating through his university uniform. He wished he hadn't worn his nicest coat.

"A witch," answered his roommate. He side-eyed Monroe to witness his shock and his awe and found neither. Monroe had heard, of course, that the City still had witches, even before embarking here on his study abroad. But the setting lacked ceremony—it was stale enough to sap his excitement.

When his roommate, a boy called Riley—born and raised in the City—said he would take Monroe out to see an underground show, he'd advertised the exhibition as exclusive, avant-garde. Monroe had made the mistake of reminiscing about the secret expos found in his home country of Miyeon, where the spaces were hidden behind moving alley-way walls or beneath cobblestones that gave way with a press, but were always, at the very least, pleasantly habitable. Walls draped in silk and floors warmed in skins, caterers toting silver trays. A host who was, at minimum, well-dressed and engaging, despite the flat, predatory cold one might glimpse pacing behind their eyes.

The man who'd taken their money at the entrance—a door merely shoved at the back of one of the dock clubs—had done so with greasy fingers and a grunt, waving them into the already-packed unfurnished room.

Monroe looked back over the teeming mass toward the stage and the imprisoned girl upon it. Tucked up into one corner of her cage. She was standing and unmoving. She seemed to be approaching middle age, but could be made to look younger if she weren't so filthy, perhaps if her dark, wild hair were brushed or if she were given a brightening-and-tightening skin treatment. Monroe could not see the color of her eyes nor where they were fixed. Her mouth seemed to be moving.

"She's almost pretty," he said.

"The nutcases always are." His roommate laughed. "Even you aren't rich enough to take a turn with her."

Monroe likely was, actually, but he didn't say it.

"I heard they bite," said Riley.

"What?"

"Witches. They like to bite."

"I'm sure the cage doesn't help cultivate their manners."

Monroe wished to return to the dorms. No, he wished to return to his country. The City was dirty and it lacked class. It often touted itself as an amalgamation of cultures, but the smear of it rendered it cultureless. He was studying here on his family's considerable dime to gather a larger view of the world and stake out a potential business opportunity for the Athalia corporation overseas. He'd been thrilled for the creative freedom.

But nothing here impressed him. People here only looked for the quick, cheap thrills—the nightclubs were unoriginal, the tourist attractions were tacky, and the chunk of gorgeous greenery that held the university campus, sprawled on the east side of the island, lacked the air of academia. It was often dotted with strung-out students, its forest rumored to be littered with junkies who didn't pay tuition but liked the greenery for their trips. Even their drugs, Monroe thought, were unoriginal. When was he going to see something *different*?

Riley continued on as if Monroe hadn't spoken. "Not that you could wring good conversation out of them, anyway. They prefer to talk to themselves, talk to the walls. It's theorized that their magic has a psychedelic effect. They're built to be naturally drugging themselves all the time. And—oh! Also—you're not supposed to keep them around each other, either. Apparently they can get rather infatuated. Obsessive."

Riley was talking too much. Monroe's eyes rested on the statue-still girl. "Lovesick."

"Yes, yes. Very, very sick. I've heard it's not *real* love, though; they often end up bludgeoning each other, which, I mean, I've gone out with plenty of crazy girls and you can't beat that kind of passion."

Monroe was barely listening to him. "They have purging machines for that, in my country. Not here?"

"Machines to purge love?"

Monroe rolled his eyes. "To purge magic. From decades ago, when we had witches."

"Did that do the trick?"

"Perhaps. Not well enough to let any of them live, apparently." He gave a thoughtful hum. "Booming business, killing witches."

"Oh, no, we don't kill them here. They go into the Sanatorium. It's more humane."

"Well, we are quite a cold, clinical people, across the east ocean, aren't we?"

Riley blinked, then forced a self-deprecating laugh. "Such a nasty stereotype, and—the Sanatorium, yes, there or bought into pockets like this—so not *so* humane—I mean, I understand the logic of calling for an extermination, they do threaten industrialization and progress—"

"Yes, Riley, witches sprout up in populations as a reaction to metropolis. Nature's last stand, its immune system response. I know the theory." Usually, Monroe relished the look on Cityfolks' faces when they attempted to overexplain things to the foreigner, only to realize he, too, had been living on the same planet, learning the same history—likely in a more formidable education system—but he was busy shifting forward.

"Hey, wait—"

"I'm getting a closer look."

Riley clamped a hand on his shoulder. "You'll want to stay back here."

"Let go of me."

"I'm trying to help you. You're wearing an awfully nice coat." The hand became a slung arm tugging his neck. Monroe could smell the liquor in Riley's whiskers. "Don't be like that. Relax. It's about to begin."

As if summoned by his words, a door Monroe hadn't noticed that lay beyond the cage swung open. Two men ambled out of it, their arms weighed with something massive and unmoving. It was only when they hoisted it onto the stage that Monroe recognized it as a dead deer. The *thud* of its body against the planks was a sudden pressure against his sternum, there, gone.

The witch's head jerked toward it.

The deer's antlers, bone bleached under the light, extended like fingers toward the crowd. Anticipation roused in Monroe's chest, juxtaposing his body that stilled around it. Waiting. The room had quieted.

One of the men who'd brought the deer stepped forward. He prodded at the girl though the bars with something resembling a fire poker. "To the flesh, witch."

"The flesh . . ." Her voice was daydream soft. She wiped at her mouth with the back of her wrist. Took a step toward the deer.

6

The man had gone on to introduce the act, but Monroe was barely listening. "...possessing arcane knowledge..."

He watched as she neared the bars of the cage. Monroe knew what was about to happen—he'd read the textbooks and watched the documentaries—knew that the witches with reign over bodily natures could perform necromancy. What else could be expected to happen now, with her creeping for the dead mass, other than resurrection? And so he waited for the deer's inevitable twitching, the lifting of its great head. Once it got to its knees, would it attempt to flee for the crowd, alive briefly, miraculously, just to be shot dead again by one of the weighty pistols set at the men's sides? It seemed, already, so redundant.

The witch knelt. The bottoms of her feet shone black.

"...one overexposed to an aspect of nature, so, purely, a freak of nature..."

When she reached one hand toward the deer, its body—

Reached back—

"...death itself!"

Monroe, at first, did believe that someone was trapped inside the deer.

That it was their hand scraping against the inner wall of its stomach, their fingers that he could see pushing outward, straining for the girl, but, no. By now its outline was too distinct not to have split the deer's soft downy underbelly; he could see the rounded nodes of the wrist, the points of nails, the softened angle of a thumb.

The witch's own hand grasped the likeness of a hand risen from the deer's side. Holding each other, deer and girl, like parent and child crossing a busy street.

Then the witch was laughing, the wispiness of her voice evaporated; she was laughing like it was the only way she could breathe, like she was trying to drink in the world.

Now she wrenched, all gentleness gone. Her teeth glinting, she was pulling and pulling and pulling, and there was the sound of bones breaking and the wet glide of flesh rupturing and from the point the deer's

7

hand was grasping hers, its skin began to thin. Delicate layers of tissue tearing back, fleeing itself. The gleam of the exposed raw shining as a bracelet, iridescent in the light.

The witch took a step back, and, in one smooth motion, broke the belly skin and pulled the deer inside out.

It was a clean, silken removal.

The spine broke downward toward its stomach, massive head swinging up as if braying. Antlers clattering up the stage. Yet there was no loose spilling of guts—the girl still had the deer's hand in hers, and the hand was attached to an arm that was attached to the shape of a human body. Sliding out of the deer's side. Bald and raw and without eyes, nose and mouth one smooth sweep of flesh, yet Monroe swore—some expression ghosted there, indistinguishable from anguish or ecstasy. He drank in the sleek, anthropomorphic outline, bulbous with the congealed amalgamation of bone and organ and muscle, and diagnosed silently, A sculpture, then . . .

The form existed only up to half its torso, which now smoothed up against the bars at the insistence of the witch's tugging, bloodying the metal.

The witch let out a choked noise, halfway between a sob and a gasp of relief. She pressed herself to the side of the cage and hugged the half body through the barrier. It did not move, of course; it was the deer and the deer was not alive. It was flesh and nothing more.

The front row of the crowd had revved back, splattered with blood. Their complaints spiked air that reeked of rot; there was no ventilation or even a window to open. The miracle had been performed in a throwaway pit of the City; the patrons were already restless, disgusted and departing. The witch was inconsolable and there would be no more magic; up on the stage, Monroe stood stock-still as the onlookers flowed out around him, ignoring Riley's tugging on his arm. One of the men, the one with the fire poker, had ambled back up. He was feeding something to the girl—pills from a box.

She took them on a flash of pink tongue, greedily.

Her head rolled. Her cheek pressing back against that of the form's. Monroe couldn't catch the whole of what she was saying: "—not there—"

"Come on, Athalia—"

"What did they just give her?"

"What?" Riley squinted. "Oh, I don't know, some of the good stuff. You know." He seemed anxious to keep talking in case Monroe, in fact, did know; though, of course, not anxious enough *not* to keep talking. "Knock 'em off their natural highs into ones that won't—be as unruly, like—"

"Cause an apocalypse." He observed Riley's stricken expression out of the corner of his eye. "Oh, I was just being glib." It was an old superstition, an omen, that a witch meant an apocalypse forthcoming. But really. Whenever nature flashed warning colors, warmer summers and witches in the population, what really happened? Nothing too concerning, with a little more sunscreen and some Machines.

Such a crude solution, the drugs in her system temporary, chemical bandaging—yet apparently viable. The witch was pleasantly docile as she cradled her sculpture, whispered to it.

"What do you think it feels like?" Monroe murmured, transfixed.

"What?"

"What she's feeling."

"High?"

He couldn't help but smile, small and sad, at Riley's lack of clarity. "The whole world."

The room had already mostly cleared, making more blatant the dullness of the space. It was hardly Riley's fault, missing the weight of what was happening here. Of course people here would barely be able to gauge they were seeing something spectacular, seeing it in a cave like this.

"Go on without me."

He didn't wait to hear Riley's protest. Monroe approached the stage. Each step felt like he was approaching his future. His fate. When he got close enough to see the whites of her eyes, he murmured, "It reaches for you. The flesh."

He was surprised when she responded to him.

"Can't get it out of my head. It's my head."

Her voice came clear and sure. She was stating a fact and giving him a smile and then it was gone; her expression slackened and she was murmuring after another thought.

And so was Monroe.

He was his father's son, unearthing undervalued markets. And here it was before him. No, spurring within him—the common man's fascination with lunacy. To see someone so there, standing before you, and, certainly, not there . . . and if the someone were cleaner and classically prettier—

Monroe's gaze traced where the sculpture's torso fused to the deer. One of the proprietors had noticed him now, barking at him to stay away. Monroe would not be moved. Was it really so easy as the drugs, to make such a creature so docile? So that, when Monroe reached forward, he was able to lay his hand upon the bars, and then upon the girl herself? The blood crawling silently across the stage, staining his coat as he held her petite wrist, barely there. She, too, barely there, did not seem to register his touch. He could snap her so easily. How could a human body possess such arcane depths without disintegrating? No wonder her mind was so scrambled, and yet what a wonder she was. . . .

"It won't be like this anymore," Monroe whispered. The vacant eyes of the deer lolled at him, at once absent and sentinel. "It'll be a sensation."

FRESH

I

I

THEN

IT WAS FINE, whenever Cadence Adams found her daughters giggling and spasming on the carpet. Their pale, bony ankles elevated. Jabbing the air. A mouse had probably died in the wall again, that seemed to be happening more and more. More and more she was finding them on the carpets, or on the kitchen tile, or in the garden dirt, frothing at their cupid's-bow mouths. Sometimes Cadence did hover to make sure they weren't biting off their tongues, but mostly she just let them be. Her eldest, Vanity, could see, through the fluttering of her own eyelids, a flip-book impression of her mother, the glass of red wine perpetually affixed to her hand swirling as she walked away.

Often, of course, it was more of a stumbling, which Vanity would recall later with embarrassment, once the episode passed and her head knit back together and she retrieved the parts of herself that had scattered away. The ability to be embarrassed. How to talk. What her name was.

Once or twice, it was really a mouse in the wall. But usually, death was not tucked away behind the wallpaper, and instead lay hidden within softer confines—the head of a rat or the thimble-body of a sparrow occupying the pockets of Vanity's corduroy pants.

It was Ro, her twin, who would gift Vanity such items, small animals that hadn't run fast enough and she'd bludgeoned with a rock or a stolen spade from the gardener's shed.

Ro had always known, somehow, that the proximity to little corpses, the empty forms, was a sensation unlike any other. Vanity could only describe it as a spiritual experience that went off like a bomb in her chest. Shrapnel, and warmth.

She wasn't quite sure what Ro—Arrogance, really, but Ro often enough—was attempting to teach her. Perhaps her younger sister was just trying to get her high. Vanity didn't mind. It made her feel loved, when other people wanted to make her feel good. And Vanity's love for Ro, in turn, was the only one she possessed that didn't make her feel completely crazy.

𖤘

There were, of course, the other ones that Vanity possessed.

"I'm in love with him. And with her. I know, because I keep dreaming of killing them both." Vanity had felt the need to tell Ro this multiple times, usually after seeing Ellis and Clover at the weekly Museum Parties. Her sister was her confidant and would never tell nor warn another soul. Not that anyone *needed* to be warned. Vanity had herself under control.

"What happens next?" her sister sometimes asked, when she didn't feel like mocking. When she felt, perhaps, like nudging.

"I don't know."

"Lying."

"I'm not," Vanity lied.

"You are. You know me like you're me. I know you like I'm you. You're a liar. I'm a liar."

"Then you tell me," spat Vanity. Then she gathered up her knobby knees to her chest and said quieter, "What happens next, in the dream." Arrogance smiled. "You bring them back."

✒

But Vanity didn't know how to bring them back. Not yet.

She didn't know magic like Ro knew magic, like how Ro had known that rot and emptiness carried along such a sweet aura. Had known it'd make them fuzzy and light until the sensation spilled over and caused them to lose the feeling in their legs, froth at their berry-red mouths when they hit the earth. And Ro, of course, wasn't supposed to know, and so lived another secret between them. Vanity was her confidant, too.

All their arcane instincts were supposed to have been purged from them after being placed in the Machine as infants. As the eldest daughter, Vanity's necromancy and other flesh magic—that strange muscle memory the women of the Adams family were born with—would be returned to her by the Museum when their mother was unable to continue performing the rites for their patrons. When Cadence was dead or too old and unappealing or whatever. Then Vanity would be reinserted into the Machine, to reclaim her magic, to take her mother's place as the Museum's necromantic Spectacle.

But Ro already knew how to do magic, had somehow retained her arcane instincts past the ordeal of the Machine. This had been revealed to Vanity the morning after one of the Parties, ~~the first time she had caught Ellis and Clover passing notes.~~

~~Heartbreak was a peculiar sensation. Vanity hadn't entirely believed she would live through the night, because when she crawled into bed she was sure her heart had already burst and it was bleeding into her stomach; she couldn't expect to live for very long with such internal conditions. But then~~ Ro had shaken her awake, saying there was about to be a dead cat in the garden and it would do Vanity some good to go and see it. How do you know it's going to be dead, Vanity had asked, but Ro only went out to the garden and Vanity had followed her. Then Ro coaxed the gardener's cat with that rock blatantly sitting in the palm of her hand. Then Ro cracked it against the small head with a dull, blunt sound, one hit and it was over, and Vanity hadn't screamed, she hadn't even asked a question. Ro was her mirror and Vanity thought, I'd also kill something if I knew I could bring it back. I'd also do something horrible if I knew I could fix it. Ro killing the cat was no different than Vanity killing the cat. But when Vanity's head stopped fraying in the euphoric burst of the death, she wasn't sure how she knew this was true.

Dirt. Churning in her mouth from where her face had pressed against the cool earth.

And past the mess of it in her eyelashes, she saw the cat stand up.

It'd hobbled off unevenly into the night, tail stiff, white coat crusted in its own blood. The resurrection had made the flowers bowing in the garden around them look a bit like they were melting. Fat, iridescent globs.

As always after there was magic, there was a blank spot. Her memory curled away from her like paper lit aflame. Vanity didn't mind the break from herself. Besides. Her sister was next to her. Her sister kept her safe.

And she knew it was all Ro reassuring her. Ro telling her that this awkward, raw state wouldn't last forever. They were better than that. When Vanity was frustrated and fearful and already sick with the thought of the future, Ro simply fluttered the veil between the living and the dead and said, See. I love you. I'll show you why we don't need to be embarrassed, lovestruck, and blushing creatures. We are something else entirely. Even you, even now. There are some parts they couldn't take away.

Vanity wasn't scared of her sister, of course not. Even though she did take care pulling her hair out of the drain every time she took a bath, on the off-chance Ro might do magic with it, might not be able to help herself.

Like the other two families of witches who belonged to Monroe and his Museum, the Adams women lived in a large cottage that crouched at the start of the tree line. Theirs sat between the other two homes, all three of them spitting pathways from their front doors that ran back up the hill to the Museum in chunky veins of cobblestone. Both cottages and pathways lay well spaced, a design that reminded Vanity of the middle three fingers of a hand wrenched apart. Each home had a white picket fence and a small plot of lawn with peonies and chrysanthemum and lavender. Each had a sign stamped to the front gate—NO FLASHBULB PHOTOGRAPHY. Each had dark green shingles on a slanted roof. Each was constructed on three sides out of black brick and on one side out of a thick slab of one-way mirror.

There was some privacy, on the second floor—Vanity and Ro's bedroom and the bathroom and the hall adjoining them, with its walls made fully of brick instead of looking glass. But everywhere else, foyer and stairwell and kitchen and parlor and their mother's bedroom—its flowered wallpaper protecting the rest of the second story from the prying eyes—prying eyes.

It became a common practice, whenever Vanity was in love too much, for Ro to rise in the night to hide the teeny, diced-up forms—wrapped in napkins—because death cured such anxieties—for her to find. The sound of Ro walking around the cottage floating down into Vanity's dreams. All day Vanity would be looking at their hiding spots out of the corner of her eye, but she knew enough to suspend her search until nightfall, when the Museum's visitors trickled on home and stopped flattening the grasses past the fence.

She could always locate the presents quickly. Something in her just knew how to pull her focus in such a way where she could notice how the areas around these small instances of rot always looked a little strange. A mouse behind the loose vent of the kitchen making its grates quiver, its paint curl upward off the walls. That one day when she saw the sofa aging, threads sweating, the whole image leaking like a pipe had burst behind it, and Vanity's hand sank between the cushions to graze the velvet-soft ears of a rabbit.

Vanity could reach out and find the true, physical reality; her hands remained unstained by paint she'd witnessed smearing, feeling shelves and furniture intact and book spines solid and steady, even as they wavered before her eyes. The women of her family saw things other people didn't see. And when she was older and it was time for her to go back into the Machine, she'd come out able to do things other people weren't able to do.

"Because," Cadence Adams had deigned to explain one winter day to her daughters, "there is something wrong with us. There is something horribly, horribly wrong with us. Tell me you understand."

"We understand."

As always, the television blared before them with a gooey, romantic soap opera. Two lovers stroking their plasticky horses on a spinning carousel. The woman opening her mouth and saying with absolute certainty, "Oh, I could go around and around forever, with you by my side...."

Cadence had been on the sofa opposite theirs; she'd long made it clear her daughters would find no comfort in her, that there would be no stroking of their hair or cradling of their small hands as they were given this horrible secret of their existence. Vanity and Ro tucked up against one another instead. They often tried to slot their ribs together like the hidden gears of a clock.

Existing on the mirror side of the one-way mirror, every room in the house was doubled in size, every one of its objects multiplied by two. There were four sofas and four electric lamps and two black-and-white TVs, now flickering with two advertisements—Monroe standing in front of the Museum, slowly opening his hand, revealing a teeny square of paper. Beneath him scrolled the familiar words: STRESSED ABOUT METROPOLIS? TAKE *WORLD*. BE ONE WITH NATURE. BE NATURAL.

There were, then, of course, due to the reflecting wall, double the girls. Two Cadences and two Vanitys and two Ros, though it also looked like there could be four Vanitys or, Vanity supposed, four Ros. Cadences wrung their hands—an impressive maneuver, around the stem of their wineglasses—peering at all of her daughters suspiciously. The advertisement droned on at a cheerful, quicker clip—AVAILABLE OVER THE COUNTER, LOCALLY SOURCED: HARVESTED STRAIGHT FROM THE ARCANE BEINGS AT YOUR LOCAL SANATORIUM! TESTED ONE HUNDRED PERCENT MAGIC-FREE TO AVOID PSYCHOLOGICAL EROSION. SIDE EFFECTS MAY VARY. CONSULT YOUR DOCTOR IF—

"Have you ever had a really good psychedelic experience?" Cadence was saying. "Don't do too much magic, when you know how to do magic again, or being alive will feel too excellent like that, you know, human beings weren't meant to feel so complete, like that, you'll go mental, being so happy. Too much magic will make your thoughts run very fast and get very loud, you'll spiral and everything will seem like a grand idea, and then you might start an apocalypse." Then she must've remembered her Vanity and Ro were around five years old at the time, so she clarified, "That's not good. If you were being bad and started an apocalypse, then there's nothing your mother could do, Monroe Athalia would have to take you away to the Sanatorium and Mother could do nothing. That would be so sad."

Then she'd lit one of her long cigarettes and said she had to go lie down.

Vanity's interactions with Cadence had always been possessed of this bizarre quality. She'd ramble in a troubled and distant way about their supernatural affliction and couldn't answer any questions about anything without getting more troubled and more distant, and then she'd smoke and have to go to sleep. Now, freshly eighteen, Vanity did sometimes wish Cadence were dead, she was so depressing. But then when Cadence was dead, Vanity, as the eldest daughter, would have to go in the Machine herself to retrieve her necromancy. And Vanity didn't want to go she didn't want to go she didn't want to go.

21

✒

"Stop fidgeting, you're acting odd. It's not good, Vanity. People will point and laugh, and then you might try to hurt them." Ro was saying things like this and also some other things. Vanity couldn't hear her all the time, or other people, or notice what was going on around her. If it had been important, she'd find it out later, anyway. So whatever. It was just Vanity often got caught up in a line of her own thoughts, thoughts like broiling ink that ended up blotting out what was happening around her in the present moment.

The present moment: her sister chattering on, Vanity standing on a gray marble floor, in a silk dress. A Party, yes. The Party going on around them. People staring, like they always did. This was the Museum's weekly Party, which occurred on every week's Friday—first this soiree for the wealthy, then its Afterparty and its rites for the wealthier. Vanity and Ro would wait in the cottage while Cadence performed her role as the necromantic Spectacle and then came back home to spill herself onto the living room couch, reeking of rot and magic. Vanity and Ro perhaps thrumming and drooling in the proximity of it, their mother's spiral, that aftereffect, that aura, until Cadence remembered the pill box she'd tucked into her purse, and replaced one high with another.

Vanity recalled a flash of Cadence across the Party about a half hour ago, the glint of that silver box. The elegant tipping of her wrist, the inelegant, cawing laugh that followed. Vanity thought perhaps it was November.

"You're not paying attention to me," Ro said, or something like that. "Stop looking at them and look at me instead."

They thought Vanity wouldn't be able to see them. Did they really think she wouldn't see them?

Ellis Kim, standing with his hands in his suit pockets on one end of the hall. Clover Rao hovering at the opposite end, patting at her sparkling red dress. Bodies shifting between them, but they were glancing at each other.

Ellis and Clover, Clover and Ellis.

Their names clattered around in Vanity's head.

They were the only other two witches of Vanity and Ro's generation in line to be Spectacles. They, too, would be put back in the Machine to remember their magic, once their parent was dead and it was time to take their title and perform the rites. They were unpossessing of the Adamses' necromancy—the Museum boasted a variety of exhibitions—but their specific affinities would, too, in time, tidily destroy their minds.

Ro hung her arms around Vanity's shoulders. "They are totally obsessed with you." Vanity could hear the smile cutting through her whisper. "Scrawling your name on their walls. They're just shy, much too shy to come up and confess. Also Monroe or Wren would kick the shit out of them. But mostly—"

Often they glanced at Vanity, too. Clover's gaze darted away whenever Vanity caught it. Ellis was the one who stared back.

Vanity didn't understand how they thought of her, ~~why they left her out of their little hidden games.~~ At the same time, Vanity could do nothing but understand them. Really, she was doomed to *only* understand them, and to only be understood by them. No one else, all the normal people milling around, understood that nature had hidden threads to pull at, no matter how many tabs of World they took off the golden trays being carted around, free with the price of admission. No one else could understand, truly, that when you unraveled reality, reality unraveled you, too.

They weren't supposed to be friends with one another—witches were banned from interacting with other witches outside of their own family, since they tended to drive one another a little nuts. Especially the children, unstable, fickle creatures. It's why they couldn't be trusted with magic in the first place, had to be purged of it. Who knew what apocalypses they might create out of the dramatics of their youth.

Vanity and Ro had grown up watching Ellis and Clover grow up, watching the suits and dresses begin to fit properly, alcohol and cigarettes finding their way into their hands, the gleam of youth beginning to be counterbalanced by the tinge of haziness and hysteria of witch blood. Vanity and Ro and Ellis and Clover. Shuffling around the room at the Parties, not permitted to talk to one another, often talking to themselves, or the floors, or the walls. Certainly not permitted to pass notes. But that's what Ellis and Clover were doing, dropping scraps of paper for the other to find.

Vanity had been watching them do it for years now, tucking the notes into a plant or slipping them beneath the tablecloths for the other to collect when they shifted around the room. How long had they been performing this practice? The question constantly stabbing and stabbing at Vanity—how much had she missed?

But sometimes Clover and Ellis missed things, too. Stuck on some thought, like her. The room blotting out. And notes missed, sometimes, sometimes . . .

Whenever Clover and Ellis missed a note, too distracted with themselves to notice the other dropping it out from their sleeves, Vanity would be the one to retrieve it. To date, she had come to possess five:

Stop looking at her.

What if we don't?

What if they're lying to us.

Those were from Clover to Ellis, in her pretty, loopy scrawl.

You too

I don't remember

From vice versa. In clinical handwriting. From that day on, Vanity always thought Ellis had handwriting like a tooth being smoothly extracted. Sharp, clean jolts.

Nonsensical things, those notes.

Vanity would go home and eat them bite by bite, letter by letter.

~~Why couldn't she be a part of them? Why didn't they like her? She thought, sometimes calmly and sometimes hysterically, What is very very very wrong with me that those freaks of nature don't like me? I'd do anything if it meant they'd pay attention to me. I'd hurt them very badly.~~

No. Okay. It was okay. It was fine. She'd cross things out, she'd remember higher truths. They were going to drive each other off the rails, anyway.

And besides. She had Ro.

And Ro, looping her arm through Vanity's, now. Her twin could read her like this. Ro often knew what Vanity was thinking or feeling before she thought it or felt it; Vanity was greatly comforted by this. Ro always took care of her. She hissed at people when they got too close. Often those who weren't invited by Monroe to attend the rites of the Afterparty tried to interact with the witches at the soiree, but they never got really far, unless they paid for a reading. The witch-children were often agitated or wouldn't catch what people were saying to them, and their parents, of course, were already wasted a half hour in. When Ellis's father was alive, he'd been known for trying to bite people who spoke to him. The onlookers would laugh, their own pupils blown from the World in their systems. Witches were so nuts and it was so interesting.

Ellis's father had died somewhere between the last Party and the one currently happening. Vanity had known it had happened because she awoke one night, suddenly high with her stomach cold, and Ro had told her what that meant; also they'd found Cadence slithering up the stairs on her tummy, shrieking and moaning that soon she too would follow James Kim into that nothingness, she'd felt him slip down into it like the jelly flesh of a ripe persimmon down a throat, she would soon . . . Anyway. Tonight, Ellis would go into the Machine and come out remembering how to do magic. He would be brought into the lushly curtained back room where Monroe Athalia hosted the Afterparty for their esteemed guests, and he would do something horrific.

Vanity tried to find him in the crowd again, Ro's complaining buzzing in her ears. She remembered she'd wanted to see if Ellis was sad. She wouldn't be sad if Cadence died. She would just be terrified.

Vanity didn't find Ellis, but she did find Clover. The glint of her gauzy pink dress under the lights of the chandelier. And a note between her thin fingers, the same color as the branches of the magnolia tree that broke the air outside Vanity's bedroom window, slipping it behind the frame of an oil painting of a battlefield or some shit like that—the whole hall was strewn with magnificent tableaux and statues and whatever but who cared because all anyone wanted to see were the witches. Then she moved away.

Vanity circled the room and retrieved it.

She didn't care if Clover saw. Maybe she even wanted her to see. It wouldn't be the worst thing, if Clover hated her. Vanity just wanted to cross her mind, it didn't matter what form she took, didn't matter if the thought of her was a caress or a nail to the head.

Ro pressed her cheek against hers. "Read it quickly. No one will see. Pretend you dropped something and you're picking it up. Do it now."

Her fingers scraped at the paper. The flimsy, prohibited thing.

Vanity could smell Clover's perfume on it—sage, and something sweeter, like cherries. A tight feeling seemed to twist in her chest, then explode. She wasn't in physical pain, but she still imagined herself splattering all over the walls, slicking over the Partygoers. Mucking up the trays of food.

It was because of Ellis and Clover that Vanity was very glad to be pretty even though she didn't like having a body, the whole ordeal generally disgusted her. She didn't like having a face with orifices or being host to internal pieces that moved on their own even when she was asleep; that she had to chew things into mush and then digest them; that she was dry on the outside and wet on the inside. It was horribly distressing that she didn't have anywhere else to go. But she was glad for the pleasing arrangement of her features or else Monroe wouldn't have her at the Museum and she would have never been able to stare at the two of them. She would've been put in the Sanatorium to be harvested for World or on the Pockmarked Island in a very very deep hole and not stare at anyone ever. Weren't they such lucky ducks, Cadence crowed at times, that Monroe had created the Museum some fifty-seven years ago now and so the people liked their witches of high society, these days? So lucky that they were so gorgeous. If Vanity and Ro had grown up ugly, well, well. That really would've fucked up everything.

Good luck tonight. Remember to remember everything.

More words than there'd ever been before. Vanity's mouth watered, and somewhere off to the side, Ro was laughing, laughing. And then she stopped. Snapped her mouth shut, upon noticing Vanity's eyes were watering, too. Vanity saw her warped in her peripheral vision, staring. Oh, god. Vanity really shouldn't cry in front of Ro. Her rage—

And there was a hand clamping down on her shoulder. Vanity suffocated the note in her fist, curled away from what she thought was Cadence's touch. "Mother— Oh."

Ro showed her teeth in an unkind grin. "Monroe! How are you? How's the Party? Are we making money?"

Vanity watched as Monroe Athalia's hand drew back from her shoulder. She said nothing else to the Museum's Curator. Her gaze climbed up and up the three-piece suit to the thick, stubbled neck to the harsh gray eyes. Her hand immediately drifted to tug at the strip of black lace she wore around her throat.

"Vanity," Monroe said, ignoring Ro, which only made her grin split wider, "an emissary from Yavonia has requested a reading. He is waiting for you."

Yavonia, considered a nation practically medieval, for worshipping gods. Probably why the emissary thought he would find some piety here, at the Museum. After all, how noble the institution was, truly, possessing witches, assigning themselves as keepers of the damned.

"No," Vanity said, just because it was something she could say—air she could push out of her throat into sound, that the synapses in another brain might flash like cut wire, might flag her words as meaning something. But certainly not Monroe's. He only looked at her coldly. When he held out his arm, Vanity took it.

The reading went the usual way. Vanity held the tarot cards in her hand. She stared at the gawking emissary across the candlelit table, the noise of the main hall obscured but not eradicated by the velvet curtains draped around them. She told him, truthfully, "Your gods aren't real. None are."

The emissary laughed. They often laughed, or smiled—what a pitiful, deranged child. The eyes behind his spectacles drifted toward Monroe, standing behind Vanity. Ro was beside him, her black gaze aglow with candleflame, and Vanity felt the usual stab of vindication at the pride there.

"Oh, they really are funny!" spoke the emissary. "I was expecting incoherence, seeing the state of the older ones."

He reached and drew his hand against Vanity's forearm, as if she were a dog to be stroked. Vanity thought of biting him and then she thought of Ellis's dead father and decided against it. It was rare for a witch to die a natural death. Both her deeds now and her age later would be stacked against her, especially when she eventually had a child old enough to take her Spectacle place at the rites. These weren't rites, whenever a tourist paid for a reading. Divination was fake. A party trick to put coins in the Museum's coffers.

"...theorized that their affliction is nature's response to urbanization, which is why witches pop up in metropolitan populations. It's the magic that makes them unstable," explained Monroe—the usual spiel. "We remove their abilities until they're older. We don't fully understand how their overexposures impact their frontal lobe development, so it's safer for them this way."

"Overexposures?"

"Well, currently we define witches as those afflicted with an overexposure to nature. Think of it like a weakness to the spiritual immune system. The affinities of the witch-families we've collected for the Museum correspond to specific natural overexposures." Vanity's heart immediately began to pound. Maybe it was true, that she was spiritually weak, if her body flushed at the mere mention of them. Ellis and Clover. "The Kims are afflicted with an overexposure to the nature of the mind, so their higher magic consists of psychic abilities. The Raos, an overexposure to the nature of the physical world—their higher magic concerns, in particular, erosion and corrosion. And the Adamses, like Vanity here, are overexposed to bodily natures, particularly death and rot, which seems to lend them necromantic abilities." Monroe smiled amicably. Vanity twisted around in her seat and watched the expression with her typical unblinking stare. "Though divination is something that stays in them even after we remove their higher magic." The usual lie, lie, lie. "With a combination of the Machine during adolescence and medication thereafter, they can remain stable enough to be in society." To be here. "But we are still aware they are dangerous—"

"They could start an apocalypse," said the emissary. Vanity gnawed on her pinkie finger. Some tourists were like this, came to the Parties clutching their righteousness. It absolved them of their gawking, or something.

"We have taken every precaution," Monroe said, placating, instead of admonishing him for the ridiculous superstition. "It's all very humane. It's a modern age, and they're people, after all."

Vanity took her hand from her mouth and nibbled on the edge of a tarot card instead. She knew what it was the moment the corner touched her tongue, even though divination was all bullshit. The card she always drew.

"Forgive her," Monroe said, pantomiming pity. "The overexposure does have psychological effects. Depression, anxiety, hysteria, and violent tendencies are most common, though extreme paranoia and delusions are sometimes seen, too. Even without their higher magic. But worry not. The Museum has selected their witch-families specifically. These bloodlines are the most stable."

The emissary's gaze scraped over Vanity again. "Do you breed them?"

Monroe let out a laugh—it was a hilarious presumption. "Oh, no, we could never put the witches together. They'll often develop the habit of bludgeoning one another. We have donors. Healthy people."

"She's quite exotic-looking, I can't quite place her race. Clara, certainly, which makes sense for this end of the ocean, but also her eyes—like yours, er, I mean, from the eastern continent—"

"She's half Miyeoni and half Clara. Mixed."

"Ah, it was a good call. She's very unique." He gave a little sigh, perhaps appreciative. "It's all quite sad, isn't it, though. No matter how pretty they are . . ."

"You're not even crying," said Vanity.

"Hush, Vanity," said Monroe. "Now, Mister Volnik, would you or would you not like a reading? I understand if you have second thoughts. What sits before you, after all, is one of the beings that your religious texts warn against. Devilspawn, was it?"

But what good was devilspawn when it had no form except the shape of its ink of its word upon a page? What sat before the emissary was a beautiful young girl of flesh and bone and magic, not something read and imagined but something that could be touched. And so he did touch her, again. Stroking her arms. And so she was realer than whatever nightmares existed in his scripts. This often happened, in the City. Perhaps there was something in the air here that made people abandon their beliefs, their gods. That drove the Mayor and the chief of police and other influential persons to watch the rites. The same something that had begun to stroke witchcraft in a handful of bloodlines, generations ago, that turned what should be such blessings inside out, made them strange, and then made them poison.

"Go on," breathed the emissary.

Vanity drew a card for him. Told him what it meant. Another. Again.

It was all so dull, all so fake. She missed Ellis. She missed Clover. A scream cut through the room, slicing through the velvet drapes—Vanity recognized it, unjarred, as her mother's. Cadence often screamed for no reason, lately. She'd probably scraped a fork against her plate too aggressively, or had discovered a hangnail. Monroe would probably kill her soon, she had deteriorated and was so annoying. Still, the Curator gave a polite bow of his head.

"Excuse me a moment. Our necromantic Spectacle hasn't been herself lately." The emissary moved to push out his seat, and Monroe said amicably, "Please, make yourself comfortable. You purchased the whole half hour."

"Oh, I—" The emissary gave a strained laugh, glancing sideways at Vanity. Monroe understood right away.

"There's no need to worry. They're not violent," Monroe said. He smiled gently. "Except when they are together, of course."

This must've been of great reassurance to the emissary. Because Monroe left and Vanity stared across the table and he was reaching for her again.

She felt Ro shift behind her. Not good. Ro snapping his neck would not be good. Even if she could bring him back.

"Do you want to see a magic trick?" Vanity asked. "Here. I'll do a reading for myself."

She drew the top card. Death.

Put it back into the deck. Shuffled. Split it. Selected. Death.

Shuffled.

Death.

Shuffled.

Death.

The emissary stumbled up, out of his seat. He fled from the room, drapes billowing behind his retreat. Ro detached from her spot and dropped herself into his seat. Interlaced her fingers and set her perfect chin upon them.

"Choose for me," she said, jutting out her bottom lip. "Tell me my future, O all-seeing Vanity."

"I'm tired."

"You never want to do magic. Why do you never want to do magic?"

She didn't mean this magic, the party tricks. Ro was always trying to get her to try to perform a spell. She could whisper to Vanity how to do whatever she wanted to do. Somewhere out there in the grand hall, Cadence's scream arched again.

"Oh," Vanity said, "I don't know."

"You like the high of it."

"The animals are different." They were things being done to her, not things she was doing.

"Come on, I love you," Ro said. "I love you I love you I love you." She batted her eyes. "So don't I deserve one measly card?"

So Vanity drew one measly card. The Devil. So boring. Ro always got that.

AFTER THE PARTY. Vanity was leaned against the bathroom door and Ro was curled up in the tub, their usual ground. Their discarded silk dresses ran like mercury over the black and white tiles of the bathroom floor; minutes ago they had been elegant beings and now they were just girls again. Vanity's heels ached with the stilettos she'd kicked off halfway across the stretch of lawn between their cottage and the Museum on top of the hill. Ro still had hers on, black with green bottoms while Vanity's had been black all over. They made Ro's bare legs look miles longer, one knee dripping over the side of the tub. The light of the electric bulb that burned above the mirror shone on her shin-bone. Vanity stared at it, that white skin almost the same color as the porcelain of the tub, flesh so plump and youthful it pantomimed the agelessness of an oil painting.

Minty floss wound around Vanity's knuckles, flushing them purple. It was a picking, material sound, her working this string between pieces of her own skull. Vanity was pretending these sounds peppered her tongue like the colorful candies she wasn't allowed to have. Sugar caused rot caused spirals, after all—that's what the dentists clucked, anyway. One or another, but always a man, came in the dead of night every six months and Vanity would wake with his fingers in her mouth. If she happened to wake at all. When she did—observing her blood, pushing slow and sweet and heavy in her veins from the sleepy gas they pumped into the bedroom before the appointment—Vanity didn't really mind. She wished it happened every night, some force coming through, quietly, to pick her head clean.

It was all Ro's fault, the gas, when they were little she'd bitten off three of the dentist's knuckles, *snip snip snip*, they'd belonged to someone else and then they belonged to her. You could just take things from people like that, Ro said. Things they thought were only theirs. You just had to bite down.

↙

The twins were freshly eighteen as of the weekend prior. Cadence had cried over the birthday cake—at the teeny, five-person celebration Monroe had hosted in the dining room of his living quarters, tucked at the back of the Museum—because the age of her daughters meant that she was herself was older, and she babbled to everyone how she didn't want to die, how she was afraid of the "black place" and of "being nothing." Cadence Adams had the innate ability to have an existential crisis—what should be a deeply profound number of minutes—and turn it into one of the shittier soap operas that often flickered on their living room's black-and-white television screen.

Vanity had eaten her side of the cake, sugar-free red velvet with low-cal frosting, in slow bites. Eighteen, Vanity had thought. How long did she have until she lost her mind? She wished Cadence would just shut up; her wails were making the icing on Vanity's cake slice seem to swirl and swirl and swirl.

Ro's side of the cake had been chocolate and she'd spread it all over one side of her mouth, specifically so Wren, unable to help himself, would lean forward and wipe it off her. This bothered Vanity, because she didn't like watching other people eat or touch each other.

Wren was Monroe's son, heir to the Museum and head of security, and he was nineteen. He was an asshole and a narcissist. But Ro was also an asshole and a narcissist and so she could handle him better. She liked to flirt with him and every now and then Wren would accidentally touch her thigh under the table. It was Vanity's hope that Ro would one day eat him alive. Eat Monroe and the rest of the Museum board alive, too. Sometimes it was a metaphor and sometimes, perhaps when Vanity was hungry—admittedly most of the time—it wasn't. This she was fearful to voice to Ro because she never knew what was on or off the table for her sister. So to speak.

↙

And also she was afraid Ro might tell her about a terrible and exquisite magic that could be wrung from it, the eating of flesh, and Vanity didn't want to know. Their type of bodily magic was, by nature, intimate, and Vanity knew she craved intimacy, so, she said to herself, do the math and leave it alone.

↙

"Let's go watch the rites," Ro said now. "It's Ellis's first time as Spectacle!"

Ellis Kim had been taken from the Party early on, Vanity had watched him being loaded into a car and driven away, presumably to be placed in the Machine and retrieve his magic. Vanity had daydreamed of kidnapping him before. In such reveries he'd struggled. But Monroe or Wren had been feeding him drinks all night, Ellis had been pretty wasted and docile, wavering on his feet.

"Clover wants him to remember the Machine," Ro had whispered in Vanity's ear, but Vanity knew this would not be a thing he would do, since she had eaten the note that told him to do so.

35

She didn't feel heart-heavy with guilt—he wouldn't have remembered the Machine, anyway—no witches ever did—but she did feel jealousy. That Clover ordered Ellis around, presumably because Ellis would listen to her. Vanity wanted Ellis to listen to her, too; she wanted Clover to order her around, too.

Now Ellis had been brought back to the Museum for the Afterparty, where he would perform his reclaimed magic in what Monroe advertised as "rites." No doubt the tickets sold out instantly for Ellis's debut, perhaps from the day of his birth. Cadence could've easily resurrected Ellis's father, of course, but Monroe would've never made such a request. The freshest generation of witches were easier on the eyes, flushed with youth, and their minds were new and taut like factory-grade rubber bands. If the drugs made them drool afterward, it would gleam on pristine necks.

"We can't," said Vanity.

"Monroe's so full of shit, keeping us apart." Ro was climbing out of the tub, pulling her floss out, one thin white vein spilling out of her mouth. "What if he's lying to us? What if we don't make each other crazy? What if we could actually all be good for one another?" She was always asking questions like these. Vanity didn't see the point. But now Ro was worked up. "It's not fair," she was saying. "It's not fair. Don't we all deserve each other? I'm so *lonely*."

Privately, on the inside of each cheek, Vanity had hewn a white line of scarring with the habit of biting down on herself. She took the floss out of her mouth. Her tongue ran down the scars, first right, then left. Her mouth felt precisely clean.

"I'm going to bed. Good night."

"I'm dying," Ro said. "I'm dying and I'm sad, and you're walking away. You're so mean." She trailed Vanity up the hall, linking their arms. She was still wearing the heels, and it unsettled Vanity, them being different heights.

"We're not going."

Vanity pushed open the door to her room, but their elbows were linked and Ro had stopped walking. Vanity could push her over, but she'd never do that. It would be bad if Ro cracked her head on the wall or the floorboards and died. Vanity pictured it, Ro's head bleeding and bleeding and bleeding until all at once it had stopped and it was over, like the sun going down.

"Aw, why are you acting like you're *so* good, Vanity?" Ro jutted her bottom lip out. "You're the one who took off your shoes, coming back here."

Vanity doubled down out of instinct. "They hurt my feet."

"Not because the gardeners composted the green today?"

Vanity pressed her mouth behind her hand, like she was ashamed. Ro leaned over her and grinned. She pulled at Vanity's wrist until it came away from her face, until she could see all strong, healthy teeth in Vanity's smile.

"Don't tell," she said.

"I'd never," Ro said.

🖋

Both barefoot now. Pillows stuffed under their blankets, they made their way out of the cottage and began the trek up the moonlit hilltop, where the columns of the Museum mansion shone at the peak. Sleek marble spines. A vaulted roof inlaid with massive slabs of mother-of-pearl that looked like an oil slick at night. On the left was the shrub-lined driveway licking down onto the forested road—a little ways past that, the City—and on the right sprawled the rose garden overlooking the Pockmarked Island and the ocean beyond.

Even though they were allowed free to roam the campus at all hours, of course the minute Vanity stepped outside during the day the tourists were on her. The nights were quieter, but then there was Wren to worry about. Stalking around. He was in an especially twisted mood if he'd just come back from playing with his dogs, sleek gray things that lived in the stable behind the mansion. *Come here, Vanity....*

There were no locks on the cottage door or guards at the fence because the Museum was a humane habitat. The road that fed into downtown

37

was cut off by the electric fence that also branched into the forest line behind the domiciles; if any witch did decide to vanish into the forest they would meet ocean eventually. If they were gone for too long, Wren would unleash his dogs to drag them back. There was nowhere to run to: the City was unappealing; to all witches the concrete felt quite quite cold and wrong and to the Adams women specifically there was too much flesh that would pulse and pulse around them. The ocean would freeze them within an hour, no matter the season, and none of them knew how to swim anyway. At the Museum they were fed and lived in a nice green place and they got to wear silk dresses. At the Museum there was Ellis and Clover. And now, since Ellis really couldn't leave, Vanity really couldn't, either. She realized this as she went up the hill. She was in love and it meant she was going to die here.

⚓

There was also, Vanity supposed, the bomb, which resided alongside her ankle-bone—and all the witches' ankle-bones—which would detonate if she did make it too far past the perimeter, crippling her but not blowing off her pretty face. But this seemed, to her, a footnote, overkill, anyway. And honestly she was a little fond of it, this unnatural element that existed within her, the rest of her bound around it, altogether too natural, too teeming. It comforted her in some unnamable regard to have the option of causing damage to herself.

⚓

The twins held hands, so either could feel if the other one's feet stalled, caught in the sensation of the decay of the compost between their toes, so neither did. They checked each other in this way.

Passing the garden was more thrilling and more dangerous the more the year succumbed to fall, where the apple-sized rose blossoms began to collapse in on themselves like small suns. During that time, fifty feet away, Vanity and Ro would lie in their beds at night, tasting that slow, perfumed rot on their tongues, and in her head Vanity would think desperately Oh god, oh god oh god I swear I'm going to be sick with it.

It was never true, but the alternative was admitting how much she liked it.

Vanity knew how bad it was, for her, to like things.

Want and desire were pieces of herself that eluded her, that seemed to breathe and evolve without her permission. She never meant to fall so for Clover and Ellis, never meant for them to be in her head. Walking around and rearranging things and talking to her. And whenever she imagined hurting them—because her thoughts were calmer when Ellis and Clover lay slack and still in her head—they always got back up. She couldn't help but resurrect them.

Thus, from a young age, Vanity decided she'd dictate everything else about herself with particular care and precision. Control above all else. Flossing her teeth—that had to be right uppers to left uppers to left downers to right downers. Choosing the forms of what she consumed, measuring things on her plate into bites the length of two knuckles max—she could never pick up an apple and eat it just like that, and if she was having a meal, she had to be the one to cut up her own food. Liquid items were the most preferable, smoothies and hot chocolate and broth and alcohol. She enjoyed the feeling of these formless, apathetic items that slid down her throat without resistance, and immediately took the form of the sack of her stomach. The finger foods at the Parties were their own specific battle, and those existed in three categories Vanity had created that ranged from eatable to inedible: there were cubed things like sashimi and cheeses (ideal, clean angles), toothpick-stabbed (acceptable, barring an unevenness to the trajectory of the toothpick), and cracker things (horrible, flaky, imperfect).

But all the control she cultivated for herself would flee from her when she started to do magic, which would happen even if she resisted Ro's pressuring. She was constantly witnessing her future in the form of her mother. Cadence, coming back to the cottage post-rites, her skin glowing, eyes feverish, every movement sloppy. Knocking around in the kitchen a floor below, breaking dishes and giggling to herself.

And Vanity in her room, the lights off, pretending to be asleep while her heart beat around in her chest, listening obsessively to the ridiculous woman below and wondering what she'd been before. If she'd been like Vanity, before becoming the Spectacle, hating her mother for being her own premonition.

The Museum mansion at the top of the hill—with the rites currently being performed in the dark, curtained room off the grand front hall—had its own gravity. Ro began to inch forward, taking the lead. Only the sleekest and grandest of cars now occupied the front drive.

"This way." Ro was pushing through the bushes that bordered the back of the mansion. There was already a hewn path, footsteps stamped into the mud, which rose between Vanity's toes chillingly. The air was sharp and charged. Vanity knew that the rites were being performed just past the curtained window they now crouched beneath—the northeast corner room. Their reflections wobbled dimly in the glass. Vanity looked into the black marks of her own eyes.

"We're more natural than they are. . . . Making superstition is just good advertising. It's all part of the experience. Like with the lace-masks," Ro chattered. "We're not actually dangerous."

Vanity had a strand of hair out of place. She carefully placed it back behind her left ear. She always had to keep her long, dark hair behind her ears, it felt neat and clean that way. When she got out of the shower she brushed it one hundred times with a black-toothed comb. Ro wore her hair long, too, the same middle part, but she slept with it wet, or threw it into braids, and was always twirling the strands around so sections of it lay half-curled, wild.

"Well, say *something*," Ro pouted.

"Sorry." Sometimes Ro talked and Vanity thought it was her talking, so she'd forget to respond. "And you're lying."

Ro smiled. "Don't say sorry."

"Did you already unlock the window earlier in the Party, knowing you'd get me out here?" Vanity asked, pushing the thought back.

"Why, yes, yes I did do that."

Ro pushed at the corner of the glass. The iron hinges brushed softly against the blackout curtains within. Vanity went through first. Her dirty, bare feet pressing against the plush velvet of the curtains that pooled against the floor, blocking the room from the light of the star-dusted sky. The hem of her gray slip caught on the ledge, and Ro reached, unhooking it, and then was through the window, too.

The scent of blood and marrow, metal and rust, hit Vanity like a wall coming down.

Spectators murmured, whispers of awe sloughing in Vanity's ears, noises with strange, static corners. She tilted against Ro; Ro tilted against her. "Death," Vanity mumbled, "death in the room."

"I know it. I taste it," Ro said. "Sh."

Fingers, long and pale and painted black, reached out to a seam in the curtains. Vanity's own fingers, she realized. Some instinctual thing in her body rousing, awakening, wanting to see the others who could bend the world. Wanting to respond, Yes. I can do that too. No one taught me, but I remember. Almost. How to find the threads. How to pull them, just so. I swear I almost...

Her fingers revealed a slit in the curtains.

Vanity and Ro looked into the dark room. They were behind a woman in a yellow dress and a man in a collared shirt who did not turn around, transfixed by the tiny stage at the center of the room. Their heads—like the rest of the watching crowd—were wrapped up in a length of white lace. To separate them from the carnage, both physically and, most importantly, spiritually. Apparently.

All eyes were reduced to distant impressions like coins behind the coverings. But Vanity was wired, and she could feel them rolling around, how they followed, barely blinking, the trickle of blood off the edge of the stage, the path it carved through the crowd and out of the room. She could feel where the slickness was disrupted by lumps and chunks of whoever had just been eroded away by Lavender Rao, Clover's mother. Vanity wanted to find them, these tiny pieces that someone had once carried around in their body as a whole, smooth unit, perhaps never knowing until tonight about this ability of their flesh, that it could crumble so. She wanted these pieces in the palm of her hand, wanted to breathe on them, to make them twitch.

"I don't feel right," she murmured. "I don't feel right."

"Don't lie to me," Ro said, which scared her, and so did the bright look in Ro's eyes. Vanity looked like that, too, right now.

"This was a mistake, I'm leaving."

"Don't *lie* to *me*."

Vanity hated her. She hated the thoughts in her head. She hated her own hands. "I—"

The door opened again, a brief warmer glow of light. Then it shut and it was gone. More bodies drifted into the room. The first was a man Vanity didn't recognize and the second was Ellis Kim, wearing the same black shirt and black shoes Vanity had seen him in earlier that night, across the Party. He paused at the edge of the crowd while the unknown man was pushed up onto the stage, where he fell to his knees. His eyes were open and blank. Someone's hand was on Ellis's shoulder, that lace-wrapped face leaning in to speak in Ellis's ear. Monroe.

Ellis nodded at whatever Monroe had said.

He appeared relatively calm. Yes—why should he be nervous? He had known the day of his rites would come, just like the rest of them. No, it shouldn't be the witches who should be nervous. It should be everyone else in the room. All the foreign royals and bigwig industrialists, seeing something of genuine arcane power. Monroe could call it miraculous entertainment all he'd like—the rites were a threat. Do you see what monsters I own? It's a wonderful thing we all get along, isn't it?

Monroe cleared his throat. Then he spoke simply, "Ellis Kim. The psychic Spectacle."

It wasn't much of an announcement, and there was no applause. No need for an abundance of either. The room was filled with royalty and the richest men and women on the planet, and that alone spoke for the quality of the performance about to unfold.

Ellis stepped forward and lifted himself onto the edge of the stage. It was too quiet, the curtains eating up every rustle of movement. It was just void and the distant sound of a drum, which Vanity then recognized as her own heartbeat. Ellis was bending his head. Vanity could just see the nape of his neck, the nodes of the vertebrae set there. That almost tender curve of the skin there, that gentle encasing.

The corner of his mouth moving.

He was saying something to the kneeling, unknown man. Perhaps he was informing him that he was about to die horribly. Perhaps Ellis was apologizing. Perhaps Ellis was saying no, he wouldn't go through with it. He wouldn't play his part. He would not perform as the Spectacle. He was naturally violent and unstable like all witches were, but he was going to try to do better. Be better. He wasn't doomed, none of them were. They could help each other, he was telling the man, Vanity was sure. Help each other when their own thoughts got too loud, when they tried to spiral; they didn't need drugs or the Sanatorium or a gunshot to the head, they just needed to be around others who understood them. They could still be good people.

Ellis drew away.

For some reason, it was then that Vanity remembered she didn't know what his voice sounded like.

He turned his head.

And his black, black eyes were on Vanity.

No smile across his lips, no startlement. Just that same calm.

Behind him, the man lifted his hand. He put one of his fingers into his mouth.

Ellis did not look away from her.

A faraway pop. Soft, soft tearing. Blood flecked Ellis's cheek. Vanity tried and tried to cross the moment out but it wasn't working this time. She was seeing everything. The man was chewing and swallowing. The crowd applauded politely. The man moved on to his thumb.

"Don't go," Ellis said.

Vanity stumbled back.

She didn't know how she made it out the window, back into the cold night. Gagging on her own spit.

She was all alone. Ro hadn't even turned her head to watch her go.

It was all done ten minutes later. From her spot on the grass, looking out onto the obsidian face of the ocean, Vanity felt the man grow colder and colder and then die. With her attention on him, she witnessed a new thread uncurl from somewhere indescribable within his form. If she neared, she could tug at it and he'd come gasping back. Almost. What was the word to make it happen? It was almost there, crept forward on the tip of her tongue. . . .

If she resurrected him, whatever haze Ellis had put him under would be gone. He'd scream at the half-exposed twin bones of his forearm licked clean and white.

Vanity drew her attention away, back to the ocean. The thread became mist in her focus and then became nothing.

She hugged her arms around herself, staring out onto the water.

She didn't want to be alone, but Ro was likely sticking around to watch Cadence's performance. What miracle would their mother perform tonight?

"Vanity?"

She turned her head. And jolted back.

The image of the cold horizon was replaced with the image of a boy splattered in blood, now taking a careful, measured step back. For a moment there was silence.

Vanity could hear his breaths sliding softly up and down his throat.

On her tongue was the taste of the sweat under his clothes, the salt of it mixed with something headier, like cologne.

Her vision blurred briefly. Her head began to ring again. She didn't hate it.

Ellis Kim looked like he was lost. He touched the back of his neck. "Vanity," he said again. Said it like it was the only thing he could remember how to say. Black eyes unfocused and blown. Wired.

And then he began to laugh.

Vanity looked to the cottage waiting at the bottom of the hill. Where she was supposed to have been all this time. She could make it. Her feet shifted in the grass. Ellis shut his mouth, laugh swallowed. Then...

"Sorry." He stood framed by the dying garden behind him. "I didn't mean to scare you. I don't know how I got out here."

They're not violent. Vanity loved him. *Except when they are together, of course.* Vanity said, "Stay the fuck away from me."

"You came to watch, tonight."

"It wasn't my idea."

"Whose idea was it, then?"

"Arrogance's," Vanity said, then regretted it. Saying Ro's name always felt like handing over a piece of herself.

"Arrogance." There was the dimmest glint of recognition on his face, but following it was some other expression, one she couldn't place. "Right."

Vanity took another step back. "I have to go now."

"Please." His voice was quiet and low. He was looking at the grass, but there wasn't any shyness there. "You don't have to do that. I'm not going to hurt you."

"We're not supposed to be near each other."

"I know, I know."

He wasn't taking any more steps forward. She wasn't taking any more back. For years she'd been seeing him from across the room at the Parties, had watched him grow up, and yet she'd never been as close to him as she was now. He had an elegant face, high slanted cheekbones, monolid eyes with dark lashes, a soft mouth now half-parted.

"You live down there?" It must be a joke; he knew, of course, knew where she lived. He glanced over his shoulder, down at the cottage at the bottom of the hill, its one glass face making it seem like a doll's house from this distance, open and exposed. "I'll come say hello, sometime."

How many times had she pictured their first meeting in her head? Walking through the haze of her imagination over and over again until she bumped into pieces that were solid, she swore, nearly real. She had pictured—

Vanity tried to turn her thoughts away. Who knew what of her mind Ellis Kim could perceive now? What he could peel apart, turn inside out. But she couldn't keep the fear off her face.

"I'd never do that to you, Vanity," Ellis said quietly. "Anything like it."

She blinked at him before realizing he was talking about the self-consumption, while she was worrying about daydreams. Worrying that he would find out everything. How she didn't feel real unless she was in love with someone.

And then how she didn't feel real unless she was next to them or talking to them or thinking of them or thinking of them or thinking of them.

The man's hand was less important. After all, it was gone. She was the one still being consumed.

"Would I even know? If you told me to do something?" Vanity asked, while in her head the words rang like a bell: Tell me to do anything.

A pause. "No. You wouldn't."

"So why would I believe you?"

"Well," he said, "what do you think of me, Vanity?"

Ellis's magic was horrific. It was ludicrous, and it was incredible. He had moved like what he was doing was a sacred, beautiful act. Vanity's head spun. She could smell the blood flecks in his hair, the death dusting his clothes and skin. None of it was unpleasant. Why had he come out here, looking for her? *Stay the fuck away from me.* Had she said it for her benefit, or his?

There was a dark something inside her she kept beating back, and she wished she could say she gave it no air and no light, but it would be a lie. Sometimes she fed it from the palm of her hand.

"I don't know what I think of you." Vanity shook her head. "Nothing. I don't know you. I'm not supposed to know you."

Her words seemed to hum in the air. What was she still doing here?

She went to move past him. Their elbows brushed. Static shock down her arm. A word in her head, running around. *Please, please.* Please what? She didn't know. But she did stop walking. He's doing this to me, she thought, she lied. Always lying to herself.

"I want to," Ellis said. "Know you."

He didn't turn around, but she did. "Why?"

Seeing him standing there, backdropped by the night. The outside world seemed completely emptied out. Everyone else on the planet was inside their homes, and their curtains were drawn, or they were uninterested in windows. No one else was looking at them, and someone was supposed to be looking at them. Someone was supposed to be shouting, stay away from each other. Don't say anything else to each other. Don't you see what's happening to the both of you? Already you're not able to think straight, already you're nervous and excited and calm, somehow, so, so calm.

But it was that Vanity hated when people acted embarrassing or mundane or casual. She hated when she had to watch them eat or tie their shoes or when she heard them stumbling over their words. She was so uncomfortable around humanness. People were disgusting and disappointing because they were people, because people weren't perfect. They were built all wrong. And Vanity could lie and lie and say they were just as fucked up as she was but no matter how wrong they were built she was built worse.

And Ellis Kim.

He was something worse. Like she was.

He said, "Because you're pretty down to your gums, Vanity Adams."

Like she didn't know. She didn't smile at him.

"They arch like cathedral ceilings."

And he smiled.

Ellis had a smile like war. Like the dark thing under the bed.

"You have cavities," Vanity told him, instead of that she might be in love with him. But that would be bad. Because when Vanity thought of love, she thought of violence, too.

She looked at Ellis and wished she could act like herself for once, just to see what it felt like.

And then Ro was standing next to her.

Ellis, like Vanity, looked over.

And maybe Ro didn't like that, because Ro loved Vanity, and for Ellis to be looking at Ro instead of at Vanity was a crime, he had embarrassed her. But also maybe Vanity was just rationalizing. Ro had wandered up with the rock already in her hand.

When Ellis opened his mouth, she cracked it against his chin.

Vanity felt his teeth breaking like a lash of cold wind against her skin. He was on the ground and she was watching Ro raise her arm high above her hand. She brought the rock down one more time and it was done. One more glorious, perfect hit. Ellis's death rocked through the air and sent Vanity to her knees, over his body now, too. His expression was all wrong, he was no longer gorgeous, he was just split flesh and broken bone. He was just like everyone else. Vanity didn't register the moment her hands moved on their own. Touching Ellis's face. So warm.

The sea was swirling into the sky, and clouds were drinking up the faint glow of the oscillating surface. Holy shit, she was already so drunk off of the death, the proximity to the empty body.

"I couldn't stand it," Ro was saying. "He was so full of bullshit, I had to," and Vanity was saying, stroking his face, "I know. I know."

She pulled her fingertips away from his bloodied cheek, and as she did, something incredible happened. When her touch left his skin, droplets of crimson lifted into the air, suspended between the gap. Her heart swelled. Ellis missed her already, too. He was reaching for her.

But that was just her romantic tendency, and Vanity steeled herself to kill it. She was coherent, stable, she had to be, because Ro was nuts. Yes, Vanity remembered. Yes, she thought, I remember what this is. What this feeling is. They tried to take it away from me but they couldn't carve it out completely. They tried to purge things from my head but the flesh remembers. Remembers how it felt to be born with it, with this. Magic. Magic. Magic.

Vanity looked over at Ro. Ro was looking back at her.

Which of them started laughing first? Vanity didn't know, it didn't matter. One was the other one, sometimes, it didn't matter.

Their giggles ricocheting off of one another, cresting.

"Now you have to," Ro said, poking her in the ribs. "Do magic."

Vanity was gasping for air, clutching her stomach. Tears broke at the corners of her eyes, she was laughing so hard. "Oh—my god—you're such a *bitch*."

Ro leaned forward and they pressed their brows together. Their breathing became light, secretive.

"You remember how to do it now," Ro whispered, in this private place they created between them. "I know you do."

"I don't," Vanity said. She didn't, not completely. But Ellis's end had brought it into the inside of her mouth. The word once more balanced on the tip of her tongue, the taste of death and life and graveyard dirt. "Tell me."

Ro leaned in. Her lips brushed Vanity's ear. Vanity giggled again. The word in her head, now, tugging along with it what to reach for, how to reach for it.

"That's it?" she exclaimed, ecstatic.

"That's it," Ro said. "Do you want to do it together?"

"No, I got it," Vanity said. "I can do it."

Ro smiled. "I know."

Would Ellis be scared of her, when she brought him back?

Vanity wouldn't mind that. He scared her, too, after all.

"How do you know, Ro?" Vanity whispered. "How do you remember?"

"You don't remember that, either?" Ro said teasingly, shrugging her shoulders. Her dark eyes glittering. She still had the rock in one hand, and now let it drop soundlessly onto the grass. "I'm the eater of worlds," Ro said.

It wasn't the first time she'd said this.

Did Ro actually believe it? How much did she actually recall, after the Machine? Many times Vanity had wanted to ask, but she always stopped herself. Opened and then closed her mouth, gnawed on the inside of her cheek. She already knew the answer. Ro remembered everything. Knowing how to do magic made her brim with confidence, with blood-lust. And if Vanity asked, Ro would tell her how to do it all. Ro was a good sister. And then Vanity would change. So some part of her always stopped her from asking Ro how to do magic, the part of her that knew she was destined to become something horrific.

But just this once, it would be okay. What other choice did she have, with Ellis growing colder and colder beneath her? Just this one spell, and that would be it. She could handle a little magic. She could pull herself out of it. She could control herself.

She leaned over Ellis. Brushed the dark hair away from his ear, exposing the bone-white shell of it, and she could feel how soft the skin there was, against her lips, even though she hovered just so, without contact. Velvet.

"Say it," Ro said, somewhere above her.

Vanity closed her eyes. And that part of herself that was frightened of herself shied away. Perhaps it grinned, she thought distantly. Perhaps it had been pretending all along. "Rise."

LATER, OUT OF THE Museum doors, would depart everyone more important. The City's Mayor and his cabinet, foreign royalty, business tycoons and their glittering wives. They would file into their shiny cars that hummed and trickled down the hill, and in the backseats they would sway, perhaps stroke the limp lace-masks in their hands and thrill at what they had just witnessed. A fine night, was it not? They would think, always a lovely reminder, that nature had been cowed, leaving them to run the world. They would pay no mind to the empty lawn.

🗡

"Do you think, secretly, that you're like them?"

Wren had been leaned against the wood door of the dogs' shed when Clover Rao had approached him that particular night, three days ago, smiling. And when Clover smiled like that she was looking for war.

He'd given her a cigarette to placate her, in the hopes she wouldn't tire him today. Or maybe he just liked the way she held it. She had pretty hands.

Though she really shouldn't be smoking, he knew, since she got a little high, not off the tiny air sacs in her lungs suffocating, bowing under the tar, but the burn of the cherry. But he was fascinated with how her eyelids fluttered with each inhale. Wren would never feel the world so acutely, like they all did.

"Like who, Clover?"

"One of the royalty. One of the princes." She'd never speak like this without the delicate destruction of the cigarette at the ends of her fingers. Even such small triggering of her overexposure made her different. Wren observed. He made steady notes in his head.

But he also laughed, shaking his head. "You better bite your tongue."

Clover's own laugh was proud, was arched and cold and always made Wren think of the ceiling of a crypt. He found her self-amusement pathetic, because he knew the life she was going to lead.

"You're not your father. You can't tell me what to do." Wren couldn't keep the expression off his face, the one the aforementioned father always reprimanded him for. "Oh, and there's the satisfied smile. Someday you'll make me eat my words, when you inherit this place, yes? But you won't. Monroe is never going to die."

"Ah, but inheritance isn't always everything, is it?" Bad form, maybe, for the heir to the Athalia fortune to say this; he just couldn't help but shoot her another megawatt smile. He was referring to the Spectacle position, of course. "My father says James Kim is going to die tonight. Has it already happened? Can you feel it in the air?"

Clover snuffed out her cigarette and flicked it at him before running off.

Wren sighed. He snuffed his cigarette, too. Stretched his neck. Then ran after her.

He caught her quickly. So intriguing, that such an entity had a wrist he could fully encase in his own, that he could so effortlessly twist and snap if such crippling was of benefit. Modern technology had pried away her dangerous aspects; what was left was a beautiful shell, an antique with its gold accents scraped out.

Wren dragged Clover through the gates of the garden. The Museum's windows winking with light on the hilltop above, the glass faces of the cottage below lit with a dull gleam from the half-moon. Clover's eyes rolled all over the garden and he wondered what unseen processes pricked at her, that even though he was partially threatening her he'd become a footnote, background noise. Whenever he took a tab of World he was fooled into thinking he almost felt what they did, at least when he was peaking. But he knew even being able to assign words to describe it—euphoria, mania, wholeness, the taste of life and his own age on his tongue—marked the experience as diluted. You'd never lose your mind on World, not for long, not like the witches lost their minds on magic. The sense of lacking disturbed Wren, because he'd once believed he craved order, or at least the Museum's empire, the comforts and grandness of his father's position.

He didn't. He craved whatever the hell it was they felt.

Well, not exactly. Of course, he didn't want to be *exactly* like them—anxious, eroding, incomprehensible things. But World could certainly stand to hit a little harder, to reap what it apparently sowed. For all the sensations of *wholeness* it boasted to provide, nothing had ever made people stand farther apart.

"I want to help you," he said, making her sit down on one of the stone benches. Somewhere past the thicket of rosemary and hydrangea, fruit trees and blackberry bushes, the gardener's dog let out a series of sharp, senseless barks. Wren felt a tinge of annoyance. He despised misbehaved creatures.

Clover rubbed at her wrist and said nothing as Wren stood before her.

"I think we could work together, you and I, Clover."

The focus sharpened back into her expression, eyes flickering behind

53

her tortoiseshell glasses—though she was, of course, required to wear contacts for the Parties—from his shoes back up to his face. It was only a moment before they skittered away. Her confidence had been snuffed out alongside the cigarette. "What's that old superstition? Be wary of making deals with witches."

"We're not making a deal. You're going to want to do this."

"Why would I?"

"Well." Wren glanced over her head, down to the darkened cottages. "You want them, don't you?"

Clover did not turn around to look. But she had gone quite still.

"I don't want anything to do with them."

Fear, there, on her face. But there was no need to be afraid, Wren knew.

"No? You don't want to be around them? To talk to them?" he said, softly, softly. "Clover. I believe this could solve everything. I believe that this—that *they* can make you so much better—"

She recoiled from him immediately. "We're not allowed," she said, and that really was hilarious. Wren couldn't help but chuckle.

"Because you're such a stickler for your current way of life."

"I have a bomb in my ankle. I don't have a choice."

Wren waved a dismissive hand. "Well, if you're worried about Monroe being alerted to the proximity, you needn't be. He hardly ever checks the cameras."

"Was he sick of seeing you roll with your dogs?"

Wren grinned tightly, instead of putting his hand on her shoulders and shaking her. Her crassness wasn't her fault, he reminded himself. All the witches were socially inept, and they were prone to saying disgusting things. "We monitor the cottages and the public portion of the mansion, dear." In truth, Monroe had mentioned specifically that he wouldn't put cameras in the dog shed. Wren's reputation for being World-addled was enough without having a potential leak of surveillance footage, the Athalia heir crouched over his gleaming, hungry beasts and cooing. He

54

did talk to them, that was true. There was hardly anyone else to murmur to. "And the old man doesn't even bother with the tech anymore, he—"

"Holy shit, you're serious? You are actually serious?"

"I'm dead serious."

"You want me to—interact with them."

"I want you to be friends."

Clover flared then. It really didn't call for such a visceral reaction, all the disgust and terror and et cetera. "What *is* this, to you?"

"Don't you want to be better, Clover?"

"Am I going into the Machine, someday?"

"Yes, well, when your mother—"

"Then I can't *get* better, can I." Her voice was hard and cold. The voice of a girl already knowing the entire bleak future laid out in front of her. In that, she was just the same as Wren. But it didn't have to be like this. They could change everything, change their whole lives.

"Clover, you can. It's possible." Wren felt breathless, suddenly, with the enormity of what he was saying. This was so important; this would affect the world on a larger scale than she could conceive of, curled up in her fear of the other witches. "You're so—alone, here."

"I talk to you," Clover muttered, another half-hearted deflection.

"You steal a cigarette from me every now and then, and we bicker." Wren crossed in front of her; he held her beautiful face in his hands so she could not look away. "Clover. I could never understand you like they could."

She lifted her chin. "I don't want them. I don't want anybody, here."

"Listen to me," Wren said. "I'm sick of seeing it. All of you always getting worse. It doesn't have to be this way. You can be so much better. It is—so important, to form meaningful connections with other people."

"Whatever you're intending, it won't work." She didn't trust him; he hadn't expected her to. "When we're together." Her voice went smaller and smaller until it had dropped to a hush. "I'll barely be able to think straight."

Oh, yes, Wren already knew that.

He'd seen the way they all looked at each other from across the room. There was nothing that hit quite like young love.

"Oh, Clover," Wren said. "Who says I want you to? No, no, I want you to be reckless. Be vulnerable. Maybe you'll even surprise yourself with how good it feels to open yourself up to other people. To have them do the same in turn. When that happens, please, I'd appreciate it if you gave me updates. I'll make it worth your while."

Now she did shake him off, and Wren returned his hands to his pockets. He withdrew gladly. All he'd meant to do with this conversation, anyway, was to put it in her head.

"Well. I didn't expect you to go for this, right now. You're always so . . . careful with it, aren't you? Your head. Your heart. But it doesn't matter, anyway." Yes, Wren knew how it was all going to happen, pupils blown with World as he took in her disbelief—it would be they who sought her out, he guessed anyway. And she wouldn't be able to stay away, when it was them asking her to come closer. "I have the utmost faith you'll all be together soon. It'll be so wonderful, to have friends, you'll see."

IV
NOW

ELLIS KIM FEELS CLEAN and clear. Ellis Kim is dripping wet.

He cannot recollect why. Perhaps it'd been raining? Okay, yes, raining, during his amble up the cracked drive licking the hill of the Museum grounds. Ellis hadn't noticed. The weather or his soaked state. But, yes, he is certain he is dripping wet, now having stolen through the unlocked, grandiose front doors of the Museum, because he is disturbing the absolute quiet with the droplets coming off his dark hair. Splattering onto the marble floor in unsteady beats—yes. So it must be raining. He has it all in order. Ellis Kim is clean and clear.

The unlit ballroom smells like dust, slightly tinged with everyone they had to scrape off the floors. Even after all this time, after all the deaths, the residual magic makes the marrow of his bones hum. It quivers the bronze arms of the chandeliers hung in rows above his head, so they seem to wave at him.

Ellis waves back.

Once, Vanity had told him that he had gracefully long arms and hands and fingers to match the graceful angles of his face. He'd told her that having her describe him to himself felt like a holy moment. He'd been lying, then, of course. But he'd mean it now.

She's been dead a year today.

The anniversary was probably what had driven him to visit Arrogance in the Sanatorium—he'd missed Vanity's face.

Maybe he'd even missed Ro, too.

But it was ridiculous to think seeing the Adams twins' features would soothe something in him.

Vanity was gone.

And Ro was . . . well. Well, well . . .

Just standing on the dead grass of the Pockmarked Island, at the edge of the concrete cell-pit Clover had thrown her in, had made Ellis's vision swim. Ro had peered up at him, dirty and wild yet still very beautiful, still very much sharing Vanity's face, and the eye contact alone had Ellis pressing down the urge to jump, break himself just to be closer to her.

I left something under the Museum. Ro's sweet voice danced through his head. *Can you get it for me?*

Well, fuck no, he'd called down to her, smiling. Vanity had always said he had a nice smile. *Don't think I should, Ro darling. I just came to say hello, after all this time.*

Hello, hello . . .

Ellis shifts through halls and halls with remnants of decayed skin crusted invisibly between the cracks of the floorboards, the print of the wallpaper. In fits and starts a haze drifts over him and he comes to having moved from one room to the next with no recollection; this was not concerning. His father had taught him early on these lost moments would happen.

Ah, the late and great James Kim. Ellis quotes him now, for the wallpaper: "'There's something terrible, dark, and sick in you, it is called death, you sick fuck, you're sick, you're cruel, when you're mean it's not like when other people are mean, when you're mean you could end the world, you're horrible and hopeless and you'll go mad...'" Or something like that. Anyway. "Why am I here, Ro, you poor, poor girl? I wish it'd been you, I think I forgot to tell you that. I wish Vanity had killed you and not the other way around." Ellis is babbling and smiling to himself because it doesn't matter. His words bleed out into the dim space and then they're gone and they don't matter.

What is he looking for, again? A door, perhaps...?

He pauses just off the kitchen—the massive, steely kitchen they used for the all the Party food and not the cutesy one in the residential wing. There is a door right in front of him. Great! He might be looking for that! He opens it. Stairs descend into a darkness that smells of cool underground. The cellar. Not too much dust, here—likely from Clover coming and going to reap her white wine.

She's likely off nursing a bottle in her cottage currently, but there is someone else coming up the dark hall toward him, now. He knows it without turning around. Ellis steps onto the first stair and leaves the door open a crack, breathing and watching through the slit.

He can't remember a time when he couldn't feel other people. Most times they were the normal sort, unimaginative and mundane and generally anxious creatures, due to their unimaginativeness and mundanity, and their thoughts brushed like rough cotton against his skin.

Ellis hates that feeling. This generally makes him hate other people.

At least there were hardly any of those, anymore.

But he'd had Clover and Vanity. Ro, he supposes, also. Their thoughts like tickling a light socket with a fork, like making toast in the tub. Ellis had been obsessed with them all immediately. They'd made it so he hadn't grown up completely despising everyone.

Though that would've been better for all of them.

𝟙

Ellis, especially, had been terrible for them. Where women of the Adams bloodline had their necromancy, the men of Ellis's family possessed a less physical magic, one that influenced mentality. They carried around a kind of aura that sometimes made people act a little strangely around them. Sometimes these people would go home after the Parties and have bad dreams or hallucinations. He'd never asked Vanity if he affected her in that way. Never felt the need to. She acted strangely enough on her own.

The truth was, Ellis hadn't just missed Vanity's face—he'd made the trek to the Pockmarked Island off the coast of the City to see if Arrogance was still alive.

He'd had a gut feeling about this being the case, even though no one, of course, had ever been around to feed her. Her fault; she'd effectively ended the era of the Museum, the institution in charge of the upkeep of the Sanatorium, which consisted of two parts: a stout building with a handful of hospital beds but that mostly served as a factory for World, and then the massive plot behind it, containing a bunch of uncovered holes, concrete-lined and forty feet deep in the ground. Hence the Pockmarked Island's name. Here they'd kept the comatose witches with their long, long tubes churning out of them, feeding up toward the sky, feeding the good stuff into temperature-controlled vats, waiting for their refinement and their drip-drop placement onto paper tabs.

It'd been Clover who'd thrown Ro down into one of those holes, after her whole annihilation-of-everyone thing. Vanity had died around that time, too, of course, and that had made the surrounding week or so a bit of a black spot in Ellis's memory—maybe he *had* gone with Clover to lock Ro up?

And then—why had Ro let them?

He's thought this question before. He must've. Ellis should ask Clover about it later. But also he'll probably forget. But also whatever.

Wren Athalia looks pretty awful. His thoughts have that cotton quality, though their taste in the air is tart, blackberries plucked too soon from the vine.

"Hello?" Wren calls, voice scraped down. He peeks around the archway into the empty kitchen. A cigarette burns in one of his hands. He has a pistol in the other. He always threatens to use it—on them, on himself—but never does.

He takes a courageous few paces forward but then wavers, has to stop and throw his hand out onto the wall. Stands there for a moment, teetering, sucking on his cigarette.

Quite a shock, for Ellis to find that Ro had left him alive, when she hadn't done the same for practically anyone else. And what for? To get sloshed in broad daylight? Clover hadn't been surprised. Because Clover always knows what's going to happen and why and so is never surprised by anything.

Though sometimes Wren is useful. Clover and Ellis can't trust everything they see. It's been a while since they've died, after all.

Ellis watches Wren turn back around, thinking he should make him hurt. A lot of the time when Wren floats through, Ellis makes him hurt. But no. Ellis is busy. Ellis is looking for something.

Downstairs: rows and rows of glass bottles on wooden shelves. Directly across from the stairs. There is another door, which is great! Ellis was looking for a door.

Though it isn't as much a door as it is a doorway, hewn crudely into the concrete of the wall. Past that, darkness. The smell of earth. Ellis stands in the threshold of the tunnel, head cocking, attempting to peer down into the black.

Something down there. Some spell, reeking from there. Making the thoughts in Ellis's head start to run. He moves forward.

When he finds what Ro left behind, Ellis forgets what he is doing. It is an aftereffect of him forgetting himself.

Words fall from his mouth, and laughter.

Then Ellis finds himself upstairs, in one of the halls he'd passed through earlier. Blinking at his hands. At Wren dangling from his hands. There is blood on the both of them, from Wren's nose, gone all crooked. Wren's cottony thoughts have ignited, a field of them going up in flames, in pain, pain, pain. It is annoying.

Ellis knows how human emotions and reactions are just blobs of jelly, gelatinous masses jiggling around in a bone-dish of other gelatinous masses, really, formless and smashable as whiteheads. Subconscious and conscious and ego and id just a skyscape of clouds that tend to smear. It is easy to make them reshape, to slice the jelly into soft, shiny cubes.

He lets Wren go slack from his hands. Coughs, a little embarrassed. He thought he'd dropped the thought of going after Wren, and usually he finds himself reliable; this is out of character. Ellis is a rational person.

He wipes his hands on his jacket and wags a finger at Wren's crumpled form. "You have to admit, you deserved that." Then he goes back down to the wine cellar.

He doesn't recall going up, but this is okay. All that matters is that he does better in the future. And Clover is there to check him, too. Clover is more stable than Ellis. It's partially attributed to her personality, but also that she is good and consistent at keeping herself unsober; it's healthier to fry her synapses with something other than magic. They used to just die and come back and be peachy. But since Vanity is gone and all they've had to get creative.

Well, Clover is the creative one—the one practicing the delicate alchemy of being fucked up, the one who's figured out the temporarily grounding qualities of tattoos and piercings. Ellis has his routines, though. His daily digs. Sometimes opening the curtains. Pummeling Wren. Helping to keep the things off the gates.

He walks through the hewn doorway.

When he finds her, again, he nearly almost slips a second time. Ellis strangles his thoughts into a line and kneels down onto the cool ground where she lies.

Half swallowed in the earth, Vanity looks like she is sleeping.

However, she is totally dead. Ellis knows this. He knows it was his fault.

"So here's where you were, all this time, darling," Ellis whispers. Maybe it's, like, a necromantic thing, that she hasn't rotted? He winks at her. Even in the shitty light he can see her eyes are open. Nothing in them. Nothing there. Ellis hums as he slings her limp body over his shoulder. Her skin is ice cold. It's nice. It is like she is perfumed with roses and formaldehyde, so she smells expensive and like death. "You're looking lovely today. Did you know you're actually blackmail? You're the prettiest blackmail I've ever received, Vanity Adams." Ellis grins in the dark. "Ro really has me now. She's the only one who can bring you back. I'm going to say yes to whatever she asks. My fault for being curious. Sorry for what I might do."

II

BLOAT

V

THEN

PETRI DISHES, Wren wanted to say. *Did you know—*

He couldn't, of course. He was completely surrounded. Surrounded by the usual—drugs, alcohol, and excessive wealth.

There was the art, too, statues he watched the older witches frown at, trying to discern if they might frown back, while clusters of onlookers trailed them, thrilling as they dared each other to approach.

They were the richest of tourists, to be able to afford to attend the Parties, but tourists nonetheless. Just because they weren't dragging along disposable cameras and sunhats and sticky, sugar-crusted children did not save them from this classification. They were here, and like any of the working folks who stood outside all day shuffling between the witches' cottages—certifiable dollhouses—they were here to gawk.

But they didn't really see, did they? They never did.

They didn't see the gardeners moving in their slow, shuffling paths up and down the hill every week, spreading the special compost with its finely minced meat additives to spur up the Adamses; the candles placed in the ballroom and all around the property with the wicks delicately veined with other inflammatory chemicals to tweak the Raos; the staff riddled with histories of mental illnesses they hired to lay the meals and clean at the Kim household.

Currently, Wren was holding court. This happened every week, a group of Partygoers flocking him, these people who saw the show and never the strings, peppering him with inane questions—How *is* it? Is it just *so* interesting, being around *them*, all the *time*?

Wren would nod, he was nodding now, yes, yes, quite interesting, quite illuminating. . . .

". . . certainly very lonely creatures, aren't they?"

Wren's eyes focused immediately. He couldn't tell which of the tourists had asked the question; now all their heads were turned toward Clover Rao, looking stunning in a glittery red dress, huddled into herself under one of the paintings. She often went around looking at the art, like she hadn't seen each piece thousands of times before.

"Yes," Wren said softly. "They very much are."

"Why don't they talk to each other?" Again, he couldn't pick out which of the cluster said this. His eyes flicking over them, trying to see—but they were teeming, blending together. Had anyone even asked? His heartbeat was elevating, it always elevated when he thought about this, because this was important. It seemed fortuitous that, on a night as meaningful as tonight, when Ellis Kim would be returned to the Machine and everything could begin, Wren would be presented with the opportunity to speak on this. Something this group of people, this lucky, lucky group of people, could point to later—*I was there when the lightbulb went off in his head.*

They didn't have to know that the lightbulb had been flashing for a while now, burning, burning. . . .

"They're not allowed to," said Wren. *Why not*, someone asked, or didn't—but didn't they, with their quiet? "It's said they're prone to violence around each other, but our residents have been brought up in civilized society." His attention, too, now drifted over to Clover. Such a brash, smeared girl. "Call it nature versus nurture. We've created the perfect controlled environment here to monitor any interactions. I truly believe that if they were permitted to—"

A cold presence clawed up Wren's side.

"Ah, this spiel again," Monroe said, not lacking in mirth. Amusement. The small grouping had parted for him; he was handing Wren a glass of red wine. Wren took it—and what else could he do but murmur his thanks? "Is he boring you? This is so often a topic of our dinner conversations that I've started avoiding them. My waistline thanks him for it." Monroe clinked his glass against Wren's. "There's just, of course, the small caveat that they tend to develop the tiny habit of bludgeoning one another—"

"That's an unproven stereotype," interrupted Wren. "And—how can we even know, really, when all the witches under our care have been kept isolated?"

"Because their lives are so isolated?" Monroe made a grand, sweeping gesture of his hand around the bustling decadence of the ballroom. "They get all the social interaction they could desire—not that they very often do, that is, desire—"

"If they were just allowed to interact with *one another*, I feel they could remain stable for longer periods of their life—"

"Ah, my son, the humanitarian," Monroe chuckled, clasping a firm arm around Wren's shoulders. "He likes to play therapist with our residents."

Wren, on instinct, threw on his most relaxed, nonthreatening smile. "I'm only saying what we all already know, as educated people—no, even uneducated people could reach this conclusion. It's only common sense, after all, that it is important to form meaningful connections. It might be the single most significant thing we can do for our mental health. Even current pharmaceuticals can fall short of what—"

His father squeezed his shoulder, and Wren shut his mouth. Yes, that was going a bit too far, wasn't it? Spitting on his father's empire called for a more subtle touch.

"Well," Monroe said amicably, looking around at the benefactors with that easy, rolling charm he was so known for, "when I die, he can do whatever he likes, what will I care, right?" He jostled Wren. "What will you do, Wren? Dissolve everything? No—close the Museum gates and make it a nature reserve!"

They were like Wren's hounds, barking with their laughter.

"Now, Father, I would rather you be alive to see my achievements," Wren spoke, when it died down.

"Really, son? Because the way you've been talking, I really, really wouldn't want to be."

Wren grinned and chuckled along with the Partygoers. "Because humanitarian efforts are wasted on those not exactly human."

"Ah, there you go! I knew I was paying all those pricey tutors for a reason."

"Oh, I didn't need tutors to learn about witches, Father. My upbringing is the very epitome of education via experience."

"And how was it, to grow up in an environment like this?" queried one of the listeners.

"Well, if you're talking about literal environs, I had all the fresh air and greenery our ancestors did." Wren frowned like he'd eaten something sour and shook his head. "It makes the mind docile, lacking the stimulation of modernity."

Another incessant round of chortling. It wasn't only his father who wielded charm, after all. It was enough for Monroe to stop touching him, at least, hovering that threat.

"But really, having witches around all my life, it's been—lovely." Wren dropped his voice to a stage whisper. "I doubt there's ever existed another household that validated one's sanity so thoroughly."

It was all so easy. People came to these Parties already expecting scandal with the price of their ticket. They wanted the witches to act up and embarrass themselves—made even more entertaining by the arcane beings' utter lack of wherewithal to be embarrassed. And the yearn for spectacle didn't stop at the actual Spectacles. They flocked to Wren, too.

He was young, sure, but old enough to be married, certainly, and certainly handsome enough—inheriting Monroe's strong jaw and light eyes, all charmingly softened by a slightly crooked smile, soft-tipped nose, and faint curl to his brown hair—if he could stand to wipe the bitterness off his face. Well, *was* that bitterness they witnessed? Was the drug problem real, then, or just rumors? The gossip was nearly succulent: addicted to his father's own creation! Though, World wasn't addictive, of course. That being said, more than likely showing up to the Parties with the hazel blown out of his eyes was less than a good look. Though, again, when you talked to him—he seemed perfectly charming.

Wren was very high, standing there, flawlessly moving through this conversation.

Even though this was a big night. But the times he took World out of celebration and not out of total insufferable boredom for his reality were the better nights, anyway.

Tonight is the start of everything. Tonight is the night Ellis Kim goes into the Machine. It is the night he performs magic for the very first time, and afterward—his first conversation with Vanity Adams.

And there she goes now, having been approached by his father and the tourist who'd asked a question—an emissary from Yavonia, being led toward the back halls for a reading. Wren watched Vanity steal one more glance around the room. Looking for Clover and Ellis. Dear god, the girl really wasn't subtle with it, was she?

Soon, darling, Wren thought. *So soon.*

"What's happening?" Ellis murmured.

Wren watched the blood glint on his teeth. Then the witch's eyes rolled closed, gone again; Wren reached forward and smacked his cheek.

"Ellis, stay with me. You'll want to pay attention to this."

Wren reached into his pocket and pulled out what looked like a small silver pill. It was just him and the witch in the back of the car, the privacy divider flipped up, wheels spinning on the smooth asphalt of the bridge connecting the Sanatorium to the City and Museum estate. He held up the pill so that it glinted in the faint streetlights filtering in through the blackout windows.

Ellis had just been pulled from the Machine, most of his mind blown apart by an influx of nature, which left him overexposed to other people's emotions and tendencies. It all sounded like so much. Wren's heart went out to him, it really did.

He said, "This is the bomb my father thinks is in your neck right now." Ellis reached a hand back to his nape, and Wren added, chuckling, "Oh, there's still a bomb back there, of course. I would just rather Monroe not control it, trigger-happy in his old age and all."

Yes, Monroe wouldn't entertain the Party, not when he could send Wren away with such an important task as feeding a witch to the Machine, as implanting the bomb. The Kims needed such extra contingencies, an explosive in their head to complement the one in their ankle, just in case they ever opened their mouth to say the wrong thing. Bad thing especially, if a Kim said the wrong thing. They tended to be rather persuasive.

"You're just your father's dog," said Ellis. He didn't quite have the reaction Wren had been hoping for. But you could never expect any normal reaction with witches as it was.

"I could set it off right now."

"You won't. You're going to ask me to do something for you."

Wren watched Ellis's slack delight, the witch's head lolled back on his seat. What fresh perspective pumped through his head—what of the world could he see that Wren could not?

If Wren blew it apart, what arcane secrets would shine in the slick of the carnage?

He leaned back.

"Actually," Wren said, "I'm going to ask you to do something for *you*." No, it didn't matter that he didn't particularly like their manners, the witches, that generally they pissed him off. But Wren couldn't hold it against them. They were deeply unwell, after all. But all of that was about to change. "Talk to her."

⚡

Wren was not saying what he wanted to say.

Petri dishes—he wanted to say to the intoxicated, slaphappy tourists— *did you know that all of our youngest witches, your darlings, they were all petri-dish babies? Extracted and grown in Sanatorium tubes until they were plump little cherubs and then drained and swaddled in imported fabrics. We wanted to spare the older generation, Cadence Adams and Lavender Rao, the stretch marks, the fattening of their ankles—we all know how much their mothers lost popularity during their pregnancies—and as for James Kim, god rest his soul, well, he barely had enough focus to get it up as it was. My father thought this method was for the best. So all of you wondering why this gener- ation seems especially, entreatingly volatile—I have a theory. We've especially pissed off nature with these ones.*

We can't cure nature. But we can soothe its children.

How can you look at them and not see sick, very sick, people? How can you stand by when it's so easy to solve everything?

You'll all see it, with what comes next. It's going to save us all.

It is important to form meaningful connections.

VI

ONE DAY, WHEN VANITY AND RO were about ten, Cadence took them to the Pockmarked Island, where the City buried their dead and kept their witches in the Sanatorium. The Necropolis Forest, their destination, hugged the northern border of the Island, while the Sanatorium's cells peppered the dead earth everywhere else.

Vanity and Ro and Cadence stepped out of the car at the Necropolis gates, gray and black and red dresses, respectively, darkened in the onslaught of shade pulled from the ancient chestnut trees. The driver watched the three of them warily, the young girls teetering along, knocking into one another and gripping hands for stability, their mother attempting to guide even as her breathing became shallow. All of them were slightly nauseous and electric, an effect of being near the Sanatorium-imprisoned witches, beneath the earth about a half mile back at the Forest's edge, as well as near the Necropolis corpses, beneath the earth sprawled in front of them as the gates yawned open.

Cadence called the Necropolis "sacred ground." She had a flask in one hand and spilled gin on a tombstone and her dress when her heels sank into a patch of dampened grass. It was all totally ridiculous. Vanity knew Ro, too, saw their mother's true person and it disgusted her, but also Ro just thought Cadence was a complete joke. Ro thought everything was a complete joke. The darker and scarier parts of their existence were unserious to her because darker and scarier still was Ro herself.

"Can you feel the bodies beneath the ground?" Cadence had asked, and Ro went, "Yes," and Vanity went, "Yeah," and Cadence snapped, "Don't focus too much on them. Don't do that. Have you ever done ketamine?"

"Are you talking to me?" Vanity asked.

"Of course I'm talking to you," said Cadence, pointing her lit cigarette at her. "You're trouble. Curious. Restless." Taking a drag, clicking her tongue.

"I don't want to go," Ro said when it was time to leave.

"Come on, Vanity," Cadence ordered. Sometimes she got her daughters mixed up like this. Ro was hovering by the gates; Vanity was trying to pull ahead to the car like a good child.

"I don't *want* to go," Ro repeated, clinging to the bars of the gate.

"I shouldn't have taken you." Cadence marched over now. She had put emphasis on the *you*, because Ro was a terrible, wicked girl, wanting to be in her nature. Wanting to be here, with what rested beneath the earth making her bones hum, rather than back at the cold Museum mansion with cold Monroe ordering them around forever, with her family as his favorite freak show. Ro hated him so much. "This isn't even real," Cadence spat. "We don't have sacred ground. We have no ground. It's a fucking PR stunt. Don't you see the photographers?"

Was that the movement Vanity could barely recall, fringing the edges of the memory? When she looked back, she couldn't see the cameras flashing or hear the chattering. It was just the shine of Ro's teeth. Just the palpable quiet under the earth. Vanity hadn't known quiet could thrum, until then. Before, when she thought of death, of people being dead, she thought, Empty like a void, and now, instead, Empty like a doorway. . . .

"I want to be on sacred ground," Ro shrieked when Cadence took ahold of her arm. "I want to be *sacred*."

"You're not," Cadence hissed, dragging her away from the gates. "You're broken." Ro was digging her feet in, kicking up clods of grass; Cadence spun and crouched and clamped her hands on her daughter's shoulders, shook her. "Stop babbling. You're not making sense. You're not making *sense*."

It hadn't really been Cadence's fault, of course, being a terrible mother. They all drove each other a little mental, being witches, knocking each other into higher and higher metaphysical frequencies. Ro was giggling. She loved it when their mother yelled at her. Cadence released her and Ro darted back into the car, slid into the backseat, and threw herself across Vanity's lap. Cadence was still in her crouch, leaning a little to one side; she'd put one palm to the earth to steady herself. Vanity wondered what she was seeing. In a few minutes Cadence stood again and got back into the passenger seat of the car. "Drive," she barked, fumbling for her cigarettes. "Just drive."

Ro straightened. Vanity watched her looking out the window at the trees moving past. Then they went away and it was just the bare hill of the rest of the Pockmarked Island, the Sanatorium, its cells concrete dots between dry, yellowed grass. All the witches in the car could feel them, shivering. Cadence clicked her lighter a few times, and the air curled with the scent of burned hair; when they got back to their apartment Ro and Vanity would see she'd burned off one set of her eyelashes.

"I'll be back," Ro said to Vanity. "I'll be back."

Then they leaned for each other at the same time. Vanity's hands cupped around her mouth, marking it a private moment, just for them.

"What is it?" Ro whispered, and Vanity whispered back, "I like it too."

✒

Ellis was breathing. The stretching of his lungs sending goose bumps down Vanity's spine.

He'd been all bloody, but Vanity had pushed the red off his skin out of his clothes and back into his body, so that he was all clean. His jaw had been fixed, the teeth set right. He had such pretty teeth.

He was looking up at her, lips parted, so Vanity could see that this was the case.

It was like it had all never happened.

Her face flushed. She suddenly felt embarrassed, which made her want to make him die again. That would be okay, doing this over and over again. Reaching for him in that dark space between this world and the next to find him already drifting toward her.

Ro would've done it. Vivid, confident Ro.

Instead Vanity just covered her face with her hands.

"Holy shit," Ellis was murmuring. He was touching her legs. The initial haze over his eyes had been ripped away, she'd healed him of it. She'd done that. "Vanity."

The sound of her name jarred something back into place. It was as if she'd snapped awake. Vanity stumbled off him. She was incredibly dizzy. She gagged. She stared to hyperventilate. It was all very dramatic and horrifying to do in front of him. She wasn't going to vomit, she wouldn't, she'd rather die. ~~But yes, she was definitely going to vomit. Her stomach emptied all over the grass. Immediately the thought went to the acids there, in the bile, working their way between her perfectly clean teeth.~~

Ellis was still on the grass when she turned back, his head tilted toward her. He was smiling, licking at the blood on his teeth. Her cheeks flushed, red-hot. "Stop staring at me," she begged him.

When he didn't, and when his mouth moved, Vanity took several wobbling steps back. Ro caught her, hung herself on Vanity's frame, the giggles ringing softly in her ear drowning out what Ellis was saying. Ro was saying, "Oops. You've done it now."

"You're such a bitch," Vanity muttered.

And then Ellis's words processed: "You brought me back."

Shit. Well, shit.

He was still staring at her. Black, hooded eyes unwavering. "How did you do that?"

"You fell," Vanity said. Her sister giggled again, Vanity elbowed her. "You fell and hit your head. I just woke you up. Now get up and go away." But she didn't want him to get up and go away. She wanted him to touch her again.

Well, she didn't, it was gross and too warm. But she just wanted the image of him doing it in her head forever.

"Vanity."

Vanity removed her elbow from Ro's ribs and clung to her instead. Watched as Ellis sat up, never taking his eyes off of her. But he didn't stand. He leaned, and then he was on his knees before her. Vanity's breath caught in her throat.

"You resurrected me."

"No. No. I didn't."

"You completely did."

Vanity leaned over and picked up the rock. To her displeasure, Ellis did not shrink away. He seemed, even, to lean forward a bit.

"You have a temper, huh? I never would've guessed. I mean, other people couldn't have guessed. You're always so quiet. Sullen. Sad, you always look so sad, Vanity. It really is kind of pathetic. But I always knew, of course. When you were boiling. When you're upset, it's not like when other people are upset." He smiled. "We're alike, like that."

"It's not my fault," Vanity said, but she didn't quite know why she did. Of course it wasn't her fault, it was Ro's. Ro, grinning in her ear, that grin ear to ear.

A look passed over Ellis's face that Vanity couldn't parse. "Arrogance's, then, right?" He glanced at the sister Vanity hung on. Vanity immediately turned her body to further shield Ro, who only laughed and gnashed her teeth.

"She couldn't help it. You got too close." *You're too close.*

"Was it Arrogance?" asked Ellis. "Did Arrogance tell you how to bring me back?"

"No."

What would happen to Ro if Monroe knew her magic had survived the Machine? Would they bring her to the Sanatorium to do experiments on her, or was it a cleaner practice just to put her down? Distantly, Vanity considered the rock in her hand. Considered killing Ellis and not bringing him back. Dragging him over to the side of the cliff and letting him drop, drop down and be swallowed up by the sea. If they ever found him, they'd think he'd been too out of it after his first rites, or just depressed as fuck about all of it, that he'd stepped over the edge all on his own.

"But I don't want that," Vanity said. "Just don't tell anyone I don't want to have to do that don't make me do that—"

There was pressure in her throat and it was building. The heat of trying not to cry? She'd just poisoned herself. She'd let magic rip through her, and she'd liked it. Why had she liked it? She didn't like it now. Was she already changing? Vanity coughed. And then she was choking. "God, stop, stop," she said, not to Ellis or to Ro, so perhaps only to herself. "I can't—breathe—"

She pressed her palm to her throat, mouth hanging open as she gagged. She felt, of course, only her own flesh under her probing, but. There. *There.* Something moving? Now she was practically choking herself, trying to find it. She *needed* to find it. Whatever it was. And then she'd dig—

"Vanity? Hey—"

Ellis touched her again and she flinched away. In the motion her hand slipped from her throat, and when she desperately re-grappled, she—stilled.

What she'd felt was moving was her own pulse.

Could that be right? She swore—

"Fuck," she said. "Fuck, I'm tripping." Off him. Off his death and his resurrection, her own magic. "Get the fuck away from me."

"You cleared my head," Ellis said. She scrambled away from him, her limbs dragging against the earth until she remembered she could stand up. Did so, and almost immediately lost her balance again. He was reaching out for her. Something like desperation in his eyes. And. She'd had this dream before. It didn't terrify her so then. "Vanity—you don't understand—"

"I don't *want to*."

"Please, I'm sorry for how I was acting, the way I was talking to you, I'm—I'm not actually like—"

He faltered in his words. A look of such immense pain flickered on his face it nearly bowled Vanity over. Because of course how Ellis had been acting was what he was actually like. Even though his death had somehow momentarily purged the magic from his system, it'd be back soon enough. Scrambling him again. This state of clarity was temporary, and Vanity watched the weight of that realization collapse on him now. He put his hands around his head. Fingers digging into his scalp, and as he bowed before her, she could see the white nape of his neck. Shining.

"Please . . ." Ellis moaned again. "I don't want it to come back—"

She couldn't take it anymore. Vanity fled. Though there was nowhere, really, to run to where Ellis couldn't find her again. If Ellis wanted to.

And, despite herself—everything that went through her head was always despite herself—came the thought, small and dangerous, sighing, *Maybe he will. Come to beg me again.*

VII

"WELL! WELL!" RO WAS SAYING, as Vanity held her down on their bed, held the kitchen knife to the blue vein pulsing in her arm. "I've never felt anything like *that* before!"

"Why did you do that?" Vanity was blinking back tears. "You hurt him. You embarrassed me."

"What is Monroe always saying to the tourists? *They'll often develop the habit of bludgeoning one another.*" Ro sighed dreamily. "Oh, but didn't you feel better, after the bludgeoning? Isn't your head *so clear*?"

Vanity pressed the knife to her arm. Blood beaded along the silver of the blade. She knew of course she had to punish Ro.

"At least—" Ro went on, unbothered, always unbothered. "Wasn't all of it unlike anything you've ever felt before?"

Yes. Yes. All the small creatures over the years didn't hold a candle to Ellis.

"I lost time," Vanity said. "I don't even remember coming home."

"Sometimes you need to cross things out. It's just like pretending. You like pretending, don't you?" Blood trickling down her arm and onto the bed. Ro blinked at Vanity. "Is it so bad?"

No. Yes. Yes, it had to be.

Vanity was already starting to think back to the euphoric smear of Ellis's death, the rush of plucking him from the black place. Already missing the high, that feeling of *rightness*.

Even missing the feeling of blinking out, of not being there.

And there was something that felt so . . . *clean* about the lack of a difference. Between death and life.

Meat standing up. Meat on the ground.

"So, *wonderful*, then," Ro breathed ecstatically. "Wonderful, right? I can see it all over your face."

"Can you just behave?" Vanity cried. "What's *wrong with you*?"

"Look, look," Ro yawned. "What's the harm? He's back, isn't he?" She pushed Vanity off her easily. She ran her thumb over the shallow cut and it was gone, sealed up, and licked off the blood. Then she helped Vanity back onto the bed. She wiped away her tears. "Come on, now, darling. Didn't it feel nice, to let go a little? Isn't everyone still here?"

"I felt sick afterward," Vanity said, hiccupping. "I still feel sick. Like there's something caught in my throat. I swear there is."

"Really? Let me see."

"No."

"Come on, darling. Open wide."

"*No*."

"I won't take it from you, whatever I find back there."

Now Ro was laughing, was reaching for her jaw. Vanity scrambled away. "Get away from me. There's nothing. There's nothing!"

※

There was something.

No, there wasn't.

Vanity blinked up at her darkened bedroom ceiling.

There isn't anything. *Go to sleep.*

How could she be expected to sleep?

She got up, careful not to wake Ro, who was hidden in her usual nest: the mass of silk pillows that perpetually dominated the other side of their bed. They were still fighting, of course—Vanity hadn't forgiven her. *And I'm not sure if I will.*

She would, of course. No matter how much it frustrated her to know it.

Vanity treaded down the dim hall, pausing before the edge of her mother's open bedroom door. Slowly, she brought her head around the corner. And nearly jumped out of her skin at the flicker of movement, the swing of a sheet of black hair.

It was only her reflection in the one-way mirror that made up the opposite wall of the bedroom. Her breath rattled through her. The white ankles of an unconscious Cadence hung off the bed, the contours of their delicate bones shining in the hallway light.

Vanity continued on toward the bathroom, a room on the back side of the cottage with just a regular mirror over the sink and an actual window over the tub, frosted and fringed with stained glass depicting flowers, ivy. Sometimes when Ro gave her a dead thing Vanity would come and curl in the tub, cradling her gift, head tilted back against the lip so she could watch it all pretend to move, blossoms puckering, squeezing their pistons, ivy strangling stems, trickling out of their frame and onto the wall.

She shut the door, stalling for a moment before forcing her feet toward the sink. Curling her hands on the porcelain rim, looking down into the black eye of the drain.

"Nothing there," Vanity reminded herself. "Not a thing."

She lifted her chin and opened her mouth.

Yes, there were her teeth. Risen out of the peaks and valleys of her gums, taut and pink and pristine. Her tongue in its cradle, which she moved now, back and forth, making it tug against its leash—that thin, veiny membrane latching it to the floor of her mouth that looked, to her, like it could be so effortlessly snipped away, so that her tongue would curl back and back until it would rest in a loose coil in the base of her throat.

And, yes, her throat, where something was not growing, where nothing was.

Vanity opened wider, peering down into that self-possessed darkness, the tunnel that fed down into the rest of her body. Her long fingernails slipping on the smoothness of the sink as she leaned closer to her reflection. Tongue stretching over her bottom teeth, jaw aching with the strain.

Something moved.

No, it didn't. It hadn't. When Vanity opened her mouth again—having shut it so fast she nearly bit off the tip of her tongue—nothing. Only her, all the way down. It'd been a trick of the lights burning on either side of the mirror against the slick back there. She shut her mouth again—perhaps permanently this time, she thought stubbornly—and immediately started hyperventilating. This was it for her. She'd done magic and so she was done for, her mind was going away from her and she wouldn't be able to stop it.

She was choking again. She needed air. Almost tripping over the lip of the tub getting into it, she clawed for the lock of the frosted window, pushing it out. During the day, opening it would let in all the tourist chatter from the front yard, the staccato clicking of their film cameras, sounds clawing around the sides of the cottage. Now there was just the cool night breeze, which she drank in greedily, and. And.

Vanity stood on her tiptoes to peer out, and down.

He was standing down there, in the dark, in the garden. He did not make any attempt to hide from her. No, in fact, now he was waving at her.

"Go away," Vanity said in a small, small voice that she was sure barely made the edge of the window.

Still, Ellis responded by shaking his head.

Vanity snapped out her hand to bring the window back in. Even having her bare arm out above him felt dangerous, vulnerable. She was afraid he was going to tell her to come outside, and that she would, that she would have no choice.

I'd never do that to you, Vanity.

She hesitated. Not for what he'd said. But because of another thought that bubbled up as she looked down at him, at that lost, strained look on his face.

If Vanity left him alone for long enough, would he forget what death felt like? Forget that he liked the clarity it brought? That *Vanity* gave to him?

If he forgot—would he even look in her direction again?

It was just his proximity, pulling on her. Clouding her. Vanity knew that. Of course she knew that.

"Tomorrow," Vanity said. The single word made his eyes widen. Oh, oh, those pretty eyes. Vanity rested her blushing cheek against the windowsill. "Come back tomorrow."

🖋

Of course they made up. Ro drifting in from her evening walk the next night, smelling like garden earth. A sparrow crushed in the palm of her hand. No hiding this time—she placed the peace offering directly into Vanity's palm, which, without her particular noticing, was already uncurled to accept it. Cold, fresh death trickling up her arm. Vanity slumped back on the bed, the line of the crown molding wriggling above her. She sighed, held by the buzzing of her body. "Fine," she said. "Fine..."

🖋

"I'm staying up tonight. He said he'd come visit me," Vanity whispered to Ro.

Ro skipped up and down the steps and squealed. "Naughty, naughty girl!" She tugged at a strand of Vanity's hair. Snapped her teeth at Vanity's nose and grinned. *"Finally."*

85

So Vanity waited by her bedroom window. In her lap she cradled the kitchen knife. When Ellis came, she would stab him through the eye. That would show them both something. It would show him that she wanted nothing to do with him. It would show her that he bled and screamed like everyone else who had a knife in their eye. In this way Vanity would fix everything.

⚞

Because, certainly, there was something to be fixed.

Vanity's dreams had changed. She was no longer killing him, when she was asleep. Instead, she allowed him to do things to her. It was all unspeakably out of her control.

Ellis, cutting her hair off.

Ellis, holding her mouth open for her while she flossed, his hand on her jaw, squeezing.

Ellis, with her on that cliff's edge, again, looking lost. Looking at her.

Sometimes she dreamed of that night, but the memory came back wrong. It hadn't been Ro holding that rock, bringing it down, but Vanity. The cracking of his teeth ringing in hers.

⚞

Vanity thumbed at the kitchen knife, her body cramped in the shape of the alcove under the window. The moon slid overhead. If she looked back at the bed, she knew she'd see Ro, only her eyes and dark brows visible from under her covers and her pillows. Her question would be clear, mocking—*Still no Ellis?* And so Vanity did not look.

"You keep doing that," Ro said.

"Doing what?"

"Touching your throat."

Vanity brought her hand away. "I always did that."

"Only when you have your ribbon on."

"Give it to me."

"Oh, god, don't dress up for him."

"Just shut up and hand it to me."

"Get it yourself."

Vanity retrieved the ribbon from the bedside table. Wound it around her neck, and it eased something in her, to touch there and not just find her own skin. When she returned to the window, there was Ellis, standing down in the grass. Looking up at the back of the cottage.

"I'll be back," Vanity said.

"Do you need help?"

"Help with what?"

"Killing him."

Vanity paused in the doorway. "He doesn't just want me for that."

"Well, well, of course not, Vanity!" A shuffling on the bed. From the depths of Ro's nest floated her voice, singing, "He wants you for his resurrection, too...."

"I can't bring him back this time," Vanity said. "I can't."

Her sister didn't even bother to dignify the lie with a response.

Vanity moved over the flattened grass past the front gate. The ground was littered with the usual—crushed paper cups, food wrappers, empty film cartridges, cigarettes, gum in silver wrappers or just naked and sticky and smeared on the thistles. The cleaning crews would sweep through the estate at dawn, doing away with it all. They stared, too, so Vanity wanted to be back well before then.

"Ellis," she whispered. "Ellis!"

She peeked around the side of the house and was startled to find him already coming toward her at a quick clip. Immediately she retreated to the front door. He stood at the front gate. It must have looked like the cottage was about to collapse upon her, standing in the threshold, the entire front of it a window, exposing all the furniture above her head and the kitchen and the living room cluttered on either side.

"Can I come in?" Ellis asked.

"No!" she exclaimed, the word flying from her wildly. She breathed a sigh of relief. Yes, that was the last she would say to him, her final decision. Anything else would only lead to disaster.

But then Ellis said, "Please?" and he smiled his gorgeous smile and Vanity wanted to feel the weight of all of his teeth in her hand, and so then she was saying something else and she was stepping aside.

Then he was standing in her foyer. It was clear from the vacant way Ellis looked around that he didn't exactly remember why he had come to seek her out. Thus Vanity looked at him and thought of lying to him. Explaining that he was here because they were courting one another, that they'd been sending each other letters forever now, that he was in love with her, remember, didn't he remember that, at least, darling? But then Ellis looked back at her and she lost her nerve.

"Is Arrogance going to be here?" Ellis asked.

This was possibly the most devastating thing he could have said to her, but Vanity was comforted by the fact she was holding the kitchen knife behind her back. "Do you care if she is or not?"

"No. It's just you seem—close—"

He was cut off by his own laugh breaking out of him, and Vanity jumped, and lunged forward to cover his mouth with her hand. They stumbled against the wall. Vanity turned her head to look through to the living room, where Cadence was still thankfully unconscious on the couch.

"Shut up!" Vanity hissed, lurching with the sensation of touching him, his uneven breaths sliding against her fingers. She pushed away, revolted by the feeling of *teeming*, hand flying back against the banister to steady herself. She was buzzing. Her head was floating off her shoulders and away from her.

"I feel it, too," Ellis said.

Was this meant to be a comfort? Was he trying to comfort her? Because he *cared* about her? Just then she heard the pattering of Ro's feet from above. It sounded as if she were running back and forth really quickly. Vanity looked briefly up the stairs, sharply enough for Ellis to turn to look, too, before spitting, "Not like I do."

"No. Not like you do." A pause. "Arrogance is upstairs?"

She glanced back at him. And smiled thinly. "Oh. You're afraid of her."

"Well. Yeah." Jealousy shot through her. Ellis winced. "I'm afraid of you. Too. Shouldn't I be?"

"Yes," Vanity whispered. "But I won't hurt you like she will."

This was the truth. Or it was a lie. She squinted at him, twisting the knife behind her back. Well. It was difficult to tell.

"I just want—" Ellis started, and paused. He took in a breath. "I need to feel like that again."

"Feel like what?" Whatever he said next, it was because of her. She was the cause of that feeling, taking root in him. It felt unspeakably intimate, and Vanity needed so, so harshly for him to say something wonderful, or else something terrible; she needed his attention even if only because he was flinching away.

But Ellis wasn't flinching.

No, in fact, he was swallowing. He seemed to be looking at her mouth. At least Vanity pretended he was; she was looking at his, parting. "Alive."

VIII

ON THE NEXT PARTY NIGHT, the twins painted their nails in gleaming black and flossed their gleaming teeth and dressed in gleaming dresses, and Vanity put the silver-handled ice pick from her mother's bar cart into her handbag. Ro chuckled. Vanity took the ice pick out and threw it at her. It clattered against the tiles of the kitchen. Ro crawled after it, handed it back. Back into the handbag it went.

"Are you going to kill Ellis?"

"Yes."

"And bring him back?"

"No."

On her way out the door, Cadence, who had forgotten to speak to her daughters for several days, nursed a thermos of red wine and said, "How is being alive? How is it to have fresh skin over your bones? I hate James for dying. Lavender's going to go soon, too, she's so pathetic. They're going to kill me, don't you understand that. Monroe's going to kill me!"

She began to shriek and wail. Vanity watched the stream of lights from the cars heading slowly up the drive.

"Being alive is okay!" Ro said, clapping her hands.

Cadence was tipsy and so a little better by the time they marched up the hill, toward the Museum with its sickly spires and black brick front and the doors open and glowing and eating people like a furnace. Around the time they passed the garden Cadence reached out and stroked Ro's hair. She knew Vanity didn't like anyone touching her hair and getting it out of place, besides Ro, of course. Still Vanity watched this small, rare and so *nothing* act and felt a heaviness touch the back of her throat, and wanted everyone on earth to be dead.

Ellis first, she remembered.

"Party time!" Cadence sang.

"Party time!" Ro screamed, threading her arm through Vanity's.

Everyone standing around them on the asphalt hurried away from them.

Through the doors, then. The usual flashes of the usual grandeur: servers toting thin-necked flutes of alcohol, couples waltzing across storm-dark gray marble floor, clusters of men with their fine vests and pressed collared shirts rolled up to their elbows, ladies smoking and lounging on velvet couches, their thin cigarettes stabbed with sterling silver holders. The golden champagne fountain stood so dazzling and frothy that Vanity's mouth watered.

"Wren, darling!" Ro called, and the crowd snickered and stared and Vanity watched Wren ignore them as he neared. Cadence made some similar sound and drifted off on an uneven line.

Wren gave Ro a polite kiss on the cheek. Vanity took a glass of champagne from a passing tray. Took a sip and closed her eyes as she did it, she wanted to feel each tiny bubble explode and die against each tiny tastebud inside her mouth. When she brought the glass away and opened her eyes to the room again, it was all astonishingly bright, and Monroe was standing in front of her.

Ro's arm, hooking hers, drew her closer to her sister's side.

"*Such* a party, Monroe," Ro chattered. Monroe just looked at Vanity. His smile at her was like the water in a birdbath—Vanity could see straight through to the stone at the bottom.

Not that her sister cared, continuing to flutter her eyes and babble with her frozen, secretly cruel smile. Vanity drank more and didn't say anything.

"You're not going to say hello? Are we really just going to stand here in silence?"

"Hello, Monroe."

Wren had that carefully pleasant look on his face that only appeared around his father. Vanity couldn't imagine being afraid of her parent. Across the room, Cadence was touching one of the ferns that erupted from a standing vase. She always went to touch the ferns, probably because they used compost in the soil. In a little bit she'd go in the curtained back room for the Afterparty and rot someone alive, or maybe bring someone back from the dead—just to make them dead again, or make a sculpture that was ugly, and wet. Then she'd be given cocaine and more red wine to calm her down and she'd drool all over her neck and later on the living room couch. She could do horrific things, but she was consistently rendered too out of it to be afraid of. Vanity was only ever afraid of becoming just like her.

She looked away from Wren and into the bottom of her champagne and pretended she was sitting down there, there against the curve of the flute where the bubbles were floating up, with the Party muted and everything turned into gold.

"Let's dance," Ro said from far above the surface. "Come on, dance with me."

Vanity shook her head.

"You hate me!" Ro shrieked, like a child. Vanity's head pounded with it.

"No I don't. Don't be stupid."

Monroe said, "Now..." but he didn't mean it, because the crowd loved it, Ro screaming. They loved whispering how, at the Party last night, did you see the child-dogs were doing their strange things again? They were so weird and darling and sad and interesting. Ro had been screaming and Vanity had been sullen and Clover had been twitching and Ellis had been laughing and then going silent and then laughing again. That was what Vanity heard now, Ellis's laugh. She'd never heard his voice before that first night, but his laughs had always carried. When it got too loud and too wild like a train going off the tracks he'd snap his mouth shut, briefly, before opening it again and continuing. Vanity came up and out of her champagne and looked across the room.

His laughter stopped. He'd caught Vanity's eyes.

She imagined pushing the ice pick into his mouth and through the surface of his tongue, where it'd come out at the bottom of his chin. Vanity thought of this sensation and wrung her hands and sighed. Champagne trickled down her wrists.

🖋

"You don't want to do it yourself?" Ellis had asked, that first night he'd come to call on her. So polite. Vanity had shaken her head. He was holding her knife, she'd handed it to him. "Why not?"

"Do it in the bathtub. Don't spill onto the floor."

"All right." Ellis still wasn't moving. They were standing on the second-floor landing at the top of the stairs, and Vanity knew he was thinking about hurting her. "Arrogance seemed to jump at the chance."

"I'm not Ro," she'd said, frustrated. Just like one of the hundreds of times she'd said it, to Cadence.

Honestly her head was pounding and she *was* thinking of killing him, but she refused to ruin the image she held in her head of his death by her hands: his dark eyes rolling seamlessly back, the final sigh, the gentle slackening of his fingers from whatever part of her body he'd been clinging on. ~~Now Vanity knew people didn't die gracefully. Last time Ellis's head had snapped to the side under the force of the rock in Ro's hand and he'd crumpled. Drool had trickled past his broken teeth. She was lucky she'd resurrected him before his body had really relaxed and soiled itself.~~

"It's just—" Vanity stopped herself. Would he laugh at her?

"Just what?" Ellis asked.

"Well, it's gross."

"What? Death?" Not laughing—very serious, very much looking straight at her.

"No. Dying. Bodies. Having a body."

"You have a body."

"Yes, unfortunately."

He laughed. She'd done that, reaped the noise from his vocal cords. "How do you cope?"

"I'm high a lot." She rubbed at her neck. "Rot's okay, though."

"Oh, is it?"

"It's like . . . clean. Skeletonization's my favorite." She was mortified by herself. She never talked this much.

"Skeletonization?" At some point he'd taken a step forward. She took a step back and one of her heels inched into open air over the top step.

"The last stage. Of rot."

"Because it's all dry?" He was smiling. "And clean?"

"Yes. Very clean."

Of course Vanity had never learned this in a textbook. The first time Ro had given her a gift, as the world began to waver around her, Vanity had looked at the sparrow in her palm, still with its everything intact, feathers downy soft against her skin—she swore, almost warm—she'd seen it shuddering through what it was going to be, what it was *about* to be, what it already was, really, if she squinted . . . yes, it was certainly going all dewy at the same time it was parched, a pile of bones at the same time it was dust, if she blew it would all just go away—she had blown on it, then. Its feathers had ruffled. She'd thought it was alive and dropped it, disgusted.

"Vanity?"

"Huh? Yes?"

"Are you ready?"

"Ready for what?"

"To bring me back."

She gnawed on the inside of her mouth. "Are you sure you don't just want to die?"

"Whichever." She'd made him laugh again. He didn't exactly have a classically *nice* laugh, one other people would describe like honey or windchimes or some other cheery pretty shit; Ellis's broke out of him so sudden and sharp it was alarming and left Vanity smiling nervously, cold pinpricking the back of her neck. "It's up to you, I suppose. My life will be in your hands, after all."

That nearly knocked her over. Really—her heel slipped and she faltered back, spine kissing open air over the stairs. Ellis caught her like it was the easiest thing, his arm slipped around her waist, the only thing keeping her from breaking her neck. When he smiled again, it was more thrilled than she would've liked. He brought her back upright.

"Either way," Ellis said, "do you think we could start? If we stand around for much longer, I won't want to catch you next time."

It hadn't been exactly a threat, even though he hadn't looked exactly apologetic. He was simply stating a fact; he let it openly show on his face that he was thinking of her body broken at the bottom of the stairs. At least he was being honest.

Vanity nodded. He went into her bathroom and closed the door. She pressed her ear to its wood, but there was no noise to be heard past the shifting of his clothes as he climbed into the bathtub. At first she thought she'd missed a faucet being turned on, that the frigid cold pooling around her bare feet was water escaping the gap under the door, but as it turned out, the floor was dry; it was just his death wriggling out, chilling her toes.

𝕶

So naturally every night since then Ellis had come over to die in her bathtub. And every time Vanity knelt on the tiles to resurrect him, she looked left and right for someone to come running up to say no, no, Vanity, bad girl, you aren't allowed to do this, don't you know how horrible it is for you?

No one had, as of yet.

And then he'd be back, smiling up at her. Tears of relief prickling his eyes.

"How do you feel?" she'd murmur, as the magic pickled her brain and dissolved her. The world frothed around her, her temple resting against the cool porcelain lip of the tub. Knowing she was hurting herself for him, Vanity smiled back.

"Better," Ellis always said. "Better..." and Vanity held the *Oh god oh god I'll do it over and over again as many times as you want* in her mouth, rolling her tongue around and around the shape of the phantom words as she faded away.

Had she said it to him yet, babbled and outed herself? The first few times he'd left her alone to be out of her head. She had just barely registered him easing himself upright, drifting past her, the sound, the very distant sound, of the front door opening and closing. But lately it seemed he was lingering more and more. She could recall the flash of his sharp smile here and there, the ring of his terrible laugh against her skin. The night before last she'd come back into herself with the bottoms of her feet black with dirt, wearing his coat. And yesterday she'd come to and she'd been standing in the kitchen, two emptied cups of tea on the countertop. She'd known it had to have been Ellis that fixed them up, or at least he'd boiled the water; no one in the house used the stove, not since Vanity and Ro were little, watching their mother's hair go up in flame during a poor attempt to light a cigarette.

✒

Vanity wasn't sure if it was related to Ellis or the influx of magic she was pumping through her synapses—the new, extravagant fear of choking to death. Or specifically, picking up something and feeding it to herself and then choking to death. There was an important distinction there, somewhere.

She hadn't been aware of such a development, discovering it like one might discover the nub of a skin tag on themselves; she had not been particularly searching for it, but happened upon its habitation, the realization that she was host to it, that it had grown from her without her permission. Staring out over the colorful, indulgent breakfast table—stocked every dawn by Museum workers, plodding through the house with their shoes on—following the night of Ellis's tenth death, Vanity was sat on her usual chair, sweating. Between her and her mother, fresh fruit shimmered in the morning light, cut and fanned in pinwheels and roads that swirled up the oak surface. There was even some Miyeoni cuisine to signify to the tourists that the daughters were of mixed race—soybean soup in dark stone pots, rice and pickled cabbage chilling in red pepper juice, and hard-boiled eggs marinated with soy sauce and ginger, perfectly halved to show off the slow ooze of jammy, bright-orange innards. Vanity had wondered—passively, not particularly caring one way or another—if something as simple as a smorgasbord truly convinced the tourists that witches had not been sapped of any and all culture, that she was well traveled, well educated, well connected to the civilization of the producer of the stuff that had been injected into her mother's harvested egg eighteen years ago. Would they all be so disappointed in her, if they found Vanity didn't know the native names of the dishes? If they found they'd been lied to by the shapes of the features of her face?

On Vanity's left side—all the seats were bolted to the floor so that she had to at least show her profile to the front of the house—herself, gleaming in the mirror. Ro always elected to stand, the pale ribbons of her heels showing under the cut of her pajama bottoms, and above, nothing but her dark tangle of hair. And she was, really, very good and precise with it, never turning her face so that the gathering tourists outside could see even a curve of cheekbone; Vanity herself, when staring at the reflection, could never catch the dagger-sharp end of a smile.

Carefully, she peeled the rind off a slice of orange. When she bit down, a seed clacked between her teeth. Vanity froze. In that moment she decided she would never ever eat again.

Then she opened her mouth and tipped her head forward to let it all slide out. Trusting gravity to vacate her, deathly afraid that if she pushed it out with her tongue the seed might slip to the back of her throat. Cadence choked on her coffee as the pulp-and-spit congealment smacked wetly onto the table.

Ro leaned over to peer at it. "What's wrong this time?"

Cadence said, "How should I know?"

"I wasn't asking you. Why would I ask *you*?"

They bickered. Vanity excused herself, Cadence's squawk against her spine: "—and where do you think *you're* going?"

An inane question. There was, of course, nowhere to go when the sun was out. No doubt the tourists outside had squealed at her display, parents jostling giggling children, patting themselves on the back—*Now, aren't you glad we made you get up early?*

Vanity went upstairs and locked herself inside the bathroom. She did what she'd been doing lately, every single day, three times a day at least. Opening her mouth. Looking. Thinking—well, actually, this thought was new—Yes. There is something back there. Well, then. Not quite new. *This* was her new thought, the accompanying one: that she could see it, just barely.

That she could reach into her mouth, and, going a little ways down her throat, could touch.

There seemed to be three narrow sticks. The middle one was the longest—Vanity could put the tips of her middle three fingers against each, applying light pressure to see if they'd come loose before the fear of choking herself flashed, and she retracted, gagging. Curled up and hyperventilating on the bathroom floor, she assessed. The sticks had had a warm, slightly plush covering, but contained a structure that wouldn't give. They seemed not to possess an opposite end that connected to her, no stem fused to the tunnel of her throat or down in her guts; at the same time, she inexplicably knew they could not be extracted. Just as she inexplicably knew that they would continue to grow, that she was the one helping it along. That she would keep helping it along. Because she would not stop resurrecting Ellis.

She could not get over the look on his face, or the fact that he was lingering now, the fact that he had made her tea. How the hell could she be expected to stop, now?

So, the question was—should Vanity tell him? Was it of great concern? That there was a hand growing in the back of her throat?

🖋

Vanity despised having to touch Monroe; at some Parties, like this one, he'd request that Vanity dance with him. He was old and so he smelled like aging, which was not like the cleanness and freshness of death, nor like the sweetness of rot, but more like … "Something going stale," she murmured under her breath as the string quartet at one end of the hall swept up.

Monroe never asked her to elaborate.

She took stock of the room as she was tugged around. Clover dancing on the other side of the room, in the arms of a woman who had paid for the length of the song, or perhaps the next one, too. Her mother, Lavender, was by one of the banisters, picking at an edge with her fingernails and smiling vacantly at the air. Ellis was still staring at her from the same place.

Monroe spun her around. The room and its bright, bright colors swirled. She was going to be sick, from going around and around. Always going around and around. Every single day—the same waking and crashing, the same panic attacks and blackouts from Cadence, the same four flossings, every week the same Party. They were never going to leave this Party.

I want to do magic. The thought bubbling up from its locked box—but no, of course she looked back in her head and found it unlocked, wide open. *I want to do* magic. . . .

She just wanted to do something fucking *real.*

She shouldn't be doing this. Shouldn't be thinking this, these bad bad horrible thoughts that were going to rot her mind. Monroe spun her and she knew where to put her feet, knew what to do next. She was in the highest ranks of society, she shouldn't complain, she'd have a grand, glittering existence. Why did she have to hate everything? Why couldn't she slow the voice in her head?

Stop. Stop.

~~It wasn't good remember she was wanting horrible things remember Vanity darling dearest idiot your is mind rotting and rotting and rotting and you're doing it all to yourself this is how you are going to die this how you are going to kill yourself you are not going to be~~ okay if you keep going. Remember, Vanity? Turn rot over and what did it become? Purification—

The delicate, astonishingly precise sound of breaking glass.

It knocked Vanity's thoughts off their current path. Back into some semblance of a line.

She followed Monroe's gaze to the table next to the quartet, lace-lined and stacked with liquor bottles. The marble floor shone with broken glass; its contents were splattered up against the cream-colored wall. Ellis stood a foot away from the mess, hand still suspended in the air. It moved. Studied the liquors almost curiously, plucked another one up by its neck. He looked over his shoulder. Looked at Vanity. Grinned. Down the bottle went from his fingertips. Crash. Laughter from the crowd. Ellis reached for another one.

Wren stormed over and grabbed his arm. It was over. The quartet picked up again.

Vanity felt faint. She pulled her hand from Monroe's and pawed at her throat.

"I'm choking," she said. "I don't feel well."

"You're just fine, Vanity," said Monroe. His was silky-soothing. He stopped moving them. They were disrupting the flow of the dancers. Monroe shone with fatherly concern. "Why don't you take a deep breath for me?"

She took a breath. Oxygen rushed to her lungs and then up to her head. In no way did this provide the nutrition that her body had been begging for the past couple of days, and in that moment it apparently decided it was done. Vanity was tilting to one side and then she was blinking awake on the floor. Somewhere between the two instances, she'd hit her head on the marble planter and died and been resurrected by her mother, and now she was looking up past Cadence's tight-lipped visage to see the shocking liquid red trickling from the white of the marble lip that bowed partially over her.

Vanity blinked. The initial instinct to remember what had happened the moment prior, the moment of being dead, stemmed through her. And then she instead remembered her personality and that she didn't really care what the black beyond was like, because it wasn't like anything, and so the need to recall and understand and perhaps mourn herself or be generally horrified went away. Vanity blinked again—there was her blood dripping into her eye. She was alive again and hated it and that's what mattered.

DEATH HAD MADE VANITY briefly sober, and being sober made Vanity realize she liked herself a lot when she was high, or else she liked that she wasn't herself, that she was unaccounted for. She liked the grand, black gaps in her memory. She liked being largely apathetic to the atrocities of her life and the habitual forgetting of her jealousies. She liked misplacing that she worried over what the other witches thought of her. She liked not thinking she was a desperate and pathetic person or a danger to herself; she liked not thinking of herself at all. The things that normally ruled her bled away.

"Ellis was screaming and screaming his head off while you were dead." Cadence told her this later after she got home from the rites. Vanity was sat on the stairs in her bathrobe, clinging to the wood teeth of the banister. She had been waiting for Ro to come home, but Cadence had made it first. Her mother did not note the tears on her cheeks. "Everyone was looking over and everyone was talking about it. They *chattered* through my Spectacle! *I* was the one who brought you back! I pulled a man inside out and all I hear through the flipping of the dermis is Vanity and Ellis, and Vanity and Ellis, and Vanity and Ellis, and—dear god, child, stop shrieking! Stop it! Stop it! Stop it!"

"Not tonight, Ellis."

She did feel sorry for him. Standing in her front garden, one hand on one of the posts of the front gate, wavering after the Afterparty.

"Okay," he said. He didn't move.

"So." She looked down at her feet. Toed at the line between foyer and world.

"Go away."

"How do you feel?" His eyes shone, darting around the face of the cottage, looking into the rooms stacked on her either side.

"I'm fine," Vanity said, and it was true. But she was trying very hard not to look too directly at that, at *being fine*. She knew it'd float away soon. And what had she done with her first rush of clarity after her first death? Come home and helped herself to her mother's bar cart. Went through the house, calling for Arrogance. Had Vanity's dying scared her away?

"I mean. I don't know why I asked. I can almost see it." His eyes wandering the space around her head, not exactly catching hers. "Smoother waters. Honestly, I think it's helping me—"

"You don't help *me*," murmured Vanity. "You don't. All of this. It's just making me worse."

Ellis didn't say anything. Didn't say *sorry*; he wouldn't mean it. Not when he'd be back here soon, when her judgment worsened, when her romantics clicked back into place. Which was why she had to put a stop to this. Tonight.

Instead she thought about what Cadence had said. About Ellis screaming. Which was Ellis missing her, wasn't it, really?

She heard herself say, "I can see why you like it. Dying."

"But you don't like it."

"It's whatever."

Ellis smiled. From this distance, it was a thin, sickly thing cutting the dark. This display was not something one would normally want to spill their soul to, but still for a moment Vanity thought she might tell him about what she'd been thinking, coming back down the hill—permitted by Monroe to leave the festivities early. But what would that do, Vanity telling him she'd discovered that, actually, she didn't much care for herself? That she even found a kind of satisfaction in that indifference? Would he be kind? If so, could she stand it?

"I can't do it anymore, Ellis."

"Why do you do it for me, Vanity?"

Because you ask. Because you get this look on your face, like you need me. Because it gets me high.

Vanity sniffed and scratched at her ear and said, "Just something to do, I guess."

"I never should've asked you. I didn't know."

Red touched her cheeks, which were already pinked from what she'd poured herself from the bar cart. "Didn't know what?"

"That this was hurting you."

"What?" Now when Vanity laughed, it was rough, scraped out of her. Over the past hour a rawness had made its home in her throat; she'd been too afraid to go and look in the mirror, could barely believe she'd been actively searching all week, or even what she'd thought she'd found. And anyway, it wasn't true, Vanity had realized now, there was no hand and there had never been a hand. "You of all people should know how much it fucks with me."

"I—yes. Yes, I'm sorry, Vanity. Of course I do." He swallowed. "It's just. The way you look after. I never see you smile except after you bring me back. Smiling when you talk—you started talking to me, recently."

Oh, god. "What do I say?"

"Nothing bad. Nothing embarrassing. You're ... sweet."

"I'm *high*."

"You're sweet when you're high. You flirt with me."

She had no response to that.

"But I like this, too, Vanity," Ellis said. "When you're being sullen. And a little nervous."

"I'm not nervous." She was absolutely mortified.

"Well. Maybe I'm projecting." Now he was the one who looked at his shoes. His voice came quieter: "I really did think you liked it. Doing magic."

And then he was turning to leave. Leave her alone, like she asked. And he was never going to come back, she'd said she was done and he was listening to her.

Vanity stepped out of the cottage. The smooth white concrete of the front stoop chilled the bottoms of her bare feet. "Wait."

Ellis stalled. She ventured a few more steps forward.

"I do like it," Vanity whispered. "I wish I didn't."

"Me too." His voice was also at a hush. The fence sliced between them. "You've told me all kinds of beautiful things, this week."

Her heart thudded in her ears. "Like what?"

"Things about death. Having a body. Rot." Ellis chuckled. "Honestly, it's hard to reiterate. Also you ramble. But it's pretty. You talk about all of it so dreamily."

"Really?" About having a body? Was it possible?

"Yeah, really, Vanity. And—" His voice broke; Vanity realized it only after blinking back the sudden tears that had sprung to her eyes. Ellis had closed his own. "I think you ground me, Vanity? I mean, I—I know you do. You do. You make me remember I'm not all in my head."

"Ellis—"

"I want to help you, too. In whatever way I can."

"Because you want to keep dying?"

"I want to keep being brought back."

"God, Ellis. I don't know. I don't know, okay? There's something—" She touched her throat, helplessly. "Something bad is going to happen. Something really bad is going to happen if we keep going." Not just to Vanity. It was bigger than her, but it'd come from her, the something bad. Up and out of her. But she could not explain how she knew this and so did not say it aloud.

"Like what?"

"I don't know. I—and there's *Ro*—"

"What about her?"

"This isn't good for her. She gets excited. And then she gets paranoid. I don't know what she might do."

"To you?"

"To you."

There was a weighted pause. Almost imperceptibly, Ellis shifted. "Is Arrogance the something bad?"

A sudden chill overtook her, and Vanity hugged herself. "How could you say that?"

"How *could* I say that, I wonder?" Vanity glared at him. "Well, then, never mind. Are you saying you're not the paranoid one, between the two of you?"

"*I'm* not being paranoid."

"How do you know?"

"Couldn't you tell, if I was?"

"You're not exactly of the most reliable mindset to read."

She wouldn't even bother asking him to explain that.

"I'm not being paranoid," she repeated more firmly. "Fine. Do you want to help me? Do me a favor."

"Yes, of course. Anything."

"Look, for me."

"Look—at—?"

Vanity neared. "Just don't touch me."

VANITY WAS FEELING DIFFERENT, she was feeling normal, again, really, and perhaps she was sleepwalking. Of course she was looking for something and that something was Ro. She didn't have to go very far, just the kitchen. Ro was standing there, in the dark.

"Where did you go?" asked Vanity heatedly.

"Where did I go?" Ro's laugh was wrong, a dry rattle. "No, no. Where did *you* go?"

"I was worried about you."

"Were you really? Ellis seemed to be keeping you good company."

"You'll get in trouble, running off from a Party like that."

"No one cares what I do. You're the darling, Vanity."

Vanity bristled. She reached to find the light switch beside the doorway, hand scraping wallpaper.

"No," Ro murmured. "Don't turn on the light. I have a headache."

"Are you okay?" Vanity still hovered in the threshold of the dark foyer. She squinted into the kitchen, where Ro stood by the front wall-mirror of the cottage. For once she was facing it, but it was too dim to see her face. "You sound horrible. What are you doing? You're freaking me out. Just come to bed, please, Arrogance."

"How was death, Vanity?"

She was losing her patience. "It was nothing. Come to bed."

"Did it make you feel better?" Her sister's laugh was hollow. "Did you like it better than being here?"

"Ro—"

"Did you want to be away from me that much?"

Vanity blinked. "What are you talking about? I fainted. It was an accident."

"You showed him."

"Were you following me?" Vanity demanded. "I can have a private life, you know. You're the one always running off whenever you please, going god knows where."

"You shouldn't have shown him."

Vanity shook her head violently. "I don't know what you're talking about."

"What you're hiding. In your throat."

"There's nothing in my throat," Vanity said. Remembering the feeling of Ellis's eyes wandering her open mouth. With her head tilted back, her stomach flush against the fence, he could see farther into her than she could herself.

"Empty," Ellis had concluded.

"Are you sure?"

"I am."

"Don't look at me like that."

"I'm not. I see things, too."

"Then you're unreliable!"

Ellis threw his head back and laughed. "Well, then, if you don't believe my perspective, there's someone else you could ask." He paused; Vanity stared at him, waiting. "Clover?"

She practically jumped. "Clover!"

"It's just, she's rather level, compared to us."

"No."

"Why not?"

Vanity hesitated. "What if we do something bad? Being all together." But the word still rang in her head. *Together together together . . .*

"Bad like what?"

"I don't know." The emissary tourist she'd scared a few weeks back, with the sheet-white face, came floating back to her. "What if we start an apocalypse?"

"Well, Vanity . . ." Ellis leaned forward and whispered, "Do you know how to start an apocalypse?"

"Well, no," she said, cheeks flushing again. She wasn't sure if it was from the closeness or the embarrassment of not knowing. Would he like her more, if she did? For a brief, wild instant, she thought about asking Ro—but then Ro would actually tell her, and, oh, no, Vanity couldn't have that.

"Then it'll be fine, won't it?"

Ellis smiled at her. Vanity said nothing. Her heart was beating so fast it nearly chattered her teeth.

Ellis's eyes gleamed; his thrill stabbed through Vanity. She knew he was always here, pawing at her door, because he was addicted to death, the rush of the buildup, the slow, clear comedown of the resurrection. She knew he didn't like her as much as he liked the way she made him feel.

It hurt.

But also.

What did it matter, if it kept him coming back?

"Would you even care if we do?" Ellis's voice was eager. He was over the fucking moon. "End up ending the world?"

XI

"IT WON'T EAT ME," Clover was telling the tourists, again. Kneeling in front of the mirror of the front of her house. They thought she was talking to herself. They thought she was losing her marbles, already. But no. Not yet. And never. "It won't eat me."

🪶

Clover Rao wasn't ever lonely, which was a relief, since she'd once been apprehensive about the decision to consider everyone in her life dead to her. She needn't have been, of course. The most logical choice never failed.

Clover had constructed her life with logical choices. She took care never to occupy the same room as her mother, with the exception of Parties and brief breakfasts. She made sure to eat well; she exercised and stretched in the privacy of her room; she read books to expand her mind; she taught herself physics and biology and chemistry, at first to try to find a scientific explanation for magic (an ultimately fruitless coping mechanism), and then because she enjoyed it, comforted by the explanation of true, palpable nature, not the cosmic horror inversion of the "natural" that strangled the women of her bloodline.

The magic she'd been born with—blissfully removed from her by the Machine, like scraping out a scar—concerned the nature of erosion and corrosion, or, in other words, the tendency of things to get smaller and smaller. In this way she shared the Adamses' frequency in terms of rot and the habit of bodies to grow old and contort and collapse into themselves. Sometimes she did get a buzz off all the filthy-rich elderly that shuffled around the Parties, but she found it went away if she bit the inside of her cheek hard enough to taste blood.

And sometimes she did laugh about it, the fact that she'd be gone from herself someday, while sobbing and pulling at her hair and begging herself, *Please, please, don't go away.*

Though this wasn't very productive, so she could never tolerate the state for very long; she'd sit up and swallow and breathe and remind herself it was all out of her control, and that, remember, she was going to throw herself off the cliff when her mother died, before Monroe or Wren could catch her and bring her into the Machine. She wouldn't lose herself, thus there was no reason to cry. She filled her pockets with rocks every morning and there was no reason to cry.

There was the whole fear-of-death thing, of course, but fear of mortality was a natural human fear, and perhaps Clover sought natural human fears. Reasonable fears.

And to herself, it was always, *Be reasonable, Clover. You have reason. That's the difference between you and them.*

Ellis used to be reasonable. But then the Machine ate him.

⚹

Of course it didn't *actually* eat him; Clover was simply being metaphorical— it was important to clarify to herself that she wasn't delusional—though,

113

knowing the pipeline between imagination and insanity, she was careful to keep her allegories to a minimum—she didn't really believe the Machine was a thing with teeth and a tongue that opened, consumed, regurgitated witches.

Though—should she consider the possibility?

Ellis, frustratingly, hadn't relayed to her what the Machine actually *was*, like she'd requested, like she'd been attempting to prepare him for. Well. She'd known it'd be a long shot anyway—but sensible to attempt—that Ellis probably wouldn't remember the details under the sudden magic thundering through his head. He'd probably blacked out or shrieked as his personality shifted over to make room for other people—quite literally, in terms of his bloodline's overexposure to the nature of minds and mental; an affinity that, by definition, encompassed vast variations and inconsistencies, so it was no wonder the Kim men in particular were so inconsistent, viciously scattered, no wonder that they often died before the Raos and the Adamses.

At least Clover's magic involved reliable, describable habits. If she'd been in Ellis's place, she suspected she wouldn't even have possessed the common sense to plan on killing herself.

𝄞

So the Machine ate Ellis and their secret correspondences abruptly stopped. Ellis was dead to her, he had to be, the boy she'd known in the fits and starts of the small scraps of paper they'd left each other over the years had been dissolved. Even though he looked like Ellis and smiled like Ellis, he now bubbled with violence and senselessness and an unnamable arcane unquiet—nature revolted in the form of the only person Clover could have ever begun to consider her friend.

Vanity, of course, had always been dead to her, had never been a contender for proper friendship. The flesh witch was a lost cause from the start.

Perhaps this was why they had seemed to drift together now, Vanity and Ellis. Both already doomed things.

Clover had heard the heavy crack of Vanity's skull against the ceramic planter even from across the ballroom. Her hands had filled with cold static; she'd stopped dancing with the aging Prince of East Weneks, a ringing in her ears, until it had focused into the sound of Ellis screaming. She had drifted with the flow of the crowd, seemingly and strangely forgotten. There was Monroe hovering, gentle smile already fixed. Ellis was on his knees, soaking with the blood blooming in a ruby crown from Vanity's cranium.

Wren drew him away eventually, and Ellis was replaced by an annoyed, thinly smiling Cadence, who crouched before her daughter with none of the same panic, or reverence.

Ellis had never once looked at Clover like that.

But no matter. Clover knew that to be near the witch who occupied Ellis's body now would fray her, that her mind would come loose and she'd lose what little time she had left with herself. And it *was* little time. Ellis's father was dead, which meant Cadence Adams and Lavender Rao would be eliminated soon, making room for the next fresh-faced generation of witches.

So Clover was enjoying her final days.

During the day she was constantly pruning in eucalyptus-and-sea-salt bubble baths. She downed low-fat cinnamon hot chocolate. Long walks occupied her at night, and she bothered Wren for cigarettes. She pondered the circumstances of death; she knew the cliff was the preferred method, the only method, really. The thought of resurrection terrified her even more than death; she must not allow her body to be easily fished out like so much fresh catch gleaming on the Parties' catering trays. Thus Clover made sure every dress she wore had pockets, and every pocket had rocks. They clattered neatly as she walked around, and she was always pleased to reach in and feel their cool roughness chipping at her manicure.

Clover also spent her days considering how she might do a little damage beforehand. The most popular train of thought was burning down something. Her house. Ideally, the Museum mansion itself.

But her fantasies of arson were mostly for entertainment value; she knew that, in the moment, efficiency would be the name of the game.

All of it kept her occupied. Kept her from being lonely. Kept her from missing Ellis, and from the absurdity of experiencing that missing, since she'd barely known him to begin with. Kept her from writing him, which kept him from writing her, which kept her level.

All this to say, Clover was on one of her usual night walks, which, tonight, had turned into a sprint. She was running away from Ellis, but only because he was chasing her.

UNBELIEVINGLY FRUSTRATING. It was so unbelievingly frustrating to Clover, as she ran so hard back toward her house that she could taste blood in her mouth, that she had done nothing wrong, that she knew there was no assignable reason for Ellis to chase her and hurt her and probably kill her. Did he even know why he was hunting her down? Or had he simply seen her and been jump-started by a faint glimmer of recognition—she'd been walking up the hill and then through the rose garden, her usual route, before looping back and finding him standing at the start of the gravel pathway, both standing still at first; for a moment she thought she'd say something, but hesitated with the thought that she'd never in her life said a word to him, not one she'd taken out of her throat; and then he was moving forward very quickly, and white, cold fear slammed down over her chest and Clover had torn out of there, scraped her way through the gap between two rosemary hedges and over the wire fence, dizzy with cuts by the time she was on the open grounds again—they used to talk to each other, in a way. Yet in the weeks since his return to the Machine, he'd barely even glanced in her direction during the Parties.

Instead, his eyes were perpetually hovering on Vanity.

Clover knew this tracked. Of course Ellis would gravitate toward witches now, real witches with real magic—even whatever odd, choked variant manifested in Vanity, somehow undefeated by the Machine. Clover had always known Vanity had been different from the two of them growing up. Ellis was to thank for it. After all, he'd been the one to send the first letter, maybe around nine, ten years old. But perhaps Clover would've gleaned it eventually. It was clear to everyone Vanity was particularly unbalanced—she was honestly surprised Monroe or Wren didn't know that it was an effect of unpurged magic. Or possibly they did know, and didn't care. Vanity certainly was a favorite at the Parties, with her face and her babbling—Clover never knew if she was directing her speech at Arrogance or solely herself—and no one had actually seen her perform magic or hurt someone, so what was the harm, in not putting her down?

"Mom!" Clover screamed as she tore through the front door into the house. *"Mom!"*

"Yes, darling?" Clover jumped; her mother had materialized in the doorway to the kitchen, stroking her hands very softly and slowly against one another. She fixed that vacant stare on Clover and Clover felt an immediate dissolving force began to stretch out within her, like a yawn sliding through a cat.

"Ellis Kim is chasing me," she said breathlessly. "He might come in the house—are all the windows closed?"

"Ellis Kim..."

"You *know* him, Mom!"

"Why, yes, of course I do." Her mom's voice unspooled dreamily, light as air. "Don't be silly. He's not allowed in the house. He knows that."

"He doesn't care!"

"Well, if he does . . . I'll call Monroe. He'll come and fix it."

"And if he guts me by then?" Clover said without thinking, and then cringed, immediately knowing what came next.

"You'll come back. Cadence will come and fix it. Like last time. Don't worry."

"Like *last* time?"

"Well, I'm sure that . . . it was Mama or it was me . . . it was Ellis's papa or his papa's papa . . . had an accident and killed . . . an Adams brought me back. Or Mama back. Or . . ." Lavender looked left and right quite slowly. She did this when she lost her train of thought, which was often. Finally her eyes found their way back to Clover. A line, a small line, appeared between her brows, which Clover diagnosed as concern. Immediately she worried about it—the line, not the concern—because if a wrinkle set there, it would be one more reason for Monroe to do away with her mother. "Well . . . are you going to be okay?" She didn't seem to remember why Clover was clinging to the door, and stroked her fingers through the long and glossy chestnut hair they shared. "Do you need me to get you something? I can make you . . . a tea." She smiled, then dropped her voice to a whisper, which from her regular voice made it barely there at all. "I can spike the tea, if you would like."

Clover slid past her mother and shot up the stairs. Having a level between them evened her out; she momentarily let her weight tip against the banister, catching her breath. Below, Lavender hummed, momentarily glancing around for her daughter, or else just having a glance around. Then she shuffled backward, back into the kitchen.

Clover, looking up, saw her own reflection looking back at her, half obscured by the chandelier that hung over the foyer. Was Ellis out there, standing in the garden, staring up at her? Clover hurried into the bathroom and closed and locked the door.

She thought she might cry, but after a moment realized she refused to.

The letter was slipped under her door in the middle of the night; Clover caught the moment because she was acting sentinel at the top of the stairs with a bottle of hairspray and the lighter that Wren had gifted her. This pairing was also one of the more extravagant ways she had considered burning down the house. At one point her mother passed her on the stairs on the way up to her room. Clover at first thought that her mother's touching of the top of her head was her way of saying good night, until Lavender wobbled and laughed an apology and Clover realized she'd merely been used as a steadying post.

She'd waited for about ten minutes after the letter arrived, in case it was a trap and Ellis was waiting with his ear pressed to her front door, ready to burst in at the sound of her approaching footsteps. There were, of course, no locks on the door or the windows, save the one on the bathroom door that was easy enough to break.

Approaching it, she murmured, "You're not going to read it. You're going to throw it in the fireplace and be done with it."

Clover scooped it up using the corduroy fabric of her skirt and brought it into her room. She kept it face down on her bed for about thirty minutes while she paced back and forth, her curiosity boiling and boiling inside her until she donned the brown silk gloves she used for the winter Parties and carefully turned it over with a pencil. The sight of his handwriting collapsed something in her; Clover paused to observe whether it was a reaction of magic or of simple anxious sentimentality. After a moment of the carpeting not wriggling and the flowered wallpaper not waving at her, she diagnosed the latter, and, satisfied, promptly strangled the emotion until it no longer existed.

Clover read the letter. Then she read it twice.

Dear Clover,

I write this while my head is clear I think my head is clear because of the death which might be the answer to everything. It's been so strange since going into the Machine and you're right to be scared of it and what it does to our heads. I know I was supposed to remember what it was and how it worked and I don't. And I know you told me to stay away from Vanity and I didn't. I'm not. She's the only thing keeping me stable. But it's not good for her. You could've guessed that. So maybe I'm fucking us all over. Or maybe I'm a fucking genius. That was a joke. You're the genius we've known this. Which is why I need you and why Vanity needs you. You wanted me to remember the Machine because maybe it could help us in some way if we could make one ourselves if we could not have it hit as much but how ridiculous was that! And how long it took you to even give me that plan since even before the Machine I was already a little well you know after my entire life being in that house with him but you Clover you were always the most stable out of all of us. See but I remember that had been the plan shouldn't that tell you that something is different. Back to me being a fucking genius I think I found what you were looking for although honestly it's been more than forty-eight hours since my last death so it's all getting a little foggy again I meant to write something else did I mention it already? Death? That death is the cure?

But I guess I'm being mean that's not really why I'm writing you in the first place that was just to give you incentive to meet us. Vanity said she'll keep bringing me back and I need it but *it concerns me slightly because she has something growing in her throat but I'm not sure if it's actually real or if I'm just seeing her hallucination like I tend to see other people's. I need you to be our eyes in case we take it too far and something happens to her. So will you? Meet us? In the woods tomorrow?*

PS: I know you're scared of Arrogance but she seems to be on her best behavior lately so to speak

PPS: Sorry for chasing you I was trying to give you the letter I forgot you're scared of me now too

🖊

The most logical choice never failed, remember? Clover's hands crimpling the paper. Remember...

XIII

A MAN, WHO WAS A GOOD MAN, said, "I don't need a reading. That's not what I'm here for, Vanity." His pulse quickened. This moment, this moment was what everything had led up to, his entire life. "Would you like to leave with me? There's a boat that's been chartered to deliver you to the safety of my country. Witches are categorized as endangered species and they are not harmed, and there are entire teams of psychologists and neurologists and therapists employed for your comfort. We can help you. You won't have to be a Spectacle. You won't have to have children. You won't have to suffer any longer, I promise—"

The young witch interrupted him. "Am I the first one of us you've spoken to about this? Oh, that's good. If you try to talk to them, too, if you take me away from them or take any of them away from me, I'll do something horrific to you. I'll make you watch me open you up and then I'll eat you. Okay? Well, anyway, here's your reading. The Chariot, the Five of Cups. A journey that turns out to be a disappointment..."

Party night, and the same incessant chattering, the same pockets of the crowd high off World, having the usual revelations. Vanity, back there in the dark room, her hands on the cards.

"They call your kind daughters of the flesh, in my country," said her second tourist. Wasn't everyone some offspring of some flesh? "Can I call you that? Do you know how much I'm paying to be here? The ticket sells for . . ."

Vanity did what she did lately when she was bored: attempted to tuck her tongue back and touch the stalks of fingers scraping at the back of her throat. Of course her tongue didn't really move like this, attached to that thin-membrane leash in the damp bay cradled in her jaw. Which she had, often lately, been considering cutting. Enticed by the idea of setting it free, so it could go check for her. But for now she was staved off largely by the thought of choking. Still she believed she could taste some aura coming off of it, the hand, some foul air. Or, it should be foul. The heat of slow, wet growth. Of compost. Of heavy, sugary rot. It was air that tasted alive, like the warm buzzing of fat black flies. Vanity could almost feel it, when she pressed her hand to the ribbon wound around her throat. That humming. That life.

Today marked three weeks she'd been killing and bringing back Ellis. Well, no, *she* hadn't been the one killing him. He'd been doing it himself. Hadn't he?

"What are we doing here?" Vanity asked.

"We're waiting in the garden," Ro reminded her from her place on the stone bench. Her gray silk dress shimmering, even under the new moon. From way up here, the crash of the waves at the cliffside was soft, like murmuring.

The front drive was cleared out except for the drivers waiting for the other attendees of the Afterparty to finish up, come out from the doors grinning and chattering and reeking of death. Cadence was likely in the dark, curtained room, performing her magic, or already finished up and stumbling through the halls, trying to remember where the doors were.

"Speaking of," Ro said as the entrance opened and their mother came gliding out.

Their mother strode down the lawn toward their cottage without even glancing toward the garden. Her red mouth was opened wide, chattering to the sky. Vanity watched her go on, long white limbs swimming through the air like a beautiful phantom. Cadence was so gorgeous that it always took a moment to notice the absolute gracelessness.

"She's so pathetic," Ro tittered.

Vanity said nothing. She got off her hands and knees and attempted to brush the dirt off both. Earth smeared silk. Apparently she'd been digging. Perhaps for bone shards tumbled in the compost. Perhaps worms. She coughed.

"Do you think she's going to show tonight?"

"Who?"

"Clover."

"I doubt Ellis even gave her the letter. He wants you all to himself."

Vanity flushed. "But we need her."

"So Ellis says. Do you not remember the years of them passing notes? Not including you?"

"Of course I remember," spat Vanity viciously.

"The attention will be off you, if Clover comes."

"I don't care about the attention."

"You liar. You shitty, shitty liar."

"I don't understand you. One minute you say they're obsessed with me and the other that I should stay away from them. Make up your mind."

"You first."

"What is that supposed to mean?"

"You either love them or want them to die." Ro pointed to Vanity's hand, which she remembered held an ice pick—the bar cart's backup ice pick, the first having scattered away when Vanity had hit her head last week.

"Well, luckily for me, they can die all I want!"

The twins stared daggers at each other. Ro was the first to start laughing. Vanity followed suit. Ro patted Vanity on top of her shoulders. Then she shook her and Vanity grabbed her arms and shook her back, the both of them still wrought with giggles. Convulsing.

One of the front doors of the Museum opened a crack. There was Ellis's black suit, one half of his face, scanning the world beyond. The door opened a little further. Vanity glimpsed his expression—the blank, almost childlike gaze, his full lips slightly parted, almost smiling, almost drooling—the usual post-Spectacle performance look. He ventured farther out, paused on the first step down. No blood on him, this time. Glancing around.

Then, quickly, as if remembering what he wanted to do, he came down onto the drive and wove between the cars. On the grass now, heading for the forest border, inked black in the night. Vanity watched him go, mouth wetting, ice pick in hand. Ro was giggling. "Follow him and kill him," she whispered in Vanity's ear. Vanity made for the garden gates to follow him and to kill him.

The reasoning was the same: he was making her worse. Once she stood at his side she'd forget that. Either way, the night would end in the usual routine: with his death, and his resurrection.

But ahead of her, there was movement in the little square garden of the Raos' cottage. Vanity froze. The lights in the lamps dotting up the drive glinted off Clover's tortoiseshell glasses, caught in the glitter of her pale pink dress. Clover took off in the same direction as Ellis.

"Stay here," Vanity told Ro, stalking beside her.

"Maybe," Ro said. Smiling Vanity's smile, pressed fast under her fingers. "If you really want me to."

Vanity headed out over the green, following the dull flashing of Clover's dress. Her heart pounded in fresh anxiety as the forest rose above her, but her stride did not break. Luckily, it was just in the tree line that she saw it—a small flame. The lighter igniting the outline of Ellis's angular features in gold. He brought it to the cigarette hanging off his lips. Staring out into the forest and smoking. What the fuck was he doing?

"What the fuck are you doing?" Clover hissed at him.

He wasn't breathing in. The cherry burned and burned. He took it out of his mouth and ash crumbled and died at his feet.

"I don't quite know," Ellis said. "What are *you* doing?"

"You said—you know what, actually, don't talk to me—you—*wrote*—"

"I did?" His eyes slid past Clover. Landed on Vanity. His expression softened. Well, Vanity imagined it did. She actually couldn't tell in this light. "Hi."

"Hey," Vanity breathed.

Clover turned.

Vanity had pictured her first meeting between her and Clover many times before. She had with Ellis, too, she was sure, but he was always so blatant with everything, staring at her, unguarded expressions drifting across his face like clouds, that she hadn't needed to make up his mannerisms. But Clover was a mystery to her, and this had left room for Vanity to make more shit up in her head.

There were certain aspects that carried over from her imagination to this real-life moment now, that held true.

The glossy sheen of Clover's deep brown hair, slipping back over one shoulder. The parting of her lips, the slight uptick of their perfect little bow. Clover would meet her eyes, like she was doing now. They'd widen, and Vanity would glimpse the full circle of her brown irises. Clover would be shocked at her own influx of emotion, the guilt, the sorrow upon realizing that she'd been doing nothing but wasting time, not sending those notes to Vanity, too.

However, her eyes didn't widen. There was no surprise, no remorse. Clover simply turned her body toward Vanity's, which made Vanity stop in her tracks, cradling the ice pick awkwardly in one hand—she wasn't sure if she should hide it or not—and then Clover was talking.

"Good, good, you're here." Her voice was clinical, precise. Vanity reeled at the lack of ceremony. "Quickly, there are things to discuss. We need to—"

"You're here," Vanity said, feeling faint. "You're really here."

"I—yes. Are you sure about that? Do you have any reason not to believe I'm here? Did you believe I was here other times?"

"No?" Vanity said, bewildered. Clover had fixed that feverish look to her. Apparently she needed reassurance? Vanity felt herself blush, drove the tip of the ice pick into her palm for the distraction, or the penance. "This is the first time?"

"Are you having trouble believing I'm real?" Clover had suddenly produced a notebook, and a pen. She was scribbling something down.

"Well, no—"

Then suddenly Clover was holding Vanity's wrist, *she was holding Vanity's wrist* and using it to tug her forward and then she was pressing Vanity's fingers to Ellis's arm. Ellis jumped like he had been electrocuted. "See, see?" Clover exclaimed, and Vanity's mouth was half-open. Clover was *touching* her; she couldn't possibly hate Vanity if she was touching her. "Everyone is here, do you believe it, Vanity? Can we begin? We should. We need to hurry. God, it's already setting in, isn't it? The babbling. Anger. Restlessness. Oh god oh god my head is so loud— Yes. I'm making a note."

All her questions seemed rhetorical. Even now. Clover had not stopped talking, and though Vanity stared at the shapes Clover's lips made around the words, the ringing in her own ears was distracting. The track of her own thoughts speeding up. The three of them together . . . not unpleasant, no. Just. Loud. Well. What was Vanity just thinking about?

How had she made up Clover in her head, again?

Brilliant, clearly. Clinical, analytical, ever-watching presence. And now Vanity had to synthesize that with the creature that now stood babbling before her. Vanity squinted. She remained thrilled, of course, but honestly—what the hell was Clover on about?

A cure? Well, *that*, certainly, was all nonsense. Or maybe Vanity was distracted, or simply misunderstanding. But then Clover was drawing the ice pick away from the palm of her hand, then Clover was turning and pushing the ice pick into Ellis's heart, and *that*, of course, Vanity did understand.

The cigarette tumbled out of his mouth. He slumped back, spine against a tree trunk, and then he seemed to sit down against the roots. But really of course he was dead. Vanity felt him go. Felt him slide at once out of himself and into himself, away from himself, leaving coldness behind. Her vision twisted, in the wake of that death. Her teeth and thoughts rattled. Clover had already placed the ice pick back in her hand. Vanity wanted to lick the blood off its end, but she didn't. That would be crazy.

The world was bending. It was twisting toward the tiny hole Clover had poked into Ellis's body. She'd made a sinkhole, there. Death was a kind of gravity, everything else slipping toward it. Vanity could get to her knees, peer into the hole, and find so many other people on the other side. She thrummed in the feeling of it, of cycles complete, of graves dug. Everyone was okay. Vanity wanted to make everyone okay, like that.

Clover was still talking, really now she was taking faster and faster but Vanity was drifting after Ellis, following him into that numb black. Clover's words would come and find her later, when she got back, when she stopped tripping, she was sure. She did find Ellis, over in that other place. He didn't have eyes to look at her or skin to feel her or a mouth to talk to her; he, of course, did not notice she was there. Vanity wasn't able to put it into words, how she knew what part of the dark was him, and how she was able to distinguish him from the part of the dark that was her. But there were no words here, anyway. There was nothing at all.

"...see. Let me see. Come on, Vanity. Bring him back, now."

Vanity wasn't sure how much time had passed. It might have been mere moments. She was still on her feet, looking down at her feet. Next to her feet was Ellis's body, the ankle of which Clover was toeing. Vanity's senses, at once sharpened and sullied, could pick up the smell of her shampoo. Peppermint. Sage. The moment was surreal, and light.

"You...want me to resurrect him?"

"Why else would I have done it?" Vanity stared at her. "Oh. Yes. Violent creatures, and the like." Clover flapped her hands around dismissively. "I guess they got that part right."

"I didn't kill him," Vanity said defensively.

Clover licked her lips. "This time."

"Or any time!"

Clover's laugh was a thing that shot out of her. "And where is Arrogance, anyway? Do you consider yourself responsible for her?" Vanity's face flushed, but there wasn't any judgment in Clover's voice. Then she switched gears. "Why did you have it, in the first place, the ice pick?"

Vanity blushed. "Just in case." But then Clover's expression didn't waver, and Vanity remembered—Clover understood her. How some thoughts came up and they just wouldn't go away. "Just to have the option."

"Well, it was convenient." Clover was wringing her hands, a gesture Vanity had witnessed at the Parties countless times before. To observe it up close sent warmth punching through her ribs, right into her lungs.

"He's better, when he comes back," Vanity said. *Better than me.*

"When he comes back. Yes. Because—you remember how to do magic, don't you?"

Oh, Vanity thought. Oh, no, no.

It's not me.

Not me. Not me. Not me.

Her breath hitched.

What if Clover and Ellis didn't want her anymore, if they knew it was actually all Ro? That Ro was the special one. The one who remembered how to do magic.

She'd never been jealous of her sister, and yet the realization hit her like a mallet to the temple. Confident, cunning Ro, and Vanity, always the awkward one. The depressed one, stabbed with her anxieties and thinking up versions of people in her head who were as obsessed with her as she was with them. No, no, no. Vanity couldn't tell Clover or Ellis any of it. She'd bury the secret down into herself until she herself believed it. She needed to. Because she needed them.

"Yes," Vanity said. "There are some parts they couldn't take away."

Clover smiled.

And some part of Vanity knew it would be the end of everything.

"Prove it to me," Clover breathed.

She brushed her hand against Vanity's collarbone, was moving Vanity's hair back behind her shoulders. Perfect, she was so perfect, Vanity knew this now, being up close. She sputtered, "You're—you're supposed to check me."

"Yes, yes. For what? Wait. Don't say. It'll ruin my objectivity."

Then she told Vanity to get on her knees and open her mouth and so Vanity did.

⚹

Clover had explained it like this (it came back to Vanity later, after she'd left Clover and Ellis, now alive, and gone back to where Ro was waiting for her. Hand in hand through their front door to find Cadence already asleep on the couch, not noticing they'd been missing, a kiss happening at that moment on the flickering television screen, perfect timing, a sign. Tell me tell me tell me, Ro was saying as they both took their respective places in the bathroom, flosses wound around fingertips, stop doing that and tell me. Let me do this, Vanity said, but now she was unsure. She was suddenly unsure about everything, except for the presence of the two other witches now stamped in the middle of her life, their significance, the necessity of them. A little rot never hurt anyone, Ro said. Tell me what happened. Tell me everything. Which was perfect, really, because Vanity wanted to repeat all of it. She put down the floss. Then thought a little more about it and unspooled it into the trash bin. Ro grinning over the edge of the tub. Okay. Here, Vanity said, with the thrill of being horrible, here, Clover explained it like this):

🖎

"~~I do hate you because I don't want to be around you you make me spiral and it's horrible for me but that can't be~~ forever, right? ~~Perhaps a kind of exposure therapy?~~ Vanity? Are you listening to me, Vanity? ~~Sorry, yes, perhaps I got ahead of myself. First. Where to start? What was I saying? Yes. Well. See. We'd been discussing it for a while, Ellis and I, that he had to remember. The Machine. I thought there would be some possibility of~~ a cure, ~~there, if he remembered the Machine, if I knew what it was I could figure out how to withstand it. But~~ now there's you. Now there's death. ~~Where was I? Yes. Sorry. It is something else, having three of us here together. I observe it. I'll make a note. My thoughts usually thread together better, but now they're on a spool. Unraveling. Where was I? Yes.~~ You need to keep going. We die and you bring us back. We purge the magic from our heads until it sticks. ~~Vanity, are you listening?~~ You're ~~hurting my head. We are going to embark on a grand experiment.~~ A needed ~~experiment.~~

🖎

"There's nothing in your throat. Yes. I'll keep checking for you. Are you worried about starting an apocalypse? Vanity. Vanity? I mean, you don't *know* how to do that, do you? Tell me if you do. Well, then. It's fine."

↙

"Do you know how to start an apocalypse?" Vanity whispered to Ro. She was looking into the trash can where her floss lay curled and abandoned. She still knew Ro was smiling and smiling and smiling.

XIV

NOW

THE AIR REEKS OF FLIES and old skin. "I want ten fresh hearts."

Ellis considers this probably a bad sign.

Ro twirls her dry, black hair around the ends of her fingers. Her cheeks are pink from the cold. It might be winter.

Ellis sighs. He looks back at Vanity's body.

He's placed her on the dead grass. Her skin is perfectly white in the gray light. Across the tree-bare hill of the Pockmarked Island are the various pits of the various deceased witches—that's where the stench is coming from. Vanity's eyes are open, but Ellis had gone back and forth on that, during the car ride out of the Museum estate and over the thin bridge to the Island and its Sanatorium, with her buckled in the passenger seat and him flipping her lids up and down, trying to picture what she might prefer.

"Yeah, yeah, okay," says Ellis. "Why do you need them?"

"Does it matter?"

Ellis shrugs. It doesn't.

Ro smiles. "Did you forget so easily, that some spells require ingredients?"

"The worse ones . . ." he murmurs. Yes, yes, it's somewhere in Ellis's head. He can almost remember, ingredients . . . "The hearts aren't for her resurrection." Resurrection—the kindest of magic. Though, of course, not to Vanity. "What are they for?"

Ro only keeps on smiling.

Ellis says, slightly irritated, "So do you just, like, not die or something?"

"I'll be here forever," Ro says from below. "Even when I'm rotting. Even when I'm done with that. I will never go away, I am the silk of threads in the fabric of existence. I am more real than you are."

"Uh-huh. So you want the hearts, like, in a cooler? Individual plastic baggies? What?"

"A cooler is fine. Whatever." Sometimes she really does sound like Vanity.

Ellis ponders. He is clear enough to do that. Sometimes he isn't. Sometimes when he thinks he should think he ends up halfway across town, Clover pissed at him by the time he's wandered back to the estate because he'd vanished for hours or for days. But the foul air of the Sanatorium grounds him. He feels steady, likely stable.

Is he doing the right thing?

When Vanity is back she'll be different, after a year and some change of being dead. Ellis certainly isn't resurrecting the romantic she'd been, once. He'd done his piece to carve it out of her. She'd likely gone into the ground hating him.

Death would soften none of her thoughts. It hadn't even softened her body.

He pulls her to his chest. Her glassy black eyes roll at him. "Why did you kill her?" he asks, not for the first time. "I thought you loved her."

He knows this could not be more hypocritical of him. He strokes

Vanity's hair, which is still silky, but nearly artificially so, like the hair on a doll.

Ro giggles. "She didn't mind. She was tired. She understands."

"Understands what?"

"Everything bows to the cycle." She doesn't stop laughing, so Ellis leaves. The sounds she's making follow him all the way back to the car.

Safety first. He buckles up Vanity, then slides her eyes closed again. Halfway across the bridge, he reaches over and opens them, because there is a silken fog settled over the road, creating a dreary and colorless kind of atmosphere he knows she liked. The cityscape rises above them when they hit the mainland, skimming the road between downtown and the forest border of the Museum estate, black glass cleaving the night sky.

Even from here, Ellis can feel the scratchy mist of the thoughts of so many people looming above them. This is slightly concerning because they are really not supposed to be *chattering* like this; everyone is supposed to be dead. Sure, hunks of them are walking around, often trying to climb the fence, but they aren't thinking anything. They don't usually have moods. They don't usually feel so lonely.

It is likely that what happened was a worldwide occurrence, not just the City—not a single ship has broken the horizon for a year. He'd caught Clover walking the edge of the cliff, scanning the water. Embarrassed, she'd made the excuse that she was considering casting herself off, now would Ellis please leave her in peace to do so. Ellis had riffled through her mood before going away. It was bleak as hell, sure, but that day would not be the day. He'd left her to her wandering.

"If only you could hear what they're saying, Vanity. . . . Well, honestly, it's all pretty familiar. Well. At least there'll be plenty to get the hearts from. So don't worry. But I'll make it so you don't worry. You don't really need to know what happened, anyway. It might be worse for you to. Maybe we'll keep you inside for a while." Trauma isn't good for people. Logic like this is difficult to argue against. Maybe Ellis is a good person, after all. He shouldn't be so hard on himself all the time. "Why would you have to leave the Museum, anyway? Clover and I didn't. We haven't. Maybe that was the plan at one point, but really where else would we go? It's not bad there now. We can do whatever we want. Just maybe I won't let you outside for a while, okay? But better check with Clover on that. She's smart. Smarter than all of us. You've said that before. I don't know if she'll be down with giving Ro whatever she wants, though. She might think it's a bad idea, that you're not worth the end of the world. Again. Then, you'll *have* to forgive me *then*, right? Because you are worth the end of the world, to me. As many times as it takes. Vanity? Are you even listening?"

⚰

When the black spires of the Museum gates come into view through the misted greenery of the forest that's swallowed up the road, Ellis reaches over and closes Vanity's eyes again. Movement ripples at the corners of his vision; this he cheerfully ignores for Vanity's sake. Calm demeanors evoke calm demeanors, after all.

The close proximity to whatever preservation spell Vanity's under is starting to make Ellis feel tingly. He knows he is going up the gravel drive unevenly. He realizes when the car jolts he hadn't waited for the gates to open all the way, honestly he'd forgotten they were there. But he doesn't crash into the garden or the mezzanine over the drive that marks the front doors, going around back to the garages and the residential entrance. He parks outside, noticing it is downpouring, that it's been downpouring. No wonder it's been so difficult to see. He gets out and rounds the car to open up Vanity's door. Chivalry, at least, isn't dead.

He unbuckles Vanity and they make their way through the rain toward the Museum mansion. But the spell coming off her skin is fogging him, and he can't tell what is a door and what is a wall and what is misted, rain-streaked window. The world is one unblemished surface; it is a sleek and even photograph. Ellis kneels down on the wetted grass, Vanity propped up beside him, and waits for someone to find them.

"Don't laugh at me, darling. It only seems like we're in exactly the same place. I mean physically, yes, we're in the same place. At least I'm up at the big old mansion now; I'm lazy, okay, I didn't want to find a *new* mansion. Stop laughing at me. Clover hasn't even moved out of her cottage." He pauses. "Would you prefer your cottage?" He shakes his head. "You're such a hypocrite. You've been here the whole time, too!"

And Clover thought it was a lost cause, to look here. Or at least she thought it was ridiculous, all of Ellis's digging. What surrounds him and Vanity now is not the sleek manicured lawn she left behind—it is full of holes. At least six feet deep, some deeper, just to be sure. Every day Ellis has been digging, looking for Vanity, waiting for the day the melodic swing and pull of the shovel was interrupted by the glorious blunt note of snapped limb or shattered skull. Instead he'd made another pockmarked part of the City; he hadn't known he'd just have to wait around for the earth to open up. For Arrogance to give her back.

"Not a waste of time," he murmurs. "Not when the point, apparently, was to waste time. . . ."

Eventually the front door under the stone awning eases open. Wren's black-and-blue face is peering out.

"Oh, grand," Ellis says, standing. "Go fetch Clover."

"Is that—*Vanity?*" Wren, usually a roll-with-the-punches—figuratively and literally—kind of guy, looks strangely aghast. "You can*not* bring her in here."

"Yes I can, now that you've revealed where the door is."

"What if—Ro comes for her?"

"Uh, I don't know?" He's trotting for the entrance, pulling along Vanity. Her bare heels scuff softly up the drive. "Go and ask Clover."

They've created a well-oiled social ecosystem here: their main collaboration is the garden and the keeping of the things off the fence and Ellis pummeling Wren when the mood hits him. It works out nicely because Wren is too much of a narcissist to throw himself off the side of the cliff while also being too drunk most of the time to fight back. Also because

Clover sometimes takes to drugging him with something; Ellis isn't really sure why or with what, but it's likely the reason Wren thinks he needs to stay. Ellis, on the other hand, could take him or leave him, but defaults to Clover as the voice of reason.

Even though her reasoning here just might be that she hates Wren.

Ellis brushes past him and heads for the kitchen. He was never back here, in the residential wing, when the Museum was still functioning, only ever in the cottage or the front hall or the residential wing's dining room when Monroe sent his gracious invitations; it wasn't until the end of the world that he got to do some proper exploring of the building he had stared at all his life. After a bit it was clear that it suits his tastes nicely, though perhaps mainly due to the lack of floor-to-ceiling one-way mirror.

He's taken Monroe's master bedroom—empty since Ellis butchered him. Or at least he'd probably butchered him. They'd had to butcher rather a lot of people, who'd become not exactly people, just to clear the place out a little. Clover had pitched that they burn them; Wren had insisted on burial; Ellis hadn't wanted to accidentally bury anything on top of Vanity; Clover had said, Holy fuck, we have to burn them, they're growing back; Wren ditched the burial idea; Ellis shook his head, he'd said, amazed, mesmerized, Can you believe it all came from her?

Ellis deposits Vanity at one of the kitchen stools. She folds forward, head making a sickly sound as it drops against the black marble countertop.

"Ah, love," he says, scooping his hand under her forehead for some cushion, "if only you had known what we'd known, maybe none of it would've happened. That you were always the scariest one out of all of us..."

The light ebbs and flows across the marble; Ellis blinks, realizing he has leaned over, that his nose is in Vanity's hair. He straightens, unsure how much time has passed. He turns his head back toward the kitchen sink. Clover Rao is standing there, the dark brown fuzz of her shaved head framed in the gray light trickling from the window over the faucet.

"Did you hear what I just said?" she barks. The sharpness to her voice is not a good sign.

"No," Ellis says, smiling sheepishly, drawing his hand away from Vanity's head.

Clover's arms are crossed. Behind her glasses, her pupils are blown. The thin hazel rings threaded around them burning at him. "I said, what the fuck, Ellis, what the fuck."

"Look, look," Ellis hums, feeling lighter in the wake of Clover's insobriety. He guesses: cocaine, a microdose of psilocybin. A handful of caffeine pills. Maybe some white wine. There had been choices galore stored in the Museum for generations of witches to come—it all sends whatever haze of magic that lies inside him shriveling back like a fried synapse; the world is feeling more and more solid, individual objects becoming distinct. No wonder Clover has it more together than he does. She knows how to keep herself quiet. Ellis lifts Vanity's arm and jostles it, like she is waving, or being electrocuted. "Gang's all back together. . . ."

🪶

"Think about this, Ellis."

"I have." He thinks he must've. That counts.

"No, you didn't. You don't think about anything."

Ellis is walking backward holding Vanity under her arms and Clover is walking forward, cradling her ankles. Even though it is clear that Ellis can haul Vanity around on his own, and that Clover is a little drunk. Her hold is awkward. But she's missed Vanity, harshly, too. She is complaining and criticizing and bickering but she hasn't said no, stop, Ellis. Perhaps she will later. What would he have to do to her then? Ellis tries to picture it, to prepare himself. But nothing comes up except some image of a crowbar he supposes he'd pick up and swing, but every time he attempts to get to that point, Clover gets to it first, so over and over in his head she is picking it up and beating him to death with it.

Ellis laughs, under his breath.

Now they reach the front lawn. They place Vanity down on one of the sitting benches and look at each other across her, both a touch embarrassed. "I guess we could've left her in the kitchen," Clover murmurs. Indeed. But parting is such sweet sorrow.

Clover tugs at the brown shell of her ear, accented with gold rings and a tattoo of what looks like thin leaves overlapped, but she's told Ellis they are in fact a scatter of rib bones. Rib bones like loose change. They hadn't had to get so fancy with it, these little agonies that brought temporary clearheadedness, but. It wasn't their fault. They'd been raised as vain creatures.

When Vanity comes to, she'll look the same as she did a year ago, once she gets the flush back in her cheeks. But Ellis and Clover are all different. Clover with her hair in a buzz cut and Ellis with his longer, half tied back. The tattoos. The piercings. Ellis wonders if Vanity will flip out, have an existential crisis about the displacement, a whole year of not existing while they had continued to.

He'd like to see that. He has always liked to witness her lose it.

Though, eventually, that had stopped. She had lost that panicked gleam in her eyes, and then she was complacent and apathetic and unworried, quite, quite unworried.

"Where's Wren?" he asks.

"Stop it."

"We need him."

"No we don't. We'll just open the gates."

"But time seems of the essence. Doesn't it?"

"Just go and open the gates."

"Why do you dote on him so, Clover? Is it love?"

She didn't even dignify that with a harsh laugh. "He's the clearest one out of us."

"He's a drunk."

"I'm aware."

"What are you hoping to get out of him?" Ellis's laughter burst out of him. "No, let me guess—a cure!"

Now there was some flicker of expression; he'd struck a nerve. Anger flashes across Clover's mind, burns in Ellis like a hot wire pressed against the roof of his mouth. Instinctively he runs his tongue against it, and finds the taste set there like blood and oversteeped tea, sharp and biting.

"We're all endangered creatures now," she spits.

"Wren was supposed to die, too, I'm pretty sure."

"Well, lucky him."

"Extraordinarily lucky. Wonderfully lucky." He knows she's lying. If only Ellis could remember what she was lying about . . .

Some spells require ingredients. The words floating down to him. Who said that, again?

Clover continues, "If Wren isn't dead, it's because he's not supposed to be. I don't want to go pissing off nature."

Ellis notices one of Vanity's eyes is rolled open and the other is closed; he can't remember the state he'd put them in last. He opts to close them both now.

"Pissing off Ro, you mean."

Clover's expression darkens even further. "Same fucking thing."

They look down at Vanity's pale form lying beneath them, her purple ankles crossed. Pretty and prim as ever. She is going to start to rot soon. She'd probably love that.

"Well." Ellis lets out a breath, and gives Clover his most winning smile. "If he really is supposed to be alive, then this next part should be easy, shouldn't it?"

↙

The next part: coaxing Wren outside and tying him to a chair and then Ellis ambling down the drive and pulling open the gates. He stands to the side and hides his gun behind his back; he waves with his other hand as the things emerge from the woods. They never really had harm on the mind, in the minds that were pressed so deeply under layers of skin and limbs and woven bone—they were always just trying to get *closer*. The subsequent trampling and suffocation were just unfortunate byproducts of that.

"Yes, hi, hello," Ellis says, waving them along grandly, "come on in, he's right up there."

He anticipates their mad scramble past, the complete ignoring of him and his hospitality. Instead the things, a dozen or so, just stand there—well, some of them stand, some of them just in a constant state of kneeling, of keeling over—half obstructed by the dull light falling over the road. Their muffled thoughts stitching slowly together, clotting against Ellis—*Closer, closer*...

"Yes?" he calls. "Certainly? Go ahead?"

The things make unsure, small movements. Even though not all of them have specific, distinct faces anymore, they all face him. Waiting. It takes Ellis a minute to read them. There's not much there left to read.

"Oh!" he says. "Oh, it's for Vanity!"

This immediately begins the mad charge he'd first anticipated. Ellis closes the gate once the proper number had rushed past. How nice it is, all being on the same side.

🖋

They spend the rest of the night cracking open rib cages, bickering over the best way to remove the hearts. Clover gets really worked up over it. She wants to be surgical, clean with it. "I don't think Ro cares," Ellis keeps saying.

"I think she's just fucking with us," Clover breathes, grimacing when she finds grime splattered onto her shoulder. "Very funny. We get it, okay? It's not like we forgot."

"What do you mean?"

She gives him a bewildered expression before muttering, "God damn it, nothing. Pass me the cooler."

They're outside, going from thing to thing with their knives and the cooler. Wren is still tied to his chair. He's in that weird mood he's sometimes in, where he doesn't hate them. Ellis can sense that he's on something, just from general proximity and Wren's eyes, the irises practically blown out of them.

"What did you give him?" Ellis asks, not for the first time, he is pretty sure. Clover waves him off. Also not the first time.

Wren doesn't ask to be taken out of the chair, he's not that troubled they were using him as bait. His calm and his complete apathy for himself reminds Ellis of something, but he can't quite put his finger on what.

Ellis checks on Vanity every half hour or so. He stands over the bench and stares at her. He pretends she is lying there peacefully, just dozing; later he pretends it is afternoon and not shy of three in the morning. At some point, Ellis had gotten up to fetch her a book, laid it out open on her chest like she'd fallen asleep reading. His fingers left red blotches on the paper.

"I hate that you're in a good mood," snaps Clover at one point. "You have to cut along the *seam*—"

All over the lawn are the things opened up like cabinets and the things waiting to be opened up like cabinets. It's taking so long because the things have bodies that aren't right, bodies with too many limbs and too many chest cavities. There are dead ends and gaps where there should be organs and organs where there should be fat and muscle. What jutting ankle should lead to a thigh to a hip to a stomach to a heart leads instead from ankle to elbow to spine. Some of the hearts aren't fresh, either; they remove a few just to realize the valves have rotted, their chambers moving with maggots. Ro would not be pleased. And Ro must be pleased.

Clover is sweaty and she is still talking. He has to commit, make clean cuts, superior vena cava, inferior vena cava, trunk, pulmonary stuffs, it's not that hard. Don't saw, just push until it gives. Don't be a coward. Don't be so messy. We're not animals.

Once, high off their resurrections, Vanity had ranted about how people were attached to their bodies like flies to a web—didn't the web react with the fly's permission? Bodies had their set paths, their designated number of items, the general arrangement of those items, their unstoppable reactions to stimuli, the flush in their cheeks, the rise of heartbeats, the prickle of skin. Things that gave them away. How Vanity had hated being there, in her body, in her gorgeous features, going paler and paler as they arranged to show just how sick and tired she was with all of it, all of its habits she couldn't escape. She'd look Clover and Ellis dead in the eyes—or attempt to; really her slack gaze slid all over the place, since she was fried in her magic whenever she had these conversations—and say their magic was a footnote, they wouldn't be possible without flesh to carry them around. Flesh came first and existence came second.

Ellis, too, hated the undeniable, inescapable nature his magic revealed to him. People—when people were alive—they'd all acted ridiculously and they'd all acted the same. They were all individuals trying to convince each other they were individuals, that they saw the world in different ways, while they tried to find people who saw it in the same way, and in this way they were especially significant, they promised each other, while they privately dissolved, while they pushed away their thoughts or fell in love or tried to murder each other or themselves or said tomorrow is going to be different, it's over, I'm done with all the bullshit, and then went out and bought themselves a coffee in the morning and continued to lie to each other, Ellis knows all anyone ever does is lie to each other and it isn't even their fault, no one can convey anything precisely accurate about themselves, everyone is only ever imitating themselves whenever they open their mouths. Ellis used to look into everyone's heads and see the maze in the form of a snake eating its own tail. Passive consumption, consuming passiveness. It's all madness. It's all—

"You're getting sober, I think," Ellis says to Clover. The world is becoming stranger and truer again.

"I know that," she shoots at him. "You think I don't know that?"

"You know where to find stuff." Clover gets to her feet immediately. "If you run across Vanity, remind her she should be resting."

Clover departs, leaving blood on the front door handle. He can tell she is drawing farther and farther up the hall, away from him, because the ground stops pretending it can breathe. Vanity's presence is cold and sharp and bleeding out over him from across the lawn; Ellis has the pleasantly unpleasant thought that he might be lonely. He hangs on to the cold sensation until it blinks away, and he notices he is on his knees again, on the wetted earth, knife in his hand. Superior vena cava, inferior vena cava, trunk, pulmonary stuffs. Don't be a coward. Don't be so messy. Clover was right. It isn't that hard.

Clover comes back into the room with an unopened bottle of white wine cradled in her arms, which have been scrubbed clean. It is perfect timing, Ellis has just dropped the tenth heart into the cooler, which makes a slick, wet *thud* against the nine others. He hadn't needed to let in so many of the things; some of them had contained multiple hearts.

"Hoorah. Let's go."

"We need to get rid of the bodies."

"Why?"

"Because Wren's here." And when the things died they rotted and then they grew back.

Ellis had forgotten. He looks over her shoulder. Wren is awake with his hands tied behind him, staring at them. Blinking, face all bumpy and bruised. "I don't want to be an inconvenience," he says.

Ellis laughs, shoots Clover his thrilled and disbelieving look. "He seems fine to me."

"Ellis."

"We don't have time for one measly resurrection?"

Clover's hand moves to draw something from her coat. There is a familiar *click*, a glinting of light; Ellis blinks. He is not standing on the lawn. He is surrounded by longer thistles that seem to reach for him. He was dead and now he is not, has just opened his eyes again to the night sky, blackness crowning Vanity's head, leaned over him. He wants to reach up and touch her face, but then her finger reaches first. Touching his mouth. He remembers what it is to feel the cold bite of fear. She smiles, and he remembers what it feels like to want to run.

Clover's voice comes in through his fog. "...no time." Ellis's eyes focus on what's really in front of him just in time to see her return the pocket watch to her coat. A pocket watch, not the stopwatch that she used to carry around, that also used to *click*. Once to signal they were about to die. Once to signal that they were alive again.

Ellis asks, "Are you going to do magic?"

Clover winces, though it only shows in her hand tightening around the neck of the wine bottle. "Yeah. I guess."

Guess he's driving, then. "Do you have the stuff?"

She nods. She takes the stuff out of her pocket and hands it to him: a lighter and a needle and a gold ring, one of the hundreds of earrings stored in her cottage for the Parties. "Where do you want it?" Ellis asks.

"Don't care." Clover unscrews the top of the wine—a practiced gesture—and then stamps the bottle into the grass. Then she is raising her hands.

Ellis feels her thoughts fade out into static as she reaches for some nature of the world no one else is able to touch, the rest of the witches with her overexposure long gone.

They are all the last of their bloodlines. The end of magic.

It is for the best.

"Go away," Clover murmurs. The air around her is wavering, iridescent. "Just go away."

She isn't talking to him, Ellis knows. Still, he turns and follows the instructions, just as the skin on the butterflied bodies surrounding them begins to bubble and steam.

He goes and lifts Vanity from the bench, her book tumbling off her and landing soundlessly on the grass. He buckles her into the backseat of the car. Above the trees rising at the border of the lawn, the night sky is bruising into dawn, the weakest of stars smothered in the purples and blues. Ellis opens Vanity's eyes and draws down the window for her.

When he returns to Clover's side, there are just massive black spots burned all over the lawn in lieu of the things, and she has sunk to her knees. When he walks up she is looking up at the lightening sky, murmuring to herself.

Ellis also kneels; she tries to swat him away when he pulls her bottom lip down. "Hold still."

"I don't want it," she says.

Ellis takes ahold of her jaw. There is a dull panic beating against him like the throb of a heartbeat. "You told me to."

"I lied."

"Yes, you're a liar, Clover, I know, I know."

He drives the needle through, right beside her other ring. Really he is really excellent at this, lots of practice. Clover's eyes begin to clear as soon as he feeds the ring through the hole and closes it. Her dulled panic sharpens to a regular panic, and then Ellis observes her mind spurring up to kill it, what she would define as unnecessary, pointless energy. But Ellis knows panic is not pointless. Panic is healthy. The fact that Clover can so seamlessly quash it is not.

The habit of suppression is, after all, so addictive. Ellis enjoys it himself, too. Every time that little jolt of fear comes up, the thought that he should be scared of Ro or scared of Clover or scared of himself, it is pressed down by other, brighter words—Vanity will be alive. Vanity will be alive. Vanity will be alive.

Clover takes the wine bottle from the grass, has a swig in the process of getting to her feet. There's an appraising glance cast to Wren before she ambles past him, toward the car. Yes, he'll be fine right there for a little while.

"Be a good boy," Ellis calls as he rounds the car to the driver's seat, scooping up the cooler. "No Parties while we're gone. I want this place exactly as we left it, do you hear me?"

Clover is doubled over in the passenger seat, clutching her skull. In the back, Vanity has angled to one side, only held in place by the strap of her seat belt. Ellis winks at her in the rearview mirror. "Posture, darling," he reminds her.

When the car bumps forward, Clover opens up her door and vomits onto the driveway. Then she seems like she feels better. She has some more wine and hugs the bottle to her sternum. Dropping her temple to the cool glass of the window as Ellis begins to speed down the drive.

"I miss her," Clover says.

"Me too," Ellis says.

A few more beats of silence.

"She hates us," Clover murmurs.

"Yeah. Probably."

"We deserve it."

"I know."

"It's all our fault."

"I know, Clover."

They break the tree line, the City rushing up before them before Ellis turns right, onto the main road. The edge of the Pockmarked Island creeps into view as they ease around the northeast curve of the mainland, a pale blister on the smooth, gray marble surface of the sea.

Clover chews on some thought, slow. Then she says, voice thick, "She's probably the only one who can kill Arrogance."

"Oh, sure," Ellis muses. "Probably. But don't mention that to her. She'll think we're messing with her again."

His voice is easy, but really he's observing the strange, slick curl of Clover's thoughts. Ellis leans over this invisible, teeming mass, and divines, even when he doesn't want to. It all comes naturally to him, after emerging from the Machine, remembering his magic. You can't help but read words in front of you, if they exist in your language; you can't beat them back into senseless scrawls of ink. It is in this vein that Ellis can't miss the churn of Clover's mind. He finds some guilt there, sure, for what they had done to Vanity. But also restlessness.

And what bleeds from restlessness, if it is bleeding from them?

Well, Ellis thinks, *certainly nothing good. . . .*

If she feels Ellis observing, Clover ignores it. She doesn't care what he sees of her. She knows he won't go away.

"We should've done that already," she says to the blackened earth. "Killed Ro."

"We tried," Ellis reminds her.

"Right. Yeah. Right."

Sometimes it did come back to Ellis. In pieces.

After Arrogance destroyed practically everyone, Clover said that Ro had taken Vanity's body and burrowed down into the earth under the Museum estate. Ellis had just made his way back from the Sanatorium, finding Clover turning the earth toxic. Trying to flush Ro out, like a downpour pushing worms, bloated and writhing, up and out of the ground. But Ro had not emerged gasping for air. They had found she'd crawled up and out, by the gardens. She'd been sitting on one of the stone benches, looking out at the sea. She did not have Vanity with her.

Ellis tried to kill her, he did. He shot her in the spine and then in the head. The chunks that spilled from her just kept growing back. Clover tried her methods, too. Sometimes Ro smoldered and crumbled and it did really seem she was dead, and then the light would seem to change and her flesh would grow back, raw and gleaming and then pink and soft and pure. Ellis thought he had really lost it, that first day they spent murdering Ro. He was in hell, he was sure. Doing the same thing over and over again. It didn't help, of course, that Ro had Vanity's face. Vanity's eyes that Ellis was taking out, Vanity's eyes that would be glinting again, moments later, from the previously empty sockets.

And maybe some part of Ellis must've hated Vanity, too. To keep going, keep trying.

Hated her for loving him. For falling for all his tricks. Hated her for dying and leaving him.

Eventually both of them were fried, Clover in her magic and Ellis in his violences, and they wandered off in the consequential spirals only to wander back later, remembering what they were trying to do. Ro was still sitting on the bench. Waiting for them. The attempts began again.

"Where is she?" begged Ellis, over and over.

"Close," answered Ro.

He tore out her tongue. "Where is she?"

"Close," answered Ro, when it grew back.

The sun has risen by the time they hit the bridge, lighting the water with slivers of gold. The morning is slowly eating its own mist, cityscape emerging in the blacks and grays of dead teeth, outlines ignited in the backlight. Ellis parks at the base of the Pockmarked Island's slight hill, its incline too treacherous with the concrete-lined holes, each forty feet deep. Bad for the tires. He finds himself staring down into one, at the corpse of the witch that lies far below, halfway out of bed. Its spine curled like a question mark.

The flies are beginning to descend. By the time they near the top of the hill, their buzz is itching at Ellis's ears, the only reprieve being the soft, dreamy singing coming from the hole in the ground that keeps Arrogance Adams.

She is right where Ellis left her yesterday evening, on her cot. He wonders if she needs to sleep anymore. He wonders, more briefly, when the last time he slept was. He can't remember. Can he be sure if he is thinking clearly? "Am I?" he asks Vanity; Clover says, "Are you what?" and Vanity doesn't answer.

"Don't be rude," Ellis says to the both of them.

Then they've reached the top of the hill and the question fades out in a brilliant onslaught of clarity. The air radiates with whatever higher power Ro has become. Ellis feels at ease. Even though his hands are shaking and colors are dripping. He puts the cooler down and kicks it over the side.

The plastic hits the concrete bottom with a *clunk*, the top flying open. Hearts tumble out like jelly desserts.

Ro doesn't flinch, head still craned back to peer at them. "Hello, Clover. It's been some time."

Clover's mouth sets in a tight line.

"You have to let her come down here with me," Ro calls. "To bring her back."

Clover puts a hand on Ellis's arm. A small movement of her chin as she shakes her head.

"No reason to be scared," says Ellis.

He smiles at her as he lies through his teeth to her. It is for the best. The moment she turns away, the expression slips from Ellis's face.

When he drops his eyes back down into the pit, Ro's lips have closed and stretched.

She thinks she has him in the palm of her hand, which vaguely pisses Ellis off. It isn't her hand. The hand that holds Ellis is cold, and currently brushing the back of his knee.

"Drop her down," Ro calls. She is slithering off her bed, gathering up the hearts and holding them to her chest. Blood dyeing her gray garment.

Ellis immediately clutches Vanity closer. Her skin chills him through his clothes. "No."

"Drop her down. She won't care."

"She will."

Ro smiling, smiling. "She doesn't care, Ellis."

"How will she get back up?" He is stalling. He brought rope, slung around his shoulder.

"Don't do it," Clover hisses. "Don't, Ellis. Let's just leave."

"I can't," he says, or maybe gasps. "I can't."

He can't. He can't.

Below, Ro has laid the hearts in a small circle before the cot. Aimlessly. Now Ellis knows that it was, indeed, to fuck with them. "I want to see my sister," Ro says. "Do you think she wants to see you?"

"No," Clover says. And then she lunges for Vanity.

"God damn it—" Ellis reels back; Clover is unsteady and sprawls out on the grass. He hisses, "Stop it, Clover, just—"

"I want her back, too!" Clover shouts at him. "You think I don't? I do. I think about her every day. I can't get her out of my head. She's so loud. I fucking hate her for it. But she's gone, Ellis. Let her stay gone." She reaches one hand up and presses it to her face, over her watering eyes.

"Shut up. Just shut the fuck up," Ellis says, or laughs, whichever, whatever. Vanity's eyes have rolled halfway open, with her head tilted back. That glassy, empty stare. "I don't care if she hates me for it. I don't care."

Clover's turned away, hand over her mouth, can't stand him. Vanity won't be able to stand him. It didn't matter. They will always draw back together. The coven is unable to come apart.

They'd done that, Clover and Ellis. They'd sent Vanity to a place within herself that flinched at nothing, that blinked slowly at the violence occurring around her. She used to be so afraid of what was going to happen to her, how her mind would unravel with each resurrection. And then suddenly she wasn't. She was quiet. She was fine.

Ellis had been lying to himself, before; Vanity had not gone into the ground hating him. She'd likely been disappointed, but not particularly surprised, with all of it.

He faces back toward Ro's pit. The risen sun warms the back of his neck, paints a golden ray against Vanity's cheek.

"You're not here," Ellis tells her. He drops his head over hers, feels that cold radiating off her skin. Shuts his eyes.

You're not here you're not here you're not here yet.

Ellis drops his arms.

There is about a second of silence. And then her body cracks against the concrete ground.

Ellis loses feeling in his knees. Suddenly he is on his side, looking out into the rise of the hill and the side of the pit, before he turns his head, cheek scraping the grass.

Down and down and down—Ro is dragging Vanity's body into the center of the heart-lined circle. Vanity's neck is all wrong. One of her legs points toward her ribs. Ellis feels the guilt wash over him; it is the same thing as feeling violently sick, which he tells himself is disappointing, nothing new. Then he twists away to empty his stomach.

When he looks back, Ro is on her knees, and Vanity is on her back. Then Ro is putting her lips to the skin between Vanity's dark, straight brows.

Ellis can't hear what she says next, but he knows what it is. Knew from Vanity.

"That's too simple," he'd said to her, when she'd told him how to bring things back from the dead.

"That's the problem, isn't it?" she'd responded. She hadn't been looking at him. Her chin had been balanced in the palm of her hand. "It's always too simple."

"Rise," Ro whispers.

Down and down and down, Vanity's form jerks.

Her broken body resets with a series of bone-dry clicks. The runes and wounds on her skin go slick, and began to bleed before Ellis's eyes.

And she is breathing.

She's breathing.

She's breathing.

She's breathing.

Ellis takes out his gun and shoots Ro in the head.

Bang. Black blood sprays the curve of the wall. Ro crumples back against the bed frame and does not move again.

"Vanity!" Ellis screams. "Give me—hold on—"

He dives for Clover. The first thing she does is recoil and spit on his cheek. Ellis tugs at the rope around his shoulder.

"She's alive," he is saying, over and over and over as he ties the rope around his waist, blinking rapidly to clear the tears that have broken in his eyes. He fastens the other end to the frame screwed to the rim of the cell, the ones once used to hold the metal harvest vats. "She's here."

Clover lurches. "Vanity? Vanity!"

"Stay here. I'm going to go get her. Stay here."

"Wait, *Ellis*, Ro's—"

Ellis's blood flushes cold. Ro is no longer on the bed. There is a hole in her head and she is standing over Vanity again. Vanity's even breathing has diverged into convulsions, and Ro's hands are on her neck.

Ellis's vision blinks out.

And then he isn't looking from above.

Suddenly he is standing on concrete. He is down in the pit, over Ro. Snapping her neck. Over and over again. It doesn't matter. Ro barely cares. Every time Ellis feels the bones of her throat click back into place, she is still holding on to Vanity. Prying open her mouth. Black bubbles between the edges of her teeth. Ellis reaches for his gun only to find, when he puts it to Ro's temple, that he's already emptied the clip.

Above them, Clover is shrieking. Ellis puts his fingers into Ro's eyes. They pop. Left one first, the right barely after. She doesn't move; Ellis can't move her. Ro is smiling. White pus drips into her teeth. Vanity lets out one more violent shudder and then she coughs, hard.

Something black and moving comes up and out of her throat.

It falls onto the floor, rolls. Knocks back one of the hearts and one of the candles. Perhaps it is trying to run. But Ro is upon it. She already has her eyes back. Her filthy hands close first around the black, teeming mass, and then her teeth.

She can have it, Ellis decides.

His motions are rabid, gathering up Vanity and tying their waists together. Above, Clover grips for the other end. "Come on!" she is screaming, because Ellis and Vanity are down there with Ro, who they should've been more afraid of from the get-go. Ellis thinks of it blearily, all that time ago, the glitter of the Parties, coming awake with his cheek cold against the porcelain tub, the stolen moments in the forest, all of it threading together and tightening and tightening around his neck.

"We're going home, Vanity," Ellis says.

"Goodbye," Ro bids them. She waves. One stained palm dragging through the air. "Goodbye, Ellis. Goodbye, Clover. See you soon. See you soon. . . ."

"You're sick, Ro," Ellis says. "You're sick."

"I'm more myself now. I'm more myself now. I'm more myself now."

Ellis can hardly believe it when Clover's hand is reaching for him. The color has returned to the sky. It is midmorning, no clouds, blue stretching overhead.

"What is she doing?" Ellis asks Clover, who is still staring down at Ro.

Clover turns away before answering, quietly, "Eating."

⚹

"It's going to be the same thing," Clover murmurs. It should be a nice moment, they are going over the bridge now and the most wrong thing is set right, but Clover is saying horrible things. All of them always saying horrible things. "Killing and nothing and resurrection. Over and over and over again."

"We'll do better this time."

"We won't. We can't." She laughs, low and broken. "It's different, when it's all of us."

"I don't remember what it feels like," Ellis says.

This is a lie. It is so vivid to him. Nothing compared to that pressing descent down into the muted dark, and then air, and then light.

He remembers when Vanity hit her head at the Party. When a little thing like fainting in the wrong position made her slip out of her body, made her disappear. He had freaked out, yes. And when any one of them freaked out everyone noticed. And everyone talked about it. And everyone made wrong, wrong assumptions, like Ellis really cared about her dying, that he'd been so tremendously heartbroken over it, and not just panicking over the chance he wouldn't get his fix that night.

Really and truly, Monroe should've found a way to put *that* into a pill—*You're not you when you're not fresh from the grave!*

"I do," says Clover. "I remember. It's something that wakes in us, when it's all of us. It's out of our control." She is also pretending she doesn't want this, that she doesn't miss it. "The coven craves death. And death craves the coven."

III

PUTREFACTION

"TELL ME, AGAIN, what's going to happen," Ro said to Vanity, or perhaps Vanity said to herself, yes, she was the one lifting her fingers, counting it off: "One, they're going to die. . . ."

Vanity believed having her wildest daydreams rendered real, made flesh and bone and blood, would heal her of her anxieties. Before, when she'd pictured possessing Ellis and Clover as her dearest friends, all the frayed parts of herself had burned away into clean lines. The sadness would be purged; with her loneliness cured, she'd miraculously discover how to starve it of air.

Instead she witnessed, over the course of the week following their trio's first meeting, those frayed parts curling, uncurling. The sullenness and the bitterness boiling and boiling.

She couldn't help how she felt. But at the same time it wasn't some big deal because she couldn't ever help how anything else felt, either.

🖋

Like this: Sometimes Ro would say exactly what Vanity had said in her head word for word, and Vanity remembered she loved her so much it was shocking, it almost knocked her over. Sometimes she'd start to cry. She'd literally freak out. All good feelings felt unstable to her in this way. This wasn't a big deal—she didn't know how fine she was supposed to feel, really. Sometimes Ro felt like the only stable factor in her existence, which was completely terrifying because what existed outside of the parameters of her body she couldn't control, and also completely wonderful because the source of stability being separate from her meant Vanity couldn't taint it; Ro was unruinable.

🖋

Now that there was Clover and Clover had a plan, and that plan didn't involve Ellis coming to call on her every night, Vanity wished she'd kept him to herself a little longer. That she'd kept him dead for whole entire nights in her tub, hours that she'd roll on her tongue like sugar cubes until they dissolved, one after another.

🖋

But come to call Ellis did. Vanity's knees pushing into the lip of the bathtub as she peered past the stained glass, down into the garden where he stood, waiting. "Clover said to stay away," she said. "Until we meet. After the next Party."

Already Ellis's smile was going a little grisly. Vanity estimated around forty-eight hours between the resurrections and when he started deteriorating again. She could wait a little longer. She was testing herself. It was like waiting to see how long she could go without putting something in her mouth and chewing and swallowing.

"Okay," Ellis said. "I'm sorry if I come back tomorrow and I don't ask as nicely."

The next night he came into the house. Vanity heard the front door squeak open and stared at the ceiling above, hyperventilating, until Ro emerged from the bedsheets with a grin that sparkled in the darkness. Vanity grabbed her hand and made them flee from the room, across the hall and through their mother's ajar door. Cadence was supremely medicated and dead asleep; the twins slipped under the bed. Past their mother's dangling ankles, Vanity watched Ellis's shadow cut up the hall. Then he was there at the threshold, crouching. "I know you're there," he said. "You can't hide from me." But he was still clear enough to be afraid of Cadence and did not near, did not pull Vanity kicking and screaming out from under the bed and beg for sweet release. Still clear enough that he knew he didn't want to use magic to tell her to crawl for him on her hands and her knees, didn't want to broil and curdle himself like that, even for a moment. He stared for about an hour before drifting away. Vanity tracked the heat of his body outside to where it paused past the fence. Head likely turning back toward them, seeing their feet pressed against the one-way mirror of the front wall.

The third night she waited up for him. She lingered in the bathroom, climbing in and out of the tub to glance down into the lawn. Then she went to haunt the first floor, Ro trailing her.

Then when it was well after midnight and he didn't show Vanity put on her shoes grabbed her favorite kitchen knife crept out across the garden across the green and up to his front door, which she opened without knocking. Ellis was wandering around, looking lost.

"You didn't come," Vanity said, and his face was blank.

"Come where?"

"To see me."

He smiled that grisly smile. "I like seeing you," he said, but it was clear he didn't know what she was talking about. Vanity handed the knife to Ro and turned away. "This is for your own good," she said, but it wasn't. She'd just missed him.

Vanity hated that she'd missed him, she hated it so much that she decided after a moment she would just leave him dead, she would just leave him sprawled and leaking out on the stairs, and go through his stuff. As his death rose like mist around her ankles she wandered around the house, which was an exact copy of hers. She smelled the liquor bottles in the bar cart, stroked her fingers through silver dishes full of candy-colored pills, tipped over the ashtrays to be swallowed up by the plush of the expensive imported rug. Went upstairs and lay in his bed, located a strand of his hair on his pillow and pulled it apart into small eyelashes with her fingernails. She pawed through his closet, filled with clothes his late father had worn. The tourists loved that, they thought it was sentimental, the fresh Spectacles donning the clothes of their dead parents, they must miss them so terribly. Vanity thumbed at the cuff of a deep purple suit jacket, it was worn in small coins from where James Kim liked to bring his wrist to his mouth and gnaw. When she closed the closet door, she observed, in the mirror wall, Ro flitting around the room. Pocketing small items. A bottle of cologne. Nail clippers. A button unthreaded from a knit sweater.

Vanity went back down onto the stairs and crouched above where Ellis's head lay, limp on his neck. "You're out to get me, aren't you?" she said, hovering a fingertip over the line of his jaw. "Coming to beg me. Getting me in trouble with Clover." He hadn't needed to come pleading for her, he could die all on his own. In the comfort of his own cottage. Or bleed himself out across the lawn. Cadence would be there soon to bring him back; he'd collect the same clarity from resurrections. But he'd come looking for *her*. Vanity smiled, tugging, tugging. But no, remember? He wanted her to lose her head. Oh, well, wait. What was she worried about? What was bad about that?

"Can you not tell Clover?" It dribbled from her, when he was back. Draped across the stairs with blood on his bathrobe. Ro was all sticky with it, floating away, distracted, in time with Vanity, going away....

"Okay," Ellis said, as the paint on the paintings above him began to swirl, as the flowers of the wallpaper peeled and dangled, as her mind smeared like bright jelly and then rebelled, momentarily, and she realized she didn't understand. Why she was here. Why she kept coming back to him. And then he was holding her and saying, "Thank you so much. I love ~~it so much, I feel so much better and it's all because of~~ you," and Vanity remembered. That when it was good, oh, it was real good.

🖋

Clover's plan called for death on a schedule. It involved no blood and never any bathtubs. They would leave their bodies humanely by drinking a poisoned tea and falling asleep. They should wear their most comfortable clothes. Post-resurrection, Vanity would be supervised. She would have their company and they wouldn't leave her, even if she scared them, because she was important, an essential part of the experiment. She would be asked questions that she later wouldn't recall, but wouldn't refuse to answer. She would want to tell them everything; it was like when she held a small stifled mouse in her hand and wanted to tell the wallpaper—well, first, that it was just pretending to breathe, and to stop that, right now, you couldn't possibly understand what that meant, you'll never hurt so much sometimes you can't breathe, stop pretending that you'll never need anything, air or other people—everyone is locked in a dark and wet room.

🖋

Moments weren't vivid to Vanity as they were currently happening; they shone in her mind after they slid past her, almost plasticky in their untouchable quality. So she remembered the door of her bathroom outlined in light as she stood in the dark hall, waiting. When Ellis's death pooled around her ankles, she'd push open the door into that indomitable silence. His long legs hanging over the lip of the bathtub. His head spilled back or cradled forward in his throat. The wounds, jewel-bright, smoldering on his arm, the knife tipped out of his elegant hand.

Vanity supposed she was dreaming, now.

It wasn't her, moving into the bathroom, kneeling on the cold tile, though it looked like her hand on the door, it looked like her knees beneath. Ellis was alive, and watching her. His wounds stitched back together, chest lifting and falling with new breath. It was silent, when his mouth moved. *Don't get us mixed up,* Vanity attempted to scream from her claustrophobic, cottony perspective. *Don't you know how much it hurts me, when you mix us up?* Ellis's mouth moved again, but not with inaudible words; Ro's hand was easing it open. Then her fingers were on his tongue, and Vanity, even formless, felt the warm plushness, the ripple of his tastebuds, the blood that it had tasted when he'd bitten the side of his mouth to keep from crying out as the light had hit his open arteries. Ro was fishing for something. Ellis gagged. Then she got ahold of it, a black and slack *it,* but otherwise undefinable, a piece of the dream that smeared like an ill-dried oil painting, blurred and warped the backdrop of wallpaper and stained-glass flowers, and Ro craned her neck over her cupped palm, and ate it.

Vanity awoke. She drifted to the bathroom, where Ellis had come to die a few hours prior. She leaned over the eye of the tub. She was looking for his hair. Her fingers grasping, a few strands revealed to be hooked to a startling slimy clump, like leaves to a radish, optical nerve to eye. Vanity relaxed. Now if Ro went looking she wouldn't find anything. Yes, yes, certainly, there was the problem of Arrogance, the paranoid creature, who might embarrass her, who might fuck up everything. Vanity couldn't let that happen, she wouldn't. Ellis and Clover needed her, for more than they even knew. Vanity knew Ro wanted to hurt them. She knew Ro wanted to hurt everyone, that Vanity, as the stable sister, needed to work to be extra good.

Vanity's nostrils flared. She could smell Ellis's blood in the metal of her drain. Drawn through the ragged clump in her hand. The one she was holding up to the light, now. Trying to see red.

💉

"I can make them go away," Ro promised, trying to be reassuring. It was reassuring.

Vanity shook her head. "That's okay."

It was after the next Party and Vanity had swapped her silk dress and silk gloves for pajamas. Because tonight Vanity was going to resurrect someone and then she was going to black out and do god knows what and she at least wanted to be comfortable. And avoid the possibility that she'd find it a grand idea to peel off any article of clothing with stitching made to contain and accentuate.

They were in the kitchen, and Ro was taking exactly one bite of every fruit from the bowl on the counter and putting it back. She was smirking. She'd had fun at the Party. She never really didn't have a good time.

"Just come with me tonight," said Vanity. "I can't face them alone. I'll die."

She knew the request was irresponsible. Ro had a tendency to snap and hurt people and things like that. But Vanity wasn't sure, yet, to what degree such behavior was unnecessary. She didn't know to what degree she would need to be protected. However if Ro embarrassed her by protecting her too much Vanity knew how to hurt her enough to keep her in line. So the request wasn't as irresponsible as one might think.

"Could you believe that tourist tonight?" Ro asked. Seemingly Vanity's demands were taken as a given.

"Which one?"

"The World-spun one. She was crying." Ro was smiling. "Her nose was dripping into her champagne. She hated it. Having nature."

Vanity shrugged. Her eyes darted across the fruit bowl, at teeth marks pushing and puckering apple and pear flesh.

"I don't know what kind of witches Monroe's harvesting from, but they're weak shit. Do you think there's flesh witches, conked out in the Sanatorium? I know they've never been in the Machine, but what kind of effect can be reaped from a witch who's never used magic in the first place? Weak *shit*, I swear!" Sometimes Ro got like this. "What's the nature of the flesh, Vanity?"

"Life. Growth. Death. Rot. Arrogance, I—"

"Exactly. So what would that tourist have done if she'd taken some form of World harvested straight from us? She'd be alive. She'd grow. She'd die. She'd rot. And isn't that what's going to happen to her anyway?" Ro fished apple skin out of her gums with her tongue, then licked the teeny white counter tiles to get it off.

Vanity grabbed at her face. She looked into Ro's serene black eyes. She opened her mouth to speak, then paused. Staring into those black pits.

There was something there—yes. Something . . . what Ro had just said. All Ro had just said. A body, living. A body, growing. Overgrowing. It slithered in the dark, twisting as the limbs sprouted from smoothed flesh, as its skin fattened and pulsed, insistent in taking up space. But. Ah, no, actually. At the same time—stillness. Vanity had been mistaken. It was dead, the body. Rot, puckering. Vanity breathed in. She could smell—

"And what wicked thoughts are fluttering back there?" Ro mused excitedly, looking into Vanity's eyes as if gazing into endless pools of water.

"No wickedness," Vanity breathed back. She let go of Ro's face. There was nothing there. Never anything there. "All I ever think are beautiful thoughts."

↙

It went like this, what would lead to the collection of moments that would make Vanity's stomach sit like a cathedral in her body: Cadence passed out on the couch downstairs, and so down the stairs the sisters went, putting on their shoes, opening the front door. No guards, no alarms. All the older witches too out of it at this time of night to venture out, all the younger ones, surely, too afraid of themselves to test what was a wall and what was a line in the sand, what was nothing at all.

Vanity shivered as they drifted for the dark rise of the woods. She was counting off. She pulled at each finger as she uncurled it from her hand.

"One, they're going to die." Her feet stamping wet grass. "Two, I'm going to bring them back. Three, she'll look into my throat. Four, she'll read the tarot. Five, if all is well, one, they're going to die, two—"

"You're such a nervous creature," Ro tittered.

It was true, Vanity chattered in her head. It was true, she was a nervous nervous nervous creature, and a follower, and a romantic, they all rolled into one girl-shaped clump of anxiety, with the only reprieve being the suffocating force of her apathy for what would happen. She bit at the tips of her fingers. It was dark, and she wished they were getting lost. Ro was leading her, angling her head as she walked. Her delicate white throat as it reflected the moonlight. Vanity trudged behind, hating that the bottoms of her sweatpants had breathed in the dew of the lawn and were sticking to her skin.

"I'm obsessed with Clover," Ro said. "I never pictured it, such a grand plan! I thought she was meek. Meek as a little mouse."

"Be quiet."

"You're obsessed with her, too, I know you are. I know everything about you, Vanity."

"I know everything about you, too."

"You don't. It'd ruin it."

"Ruin what?"

"All of it," Ro chattered. "I can't wait to end the Museum. Do you really think Clover can figure it out? Do you really honestly and truly believe her?"

"She can do anything," said Vanity, only because it was absolutely true. Clover, with her grand plan. And Vanity all her life just fuming and complaining and thinking well, that's it, all I can do, I'll just do a lot of drugs until I die one day. But Clover was a genius. They should pretty much do whatever Clover said. "And this is about finding a cure, not ending the Museum."

"Are you sure? Are you sure that's what we're doing?"

"Yes. Yes." She knew what they were doing. "One..."

Vanity stopped walking. Now the grand cold mouth of the forest gaped open in front of them. Ellis said he would walk with her. They were going to hold hands.

"You don't know Clover at all." Ro could change on a dime, like this. Her voice suddenly hard. "You don't know what she might do to you."

Vanity covered her face with her arms. All she knew was that they would be looking at her. Needing her. "One they're going to die two I'm going to bring them back three she's going to look in my throat four—"

"Didn't you bring me, for this? To tell you what you need to hear." Ro's hands landed cool on Vanity's wrists. "They are obsessed with their own deaths, and they're using you." Ro's teeth flashed in the shadows. "Though, who isn't?"

"No. No. They love me."

"Do you really think that's true, you sick little freak?" It didn't matter what Vanity thought. She thought it had to be true, she thought, It has to be true or I won't be able to take it I won't I don't know what I'll do but I won't—Ro wrapped her hand around Vanity's head and kissed her fiercely on the temple. "You're very dear to me. I'll watch, for you."

"Watch for what?"

"Lies." The word sliding along Vanity's temple, dropping a shiver down the length of her body.

"They wouldn't," gasped Vanity, even as she was nodding, as she was telling her sister, Please protect me. Please don't let me go away completely. I don't know how to help myself. I don't know how to not like getting worse. "One—"

"Please don't start up again."

Vanity bit it down. She curled her fist until her bones ached. "Death. Resurrection. Wellness checks. That's all we're doing. There's no reason for her to lie." She'd do anything Clover asked of her. "There's no reason."

"Oh, sweet, sweet girl. You're terrified, aren't you? Don't worry. I'll be here, like I've always been. I'll carry it around for you, like I always have. You remember the good. I'll remember the bad." She took Vanity's hand, squeezed it. "Yes, here, my darling sister. We'll do it like this. You be the romantic part, the one that falls in love. And I'll be the rational part." A rare tinge of sentimentality nestled in Ro's voice. Her eyes looked almost wet, though it might have been the reflection of the moon over-head. Well, then. Maybe she just looked ecstatic. "The one that wants to hurt everyone."

Vanity relaxed. Everything would be fine. Death. Resurrection. Well-ness checks. She would go away for a little while, but she would come back later, when Clover knew how to fix her. Until then she would know what was happening to her even while she was gone, because they'd be looking after her. There was no reason to worry. It was only goodbye for now.

"Hello, darling," came Ellis's voice behind her.

Vanity turned her head back, finding the post-Spectacle glaze written all over his face. He wore the warm, rosy scent of someone else's blood, and his father's purple coat. His dilated eyes sliding over her. He was high, but see, *Ro*, he remembered her, what they meant to each other, she was sticking to him more and more.

As their fingers found each other, Vanity shot Ro one last triumphant look. *See? See? We won't hurt each other.*

But what she meant was, not in a way she couldn't take back.

XVI

HEAD TIPPED BACK TO A SKY full of ink and weak stars, and then Clover dropped her chin. They were coming out of the woods and into the clearing now. Wearing pajamas, holding hands. Clover's hands bunching in the quilt spread under her knees, flattening the thistles erupting in this small blank spot in the middle of the forest, the usual fear of them spiking. Vanity, with her head turned, chattering to Ro; and Ellis, with his head turned to Vanity. Watching her.

Clover identified the problem, that Ellis was pretending to be in love with her, and filed it away for later observation.

Things for the experiment, she went down her list: A quilted blanket. A stopwatch. A stack of tarot cards. Two thermoses of oversteeped green tea. Her notebook and her pen. A knife tucked in the depths of her massive sweater, just in case.

Clover gestured weakly around the clearing, as if welcoming them into her home. She'd never actually do that. "Well," she spoke. "Shall we start?"

↙

"The tea takes longer," said Ellis, who was also a thing for the experiment, and then he was dead. He tipped over, thermos coming loose from his hand. Vanity—looking like a marshmallow in her pale yellow sweatpants and sweatshirt—gave a peal of hideous laughter, as she was prone to do, and curled closer to him, like worms drawn to softened and buried form. She settled into a very serious look. Wetness peeked from the corners of her mouth.

Now it was Clover's turn. She hugged her notebook to her chest. She swung the stopwatch out. Vanity's eyes flicked up. Her black eyes following the chain and then the weight.

Clover snapped it open. She lay down on the quilt. She opened the thermos and drank the poisoned tea. She pushed herself through the actions so she would not think. She must not think. She could not trust her mind around them. Her mind, her most precious private fortress. She'd ranted, in their first meeting, she'd said so much to Vanity. Too much. Unable to help herself. Not again. She'd stave off the urge with logic: there wasn't a need for words. Look. At Vanity's face. At Ellis's still-warm body limp at the edge of her peripheral vision. They trusted her. Trusted her to cure them.

Or, at least Vanity did. Ellis was just along for the ride. Clover didn't know if Vanity understood that. Did she even know the expression on her face was so blatant, when she looked at him? When she looked at Clover? It was so openly dreamy, the face of a lovestruck soap-opera starlet, perpetually on the edge of pretty tears, that Clover might even trust her, too.

"The tea takes longer," Vanity said. "Aren't you scared? Next time, we could use a knife instead."

"He'd use it on us."

"He won't he won't. Ellis won't hurt us."

"He will, Vanity." Clover couldn't stand her eerie, pinned gaze. "See." She made an awkward motion of jostling around the stopwatch, trying to keep the nervousness out of her voice. "When I get back, I'll time how long it takes for one of us to hurt another."

It was a joke, but judging by Vanity's earnest expression, it clearly didn't land. Did she actually believe it? Maybe it would be better if she actually believed it. There were things Clover was meant to tell her and there were things she wasn't. One of those things being that the stopwatch was actually for timing how long Clover stayed gone. How long Vanity left her dead.

It wasn't to be cruel to her; for the purposes of the experiment, of course, there were other factors that Vanity shouldn't know. Her idea of the experiment should remain untainted. If one knew the behaviors that were being monitored, such behaviors might occur unnaturally.

"Do you have to die, too?" asked Vanity. She was touching her neck, tied with the usual black ribbon.

"What? Are you going to be lonely or something?"

Clover observed her blushing. She opened her notebook, but her movements were already growing sluggish. Her pen drew an indistinct scrawl across the page. She closed it again, hugged it to her chest. Later . . .

"You *are* going to bring me back, aren't you?" On one hand: a ridiculous question; Vanity was clearly addicted to the resurrections at this point. On the other: it was Vanity. Vanity, with her fixed gaze, with the perpetually distant look behind it. Vanity, who was a lost cause already.

God, what was Clover doing?

"Yes," said Vanity. "I'll bring you back. I promise."

This meant nothing to Clover.

"This." Clover tapped at her notebook cover. It was made of reliable black plastic, chemicals rendered together and made practically immortal, compared to the human lifespan. "Vanity? Don't read this. It'll—mess up the experiment. Tell me you won't."

"Okay. I won't."

"Don't let Arrogance do it, either."

"Well . . . okay."

A laugh trickled out of Clover. "Yes . . . oh, yes. That was entirely convincing." Her fingers clenched the stopwatch, sending the *tick-tick-tick*s spilling into her palm. It was time. "Oh, god," she realized. "I'm scared. I'm scared."

Vanity held her hand and said, "Don't be," and then Clover wasn't. Being anything.

XVII

"DESCRIBE HOW YOU'RE FEELING."

Ellis was staring up at the blank sky and Vanity was staring down at him. She was unsure who Clover was talking to. Later, she wouldn't remember this. Turning to look at Clover's throat. Watching the vocal cords scrape and sing under the delicate skin.

"Stopwatch..." Vanity murmured. "What's it for?"

"To time." Clover shook her hand, the hand that held it. "How long it takes."

"How long it takes..."

"How long it takes for what?" Ellis finished the thought for her. How horrible. He was there. In Vanity's head. She clutched her head.

Clover said, "Answer the question, Vanity. How are you feeling?"

Vanity was digging. Digging in the earth, and there wasn't the open night sky above them anymore; she was somewhere in the forest. What time was it? What was she looking for? "What are you looking for, Vanity?"

They were standing around her, looking down, as she cut her hands on the undergrowth. She found something. Perhaps it had been a rabbit, at one point. Vanity pulled it free, dirt smoothing in its matted gray fur, stiff, half-whole.

"Don't you ever wonder how they get past the fence?" she murmured to Ro, who was close. Breathing down her neck. Vanity swatted her away.

"I assume they live here to begin with."

"Clover. Let's just get her home."

"Don't touch her. Let her behave naturally."

"I don't like this. This isn't what you said we were doing."

"I like this," said Vanity. Cradling the rabbit to her chest. Breathing in its rot. It was sweet and it was perfect. Just as it should be. "I like this a lot."

Clover had opened her notebook. She was looking at Vanity and her pen was moving. Writing about her? First she flushed with attention, then with horrible self-consciousness.

"What the fuck are you scrawling on about?" This was Arrogance, sitting on the clearing grass beside Vanity, having returned from whatever promenade she'd deemed more important than the resurrection club. It was either the first meeting or the third or some other number.

"Notes," Vanity snapped. "Leave her alone, Ro."

"She's not exactly an unbiased observer," said Ro. And stood up. Vanity stood, too, out of instinct.

"Shit," she said, looking up at them. "Time?"

"What?" Clover breathed, already scrabbling away.

"She's about to hurt you. Stop the clock."

"Oh, yes, right..."

Ro had already lifted her hand.

Honestly—where the fuck did she keep getting the rocks?

Either that time with the rock or some other time where Ro hurt them some other way: when they were back and blinking and good Vanity had grabbed Ro's wrists and said, "Say you're sorry."

"Excuse me?"

"Say you're sorry. To both of them. Arrogance. Just *say it.*"

"Even if I don't mean it?"

 ↯

And so every night now Vanity wound dry floss around her fingertips, pulled it until they flushed purple, until Ro's giggles crested, and she dropped the string unused into the trash. She wanted those delicate black spots of decay in her head. She wanted her physical to match her mental so viciously. Slow, dark withering. Ellis and Clover were so sweet, she was sure. So sweet they were rotting her teeth.

 ↯

Distantly, Vanity knew it was all batshit, what they were doing.

What did they think they were doing, exactly? Often she forgot. Often, it seemed like it didn't matter.

Some version of roulette, yes. Tipping one another further and further toward their edges, yanking one another back. This was supposed to help them. It would, because Clover was sure of it.

 ↯

The question, always the same question—what had Vanity been acting like before?

 ↯

So went their encounters, their resurrection club—death. Beckoning. Black spots. Rising out of it—murmuring, and dirt on her hands, and a foul taste in her mouth, and blood on her clothes. Where had that come from? Anyway. What else? And going home, sometimes.

ℒ

Vanity had decided to follow Clover home. It was more and more often that Vanity was making this decision. She wasn't exactly sure the purpose of it. And Clover would do what she always did—turn around and pick Vanity out of the shadows.

"Vanity?" Clover would start. Then Vanity would take a step closer and Clover would take a step back. "Arrogance?"

The second name always ringing with apprehension. Because Vanity was the lovely and good one and Ro was the violent and horrible one.

Later, Ro would bring her a gift, Vanity would find a dead thing or a bottle of cologne or nail clippers or a button in her pocket, and Vanity would take her arm and hurt her. "Stop it, you have to stop killing them. They're scared of you," and Ro would say, "They're killing themselves anyway, and of course they're scared of you, and they love it, " and—or— was it Vanity, saying this?

She squinted. She *was* holding Ro, right? It was hard to tell in the unlit bedroom, with her stomach scraping the carpet. It was getting difficult, sometimes, now, for Vanity to tell them apart. They did look *so* alike, after all. Really, Vanity couldn't blame Clover for mixing them up.

ℒ

Cadence was pulling her arm. They were marching up the hill to the peak where the Museum glowed, the bitter wind lifting off the sea attempting to shove them back down to the cottage. Vanity turned her head and saw the City twinkling past the curve of the landscape, its glass spires so very dark against its glittering shards of light, and all this light embarrassed them, exposed them as being inhabited, and so Vanity, tripping over her feet, thought, All those people swallowed up by metropolis, I really and truly feel them teeming, their tiny, wriggling bodies suspended, they stand on concrete instead of earth and so they stand on nothing—

"—lately, a *total* basket case—"

This was from Cadence. Vanity and Ro and Cadence were standing in the dining room of Monroe's living quarters in the back of the Museum mansion and her mother was saying Vanity was not fit for the Spectacle role, not at all, clearly she was too far gone already and Cadence needed to live at least a few more years before Monroe started to think about killing her.

Vanity tuned her out.

On Monroe's dinner plate there was a steak that Vanity observed to be in a state of growth. Was it true? As Cadence got more and more worked up, the slab of meat seemed to pulse and bulge and expand, squishing the mashed potatoes, suffocating the peas. Vanity blinked and looked to her mother's strained face, the lipstick that had pilled at the corner of her mouth, then at Monroe and Wren on the distant side of the sprawling dining table. The patriarch stared on with practiced placation and the heir with a pinched amusement quickly souring as the rant continued. Was it really happening, the growth of the steak?

"Vanity? Vanity?"

Vanity would've missed Wren saying her name if Cadence had not begun to shake her arm. Vanity made eye contact with him. Anything to stop looking at the steak. There was something behind his steady focus on her that she didn't bother to decipher; she assumed he was imagining her naked or being torn apart by his dogs and so moved herself along.

"Is all this true?" he said. "How are you feeling?"

"Well?" Cadence demanded. Her laugh was high and triumphant. "Speak. Say something for yourself."

Vanity was in the forest. No, she was thinking of the forest, the clearing. In the clearing, Vanity could act like herself. Could lose herself.

And she did, perhaps.

It wasn't Clover and Ellis's fault, that both love and magic were smearing her. The bad, bad, bad thing that she knew slept in her depths, uncoiling, stretching out. Sometimes, startling awake in the middle of the night, Vanity thought it had finally spilled out of her, tangled in her limbs and breathing under her covers. But it was only Ro's ankles, hooked around hers.

Vanity wondered: before, had she also been dreaming of eating them alive?

"Pardon my mother," she heard herself say, felt the apologetic smile sliding across her face. "I'm not quite sure what she's talking about."

*

"Open your mouth. No. You're good. Nothing there. Promise."

*

At night, Cadence had taken to pacing the house, clawing at handles, looking for her daughters. She might be thinking of killing them, that would buy her some time. Had her mother, Vanity's grandmother, attempted to do the same to her? Some comfort, then, that all of this had happened before. Everything just went around and around in a circle. Mothers being daughters, mothers throttling daughters.

*

A Party! Another! Another! Another!

*

"Last time you described that it was difficult to get your bearings. That events seemed out of order, or in pieces. What does that mean, Vanity?"

*

The sweet, staccato *flip flip flip* of tarot cards. Spilling out of Clover's hands and onto the quilt. Vanity couldn't look at them, couldn't stand finding the gut-punch of disappointment for herself, just waited for Clover to diagnose "We're way off" or "We have a lot longer to go."

"Longer to go for what?" Ro asked, frowning and embarrassing Vanity, and so Vanity had to shoot back, stressing her smile even as the rest of her fell away, "The cure, Arrogance," and then she did fall away completely and she wasn't sure which sister was saying it, saying, laughing, utterly confused, at the idea of a cure, "But it feels so good? But it feels so good?"

Rare moments of realizing the present moment: Vanity looked up from the glistening slab of her steak. The dining room's wall of windows faced out over the edge of the cliff and onto the stormy, churning oceanfront. It looked like a moving painting. The room was lit from multiple chandeliers suspended above the elongated, skinny wood table that sliced up the middle of the space, gleaming with silverware atop lacy place mats. Ro, on her left, was picking the silver covering off her dinner. On her plate was a heart. Thudding. Valves puckering, easing open.

Vanity blinked. It was gone.

Ro grinned at her and stuck her fork in her steak. The smell of it was nauseating. She already felt so full, but she couldn't recall the last time she'd eaten.

Flies buzzing. No, no. People talking. Cadence's fraying, shrill voice. "—served the Museum for all my life!"

"Vanity, did you hear me?" Monroe rumbled.

"She's too dull to take my place. She doesn't have my flair! You'd bore the others, with her."

Vanity cut up her own steak and then pushed the cubes together, so it looked like it wasn't separated at all, one whole part of one whole cow.

"I wish it was just you. Dying," said Clover to Ellis. And Vanity was there, she presumed. Somewhere.

"Sure. Whatever. It can be."

"It can't. It can't."

𝟙

"No, she's around here somewhere. Why do you want to know? There's not a lot to know. Ro likes to take long walks. I assume that's where she is. She doesn't like you guys."

𝟙

Clover always brought a quilt, which Vanity thought was a darling touch. She kept stroking the blue-and-purple crisscross pattern, still blushing. Had Clover pulled it off her bed? The individual threads seemed to wriggle under her fingers, but she breathed in and out, trying to steady herself. She wondered if it worked.

𝟙

"Because she thinks you're trying to hurt me."

𝟙

Vanity kept waking up with a weird taste in her mouth. "Did you guys feed me something?" she'd ask them, when she saw them again, again.

"No."

"No."

"Arrogance. Did you feed me something?"

"No, Vanity."

"Did they? Did they?"

Then they were dead again and Vanity didn't stop talking to them. "You're out to get me, aren't you?" She knew she had all night to argue with them. Their bodies could go cold because they'd be warm when they got back anyway. So she accused them and sometimes she'd strum their vocal cords and make their stomachs contract at the same time to smooth out that last bit of air, say things in a final wheeze that didn't really sound like them but were totally close enough, okay, Ro?

⚑

Clover and Ellis couldn't really mind, not really if they never really mentioned to her, anyway, if they were put off by sometimes awaking in different positions, halfway across the field, stacked on top of each other, rolled over onto their stomachs. As if different positioning would yield different answers. "Are you hurting me? Are you hurting me?"

⚑

"I'm sorry we don't go out and do anything anymore, Ro. I don't want you to be bored."

"I'm not bored, dear sister. I want to keep going, around and around. . . ."

⚑

"My first time doing magic? When Ellis died. The first time. Yes, really. Oh. Ro's first time. Does it matter? She's not even here. Well . . . hard to say . . . knows as much as me, I suppose. I don't know, okay. Fine. I don't remember the exact details. We were around five. We were fighting and— No, not often. I mean we bicker. So she— I don't know. Little things. But we always make up. She brings me things. It's . . . well, is it important? It's private. Do you want to know the story or not? Then stop interrupting me. It's fine. It was after a Party and she was being insufferable and Cadence was being insufferable. And— No, of course not. *I* was being perfectly lovely, I'm sure. Funny? Oh. Did you really just call me funny, Clover? Oh. Well, that's . . . ha . . . well, anyway . . . I . . . Ro was trying to prove a point. Earlier that day Cadence had given us some big speech about being fucked-up creatures and it hadn't sat well with Ro. She said we were invulnerable, perfect beings. And I didn't believe her. I still— Ellis, oh my god, can you let me finish? I was just about to say that I still don't believe her, because how— *I'm a perfect creature? Did you really*

184

just say that to me? I...it's...so...I don't remember where I was at. It's all your fault. It really is. Well. Bottom line is that we were arguing and then Ro was cutting off her ear and then she was growing it back—well, I didn't see her cut off her ear really but she woke me up in the middle of the night to put my hand to the side of her head and at first I thought she'd gotten something in her hair, like gum, but what I felt was moving and I flicked on the lamp and saw it was it growing back, her ear. I saw the blood on the pillowcase and then the knife and the ear on it, but then she took it, I don't know what she did with it, I didn't ask, it was hers and none of my business. I don't remember. The right one. Or the left one."

It took around a month without touching her floss to get the first cavity. Vanity tongued at it, the tiny bloom. Rot in her head, clearing her head. One night she dreamed she was lying back on a leather-plush table with Clover and Ellis leaning over her, both in blue surgical masks. Open, Clover instructed, and Vanity did, because she did whatever Clover told her to do. The saw, Clover requested, and Ellis handed it to her, over Vanity's body. Where's Ro, Vanity asked. Don't take it away, Vanity said, afraid suddenly. They were going to dig out her rot and she didn't want them to. She was at once looking up at them and down at herself, down into her own mouth. She could smell the cavity across her left back molar. It was yawning and beautiful. Alive, pulsing. Don't take it away, Vanity said again, still opening wide. It's making me better, don't take it away. You'll like it, Ellis said cheerfully, and Vanity relaxed. Right, right. She trusted them. Needle, Clover said. Vanity watched the syringe dip inside her mouth, heading toward the back molar, so clean-edged and foreign to the weird plushiness of the inside of her head. She felt fear again, but she didn't say anything. She held completely still. Clover pushed down. Out of the tip of the syringe beaded something pale and viscous. Not the chemical filling. Vanity wept with relief. Flesh smoothing out over the cavity, spilling into its dark crevices. Not destroying or replacing, just holding, caressing. Clover and Ellis were taking care of her. They always knew what was best for her.

🪶

Vanity was drooling. She didn't quite know where she was, but the stars were above her and grass tickled her thighs. Shorn grass, not the clearing thistles they'd started off the night in. What day was it? What season, now? How long had they been doing this? In her ears: the frantic barking of dogs.

"Here, Vanity. This is for you."

"For me?" Vanity whispered, taking the gift. It was warm and weighted.

"For you," said Clover. Vanity's head and body tilted, trying to look into the structure she was leaned up against. Into the dog shed. She only glimpsed Ellis, stepping in her way. And then Clover was holding her face. Her thumb on the corner of Vanity's mouth. Vanity melted, and melted further when Clover went, "Hey," and then, gentler: "All of this is for you."

XVIII

DON'T FORGET WHAT THEY ARE.

His father's words rang in his ears, louder in the silence of the woods. Branches veined the night above his head, rasping in protest when the wind moved and tangled their dry limbs.

Once, the island the City had sat on had been all trees. But Wren had learned from World that change was nature's most reliable pillar, knew from that high that nothing lasted.

Now there was only the Necropolis—its plots filled about a century ago, cremation being the modern-day convention, and so solely serving as convenient fodder for the lore of the Adamses, a nice setting for their "sacred ground"—and the woods that engulfed the western stretch of the Museum estate. Everywhere else was made bald, and then glittering. Child wonderment had drawn Wren to the woods when he was small—he'd liked how the sky disappeared—but then he'd gotten older and he'd noticed that he wore very fine shoes. A few times on World he'd wandered back, seeking some kind of fulfillment in the churn of the root. But it'd been overwhelming, the senselessness he felt within the wildness tangled around him. Disoriented, when he'd broken the tree line again and the Cityscape was suddenly there, rising past the curve of the hilltop, and he'd fallen to his knees with the acknowledgment of how all those spires slotted so nicely into the sky, like keys. And, again, the thing with the shoes.

Wren hadn't returned since.

But he knew where the clearing sprawled.

In his left pocket, he had the device that would blare if the witches went past the wall and detonated themselves, though it sported a button he could press anytime to the same effect.

He reached the clearing. Vanity was standing in the middle of the thistles, alone.

Her head was down and her spine was curled. She was talking, it carried to him like whispering, but he couldn't make out her words. It was very dark now that he'd turned off the windup flashlight he'd used to guide himself through the woods.

Wren took a step out of the tree line. Then another. His eye scanning the clearing. He could see no one else. The ring of forest around them moved slightly in the breeze, leaning, like they were standing on the cornea of a being beginning to blink.

"Are you hurting me?" Her words strained by her sob. Angry, heartbroken words. "When I would *never—do* that to you."

"Vanity," said Wren, softly, unable to help himself. The absolute heartache in her voice strumming something in him. She looked so lost, so lonely.

For five seconds, all was silent. Wren didn't breathe. The breeze had seemed to halt.

It was only her face turning toward him. Slowly. The tears he'd heard in her voice dappled all over her face, making it gleam as her mouth fell slightly open. Greasy, almost. The thought rose in him, out of habit and disgustingly disconnected from what was happening, that she needed to keep in the routine of washing her face. They couldn't have her breaking out.

"Wren," she murmured, as if just remembering his name.

Her voice reminded him of what was speaking to him. A poor girl with a mind like a spiral, rendering the world a bright, confusing smear. That was it. She was disoriented. He spoke as gently as he could. He could smell the blood in the air. "Are you all right, Vanity?"

"I don't know, I'm not sure," Vanity murmured. "I don't know I don't know I don't know."

"Try to describe how you're feeling—"

"I hate that question! I hate it! They're in my head—they won't *leave*—"

How Wren felt for her, the panic so weighted in her voice he felt he could bite down on it. She'd never felt anything like this before. She'd never been anything but lonely.

Wren was going to cure that. He was going to soothe such cruel natures. And after. After, they would all be so much better. They would question how they acted in the first place, how uncareful they were with one another, with themselves. It all lay in how they connected with one another.

"Oh, Vanity," Wren spoke softly, over the heart in his throat. "That's how it feels, to be in love."

She was very still for a moment. And then she was nodding. *Yes*, Wren thought, *good*.

Then he asked, "Where are the others, sweetheart?"

The effect was immediate. Vanity laughed, high and panicked, the sound so wiry and wrong against the gentle creaking of branches, the cold arch of the sky.

"Right here!" she said. A jerking motion of her head. "I didn't do anything."

The thistles on either side of her quivered. In the breeze? From some other movement?

Wren fumbled for the flashlight. It clicked on, white-yellow circle on his shoes and then sliding up across the clearing. It landed on her face first, and then on them: Clover and Ellis, suddenly there, standing at her sides.

They were . . . they must have been lying in the grass, Wren thought, trying to calm his breath, they had been lying in the grass and had gotten very quickly to their feet.

They looked stiff, like their knees were locked. Clover's hair hung in her eyes, threaded with loose grass. Ellis's were closed. But his mouth moved, the skin pulling back to a grin. His pristinely white teeth gleaming in the circle of light, which threw their shadows all the way back to the opposite tree line.

"Are you . . ." The words died in Wren's mouth. Are they what?

Wren stumbled a step back. Vanity's spine straightened in one jolt, a snap of movement.

"You don't understand," she whispered, taking a step forward. Her face shining greasily. Wren had already decided to run. "They're the ones hurting *me*."

✒

The scent of dried lavender had been present in Wren's life for all of his life, so that he could barely identify it any longer, save for when the heat kicked on in the mansion, vents stroking from the dead flowers a faint haze of dust and sweetness. That and a rustling sound like small, dry laughter.

But that was only in the front part of the mansion, the ballroom and the rest of the Museum that was left open to the paying public. In the sprawling living quarters that lay in the back of the building there stood no doorways adorned with dried herbs, no cinnamon bark delicately threaded through wallpaper, no candles with globs of sweating wax disrupting fabricated runes—all details that Monroe had presented to the tourists as ancient witch tradition, alongside the tarot card readings, the rites. All of it was a manufactured culture, made more interesting when melded with reality, with the Kims' household with shoes neatly placed by the front door, these silly, darling habits that now bled into the Adamses' with the latest generation. Foreignness was just so captivating, these pieces brought along across the great, cold sea. As Wren grew older, he had a vague understanding that he had a stake in such culture, that the blood in his blood and the blood before that had existed in Miyeon, pumped through limbs that moved to perform traditions so habitually they only called it living.

That's all they did here. *Perform tradition.*

All Wren had was his father, and the Museum, and his dogs. He'd never set foot in Miyeon and only knew what his father had cherry-picked for public consumption.

The living quarters smelled like wood polish, not lavender, and when the heat kicked on, it aggravated from the pristine surfaces the tangy smell of chemical cleaner.

His father's office got the worst of it, alleviated only slightly by the heady warmth of cigar smoke. Earlier that evening, before he'd been sent into the woods, Wren had spoken through a sliver of the ajar door.

"You called for me?"

"Don't hover."

Wren entered. Monroe was seated behind his great oak desk before a scatter of papers, wreathed with smoke and framed by the sea-facing windows. It was dark and starless outside, and Wren could only see cliff and then great, black void. He was tense but didn't show it. In private, his father's jovial smile was replaced by a neutral, impassable expression, except when something was wrong. Then he looked disturbingly serene. Wren had only seen his father look like this once, when he'd almost gotten kicked out of university his first year. Apparently, he'd showed up visibly high for one of his classes and babbled about human interconnectivity during a presentation that was supposed to center premodern psychological schools of thought and its origins in philosophy. Wren

191

still was of the firm belief that he hadn't been saying anything off-topic, original, or untrue.

Whatever had unfolded now was clearly more severe. Monroe was so eerily calm he almost looked complacent, lording from his high-backed chair.

"The youngest generation has been meeting in the woods. You'll send the dogs." Then Monroe nodded and his gray eyes went back to his documents.

Wren stood unmoving, blinking.

"That is all," Monroe said, without looking up.

"What?"

"The dogs, Wren. You haven't trained them for show."

"You want them dead?"

"Just for the night. I'll call on Cadence in the morning."

Still, Wren did not move. His mind was racing. All of them together, Vanity, Ellis, Clover, in the woods. When had Clover been drawn in? Had the other two sought her out on their own? How long—

"Wren."

"Yes?"

Monroe's calm was shifting to visible irritation. "Do as I say."

"I told them to meet."

"What?"

Wren steeled himself. "I told them to be friends."

His father stood very quickly and rounded the table. Something in Wren jolted, the child self he carried around in him that only stirred when his father neared like this, only stirred to flee. But Wren found his nerves miraculously steady, even when Monroe was looking in his eyes, looking for the dilation, the trip. What were they doing, out there in the woods?

"How long have they been meeting?" Wren breathed excitedly. "They're—"

He was cut off by his father backhanding him. Wren careened into the arm of a chair, caught himself awkwardly on the seat. Monroe advanced.

"Have you lost your mind? Have you forgotten what they are?"

"Terrifying creatures. Mad creatures," Wren answered without hesitating, over the taste of blood in his mouth. "Yet Ellis still screamed her name when she hit her head." Then, softer: "Do you remember how they all looked over, the tourists? Do you remember how they flocked to his rites afterward?"

Monroe would never believe Wren's theory that the witches finding connection in one another would better them, if only because Monroe did not want them better. Monroe would not profit from having them better. Having them in love, however...

"I could punish them for this," said Wren. "I'll send the dogs, if you wish it. But if they have been meeting for a time now, like Ellis's reaction suggests, then perhaps they don't have the calamitous effect on one another that we previously believed. Perhaps their relationship could be something sustainable."

He could see in Monroe's expression that his father was filling in other words. Marketable. Sellable. Yet when Monroe's mouth moved, it was only to say, "Vanity."

Vanity.

"She's..." Wren shrugged. "She's hardly been a stable one to begin with."

Yes, of course, she had been faring worse and worse these last handful of weeks, not eating, having her murmuring and twitching fits more and more frequently. Monroe perhaps thought to blame it on her proximity to the others, but. No. Wren knew companionship was medicine for the mind above all else.

"Anxiety over her ascension to necromantic Spectacle," he offered. Then he paused, relaxing his expression into thoughtfulness. "Or...well. If love is bound to feed anything in a young girl, it's her nervousness and her strangeness, no? That's what I've seen from the television soaps. And the shorts in the newspaper. And all the popular books of our time."

Monroe's expression was becoming thoughtful. Wren swallowed, anticipatory. He, too, was thinking of all the possibilities, no matter how distant they stood from Monroe's reveries. His father could never see the big picture; he lacked creativity, scraping from the top of the cream. He sold culture and violence and World, and all of it was charming or shocking or addictive, but certainly nothing that wasn't already there. For the witches, Wren knew, Monroe was picturing a glittering courtship, a wedding with tickets costing a year's rent in the gaudiest district of the City, international coverage of the sickest and darkest of people proving unimmune to the lightest parts of humanity, all under the glorious, generous patronage of the Museum, of course....

Wren didn't want a story. He didn't want performance. He wanted the real thing, which was a healing thing, which was . . . perhaps possible now, now that his father's expression mirrored his own, gears turning.

"It could be a sensation," Wren breathed, the final push. "*They* could be *the* sensation."

The last of Monroe's serenity evaporated, though stinging heat still radiated from Wren's cheek.

"Go see for yourself, what the children toil with, within the woods," spoke Monroe. "Don't forget what they are."

"I'll bring a dog."

"You'll bring nothing and no one." His father had returned to his chair, his documents. "It is important to know the fruit of your labors."

✒

Wren stumbled out of the forest and onto the green, the Museum at the top of the hill—twinkling like the crown jewel of the place—and vomited. His sick splattered the dewy grasses brushed around his shoes. He'd run. He hadn't meant to run. He had reacted as if . . . It was just, he'd sworn . . .

Strange dreams. He'd been having strange dreams, as of late. Horrible things he would not give air to.

He had to be the one who had his bearings. So that he could cure all of it. Yes.

The night air refreshing him, cooling the sweat built up on his forehead and under his clothes. He breathed. It all lay in how they connected with one another, remember? If something in that connection unsettled him right now, if something ran in him that screamed *wrong wrong wrong*— it was only his father's superstition, not Wren's own.

Wren wiped his mouth with the back of his hand. He would brush his teeth, put on a clean suit, report back to his father that all was well and friendly.

Then a voice came out of the dark forest behind him.

"Wren?"

Clover? His heart palpitated. How could it be Clover? He swore they'd seemed . . . He suffocated the image before it could come back into color. No. A hallucination, the World still floating around in his system triggered by the three of them. He forced himself to turn around. "You're here?"

"Can we talk?"

She was coming out of the woods now. Dirt and leaves sticking to the cool satin of her pajamas. The other two witches nothing but rustles of movement behind her. Ellis was speaking softly to Vanity, both of them just shadows in the woods, Wren couldn't make out the words. Yet Wren saw. How the world leaned for them, curled around them.

He flicked his eyes back to Clover. "Are you okay?"

"I'm alive, aren't I?" She gave him a perfect smile. Perfectly alive. "You were right. We need each other."

XIX

WELL, REALLY IT WAS ONLY because Vanity knew her so well that she had to do the right thing and lie. Lie to Clover. Because she knew sometimes Clover got nervous, when she was alive again and she was in a different position, off the quilt or halfway across the field or in the forest with her ankles tucked into the undergrowth, arms splayed like a martyr's.

It was only because Vanity was trying to understand them and it was easier when they were dead, when they were simpler like that, and she could make them smile at her. Crawl to her. On their hands and on their knees.

"Ro did it," Vanity would insist when they were back, tumbled into different positions, when sometimes Clover held her head and breathed very fast and pushed out tears very quickly from her eyes. It was the best thing to do because Ro wasn't there to defend herself—because at that point post-resurrection the magic was hitting Vanity's head, and when Vanity wasn't there Arrogance wasn't either.

🖋

"Where do you go?" Vanity asked her, once. It might have been a long time ago.

Ro was in the bathtub, and then she was up and holding her chin against Vanity's neck. Did Vanity still have floss threading her hands together, then? Or had this been the point she'd abandoned it completely?

"When?" asked her sister.

"When I'm high. When I'm not there." Did the cavities already twist and churn in her molars, peppered rot? Would she—or was she—remembering this truly? Ro smiled, or maybe Vanity smiled.

It didn't matter. There wasn't a difference, Vanity struggling to pick herself out from the mirror, from the tangle of girls, of limbs and teeth and beauty. They were both liars, and so there wasn't a reason to be scared when Ro said, "I open your mouth and I crawl down your throat."

🖋

And besides. Vanity liked when Ellis looked at her out of the corner of his eye and then maybe winked at her; of course *he* knew when she was lying about moving them around. And as she floated farther and farther away from herself she'd cling to it, this secret between them. Vanity could keep secrets, too, like how ~~he didn't actually care about any of this, what Vanity did when they weren't here, what Clover did when they were, all her questions, like how he didn't actually give a shit about any of them, he just liked fucking with them and even getting fucked with, which is why maybe Vanity was confused about what was happening, about whether or not~~ he was actually in love with her. Vanity was in love. Wren had explained that she was, that night he'd caught them in the woods and hadn't blown them all apart with the press of a button.

As she did with most things these days, Vanity had to focus very hard in order to discern what was happening. She was getting it mixed up again.

197

The cold night was pulling at her skin, and—no. It was the cool gray silk of her dress that was chilling her. The grasses of the clearing tickling her knees, except they were silky, like the threads of a tablecloth. And also the clearing of the forest looked an awful lot like the dining room of the Museum. Sort of. The electric chandelier had been replaced by candles, their necks cut with runes, the table strewn with bouquets of dried lavender. And usually when she ate here it was her and Ro and Cadence and Monroe and Wren, and it was generally a horrible time. But instead it was her and Ro and Ellis, and she realized she'd come to in the middle of being excited, even thrilled.

She'd never been excited in this room before and she didn't let it show on her face, she kept it a secret, she tucked it between her back molars and chewed on it like Ellis chewed at the skin of his chicken across the table from her.

Vanity immediately started blushing.

And Ellis said, "You're blushing," to which she said, "It's been a while since we've been alone," to which Ro said, "You're not alone," and Vanity responded, suddenly wholly frustrated, "You don't count!"

But really she was relieved Ro was there, seated on her left. She leaned over and whispered, "What's happening?"

"Sh." Her hands were on Vanity's face then, turning it toward the tall mouth of the doors, which were flung open. There was a thick velvet rope slung across the entrance and there were all these people smiling at them.

"Look at her, turning green with envy," said Ro, though their mother wasn't actually green, of course, of course it was just Vanity squinting a little and seeing through her skin, where she wasn't just green but a myriad of hues that swirled around each other, dancing with wet heat and heartbeat. Cadence was posted inside the dining room but hovered with her back against one of the opened doors. What was she doing standing, there, all fidgety, in her Party clothes?

"To have a date without an escort would be scandalous," murmured Ro in her ear.

"A date? What date?"

The grasses moved against her knees. Vanity picked at her ribbon, looking at the slab of meat on the plate in front of her, garnished with parsley. It was Clover. She'd gone out a little before Ellis, this time. Now Vanity would make her move a smidge, like she always did. Well, maybe she shouldn't, with Ellis still alive and watching. Even though she was doing nothing wrong, it was only to understand Clover, to know her without touching her: the intimacies tucked within her form, where she knotted together and where she softened, what hidden pieces could be made to sigh and unfold. In this way she knew where Clover lived and momentarily Vanity could live there, too, instead of her own body. For once she was brave and grazed Clover's cheek and her fingertips came back slick with something heavy and fragrant, like oil.

"She's not eating?" Wispy threads lifting from the crowd. "She looks positively sick. Why doesn't she stop touching it, then? The girl really should..."

"Eat?" Vanity let out a nervous peal of laughter. Then she had stood and was screaming. "How could you say that? Oh my god, that's disgusting. That's horrible!"

Most of the day had been spent contemplating why their mother was still kicking. Vanity knew that Cadence, despite all her bitching, didn't really want to be alive—in reality, the prolonged life was making their mother more and more nervous. The unexpected continued being-alive had only left Cadence with more time to anticipate her death. This anticipation often took the form of drugs.

"Why is she still here?" Vanity whispered to Ro. Ellis's father had been dead for a while, some bizarre accident should have befallen her by now.

The twins had been clinging to the banister. They could see the television going in the living room mirror, their mother's favorite black-and-white soap playing, the starlet throwing her skinny arms around her lover. The tearful exclamation accompanying: "It's so *nice* to finally have a moment alone *together*." But you couldn't really have that, could you, Vanity thought, a moment alone, together.

The twins could also see Cadence in the other room, too, she was on some sort of rampage, she had stripped off all her clothes and had moved all the furniture into the foyer. When the workers crept through in the morning to set out the breakfast, they got a free, if slightly obscured, show. She only went upstairs to put on some clothes when Ro told her she could see her stretch marks.

By the time she returned downstairs, the furniture barrier had been dismantled and redistributed, the cottage was clean, and there was breakfast and tourists to please. Today, it seemed, for an unknown reason at that time, that their cottage had been quite popular—for a while Ellis's had become the favorite daytime attraction, people flocking to see what he did all on his own, perhaps, what he would do in a grieving state that Vanity knew didn't actually exist. Other than that, though. Who knew what he got up to during the day. Vanity didn't know him at all.

↙

"Why are you doing this?" Vanity hissed at him. She'd sat back down. She'd stopped poking at Clover, which was not actually Clover but half of a roasted chicken. It smelled of lemon and pepper and not sweet humming death at all. Now Vanity's suspicion had crept in. It still managed to do that, sometimes.

Ro banged on the table and shouted, "Why are you doing this, you sick fuck? You want attention? You want to get your rocks off, right? Stop grinning. I said, *stop grinning*, piece of—"

The crowd rattled with laughter. They loved when Ro was obnoxious. Under the table, Vanity took her dinner knife and pushed it a bit into the side of Ro's knee until she shut up.

"I don't want to get my head blown off," said Ellis. But then he winked at her and she knew it was a lie. Her blush had come back; there was

200

no death and resurrection involved with this. He was here because he wanted to be here, looking at her across the pile of slick bones on his plate. Still, the anxiety thrummed through her. She was shaking her head. No. No. No.

"Where's Clover?" Vanity subtly side-eyed her chicken again before making herself stop.

Ellis went very still. "Should I be jealous?" He spoke in a careful way. "This is about you and me."

"No it's not. We need her. That's what this whole thing is about. That's what I thought we were doing. What are we doing now?" Vanity's breath was suddenly rocketing through her. She shook her head until the room spun around her, and then she shot across the table, quieter and sharper, "All of us should be together. That was the plan. Why aren't we sticking to the plan?"

Ellis moved as if through water, lazy stretches of his limbs, slow tilting of his head. His smile spread like melting butter. "And what was the plan again, Vanity?"

Her mind flared, images squeezing from her head, dew straining from damp morning air to lie fat and sweet on her tongue. The scratch of the thistles. The dome of a starlit sky curved over her head. That absent place where she found Clover and Ellis again and again, that void, that stomach. The trembling of her limbs in unstable euphoria, the way she sweated, the way the world sharpened around her until it collapsed under all its exquisite detail, until it was gone and all was quiet.

Quiet and dark and blank in her head, for a moment, as that dew swelled in her mouth, dribbled down her throat. Her teeth, automatically, on their own, ground down on something that was warm, and then warmer still, when it popped.

Vanity tasted blood.

All of this is for you.

She gripped the tablecloth and gagged.

"We were—we're—" *Finding a cure. A cure for magic. A cure in death.*

But that's what Clover was doing. What was Vanity doing? What was Vanity *doing*? All she found she could do was repeat herself. "All of us should be together."

"Like they are," offered Ro.

"Yes, like—" Vanity stopped short and shut her mouth.

Ellis leaned forward, eager. Vanity waited with the dinner knife still weighing down her hand. "Like who is?"

Ro was referring to the crowd teeming past the doors, fighting to get a view. The lines between bodies were obscured, there were so many of them—there was really no distinction. They were all one creature, really. Of many mouths and many heads. Before Vanity's eyes, the creature seemed to grow. It seemed to like to grow, taking what was separate to make itself whole.

"What's *wrong* with them?" Vanity whispered feverishly to Ro.

"Oh, I don't know," said Ro, even as the tip of the knife warned against her knee again. "They seem all right to me."

Was something worse happening? Was it because of this—Ellis sprawled before her like a king, head tilted, arms open and draped on his chair's rests, the pale lengths of his wrists shining in the candlelight. Still smiling and smiling at her as Vanity blinked rather quickly, trying to organize how she felt. Again she rose unsteadily from the table. She leaned over and pulled her sister's head close to hers. Ro made a rattling noise like laughter, or it might've been the sound of their temples knocking together.

"Is this real?" she whispered to Ro.

"Is what real?" Ro responded, staring toward the back of the room with her depthless black eyes.

"You said you'd watch for lies."

"Do you really want me to tell you?" Ro's smile sliced up the edges of Vanity's peripheral vision. "When you're only lying to yourself, wanting to know this. You haven't cared about yourself for weeks."

They're the ones hurting me.

She'd said that to Wren. But whatever part of Vanity that was scared of them or wanted to run or wanted to stop barely felt like her at all anymore, just a mistake, an accident, she didn't mean it, didn't mean to be ungrateful.

"Well, then, dear sister, how about instead I'll tell you everything that's true? He's obsessed with you. He can't leave you alone. When he smiles at you he means it. You're the best high he's ever had. And no, it's not the death. It's you. All you, Vanity. It's not what you do to him. It's what he does to you. It's what you let him do to you."

"Why do you have to be so mean?" Vanity already knew that she would hurt Ro later, when they got home, she'd take the dinner knife and then when Ro was asleep she'd make a series of calculated marks across the soft recesses of skin between her ribs. Ro seemed to be acting worse and worse and so Vanity had to do things like that more and more lately. Even though she knew she'd set it right like this later, she couldn't help crying now. Ro pushed away from her, disgusted.

Her arms and warmth were replaced by other arms, other, hovering warmth.

"Is she making you sad?" Ellis whispered in her ear, sending prickles down her spine. The crowd immediately revved and surged. Flashbulbs burned white. Vanity practically seized.

Cadence let out a series of scoffing noises, marching over to the two of them.

"No touching," she barked as Vanity's stomach churned.

"Ah, Cadence," Ellis said easily. "I never took you for a prude."

Her mother seemed ready to bark something else, but Ellis stretched himself to his full height. Cadence cowered. He was no longer the senseless little boy, charming in his youth and powerlessness; he was now a senseless man, and those were among the most dangerous kind.

"She doesn't like to be touched," Cadence said, quieter.

That was right, Vanity didn't like it. She used to not like all these things, she used to need control. Ro's mouth moved silently. *He's. Fucking. With. You.*

"Get off me," Vanity murmured. "It's not supposed to be like this. We're all supposed to be together!" She lurched for the table, rattling the edges of her plate. The lemon pepper chicken glistened with the movement. Or was it moving? "Clover?" Vanity shouted. "Clover!"

"Sh," Ellis cooed. "Sh . . ."

She shut her mouth. That was right. They had to be secretive about it. About the club, about the things they did in the club. One they died two they came back three they looked down her throat. Vanity frowned at Clover. That was all? She wasn't missing one? It felt like she might be. She almost asked Ro about it, but it would be bad if the others heard, so she just went over the list again: death, resurrection, wellness checks. Vanity relaxed. Nothing bad was happening, they never did anything too bad, not anything that stuck. She picked up her fork. She pushed it into Clover, because Clover never cared, not when she was still like this. When Clover was back again she'd be brand-new, it didn't matter how many holes Vanity put into her.

But they were being watched now, Vanity knew. So it was important to perform and do what she was supposed to do.

"It's so nice," she said to Ellis, pushing the prongs of the fork deeper and deeper into Clover, "to finally have a moment alone together."

EVERYTHING ABOUT THEM was charming. Even their lapses in conversation, when Vanity talked to her food or argued with Cadence or Arrogance or Ellis clutched his head, screaming about the voices. Then he'd trail off into laughter. Vanity laughed along with him. The crowd tittering. Their flashbulb cameras searing white.

All of this Clover would see on the television screen every single night. Sometimes she knelt so close to their silver faces that her hair curled from the static. Because this was for research purposes, she always had her notebook in her lap. The commercial would end with the flashing words COME SEE THE LOVER WITCHES and would come around again in ten minutes. Clover used these intermissions to jot down her observations: *You stupid creatures. You stupid creatures. You stupid creatures.*

Club continued as per usual. Well, didn't it? With Ellis and Vanity always staring at each other. They'd always been doing that. Always showing up, holding hands and gawking and gawking.

"You're home late, again."

Clover jumped, then quickly shut the door she'd been slowly closing, peering out at the thinning and thinning gap. She'd been staring at Vanity, hovering by the corner of the fence. She always followed her home like this, after club, when Clover wanted nothing more to do with her, was sick with her being near, sick of the wetness of her lips as she babbled. Clover blinked her eyes to clear their dryness. The hours seemed countless, by now, that she'd spent staring at Vanity.

"Needed some air," she murmured, turning. Lavender was standing in the center of the stairs, one hand braced against the wall.

"Oh. I could've gotten some air, with you."

Clover smiled thinly. "Next time."

All her life she'd witnessed Cadence Adams snapping at Vanity and James Kim at Ellis—until James died—at the Parties, but her mother never spoke to her with the same tone. She wasn't capable of it, which damned her. Or, at least, Clover damned her for it. If she'd been screamed at every so often maybe she wouldn't be so disgusted with her mother. Lavender's gentleness confused her. Clover couldn't cope with it, with the hand that reached out to touch her hair as she tried to pass on the stairs. It should be simple—Clover treated her badly and so Lavender should treat her the same. Instead her mother's manicured fingers caught her curls and then the tip of her shoulder, and Clover jerked away, and Lavender stepped to the side to let her by.

"Honey," Lavender said. "You know...you've been in some mood, lately...."

Every word trailed. Clover ground her teeth irritably, waiting, then realized the words had ended, lingering threads of thought like cobwebs broken off in the wind. "No I haven't," Clover said.

"Do you feel left out, by them?" Lavender glanced at the mirror holding up the front door, as if she could see into the yard like people could see into the house. But there was no one there, in the dead of night. And lately, only stragglers during the day. The Kim and the Adams houses had spiked in popularity, following the courtship. Not that Clover minded. What did the tourists expect to see, anyway? Ellis writing Vanity's name over and over again on the walls, Vanity tripping over her own feet, balance obliterated by her crush? That couldn't be what was actually happening. Was that what was actually happening?

Clover went into her room, discarding her things. The notebook, the stopwatch, and then her body all falling soundlessly onto the bed. She felt hot all over, like there was pressure building up in her head without the headache. She curled into herself, watching her fingers make light indents on the comforter. A shadow moved under the door, right to left, left to right. But her mother did not knock.

Her complacent behavior reminded Clover so much of Vanity.

Though, lately, everything reminded Clover of Vanity.

Right now, Vanity was standing outside, staring up at the house. She'd grown used to Vanity following her home, at one point. It scared Clover shitless, of course, but routines were reliable, and reliable was preferable.

Clover never elbowed her way past the tourists to see Vanity and Ellis taking their meal together, nothing like that. Sometimes she glimpsed them when they made it into the ballroom, when they were dancing, which was just Vanity tripping over Ellis's feet and everyone applauding when he caught her. His hand against her waist, so small that Clover knew she could close her whole arm around it, their ribs coming together. Of course she'd never try.

Clover had died thirty-seven times. Either by her hand or Arrogance's. But whichever. Dying was always the easy part.

At first, she'd been wary of coming back changed, clutching morals or pacifism or something else as obstructive, but.

It was always just her, here again.

And Vanity leaning over, always.

Vanity, who was definably in a state of dissolvement.

Those heavy black lashes opening to reveal pupils like lakes of ink. The blush spilling in her high cheekbones, her elegant hands dragging through the dirt, her mouth opening, so—good. Always doing what Clover told her to. Trusting Clover completely.

To cure her.

To undo all the bad things being done to her.

Undo them like Vanity herself undid death, turned it inside out so Ellis and Clover came tumbling back. She always did it so beautifully. It was her art. And the fact that it was making her completely lose it was only beneficial. It made her less inclined to run away.

And really she should be running away, very far away. From Clover.

Clover couldn't have that. She couldn't have that because they weren't done yet. Clover wasn't done with her.

She wasn't addicted to the resurrections the same way Ellis was, no, she did not crave that clarity. Clover was already so clear, all the time. But perhaps she was addicted to the awe of coming alive again. To the shock of Vanity's hands on her face. To her breathless babbling, to the light in her eyes when she was wired.

Clover didn't have very many feelings that took off running in her that she couldn't just put a leash on and tug back. The ones that managed to get away from her—the panic attacks, the cold fear that overcame her when she came back to life in a different position—died quickly.

So. This wasn't some crush.

"A parasite," Clover reminded herself, watching her own fingers curl. Something feeding on her. Something to rip out. Later.

✦

"There have been some complaints that Vanity's not eating."

Immediately Clover was scowling. "How are her eating habits any of your business?"

"My, you're defensive on her behalf. That's a good sign." They were taking what was becoming their usual stroll around the rose garden, Wren walking with his hands behind his back. After he'd caught them in the forest, Clover had said this was the better way, they'd converse and she'd update him. He didn't want to interfere with the process, after all, did he? The development of their *friendship*. "And it is actually, quite literally, my business."

This wasn't ideal. If Wren recommended Vanity be scheduled an appointment with a feeding tube, who knew how that would set things back.

"My concern is that this might be a reaction to a larger issue. If your group is experiencing some kind of tension—"

"No," Clover said. "She's been eating. She eats when she's with us."

"Does she?" queried Wren. He'd stopped walking. "And what does Vanity eat?"

Clover leaned to inspect the thorns of a winter-dead rosebush, stems glossy and firm even under the bite of the cold. "Cakes."

A dry smile lifted Wren's mouth. "Cakes."

"Yes. Why do you think there's been so many cakes ordered to my house?"

"Lavender is quite fond of them."

"Well. So is Vanity."

"So that's what you've all been doing in the woods? Eating sweets." He was amused, but not thoroughly. Clover knew what was happening, reading it in his stillness, which only pretended to signify calm. He was waiting for her to dig a bigger hole.

Clover remembered the first words that had sputtered from Vanity's mouth, when she'd been brought back that day. *Wren saw us*. But following him out of the woods, it was clear he hadn't known what he'd seen, exactly. Clover wanted to ask. And she didn't want to ask. What Vanity had been doing with their bodies, bodies he hadn't known were empty, empty of them? Because, of course, how could he think that, when Vanity didn't remember how to do magic yet? Did Vanity talk to

Clover? Scream at her corpse? Did she stroke her hair? Did she hold her like she sometimes did in Clover's dreams, hazy, cramped dreams where Clover pushed and struggled only to find she was sinking deeper into Vanity's stomach, cradled in the space of her rib cage, and that it was warm there, so soft....

"And we've been getting high," Clover said. Better to throw in a bit of truth, right? "Ellis has things to spare now, and he brings us loads to try." On instinct she had forced her body to relax around her hammering and hammering heart, but upon thinking about it, pivoted, sliding into the slightly defiant expression of a caught child. "You don't actually care, right? There's no way you actually care, that would be massively ironic. And recreational drug use is good for bonding." Clover paused. "Vanity talks more, when she's high. She's actually opened up a lot." All true. All true...

"About what? Her dreams?" Wren's eyes drifted for the cliff's edge, and then, before Clover could answer: "I've been having dreams...."

"What?" Wren was looking at her as he sometimes did: his expression open, thinly anxious. She thought it pathetic how he sought her for company. But this time she did not laugh, as she had done before. "Dreams of what?"

"That I was..." Then he seemed to catch himself. He shook his head, that crowd-pleasing smile settling once more. "Apologies. It's quite grim, I'll spare you."

Spare her from grimness. Sure.

Clover realized she was waiting impatiently to go back to his prior line of inquiry, to ask about Vanity's dreams, so that she could lie to him and tell him there was little to say. Even though there was so much she could say. So much Vanity had told her after the magic hit her head, gorgeous and horrifying whisperings of the sick, teeming curl of life and death and rot. Littler things, too, things that didn't matter, things that should've fallen out of Clover's head as soon as they were said, yet—stuck with her.

Like the disgust Vanity held for her own body, the claustrophobia. The way she believed her mother favored Arrogance. The dreams she had, so vivid she awoke and simply brought them with her, pretended they had actually happened until they did, they had, hadn't they?

How she dreamed of them, of killing them.

And, sometimes, of eating them alive.

⚶

Yesterday, or maybe the day before. Or maybe it hadn't happened yet; it was either death or them, together, that was scrambling the timeline. Whichever time, whichever direction—Vanity had been following Clover home as usual and then suddenly she wasn't. Clover had turned around on her front stoop and Vanity, her shadow, wasn't in her usual hovering place by the fencepost. After a moment Clover's hand left the doorknob. She crossed the front yard.

After all, an interruption in the routine, was, certainly, something to investigate.

Vanity was standing a little ways past the house. Doubled over. Ellis was beside her, hands rubbing unsure circles on her shoulder blades. "There, there," he said meekly. "Let it out."

"Oh, god, what is it?" Clover spoke quickly, walking up. She immediately cast her gaze up the long stretch of hill toward the Museum. It felt too exposed out here.

"Let it out—" Ellis repeated, as Vanity heaved, opened her mouth—Clover scrambled forward.

"No!"

Ellis stumbled back; she realized a beat later it was because she'd pushed him. Her arm was around Vanity's shoulders.

"Vanity," she said, "it's bad for your teeth. Come on."

"Where are we going?" Ellis asked.

"Not you. You stay out here."

"Oh, no, it's fine," Ellis said, trotting behind them. "I don't have anything else to do. Coven was the only thing on my list tonight, or, any night, for that matter—"

"We are *not* a coven," Clover hissed. Vanity was hobbling along, tucked into her side, looking quite green. Her skin was hot to the touch.

"Sorry. Death club, I mean. Anyway. That was the only thing, so I'm free to come along."

"That's not why I— Fine, fine. Come on."

They looked ridiculous, clustered together as they went through the white picket fence and up to the door. Clover opened it and peered in. Lucky—the first floor was dark and empty. A light shone from underneath the bathroom door on the second-floor landing, the sound of rushing water and Lavender's lilted, stop-and-start singing. She was drawing a bath—they had an hour, at least.

"In the living room," whispered Clover.

By this point Ellis had taken hold of Vanity again, too, and they half walked, half dragged her through the foyer. It really wasn't that much less exposed than standing around outside, with the viewing wall and all, but at least it didn't face up to the mansion.

They plopped her on the couch. Then Ellis plopped himself right down, too, slinging his arm over the top of the backing, Vanity's head rolling into the crook of his shoulder. His eyes swiveled around the room. Clover stood above it all, breathing heavily. Okay. They were in her house now, and she'd been the one to let them in. Why had she just done that?

"Are we sure that's Vanity?" Clover whispered.

"Yes." Then he frowned and Ellis grasped her face, the glazed, half-closed eyes rolling up to meet him. "Well. I'm pretty positive. Ro doesn't get sick, right? That's like, not a thing she does."

"You guys are such dicks," Vanity mumbled. It was definitely her. Ro hardly deigned to talk to them.

"I'll go get you something carbonated."

"No."

"Stay here."

Clover went into the kitchen and returned with a can of soda water her mother liked to mix with—anything. She cracked it open and waved it in front of Vanity's face. "Drink."

"No, please, I'm so full," moaned Vanity, recoiling into Ellis's side. "I ate too much. I just want it out of me. I feel like I'm about to split apart."

Clover's eyes flicked to Ellis. He gave a small shake of his head. "You didn't eat anything, Vanity," he said, very quietly.

She squirmed away from Clover's attempt to pour it into her mouth. "Don't make me."

"Just a sip, come on, it'll make you feel better," Clover said, strained. "I promise."

Finally she stilled. She took a small sip, her hands not lifting to touch the can, Clover leaned over her. She swallowed. Good.

"Let that settle."

"Peachy," Vanity said miserably, her hand massaging her throat.

Clover sighed. "There's nothing there, Vanity, I already checked today, remember?"

"No, you didn't. You didn't check because we were dancing."

"What?"

"Ellis and I were dancing. I opened my mouth for you but you weren't there."

The image floated back to Clover: yesterday's Party, Ellis and Vanity in the ballroom, Vanity's mouth stretched open. "I was trying to do it subtly, so everyone else didn't notice."

It hadn't been subtle. She'd fissured her plum-dark lipstick, Clover had seen it. She had glimpsed the shining red inside of her mouth. She'd told herself in her head that it made Vanity looked sloppy, her jaw slack like that, but it was a lie.

"Oh," Clover said. "Yes. I must've missed it." She was looking sideways at Vanity, now. Vanity was looking at her full-on. God, the eagerness on her face.

"I won't get us caught," said Vanity. "I'll make sure to hide it. They won't know what we really mean to each other." Then she started to cry.

Clover, uncomfortable, quickly said, "Well, here, I'll check again. You don't have to do that."

"Okay."

Vanity lifted herself a little from Ellis's side. Opened her mouth. "Nothing," said Clover. "Here. Drink more."

Now there was silence. Clover didn't like it. She went to switch on the television, then took a seat on the couch next to Vanity. For some reason this made Vanity laugh, the shrill, sudden laugh she did sometimes that sounded almost panicked. Then Clover felt a warmth. Vanity's arm was flush against hers, flush against Ellis's. The black-and-white television droning before them, casting their shadows up the walls, larger than them.

The newspapers called the Museum residences things like *Quaint, Cozy,* and *Adorable.* It was hard for Clover to gather this impression with one wall that doubled almost every room, but—had she ever actually sat here before? Just—watching some soap opera. If she had, she'd have done it alone. She'd have been very careful to do it alone.

Subtly, she turned her head to the side to glimpse them in the mirror. Vanity sipping her soda. Ellis's arm outstretched, so the crook of his elbow was behind Vanity's head, his fingers dipping into Clover's hair. The television's music was sweeping up, a woman falling into a man's arms, the perfect teardrop rolling down her perfect cheek. Ellis took a sip of Vanity's soda. The scene just seemed so natural, like they'd been here a million times before. Both totally transfixed by the television, the music cresting, now.

Wren often ended their walks with inane questions. *Do you see what I mean about meaningful connections? Aren't you feeling better? Doesn't the world seem less bleak?* And the horrifying truth Clover never told him—it did. The world had exploded into vivid, startling pigments. She was noticing so many details she'd missed before. She'd never allowed herself close enough to see that Vanity's hair was really a very deep brown instead of pure black, and the same for her eyes, ringed by crow's-feet that radiated the palest lavender hint out of the bruised hue. And Ellis—he had hands so pale they were almost translucent in the right light, and the veins there were fine, and green.

Clover knew the most poisonous creatures wore warning colors.

She wondered what colors she wore. Wondered if Wren could ever see them, flashing. How she hated him. Hated that he'd come into the woods during their club, trespassed like that—it was like he had seen her without clothes on. It felt like he was messing everything up. Ellis and Vanity ogling each other at the Parties, that was all his fault. Couldn't he see that they were bad for each other, like that? That Vanity was performing, and it was confusing her? He should've just left them alone. She could just be herself, with Clover.

"I wish I wasn't so totally disgusted by it," Vanity murmured.

"What?" Clover turned her head back to the screen. The leads were kissing. "Oh."

"Very slippery. And that's lot of bacteria."

"What about on the cheek?" Ellis asked.

"No."

"Hand?" Vanity lifted her hand and considered. Turned it over. Back again. Clover watched the gesture; it was clotting an odd feeling in her chest, a deep-set tightening.

"Hand would be okay," Vanity concluded. "Wrist is better."

"Gimme," said Ellis. Vanity immediately turned scarlet.

"Absolutely not!" she gasped, bringing both hands protectively to her chest. But Clover could still see it. The strip of skin running up her forearm, half shadowed, half washed in staticky light. It looked so soft, there. Clover wanted to press her fingers to it. But there was no logical explanation for that. She had no reason to check Vanity's pulse right now.

"You need to leave soon," Clover heard herself say. "You do. You really do."

✔

"We're missing a piece." Clover had spoken softly, because Vanity had fallen asleep. Her head on Ellis's shoulder, hands interlaced on her stomach, features washed by the television's glow.

"We're not," Ellis said. He sounded so sure. He didn't know he wasn't sober. Couldn't see that he became unwell as soon as he touched them. Clover could see it clearly. She was the only one keeping them afloat. "We have everything we need. I'm better. I'm all better."

Clover shook and shook her head. "Being in love doesn't fix you."

XXI

"PLEASE TAKE A SEAT, VANITY. There have been some complaints that you're not eating. Why aren't you eating? Well, I'm asking because I'm very concerned. Everyone is very worried about you. No, dear, I think you look beautiful. No, no, now, I know that's a lie, Vanity, and please don't lie to me. You can't feel full, we know you haven't been eating. The kitchens can make you anything you want. We all just want what's best for you." When Monroe smiled his eyes crinkled at the corners; he had lines there, pantomiming a joyful life. Vanity wondered, was he really joyful? "...alternate measures..." Was he truly satisfied with his life, sleeping in a cold, empty bed every night? Vanity nodded and tuned out his ramble, trying not to sit there grinning to herself—she was the luckier person between the two of them and Monroe didn't even know it, he was thinking, Poor creature, and she was thinking back, Poorer creature, poorer, lonelier creature... "...don't *want* to have a tube down your throat, do you?"

And Vanity, shaking her head, frowning, no, no, I want to get better, of course I want to get better, after all—who doesn't want to get better? Who in their right mind would have the desire—the deep-set gnaw of need in the marrow of their bones—to get as bad as they could possibly get?

*

But Vanity hadn't lied, she did feel so full, all the time. Sometimes the worst of it would hit her after the resurrections, she'd come out on the other side with her fingers probing her stomach, so stuffed she was sweating. "Did we eat anything, during club?" she'd murmur to Ro, when Ro bothered to be there, and her sister would always respond, "I had dinner."

At home Vanity would strip in front of the bathroom mirror. She turned from side to side. She was bloated, she was sure. Well, almost sure, as her knees touched cold tile and she bowed before the toilet bowl. But her fingers hesitated at the threshold of her teeth.

Clover had said it was fine, and Vanity didn't want to find any reason to call her a liar.

*

But other than that discomfort it was all going along very well, very secretively, even though there were all these people watching them, now. Even though when Ellis touched her, when they were going around the clearing—no, the ballroom—it must be so clear to everyone, how intimate they were, it was clear how often Vanity held his soul in her hands, even though her hands on his skin now did make her nauseous. Opening and closing her mouth as he spun her, slowly.

"Nothing there," he kept on saying, even though Clover was the one who was meant to check. "We're not where you think we are."

Ellis seemed distressed. He'd been showing up late to club, though he always came to the clearing sooner or later. Sometimes, when he was back in his body, he cried. He told them they should stop. When he said things like that, Vanity was already drifting away, and it fucked up her high, really, when the last thing she could remember was him and Clover beginning to argue.

"I hate that they're watching," said Vanity under her breath. They were the reason he was so uncomfortable lately, with their sentinel eyes. "Pretend it's just me and you." She wanted to put him at ease. Vanity was sweating. She was wearing a pretty dress instead of her sweatpants, which was wrong. She could feel his heartbeat through his skin, crawling up through the soft teeny tubes of his veins. "And Ro and Clover." That's what it was supposed to be, she remembered. Just her and Ro and Ellis and Clover.

*

So of course the next time Vanity looked around and found they were truly alone she had to take advantage, had to make it last so Ellis would feel better. When they were dead from the tea she wandered back through the forest and Ro helped her break the lock on the gardener's shed to get the shovel. Returning to the clearing, then, to dig. She laid the quilt in the hole first and then her and Ro rolled them in and covered their faces and covered them up. Vanity lay over the pressed earth and fell asleep. She did not dream.

When the misty dawn light lay gauzy over her face Vanity awoke. The night without magic had made her clearer, made her feel guilty and panicky and craving a hit, and so she dug, following the *tick tick tick* of Clover's stopwatch under the earth. Ro was no help, stretching lazily in the grass.

"They're going to kill me," Vanity said, but no. They were going to hate her, which was worse. "Fuck. Fuck."

"I mean," Ro said. "It's a weekday. Slow tourism. You could probably just leave them."

"And do what?" exclaimed Vanity, exacerbated.

Ro shrugged. Newborn morning light uncurling against the sky above, reaching. "What you usually do."

⚥

Vanity didn't remember walking. But then she was standing on the usual threshold. How was this the usual threshold? But her shoulder found its comfortable place against the wood post, peering in. This dim, slightly humid space that smelled of animal and hay. The dog shed.

Wasn't she afraid of this place? Or did she have that backward, too? It seemed more like the dogs were afraid of her. Their sleek gray bodies cowered against the back wall, their whines sharp and arching in her ears.

"Are you looking for something?" Ro asked, almost eager. Vanity remembered she was there, leering, that her sister was who the dogs were scared of, not her.

Vanity's eyes slid across the dim space. Then she shook her head. No. There was nothing for her here.

⚥

"I'm sorry," she said when they were back, as Ellis coughed up black debris. Clover peering at her, dirt in her long eyelashes. Finger slipping against the stopwatch.

"What time is it?" Clover murmured, then tipped her head back toward the light. She stumbled to her feet. "Fuck, I have to get home."

Ellis grabbed Clover's wrist and went, "Wait a minute. I'm—"

"Fine?" Clover spat the word. Vanity beamed, but then Clover was shouting at her, "All fucking night, Vanity?"

She said she was sorry again. That, like she sometimes did, she'd placed presents in their pockets to make up for it. She watched the world waver around Clover, watched the flush of her anger pulse red over her skin, then rainbow. Vanity giggled. Ro had already run away, already crawled down her throat. That was the sensation she was feeling, palm against her neck, the warmth moving in it. But Ro had just been kidding about that, Vanity reminded herself, but laughed harder anyway.

"This is it, Clover," Ellis was saying. His hand still around Clover's wrist. "This is what you were looking for—the *clarity*—"

"No," Vanity said, understanding suddenly, gasping, "No, no, no."

"We just need to be dead longer." He was still talking, ruining everything. Vanity had ruined everything. "This is what I'm supposed to feel like. This is what I'm supposed to feel like all the time."

"No! Don't go." She was talking faster and faster, trying to keep up with the pulsing of their bodies, the churn of their blood. "You're not fixed. You're not cured!"

She nearly burst into tears of relief when she saw Clover shaking her head. "We don't know. Do we need to be buried? Does it need to be nighttime? Is—"

"I'm so sick of this," Ellis spat. "What the fuck are you doing, Clover?"

Vanity watched her cupid's-bow lip pull back from her straight white teeth. "Why don't you just make me tell you?" She ripped her hand away when Ellis didn't answer, tried to wipe the dirt from her sweatpants. Clover leaning over her now, snatching the thermos and her notebook from its place on the thistles. "That's what I thought. Come on, Vanity. We have to go now."

So Vanity stood, and had the sensation that she continued to stand, even when she was all the way up. She was floaty. Clover, ahead of her, dug the dirt out of her mouth with a fingernail. Behind them, Ellis followed, footsteps dragging, then quickening.

XXII

"WHAT ARE YOU TRYING TO DO, CLOVER?"

They needed to stop following her home like stray dogs. She didn't know how Ellis had gotten into the house. Probably through the front door.

"I'm trying to find a cure." It was night now, and she'd washed the dirt from her hair as soon as she'd gotten home early that morning, but she always felt the need to take a shower after the tourists went home. Her hair dripped onto her bare feet. She closed the bedroom door behind her.

Ellis's features were bathed in darkness from the corner of her room. Clover still saw the tilt of his head, and his voice came soft and steady. "For us?"

"Of course." She took her time, opening her closet, taking out her things. "Clearly it's working. You used to be all over the place. Look at you now, with intent, of some kind. That focus shows improvement. Murderous or otherwise."

"I don't want to hurt you." Oh, and the audacity to sound so *wounded*. "You always think I want to hurt you."

"Well, perhaps I'm beginning to be wrong."

"So death makes us level. How does that help her?"

Clover rolled her eyes. "Vanity seems rather happy, lately, I would say."

Ellis stood up. Clover was casual, turning on the light. Moving in front of the mirror that hung on the door of her closet, her hands working through the knots in her hair.

"You never thought she was coming with us, in this."

"Vanity can't get better."

"She can. She hasn't even hurt us yet. Not really."

Clover couldn't help but laugh at that. So Ellis put his hand on the back of her neck and slammed her against the mirror, so hard it cracked.

Clover was calm. There was no reason not to be calm. If Ellis was getting better, he'd be less prone to actually killing her.

And if he did kill her? Well. Death had lost its stakes anyway.

"Arrogance won't stop hurting us." Her breath fogged the spiderweb cracks. "And there's no Vanity without Arrogance."

"What does this end with?"

"A cure."

She was, of course, being intentionally obtuse. She had to preserve the integrity of the experiment above all else.

"I wouldn't," said Clover, when Ellis's mouth opened. "Using magic would upset your delicate sobriety. You wouldn't remember what I told you, anyway." Sometimes she heard the sound of her voice and realized a part of her enjoyed this. Enjoyed how clear she was by comparison, the satisfying reminder that she had all her ducks in a row, everything under control. "I'll make your head spin."

He glared at her. "You don't know that."

"I do." She tapped one of her fingers against the mirror, against another set of delicate cracks. "You lose it, every time."

Ellis's grip loosened and then slid away. Clover pressed her hands against the closet door and peeled her cheek away from the mirror. She could hear him breathing rather hard. Like he was so furious.

He had once put his trust in her. Throughout their childhood, Clover had told Ellis to stay away from Vanity. And up until the Machine, he'd followed her instructions. He knew why he should be afraid.

Clover knew why she should be afraid.

And yet they couldn't seem to leave Vanity alone.

↙

Clover had a theory. Wren had mused to her before how World tricked nature into not planting new pockets of witchcraft into the population, but what if he was wrong? Both the Museum and the City had been lulled into a false sense of security. Though Clover would inherit magic that dealt with an overexposure to nature's processes of deterioration, she knew its tendency toward resilience, too. She could see it everywhere, in the ivy that attempted to strangle the sides of the cottages and the mansion that the gardeners fought back with shears and with poison, in the rabbits spawning incessantly in the forest, in the stoicism of the sea as it tried to tear the City from its foundations.

Clover could see it, she believed, in Vanity.

In whatever she was—a witch, yes, but clearly a variant. As with all of them, the natural pantomimed the horrifying unnatural, but Vanity was the revolt of the world incarnate, death made flesh made girl unraveled, and this revolt had withstood the Machine.

And, perhaps the most terrifying part of all of it—nature had seen fit to bestow upon Vanity an unspeakable loneliness. A craving for their company.

And now, before Clover's eyes, it was infecting Ellis, too, a poisonous infatuation so potent it withstood even his deaths. This tendency to protect one another. Nature didn't simply desire the existence of witches any longer, to teem and to embody. Nature desired a coven.

224

Not to be said that it wasn't affecting Clover, too, this coven tendency. It was important to observe this; though resistance was necessary, denial was obstructive. Perhaps if she was as foggy-headed as Vanity, yes, she would declare that the wriggling worm of this thought pattern was something romantic, that they were on her mind. Always. But Clover championed logic above all else, and thus was protected by the fact that love did not fit in them; witches were simply not built for it; or else she was not built for it; she dismissed any longing either as the infection of the coven tendency or as her own need to continue the experiment. And so when she touched Vanity's hair or Ellis's hand or thought her terrifyingly strange and him horrifically attentive, or else thought about them constantly, all of it because Clover was seemingly unable to *not*—it was either to take a note, or because something had invaded her, causing her to act unlike herself.

🖋

"You already know everything that's about to happen, don't you?" Ellis asked quietly.

To an extent, yes—Clover knew a general "everything." She supposed she was painting with broad strokes. She'd bought time, with Wren believing she had coaxed them together all on her own, that she was facilitating meetings with no other purpose than close proximity. With Monroe holding the sham dates.

It had to be enough time, for the cure to grow.

For it to ferment in Vanity's throat.

"You asked me for my help. I'm giving it. I promise I am."

"I don't believe you." She knew what was coming next. "I saw your notes."

Yes, he'd wrenched them from her hand this morning as they made their way back through the woods. And then he'd given them back. Left without saying a word, leaving Clover to direct a drooling Vanity home.

A whole night lost. She hadn't felt up to asking her usual questions, or why Vanity had buried them—there would be no rational answer. There never was.

What Ellis had seen in the notebook had been three columns, spanning many pages now. The first column specified the date. The second column was the amount of time spent dead, recorded from Clover's stopwatch as soon as she was resurrected. The third was a brief description of Clover's mentality, and Ellis's mentality, predicted by his demeanor—how long it took them to feel their overexposures again. The descriptions were less and less detailed as the days went on, Clover wasn't sure if Ellis had noticed that. But he'd definitely seen that she'd known all along, hypothesized from the get-go, that the longer they were dead, the longer they stayed clear. *But so what?* Clover wanted to spit to him now, had been spitting more and more to herself as the weeks had turned into months. *What does it fucking matter, if it doesn't stick?*

Death never stuck to them. No, death was always the easy part. Vanity reached out and peeled it off, blew it away with a sigh. The hard part was when you woke up and she told you she'd missed you, expected you to love her and smile at her and heal her, like she was just a girl with a dark streak and a tender heart, and not someone who had left you dead and buried for seven hours and nine minutes because she'd felt like it. She swallowed nights for you, like that. She collapsed time. And she flinched away when you screamed at her for being a fucking freak.

Clover hated her for everything, but she hated her more for barely noticing how much Clover was afraid of her. Vanity always thought Arrogance was the scary one, the vicious one. She said it all the time, when Ro wasn't there, and it made Clover sick to her stomach, every time.

"Death is the cure," Ellis said quietly. He'd written that to her, what felt like forever ago, now. Lifetimes ago, ha ha. "We already had the answer. Why the fuck were you doing—all that other shit?"

Rich, that *you*. He was there the whole time, for all of it. Every resurrection. Every trip up to the dog shed.

"It's not enough," she snarled, lips pulled back from her teeth. "I told you that. We're missing a piece. We need something more permanent."

"More permanent than death." A laugh behind his words, because, obviously. "I'm out. I'm done." No, he wasn't. He'd said it all before. Said how he was disgusted with her, finished with her, how he was going to leave her all alone. As if any of them could leave each other alone. "You stay away from her, Clover. I mean it. I'll hurt you." Yes, yes, and around and around it went. This was a merry-go-round and it was spinning too fast at this point for any of them to step off.

"What does it matter, if I keep my distance?" asked Clover. She knew her smile was cruel. She'd smiled like that before, they'd done all of this before. And Clover was tired. So tired when she said, "Vanity won't."

She didn't know how Vanity rationalized her gravitating toward them, but whether she defined it as romance or hatred was equally dangerous and equally wrong. Vanity was puppeted by arcane forces. It frustrated Clover that Ellis couldn't see that. The more time he spent with Vanity, the more he seemed to forget that Arrogance was there, too.

And Arrogance, of course, was evidence of all of Clover's theories. Evidence that, in this generation of Adamses, you peeled apart a girl and would find—in the slick under her skin, in the shape of her thoughts, in the fresh, warm curl of her breath—revolting nature, nature revolting. . . .

XXIII
NOW

ELLIS WATCHES THE rise and fall of her stomach.

Both he and Clover had crawled into bed with Vanity, no discussion about it. Eventually Clover had dozed off, too, and now it is only Ellis that lies with his eyes open. He'll wake them if the end of the world is starting.

Or maybe he won't. He'll see what his mood is when the time comes.

Eventually Vanity opens her eyes, dark, gleaming disks. Clover's head is in the crook of her neck. Ellis says nothing, watches Vanity breathe in.

Then she turns her head toward his. Their noses brush.

"Your hair is so long. Are those face tattoos?" she murmurs. "You look so stupid."

Ellis waits.

"I hate you for bringing me back," she says.

"I'm sorry."

Vanity looks back toward the velvet canopy over the bed. They're in the residential wing, its sprawling master bedroom. Ellis guessed it was only ever Monroe in here—if the old man hadn't possessed such a shriveled little heart, maybe he would've thought to be lonely. All the curtains have been drawn. Not just here, but all over the mansion. Ellis made sure.

"So," Vanity murmurs. "What now?"

"What do you mean?"

"What do you want with me?"

There is a bitterness to her voice Ellis hasn't experienced before. It lies tart on his tongue and he shivers with the taste. He doesn't ask, *What makes you think we want anything from you?* because, of course, the answer would be *Everything.*

Before, her beats of despising him could never hover for very long. Her only sense of self-preservation had been in the form of Arrogance. For Vanity, there was a certain satisfaction to feeling shitty, it was like penance for being so disgusted by everyone and everything. All of this she had told Ellis, little by little, once they'd gotten the resurrections going. He'd figured out pretty quickly that she couldn't always tell when she was babbling, that half of what she thought she said in her head she'd fed into the air.

Ellis loved her so much.

She hadn't stood a goddamn chance.

"I can't believe you're right in front of me," Ellis breathes. He won't tell her he loves her just to soothe her. He won't tell her because he's tainted the meaning for her. And honestly, he's fuzzy on the meaning itself. Was it love even when he loved watching her lose it, too?

Instead he puts his hand on her cheek. Instead he holds still while Vanity turns her head and bites down into his palm.

He pockets the sensation of her wanting to hurt him. His blood pools on her lips, dyes the pillow red. His hand's a ragged mess when she's done. Ellis offers her his other one. Vanity just closes her eyes.

"Do you remember what happened?" Ellis asks.

Silence for a few heartbeats. Ellis can hear the blood pushing and pushing in his ears. Then she says, "You were dying in the woods, and I was bringing you back. We were in love. We were getting married."

Ah, yes, that's right. How ridiculous. "That's not really what I meant." He doesn't know if this is still her trying to hurt him.

"How long was I dead for?"

"A year."

She's crying, a little. She probably feels very clear, clear as ice, or vodka. But this also means she's horrified, properly horrified, like they should've been the whole time.

"Where are we?"

"The Museum."

"Why?"

"Ours, now. All ours."

"Clover's idea, to stay?"

"Clover, Clover. Always with the plan. Always with the following through of that plan." He considers. "And, well. Where else is there to go?"

"This is all her fault."

"I know."

"Yours, too."

"I know."

One of her hands wraps around his wrist, the bloody one. It is a jolt, an instinct.

"Mine too." For a moment her chest rises and falls very quickly. "Mine too, right, Ellis—"

Her panic scatters and beats on his skin like hail. Ellis panics, too. That's what they do. One hurts and the other does, too. One snaps . . .

"It's okay," Ellis lies, voice shaking. He props himself above her. Her irises are lost in their whites, going everywhere, unfocused. "Hey, hey, Vanity, it's okay."

"I remember what I see isn't always there. What I remember isn't always true. It isn't always true. Is that true?"

"Yes."

"But everyone is dead."

"Yes."

"It was Ro?"

He hesitates. "Yes."

So she doesn't remember what happened, not everything. Why and how Ro snapped. He knows she doesn't know because she is still in the bed with him. She is able to touch them both without recoiling.

"She took something from me," Vanity whispers. "I felt it in my throat."

Cold prickles down Ellis's spine. *Open wide . . .*

Ellis laughs. His hand throbs and throbs, the raw bits screaming at the intrusion of the open air. For a moment he is sure he has loved her since he was a child, but he remembers this isn't true. What is true is that she is like a pin stuck between his ribs. Sometimes he imagined taking out this pin, but just so he could push it back in again. This year without her had been hell, but Ellis doesn't know how to tell her that, he doesn't have any detail to describe any of it. It is just one big bloody, cackling blur. The swing of the shovel. The bloodying of his hands against Wren's skin. The indomitable silence radiating from Clover's home. It'd be lying, saying this year had almost killed him. Because really this time without Vanity had been nothing. It hadn't meant anything, Ellis hadn't existed during it. Now she's back and he's becoming real again, he can feel it, he is a picture processing and she's the one holding him up to the light.

"So. What's Ro going to do?" Ellis asks, because he's curious.

"How am I supposed to know that?"

"You, of all people, should know that."

This last bit is spoken into Vanity's neck by Clover, whose hazel eyes are open now. All of them awake now, all of them together. For a little while they go quiet again. Just breathing in the same space. Proving to each other over and over again they are alive.

After a little while, Vanity says, "I think the world's about to end."

"It already did," says Clover.

"We're still here." Her voice turning quieter and quieter. "God, god. We're always here, again."

231

Clover's thoughts turn, then—a jolt of rising, frigid tide. She opens her mouth. She is about to ask for death, but they said they weren't going to do that anymore, remember? "Vanity, do you think—"

"Do you guys want to try to stop it? The end of the world?" Ellis asks, trying to be casual, like that craving part of him doesn't jolt then, too. "I'll do whatever."

Vanity sits up suddenly, holding her head in her hands. Her misery presses Ellis down into the bed like a weighted blanket.

Clover glances at him. He meets her eyes and so she looks away, putting her hand on the small of Vanity's back. Vanity shuts her mouth and breathes in, one rattling intake of air.

"Hey," Clover says gently, rubbing small circles. "Hey. Do you want to get really fucked up?"

A grand idea. Because there is absolutely nothing else to do.

Vanity is right, about all of it. That they can't stop what's coming. Ro is nature incarnate, and nature isn't something that stays dead.

Though, truly, none of them are.

They really just should've killed her early on, instead of it being mostly just Ellis and Clover dying, over and over and over. But how else could they discover what Vanity could do? How else were they supposed to get to Ro?

⚰

Vanity doesn't specifically want to do a lot of drugs. But she does want to feel numb and pretend her being alive and the circumstances around her being alive aren't actually happening. Getting fried goes in that general direction.

She is sitting on a kitchen stool. Someone has pushed a crumpled carton of cigarettes into her palm before dumping her here. She doesn't quite remember what to do with them. Vanity pulls one of the white cylinders from the package, puts it in her mouth and chews.

There is some kind of chattering sound happening then—Ellis's laugh. Vanity spits the cigarette out as a wet blob onto the marble countertop.

Selecting another. It goes in her mouth properly this time. Clover is leaning for her, now, lighter in hand. *Click*, the glow of a flame. There was a time Vanity would have adored such attention from Clover Rao.

Vanity can observe it in herself, the ghost of the old habits of her body. Here is the scorched earth of her adoration.

Vanity watches the flame destroy the end of the cigarette, eating its way down. She takes it out of her mouth and presses the glowing cherry to the back of her hand. Screams, even though the pain feels far enough away from her, detached from her. Really, this is just for the feeling of screaming.

Ellis laughs louder. Clover takes another bump from the field she's divided into generously, orderly white lines on a porcelain plate. All that orderliness blown apart in the arena of her body. They know Vanity is okay. Or at least as okay as the two of them.

Ellis smiles at her. Clover does her closest version—her body angled toward Vanity with her head facing the opposite direction. Candlelight has erupted all over the room; the drapes are drawn. Vanity doesn't think this is a mistake. There could be anything out there. Or this room could be the only thing left.

"Did you see a white light?" Clover is asking, and then throws her head back and laughs.

Vanity stares and stares at them.

Vanity thinks, as they pay all kinds of attention to her, as they get her high and fill her glass and move in their awkward currents around the kitchen, she thinks, with excruciating clarity, I was in love with the both of you.

She thinks, as she has thought before, Death couldn't cure it.

She thinks, I wouldn't have let you go. I would have turned the other world inside out, looking for that love, I would've made death unnatural, bruised and blushing and wrong, if it had tried to take you two away from my head.

So I know.

I know you both did something terrible to me.

↙

Well. More terrible than the usual terrible, anyway.

↙

She'd wanted to shower first, before their little Party. First she'd stripped and stood in front of the mirror, because that had been habit, once. Touching her skin, frowning.

There were marks. Faint ones, invisible, really, they'd been long healed over, but Vanity could feel their weight. They were all over her arms and legs and stomach and chest, some small and some sprawling and some sporadic, like pinprick freckles.

Had those always been there?

So much of her memory had been blotted away, even before this last bout of death. She'd been so smeared. She'd lost herself completely, in them, to them.

Once, that glorious unraveling had been everything Vanity had hoped for.

Apparently it had led to the end of the world.

Vanity didn't remember the specifics, but she'd gathered the context clues. That they were the only ones left, or close to it. That it was Arrogance who had made the apocalypse.

Who had been the apocalypse.

Hadn't Vanity always known it was going to be Ro?

Her sister could've done away with it all years ago, but she had never taken the Museum patronage as a burden, no reason to treat mortal cruelties that seriously; she enjoyed the luxury, enjoyed treating the estate as her playground and scaring the tourists and goading Vanity. But Ro loved her. She would've done anything Vanity asked.

Had Vanity asked?

She could picture it: Ro looking over, hazed and high on the carnage, with all the adoration Vanity had sought in other people, and saying, I'll start it over. I'll eat the world and start it over, for you.

But Vanity has always been good at imagining things.

Here is her last memory: It was dark, and she was choking.

🖋

There is a disorienting kind of darkness settled into the mansion—the faintly glossy surfaces and glint of fabric and shimmer of wallpaper pantomiming light, coherence, but Vanity knows if she pins her stare on anything she won't quite be able to make it out in detail.

As they move farther and farther away from the candlelight flickering in the kitchen, the shadows deepen from gauze into ink. By this point she is quite fried. Ellis reaches for her hand—it's unexpected and she hasn't braced herself, and through the skin of his palm against hers she can feel his nerves throbbing with the beating of his heart. She jerks away.

"It's a lot," she mumbles.

"Yeah." He cradles the dejected wrist to his chest almost shyly. "Sorry."

"Where are we going?"

"I don't know. Following Clover."

"Clover. Where are we going?"

"What? Why?" Clover has a cigarette in her hand and they're trailing after its cherry like a beacon. "Why do you think I know? Why are you following me to begin with?"

Vanity's hand brushes heavy velvet drapes. She stumbles a little, teetering left, and her other hand brushes the same. She's been here before, in this hall, with its tiny, curtained rooms. The satisfying bridge of the tarot collapsing in fingers, rippling through her. She drew one card and then she drew another. Frowning and then smiling.

"Where are we *going*?" Vanity said, harsher this time.

"I don't know, okay? Okay? Nowhere. We're going nowhere."

Clover's body hits doors and then goes through them. The stuffy lightless air of the hall opens up to the sprawling lightless air of the ballroom. Vanity's foot immediately kicks something soft and then something hard—a pillow, and then Clover's shoulder. Clover's on all fours, her hands searching the low seating area. Then a match strikes and finds a wick in the dish of candles on the tea table.

So then they are tucked away in the corner of the ballroom, oppressive dark hovering over them. This place that was once filled with light and music and richness and, apparently, culture. Vanity is settled back now, into a pink puffy pillow. It all reminds her that she is not supposed to be here. She is

supposed

to

be

dead.

And then the thought softens, filters away.

Instead Vanity thinks, Existential dread exists in the system of the form. Bad thoughts can be obliterated, they float in a vat of chemicals that can be altered, shaken like a misbehaving child. Everyone playing alchemist all their lives, introducing things to their system, and what a system it is, how resilient, how receptive. You could change your whole person, if you controlled what you brought into your stomach, your lungs, your veins. The mind is subservient to the body. She should say this. "The mind is subservient to the body," she murmurs in Ellis's ear. "That's why you shouldn't have fucked with me."

He makes this little noise in the way back of his throat, it's like she can reach into his mouth and pull it out like a bead of gold. She forgets that she doesn't exactly love him anymore and doesn't know why; she recalls how she likes the line of his jaw. She likes the way he looks at her.

There is a bottle they keep passing around. There is smoke, breathed in and out, terraforming. There is powder on the table and then powder in Clover. "You know I can feel your synapses shriveling and dying when you do that," Vanity murmurs.

"Me too," returns Clover, sniffing and dropping her head back. "That's why I like it."

"Why don't you go back to the Machine, Clover? Why don't you save yourself? You never wanted to be like this."

When Clover ignores her, Vanity laughs and laughs and laughs. She is thoroughly amused; Clover's apathy is so *familiar*. Ellis smiles at the sound. His smile is easy; his smile is so nice. His spine is leaned up against the same pillow as Vanity's. She can feel the heat whispering from his arm across her shoulder blades. Sleeves pulled up, a tattoo there. Something dark and sprawling. Inked under his left eye: DON'T PANIC! On his forefinger, his trigger finger: PANIC!

Vanity says, "There's something you're not telling me."

Clover says, "Of course."

"How do you know I don't already know? I was dead for a year. Wasn't that the whole point of the experiment? Finding a cure in the black?" Clover tries to stand up, and Vanity hooks her elbow around hers. "Remind me—how did that work out, again?"

"Just peachy," Clover says evenly.

"Well, how about we trade, then? Don't you have something you want to ask me, too?"

"No. I don't."

"You don't want to die?"

"Let go of me."

"Because it didn't turn out like you wanted it to, the last time, right?" Again Clover tries to get away; Vanity keeps her anchored. There's something burning in the back of her throat and it's not the liquor. Not the scrape of a hand. It's anger. Just anger, finally. "Why did you bring me back, then? You want me to *save* us again, don't you?"

"Not like this. Not like that. I can't do it anymore." But Clover wants to; Vanity could see it all over her face, the slight pant of her words, the way she hooks on Vanity, too. "I just want us to stop."

"To stop what?"

"Stop going in circles!"

"Then you shouldn't have brought me back."

Clover finally breaks away. She stands above them with her chest heaving. "I know! I know!" Her eyes flick from Vanity to Ellis. In the weak light, it makes her look half-terrified. Her arms looping around herself, Clover laughs, a startling, rattling laugh. "I thought I was going to be able to leave you alone. But I couldn't. I couldn't even leave. All I've been doing is sitting here waiting for you to come back, and—I don't even love you! I never did!"

"God, Clover," Ellis attempts, but now Clover has momentum. Vanity shuts her mouth and lets it happen. She wants to hear all of it.

"We're nothing but parasites on each other, do you hear me? We've been built to be obsessed and I don't want it in me. All we do is feed and we feed. We fed you the most, don't you remember that? Do you remember—"

"Clover!" Ellis barks.

She recoils, blinking; Vanity turns to scream at Ellis, and Clover takes her distraction as an out, turning and fleeing, swallowed up by the black of the ballroom. Just like that, the fight bleeds out of Vanity. Slouching back. Well.

Vanity thinks to herself, Actually, none of this just happened. She drops her head toward that blissful numbing powder. She is a god leaning over the world. She is bigger than all of it.

She travels from one minute to the next without being exactly sure where she'd been, or what she'd been thinking, the beat prior. In this sense it is all like being dead. There is more liquor. There is Vanity ricocheting between nursing her crushes and holding utter disgust for them; there is a brief moment of panic where she swears she glimpses Ro's white limbs cutting through the darkness. She screams and screams. Ellis comes and collects her. He deposits her back into the plushness of the sitting area.

Clover is nowhere to be found. Vanity pushes back the previous moment with another cigarette and another drink and then it is easy to pretend that it had never happened in the first place, so easy that she keeps going back in her head, blotting out everything bad that has happened. No Ellis. No Clover. No Monroe. No Wren. No Arrogance. No mother. No magic. No Vanity. There. When the past begins to tug at her again, urging her to ask questions and answer them, she'll look back and only find a clean, gray fog. The beginning of her life was waking up in that bed a few hours ago. She has never done horrible things.

"It's the end of the world," Vanity says to Ellis, and Ellis says, "Yes," so she brings her lips to the hollow of his neck. She is finding things, against his skin. Familiarity, and cruelty, her own disgust, a void where lust should be. All clattering against the clean slate in her head. Her eyes watch her hand glide his to her thigh, under the table. It is not her hand, not really, it is something she is pulling with a string, controlling, but not exactly being. There is hatred. There is claustrophobia. There is shock and disgust of being touched, the warm ache of being touch-starved. There is need and guilt and embarrassment and *need*. There is a gasp in her throat as Ellis touches her briefly between her legs. There is Vanity Adams. There is no Vanity Adams. *You're me.*

"I'm sorry, I'm sorry." God, why was he *talking*?

"Shut up."

"When you died—"

"You're ruining it." She lets him go, dragging her wrist against her wetted lips, already fumbling to take out her cigarettes. God, how the room spins.

Ellis brushes a hand back over his hair. "Vanity."

She is so sick of him. He is leaning into her, like she has gravity.

"Just kill me," she whispers. Feels him freeze. Good. "Come on. You can be creative with it. Make me step off the roof. Make me eat my—"

"Stop, Vanity, please." His voice is strained. His hands land softly on her wrists. "Stop."

"Tell me you haven't thought about it. Ellis. Ellis? Tell me you haven't hurt me before."

"I can't." He has closed his eyes. *Don't panic!* "Okay? I can't."

A flash of vindication, and then it's gone. "Describe it to me."

"*Stop*, Vanity." His words vibrate the air. She shuts her mouth. She doesn't have a choice. But he can't stop the thoughts in her head, screaming louder than she ever could. Bubbling up from that dark place, from the murk of her death, or where she locked them away all on her own. He was always saying he was going to stop. Always saying he wouldn't hurt her. Usually while he was hurting her, or just after.

You'll want to see . . . smiling, with his hand warm around her waist, as he opened up Clover's journal . . .

Don't. Panic!

Vanity panics.

She is somewhere else, suddenly. She is in a dark place, and she is choking. This time it amounts to something. She comes apart and then back together, and somewhere in between, the world ends, everyone is gone but then everyone stands up, walking on stranger feet in stranger forms, seeking each other, seeking her—

Vanity pushes away from him, gasping, stumbling away from the candlelight, and heads into the black. Ellis holds his head and does not follow.

ϟ

From the curtains being drawn and everything, Vanity had expected a general kind of hell. The outside world is startling, the sky grotesquely huge above, patterned with bruised-colored clouds. But things are generally where they should be. Earth under her feet.

Earth with holes.

Hundreds of them, gaping all the way down the lawn. They're like eyes that stare unblinking at her; she rubs her own, bloodshot and dry. Then she moves for Wren, who is tied to a chair on the drive.

Vanity greets him. "Aren't you supposed to be dead?"

He gives her a messy smile. "That's a touch hypocritical, coming from you."

She leans over and unties him. He doesn't lunge for her. Wren just tilts over to the side and vomits a little. His hangover is sticky all over his body, inside and out, headache flashing in yellowish pulses of light haloing Vanity's vision.

"Can you make it go away?"

"Oh, yeah."

"Well. Go ahead."

He's joking, but he seems to enjoy pretending for a moment. His hand waving through the air, commanding. Then he turns in a slow circle and starts to shuffle back toward the mansion.

Vanity trails after him.

"Have you left me anything in the house or did you lot drink it all?"

"You're alive, so you had something to do with it. The apocalypse." Vanity grabs at his arm. "Wren."

"Maybe I'm just tragically unlucky." He doesn't try to shake her off, instead he pats her hand amiably, which makes her recoil. His eyes roam her up and down, keeping his pleasant expression. Vanity is suddenly breathing rather hard, something is very wrong here very wrong well more than the usual amount of wrong, she's missing more than she thought she's— "They kept me foggy about all of it, too. Clover still does."

"How?"

"She gives me very lovely drugs that make everything seem fine."

"And you take them. Why would you do that?"

"Didn't I just say? Everything is fine." He winks at her. "My addiction is one of my own making, after all."

"I don't understand."

"Regardless. I'm sure you can relate."

Instead of going into the mansion Wren trails past it, heading for the stone pavilion that overlooks the City, on the opposite side of the hill from the rose garden. Vanity has never set foot here. The metropolis sprawls so vast that it almost touches either corner of her peripheral, her right streaked by the barest cut of ocean. If she turned in that direction— the Sanatorium on the Pockmarked Island, the Necropolis.

Ro is there, somewhere.

"You ruined the world," says Wren. Adding thoughtfully, unvengeful, "It was barely even your world."

"Seems pretty there to me," Vanity murmurs, but he's right. She'd never known anything else but this stretch of lawn, the four buildings and its forest. She'd never even really entertained any fantasies of running away. "You hardly left this place, either."

"You're certainly not wrong about that."

"Why haven't you? Get a boat. Go the fuck away."

Wren looks at her sideways. "Why don't you?"

"I just got here," Vanity snaps, and then quieter: "I just might."

They stare at the landscape for several beats in silence. Both of them sick as dogs, tilting in the startling wind. Vanity cannot conceptualize being anywhere else. With anyone else.

"Do you know where we got the Machine from?" Wren asks. The topic change is abrupt, but Vanity just shrugs to let him know she doesn't care. He continues anyway. "A long time ago, when witches sprouted up in the population, they didn't come so mentally volatile. Early warning signs, some people theorize. Whole groups of them came together, in an area that early Miyeon would later swallow up. It was largely stable, developing their own practices and culture. They're the ones who created Machines, the ceremony of putting infants into it to be returned when they had been taught about the world properly, when their brains and bodies were fully developed. But in other parts of the continent, as progress barreled and barreled forward, more volatile variants of witch-craft were seen—the point in history that began to see the largest scale of extermination. The society of witches presented their Machines as an alternate option. It was highly unpopular, though, on both sides; some

witches did not want to give up their magic, and the results were...
well." Wren copies Vanity's shrug. "It was better just to do away with all
of them. Witches fell into antiquity and then—vintage, I suppose, by the
time my father set foot in the City for the first time. And he knew how
to build a Machine—it's a very simple blueprint, actually, if you recall—"

"I don't." But Vanity has her magic. Knows she'd gone in, at some
point. "Why are you telling me this?"

"Because all of this is entirely unreal. Don't you see that, Vanity? He
didn't want witches in cages because he wanted *authenticity*—natural
reactions and whole lives put on display. But he ruined that immediately
by winding decadence around your afflictions. He ruined that by creating you, by intentionally making a face like yours. He built a Machine
with none of its ceremony attached, stripped of its origins, none of its
original intention. He created World, and it just reminded me all the
more that it could never measure up to the real thing. I wanted it to be
more. I was so close.

"No wonder magic spoiled you quicker and quicker down the bloodlines, no wonder the Machine failed, with you. No wonder you're so out
of your mind. You've never lived once in reality, you've never once come
up for air. You're likely unable to, now. You're built to be drowning."

In her own self. And in them.

Vanity is numb to it yet knowing of all of it. All she can think to say
is "It did work, on me, the Machine. Just not on her."

Wren seems to spasm then. Vanity jumps, the odd hypnosis that his
ranting had draped over the moment shattering; Wren spins at her with
a stricken expression on his face. "Oh, god, Vanity—oh, god, are you
serious? You don't even remember who Ro actually is?"

IV

ACTIVE

WREN LEANED AGAINST the daughter of some aristocrat and told her about the world. Perhaps a new World. She was getting irritated with him, clearly, she kept trying to change the subject, but Wren pressed on. He was in high spirits. It *was* a Party, after all. And not just any Party. The Engagement Party.

They swiveled around the sparkling ballroom. Wren reached past the woman's shoulder to take a tab of World from the golden tray of a passing caterer. He grabbed one for her, too. For all her complaining, the pink length of her tongue flicked out immediately. He pressed the paper square to it, felt the heat of her mouth. Now, the woman said, they could both talk about whatever they liked, they could know they were having a deeply meaningful conversation even while they were essentially ignoring each other, it was significant enough to share this moment—Wren let go of her when the tears began to stream down her face.

He went off to find Clover. Clover understood him. Her face shining brightly in his head.

Instead Wren found Monroe, surrounded by a shroud of smoke. Wren only approached because he thought Monroe was with Clover, until he blinked through the aroma of cigars and Lavender's face floated into view, her gloved hand dutifully wrapping his father's arm. Even with the drool beading from the corner of her lipstick, the glaze in her hazel eyes, she looked particularly radiant and youthful next to Monroe's shriveling, rugged face. Someday Wren's face would look like that.

He tried to get away. Monroe caught him, strode forward and grabbed his shoulder with Lavender still in tow. Champagne sloshed out of her drink and onto her shoes, which were tall and black and twinkling.

"And the one who made all of this happen!" Monroe was saying. Patting his shoulders.

All of this. Monroe was referring to the increased ticket sales, the sprawling wait list for the Engagement Party, the sold-out wedding to come, which would be hosted next week. He was referring to the superficial. Wren wanted to grab his old face and twist it on its wrinkling neck toward Vanity and Ellis, in the middle of the ballroom, locked together in a stumbling dance for the next half hour, then a five-minute break, then another half hour. Couldn't he see the way they looked at each other, that this was *real*?

"...runs in the family," Monroe was saying, and so then Wren was thinking about things running, running in his veins, running around in circles.

He thought about how, later, his driver would chauffeur him off the estate and down the road that wound the hill and fed into the City proper, where Wren would then go to the clubs and take tabs and rack up a bill that could feed a small family for a year. Then he'd return home and tend to the dogs with bright strips of raw meat and considered what killing his father might offer him. Monroe had used his inheritance to buy his old University and its property—now the Museum grounds that

Wren stood on—and moved the Uni into a cluster of skyscrapers that sat low by the docks. What would Wren purchase, with his inheritance? What did he want? To go away all the time, like how everyone wanted to go away all the time. Lucky you could pay a little money for a tab of World to make anything a spiritual experience, even if it was a concrete jungle, or loneliness, or the same thing over and over again. Always the same thing, over and over again.

Wren didn't want to become his father. He wanted to feel, for once in his life, that he'd done something real.

Wren broke away. He found Clover haunting one of her favorite corners, one with a lot of cushions, where she would never sit down but could always find tourists to give her cigarettes, and dragged her onto the ballroom floor.

"Are you having a lovely Engagement Party?" he asked her, halfway into the dance. She said nothing. He went on. "Ah, yes, it's all progressing nicely. Though, Vanity's getting a *bit* disruptive. I don't really understand why she keeps talking to her dinner. She brings up your name a lot. And opening her mouth during the dances like that, all the time—is she doing it now? It's fine. It's just getting rather inelegant. No, really, it's fine. Monroe doesn't think anything's amiss."

"Why would he?" asked Clover, carefully. Wren gave her a complacent smile, one that said, *I've kept quiet. You go on doing god knows what in the forest.* He himself still didn't quite know; it was their business. Though his first guess, of course, was sex. He'd told Clover she could come to him if anything happened that made her uncomfortable.

"And don't worry. You can call him *Daddy* in front of me," she shot back, in a mood, again. One of her hands still held a cigarette, which she sucked on in beats. "I won't judge."

Wren admired Clover like he admired the sheen of his dogs, how they consumed recklessly, void of any desire to taste and savor. He liked that she talked to him. Even if it was just them monitoring each other.

Clover rolled her eyes, sensing him watching her. Probably seeing his blown pupils. She tossed her perfect, glossy hair over the delicate peak of her shoulder. "Does it even work for you anymore, taking World?" she spat, out of an unproductive spite. And here Wren thought she despised wasting energy. "Do you even have any synapses left?"

She was right, of course, Wren was a little high, but it'd been a while since he'd been remarkably so. At least he could still sense the warmth of the smoke she sucked down in her chest. He could feel the pull of gravity on himself from both the earth below him and the moon above him. Though, where this had once massaged him, it now only pulsed in his fingertips like a dull throbbing.

Wren sighed and he tutted, dabbling in pettiness. "Feeling left out, are we?"

He was referring to the witch-couple that Clover was clearly pretending not to stare at. Ellis and Vanity were still making their slow, awkward turns around the sea of tourists. Heads clunking together, talking low and frantic. Wren didn't understand it, why Clover was clearly afraid of them yet still gravitated toward them. He longed to understand it. He wanted to look at other people like that. Wren wanted it far more than having other people look at him.

"You're twitchy," Wren observed. "You're never twitchy."

She was quiet. Then, in a sudden burst: "They don't even understand—they barely *register*—what's *happening*, right now, don't you get that, you smug fucking—"

Smug? Him? Yes, Wren supposed he was smiling, but now it was in a placating way, because now Clover was yelling. Heads swiveled. He gripped her hand and her waist tighter. "Be *quiet*," he hissed, trying to keep his head, which was spinning more as she got worked up, "Clover, I swear—"

"You don't believe me. Of course you don't believe me." She managed to wriggle away from him, it was all the thousand-thread-count silk she was wearing that slipped past his fingers like a live eel. "You think we're helping each other? That we're *fixing* each other? Do you want to see just how much we've *fixed* each other?"

Yes, because Wren was curious, in this state, curious about everything. But the other part of him, the part that was his father's son, was still smiling and shaking his head, still trying to touch her and make her behave. He spoke, kindly, gently. "Clover, honey. Let me get you something. Anything you want, to calm down."

"Oh, were you trying to make us *calm*, this entire time?" She was walking backward as she talked. Arms striking out at her sides, knocking into tourists, caterers. Her gloved wrist hit a tray, sending olives and cubed cheese spraying across the crowd. Wren followed her, the light that shone off her dress, her little trail of chaos. "Let's see how that worked, shall we? Let's see let's see let's see . . ."

". . . might try to hurt them."

"What?" Vanity murmured. "What did you say?" Ro's words processed. Vanity flicked her wrist, waving it off. Then immediately turned to worrying at the black ribbon at her neck. "You've said that before . . ."

It was a Party—people were buzzing about how it was a *special* Party, but Vanity wasn't sure why. Were they trying to call the club meetings a *special Party* to throw her off, make her slip up? She was in Ellis's arms, Ro trailing close by, just close enough to whisper in her ear and knock into people. Their disjointed dance carrying them in a slow clock-swivel around the room.

Had Vanity remembered to blame Ro for what happened, for them being buried all night? Because it *had* really all been Ro's idea, wasn't it? It was hard to remember.

Either way, Vanity had hurt her. She promised Clover and Ellis she did, even though they sometimes got these looks on their faces like they wished she wouldn't, even though it was all for them. Usually, Vanity would hasten to explain before she started to slur too badly, she'd go, "Later, I'll hurt her, I'll push her down the stairs or I'll cut her up, but I don't know, she doesn't listen to me, but I promise I'll try harder, or I'll tell her not to come anymore." Then she'd shut her mouth and look at them both anxiously, as they exchanged that look between them, astounding evidence that the private bubble of theirs, which Vanity had thought she'd popped and rewound around the three of them, had actually gone unruptured, and it was all of it Arrogance's fault. "Don't tell her not to come," Clover always said. "Don't hurt her, Vanity," Ellis always said. It was something along the lines of We need all of us. Or it was something along the lines of We're scared of her. Or We like her better than you. Or We know you're a big fat fucking liar and that she's been the special one all along.

*

But that wasn't right at all because Vanity was becoming special, too, when Clover said Open your mouth Vanity did because she was such a brave girl, now, wasn't really afraid anymore, except of course of course of disappointing them, of losing them, and so even though she was seeing the hand in her throat in full now. There: way way way back in all that darkness, or sometimes coming to rest on the curve of her tongue, sometimes slack and sometimes twitching, sometimes picking at her molars and sometimes away from her altogether, attached to a body that walked around in the dead of night, sleepy, she followed it around the cottage, out of the bedroom and downstairs, she went into the kitchen, she knelt in front of the mirror, she reached, she spoke, Come back, and remembering there was nothing there, just her hand outstretched for her own, she moved it, and watched, and it was exact, she was sure, no delay between real and reflection—and why would there be? Vanity smiling sadly. Silly, anxious girl. Nothing terrible was happening. . . .

*

They had to be subtle about being in a club meeting because there were a lot of people, standing around in Party attire in the clearing, it was ridiculous, to try to fool Vanity like that. Ellis was still dancing with her, sometimes he tried to get ahold of her face and make her listen to him about something, something about how *Don't show up to club tonight*, something about *stopping*. That was ridiculous, that didn't make any sense.

Had she brought Clover back, too, already? Vanity looked around, squinting in the harsh moonlight.

There she was. In a backless green silk dress, walking backward, then turning as if feeling Vanity's eyes on her bare spine. Then she picked up the pace. Clover's hands first pushing Ellis away from her, then landing on Vanity's face, so Vanity was glad everyone had chosen to wear gloves tonight.

"Tell me what's happening, Vanity," Clover was saying. She shouldered off Ellis's grasp on her arm— "No, no. Vanity. Look at me." Her smile was brilliant, if not, Vanity thought, a little strained. Sometimes she got a bit tense, when she was alive again and it was question time. "Do you know what's happening right now? Where we are? What this Party is?"

Vanity was confused about what answer she should give. *Party*—Clover wanted her to keep the guise up, yes. But of course it was actually a club meeting because she and Ellis were paying such attention to Vanity, and they weren't allowed to do that at the actual Parties. But with all these people watching, why would Clover ask such a direct question?

Vanity was afraid of saying the wrong thing. So instead she just opened her mouth, very very wide.

Ro shrieked laughter, somewhere from her peripheral vision.

Clover's flushed cheeks immediately blanched. She stopped touching Vanity, recoiling, gloved hand over her mouth. Vanity shut her own mouth so fast it hurt her teeth. Tears immediately sprang to her eyes, fear clawing cold across her skin.

"Oh god oh god what is it is it there? Clover? Clover?" Clawing at her throat, fingers catching on her ribbon, the sudden onslaught of her terror squeezing black spots into her vision.

"Nothing!" Clover was screaming now. "No, no, no, there's *nothing*, Vanity—"

Ellis was looking at Clover and then looking at Ro and then looking back at Clover and so of course Vanity's thoughts went why why why isn't he looking at *me*? And then Ellis looked at her and she looked away.

Wren was here now, too. Monroe's gray head also bobbing toward them, over the sea of other heads. Vanity wiped her warm cheeks. She tried to smile ear to ear. She was so upset. So embarrassed, and she couldn't even blame Ro this time. She wanted to crawl out of her body and leave it behind, she couldn't stand it, that she was forced to carry around the evidence.

And because Vanity was getting all worked up, Ro was getting worked up, too. Vanity was saying sorry and sorry and sorry, and then her sister smacked her on the shoulder and said, "What the fuck is she trying to do anyway? Clover. Hey, you motherfucker. Yes, I'm talking to you. Do you really know what you're doing?"

Clover seemed to freeze. Vanity didn't understand it. Was Clover looking at her, or at Ro? *Look at me.* The crowd was murmuring about love triangles, about jealousy. Vanity shook and shook her head.

"Are you really so scared of it, Clover?" Ro's arms tugged at Vanity, picked at her clothes. Vanity couldn't speak over the heat in her face. "Scribbling in your notebook. Fiddling with your stopwatch. Running away from all of it...do you think that's actually possible? How far do you think you'll really get without it?"

"*Ro*," Vanity whispered.

"Without what?" Clover asked.

"Without your nature."

Clover laughed.

In the harsh glow of it, it took Vanity a moment to realize that her sister had begun throttling Clover.

And Vanity, mortified, was shouting, "Stop it, Arrogance, stop it!" But Ro kept going, and the worst part was Clover was letting her, letting the teeth rattle in her head, and Ellis was, too, both of them staring at Ro like looking away was impossible. No one in the crowd moved to do anything. The camera bulbs began to flash.

"This is—" Clover's words pushing through her clattering teeth—why was she *smiling?* Smiling like she was thrilled. "You're kidding me—"

"Abandon it." Ro's voice was at once calm and simmering. Devoid of anxiousness, completely sure in her thoughts and her actions. Vanity thought wildly, I could never ever ever look like that.

"Abandon what?" Clover breathed. "Tell me."

"Arrogance, let her go!" Vanity was screaming, sobbing.

"No, Ro, don't let me go." *Why* was Clover egging her on? "You're talkative today—you never talk to *us.* Why don't you ever talk to us?"

"Clover," Ellis snarled, startling Vanity with the total lack of amusement in his voice, in his expression.

"Because you're nothing. You were made nothing." Ro's teeth shone as she spoke, illuminated by the white-hot flashes of cameras held up to tourists' eyes, and in those flashes Vanity saw her sister's smile change in uneven beats, from black rot to pristine bone and back again. Death and life and life and death. "So abandon it. Your sense, your self. She can't be the only one. That's not how a coven works. Put it all on the altar of the world, for your *cure.*"

Vanity didn't understand what was happening. Why Clover's expression was of the gears, those brilliant gears in her head, turning and turning. Ellis's hands were around her. Trying to drag her away.

"The altar of the world," Clover breathed.

"No," Vanity said. "No, no, no."

Clover's hazel eyes were still on Ro. It hurt Vanity so much that she imagined that Clover was making eye contact with her, instead. She swore she could almost see it.

But then her imagination faltered. Clover wasn't looking at her with adoration. It was almost hungry, like Vanity was a bug she'd trapped under a magnifying glass.

"It's fine," Vanity was gasping. Not sure if she believed herself, now.

"Arrogance, it's fine it's fine it's fine. Please."

At last, Ro's hands dropped away. She stood up, twisting, to smile at Vanity.

"What did you do?" Vanity whispered. She would hurt Ro later. She was comforted by this promise to herself.

"I don't know," Ro whispered back. "What did *you* do?"

NO STARS. Vanity was coming up on the clearing, the bare branches above her head thinning and thinning until the sky was a glorious pool of ink she felt she could slip up into.

Vanity breathed in deeply. And tasted blood on her tongue.

Down on the grasses on the opposite side, Clover was throttling Ellis. She was hitting him over and over and his laughter was arching and stopping, arching and stopping.

As if she were shy—was she shy?—Vanity stood there at the threshold of the open space. She tugged absently at the collar of her shirt, eventually nearing, just to the point where she could feel the heat coming off both their bodies, and sank down to the ground. Held her knees to her chest.

Clover straightened, momentarily, from Ellis's sighing form to wipe her forehead with the back of her hand. Vanity watched the sweat shine on the contours of her neck, briefly cooled by her posture. Clover cleaned her hands on her legs, now covered by sweatpants instead of the green silk dress she'd been wearing at the Party—tonight's Party? Last week's?

The blood leaking into the air made Vanity fuzzy, so fuzzy she felt sleepy. She nodded off. When she came to, perhaps five minutes or so later, Ellis was still alive and bleeding and Clover was crouched nearby. She had her notebook open on her knees, frantically scrawling away. Vanity squinted. Ro was behind Clover, reading over her shoulder. But no. Vanity blinked. Arrogance wasn't here, of course. She'd been punished and had hung back with her tail between her legs.

"Why?" Vanity thought to ask.

"Why are you back here?" murmured Ellis. His head tilted on the grass. He shivered. He was in great pain and it vibrated the air around him. "I told you not—not to come, tonight."

"Did you? When?"

"He's ruining everything," Clover spat. "We don't need him anymore. I've figured it all out."

"Vanity, please," Ellis said. Tried to prop himself up on his forearms. And his mouth moved again. Saying...

Vanity blinked; it was like she'd missed a moment. And then Clover was storming over to kick Ellis in the head, which killed him, the cold wave of it sending Vanity down onto her spine, and she did then slip up into the sky for a moment, and it was, like she'd suspected, totally glorious.

When her focus returned again, she was leaning over Ellis. Moisture at her mouth; she wiped it with the back of her hand. And then wondrously Clover was grabbing her jaw. Vanity's body knew the routine; she opened up good and wide. She could see the clots of cloth sticking out of Clover's ears now, out of her hair—so that's how she'd dodged Ellis's spell. His request. That was ever-clever Clover for you.

"Nothing." Always nothing.

"Are you okay?" Vanity couldn't help but ask, because she could feel in Clover's face swelling tear ducts, wetting and wobbling. "After Ro attacked you, last week."

Clover said nothing for a moment. Then: "Two hours ago," and Vanity wasn't sure what she meant, so she just shrugged. Clover said, "Don't feel sorry for him."

"Okay."

"You—" Clover shut her mouth abruptly. A look that Vanity hadn't seen before had flown to her face. *Concern*, Vanity hoped. Eventually what she fought out was "Honestly? I tell you how to feel and you feel it, just like that?"

"Well, yeah."

"How on earth can you think so little of yourself?"

"I don't!" But really she only said it because now Clover suddenly looked furious with her, disgusted. Vanity couldn't understand why she was so upset. "I don't," Vanity said again, then quieter: "You die all the time."

"Not just to throw myself away!"

"But you were going to, before. When you used to carry around the rocks." She used to find and replace them with a dead thing, gifts while Clover's body went colder and colder. But Vanity had stopped finding them. Clover had started wanting to live. *I did that.*

"Stop crying," Clover screamed. "Stop *crying!*"

"We're helping each other," Vanity sobbed. "We're already helping each other. Don't listen to Arrogance. We don't need her."

"We *do*, Vanity."

"No! She's too dangerous. She won't come back. I hurt her and she won't come back—"

"God, god, Vanity, I don't want to hear it! I hate hearing it!"

Vanity blushed, but the heat did not seep to the rest of her body. "I'm just trying to protect you."

~~And then Clover said the worst thing. Looking at Vanity like she was the worst thing. "I don't want you to hurt her."~~

~~The words dropped down into the dark tangle of her guts and dis-solved her.~~ "But I hurt," Vanity said. ~~"For you."~~

~~For a moment Clover seemed unable to speak. The line of her shoul-ders trembling. Then her voice came, scathing and accusing. "Do you even know how much? Maybe if you cared about yourself it would be different. Maybe if you didn't just lie down and take it. Maybe if you left us for dead." She wiped her eyes. Smeared her mascara. "You hurt. For me.~~ I know. ~~You haven't ever asked me for anything. Not my affection. Not even a cure. You love me like I deserve it and I hate you for it."~~

Vanity said, "As long as you know, it's enough for me."

"I know," Clover repeated, like she was tired, so tired.

Vanity brought Ellis back. He came to clawing at her arms, begging her to leave. No spell attached to his words.

Vanity was tired, too. Turning her body toward the forest.

"Where are you going?" asked Clover quietly. "It's my turn."

XXVI

"AND HOW WAS YOUR NIGHT?"

Vanity looked at Ro furiously. She'd draped herself over the fence in the front yard of their cottage, picking at the paint with her nails. Some of the tourists took to scraping out things there, initials and hearts and a few more pointed inscriptions: *Undress more. Kiss me, Cadence. Eat, Vanity, Eat! Halfie half gone!* "Did you miss me?" Ro was cooing. "Do they like you without me? Who you are, without me? Oh, don't have that look. I only ever tell you what you need to hear."

Vanity followed Ellis's instructions. He needn't have made them a spell. She'd do anything he asked of her. The thought pushing that terrible heat to her face all over again, as she trudged across the green. *How on earth can you think so little of yourself?*

Stupid stupid stupid.

She pushed through his front door, through his front hall. It must've been raining, because there was something dripping down her neck. It was almost dawn. She'd spent her spiral off his resurrection slumped in the bathtub, watching the stained-glass flowers dance, until even Cadence had given up banging on the door. It used to be so simple, like that, getting high on gifted dead things, it used to all be just for fun, just to be somewhere else.

Now more and more it was just realizing where she was. Going around in circles.

"I forgot to do something," she'd murmured again and again to Ro, who watched her from the bathroom floor. "Death, resurrection, wellness checks. What did I forget to do?"

Her sister's temple had tilted against the lip of the tub. Her black eyes rolling and rolling at her. "Eat," said Ro, like Vanity was being ridiculous. "You forgot to eat."

"We're done, Vanity, we're done." The usual things, trickling out of his mouth. He'd been waiting for her, sitting on his stairs, still in the dirty clothes he'd died in. Some thistle particles caught in his black hair. Some floating down on Vanity as he crossed the hall and took ahold of her shoulders.

"You're not done," Vanity reminded him. "I'm not done."

"Clover's using you. You don't even know for what."

"You're using me."

He hesitated. "Tonight was the last time."

"Ellis, I don't care." What Clover wanted with her. What Ellis wanted with her. All Vanity wanted was that want. "I just don't care. Do whatever to me."

"We're leaving tonight."

"We can't."

"We have to. It can't be like this." His tone implied desperation. "*You* can't—"

Ellis released her. He took a step back, and she could feel the rush of air in his lungs, felt all the delicate, lacy patterns of membrane sigh and drink in, and Vanity shivered, goose bumps skimming her entire body, and then Ellis lunged forward again, gracelessly, desperately, he was putting a hand around her throat. She stumbled, her back hitting his front door. Her arms hung limp at her sides.

Vanity suspected Ellis meant to be pressing down, but he wasn't.

"It won't change anything. It always comes back." Heat pricked her eyes, but her voice was bare and even. Her face arranged itself in the blankness she felt. She reached around his arm to touch the tears on her cheeks and blinked and licked them off her fingers. "I can't get out of my head. Don't you understand that I'm stuck here? You're stuck, too. Over there. And we can't leave." His face drew up in pain; she was causing that, she didn't even have to use magic, to make his form react so. "So what does it matter. I love you when I'm sober, too."

"I have to try."

"Because you care about me?"

"Yes, Vanity, yes."

"Then don't bring me back." She was so tired. "You have no idea what it feels like, not like I do. We have nowhere else to go. We have nothing else to do."

Vanity imagined, then, that Ellis broke her neck.

She imagined blissful nothingness, and then light. Coming back with Cadence leaning over her with an irritated scowl. At first, she might believe it was snowing, though it'd turn out just to be the cigarette crumbling from the edge of her mother's mouth—Ellis had left her laid like a doll on her front door stoop. He'd draped his coat over her in case it rained again.

Vanity blinked, the daydream clearing. Then she was back, and Ellis was pulling away. ~~He'd seen it all happen in her head and that's why~~ he was smiling. It was a sad smile. Tears flecked his eyelashes when he blinked.

"Honey," he said, "anything you want." Then his hand slipped into hers. Its warmth still echoed on her throat. "I have to show you something."

So she followed him upstairs, into his bedroom. She'd been in here before, to steal; the space was simple, a copy of her mother's bedroom with less frills and mess—a desk, an unlit crystal chandelier, the headboard of the bed against the one-way mirror. No knickknacks, no paintings, no books. Only an emptied glass sat on his bedside table—now Vanity could smell the vodka on his lips, and, if she focused, in the lining of his throat.

Vanity, then, was vaguely aware it wasn't just rainwater dripping off her. That there was blood, too. It was making the collar of her shirt sticky.

Vanity sat on the edge of his bed. He stood before her, and leaned so their faces were very close. Studying her. Did he see something she couldn't? She glimpsed her own reflection in his eyes and dropped her gaze.

"We've been changing you," Ellis whispered. "Maybe it's flipped. You're changing us now. And it scares Clover. But it doesn't scare me. You've helped me more than anything else ever could. So I want to help you, too." His voice was so gentle. "By making you understand that you should run."

Vanity said, "I don't want to change you."

"You should."

Ellis approached a desk made of rich cherrywood, gloss excessively picked and scraped at, and opened its drawer. The contents curling up toward the open light.

There were notes, *the* notes, between him and Clover over the years. There must've been about a hundred of them. Vanity's eyes stung. She gathered her legs up so she could hold her knees to her chest.

On top of the notes was a notebook; this Ellis removed. He sat back on the bed and put it between them. Vanity recognized it instantly. It was Clover's notebook, the one she'd carried and scrawled in every club meeting. Clover was going to take these notes and squeeze them and use her brilliance to create a cure and save them all.

"You took it from her?"

"That's the only reason why I went out to the woods tonight. You weren't supposed to be there. She doesn't know."

"I don't want to see."

"Yes, you do." Ellis put his arm around her waist. "You'll want to see."

"I don't." But she was already practically looking, seeing the uneven lay of the cover, that there were pages upon pages that'd been raggedly torn away. That what was left behind was frantic and fresh, new ink that smeared...

"Please, Vanity?"

"We shouldn't." She was leaning forward. And Ellis, such a gentleman, was opening it up for her, letting the light reach the handwriting, that gloriously bold scrawl in which they'd find salvation....

THE MACHINE THE MACHINE THE MACHINE THE MACHINE
THE MACHINE THE MACHINE THE MACHINE THE MACHINE
THE MACHINE THE MACHINE THE MACHINE THE MACHINE
THE MACHINE THE MACHINE THE MACHINE THE MACHINE
THE MACHINE THE MACHINE THE MACHINE THE MACHINE
THE MACHINE THE MACHINE THE MACHINE THE MACHINE
THE MACHINE THE MACHINE THE MACHINE THE MACHINE
THE MACHINE THE MACHINE THE MACHINE THE MACHINE
THE MACHINE THE MACHINE THE MACHINE THE MACHINE
THE MACHINE THE MACHINE THE MACHINE THE MACHINE
THE MACHINE THE MACHINE THE MACHINE THE MACHINE
THE MACHINE THE MACHINE THE MACHINE THE MACHINE
THE MACHINE THE MACHINE THE MACHINE THE MACHINE
THE MACHINE THE MACHINE THE MACHINE THE MACHINE
THE MACHINE THE MACHINE THE MACHINE THE MACHINE
THE MACHINE THE MACHINE THE MACHINE THE MACHINE
THE MACHINE THE MACHINE THE MACHINE THE MACHINE
THE MACHINE THE MACHINE THE MACHINE THE MACHINE

⟑

Ellis was holding her. He was playing with her hair, taking care with the side of her head, where the bleeding had slowed but the skin still glistened, raw. Before Vanity had come here, she'd been home, home pulling back her hair, looking left looking right, and, landing on the left, folded her ear forward. The angle was shitty and she couldn't see it, what she thought might be there, and, having collected a knife from downstairs, placed the blade in the velvet crook of her ear and slid it back and forth and back and forth until it had come away in her hand, and there, after she'd cleaned away some of the blood, there was the scar, a clotted silken length of strengthened tissue, because she'd gotten it wrong, she'd lied to Ellis and Clover that one time; it hadn't been Ro who cut her own off all those years ago, in argument, in punishment, in proof, everything bad that happened to her Vanity had done all by herself, she didn't need anyone else's help, so was it very very very wrong that she looked at Clover's handwriting and was nodding, of course, it was the Machine, sure, the altar of the world, what else, what else could Vanity really do, she was unreliable and must therefore rely on other people, even if Clover was saying there wasn't a cure as much as there was what was always going to happen, even if Ellis was saying I'm sorry I'm sorry it's all my fault that you're like this, can you look at me, I swear Vanity this isn't what I thought she'd be like, Vanity was thinking, Well, whatever, what were any of us going to be like, anyway.

XXVII

THE LOVER WITCHES were found just past the front gates, which, of course, at any hour could be pushed open, strolled through. The groundskeeper squared his feet. This was an essential step before switching on the hose, which released a powerful stream of water that carved away the blood and brains and bone splattered across the stone lions that bordered the entrance to the Museum proper.

He would only clear away the larger chunks. Speckles were to be left, ones that would show up subtly, artfully in the photographs, once the Museum opened—only an hour later than usual—advertising the special event. The temporary border of plasticky chains was already being looped around the bodies; the groundskeeper's first task of the day had been to trim the branches of the trees above to allow in more light.

Some professionals had already come and gone, blotting makeup over Vanity Adams's face, arranging their limbs. Since she'd been wearing sweats, they'd stripped her clothes and redressed her in something nicer, slacks and a sweater and boots with a slight heel; the groundskeeper had averted his eyes the best he could. After all, even though she was elements of nature incarnate, the witch's body still looked like that of a teenage girl.

As a younger, fresher man, the groundskeeper's stomach had turned, but now he only appreciated how efficiently his power hose cleaned the lions' stone eyes, the lines of their grinning teeth. He'd been here for decades now, after all, and he'd seen it all. Why, what James Kim and Cadence Adams and Lavender Rao used to get up to in their youth! No reason to linger on all the senseless events. And, anyway, the groundskeeper was close friends with the gardener, who swore up and down that Ellis had murdered his dog.

*

Later, Monroe explained to Wren, after the young lovers had been properly documented, the crowd would witness their miraculous resurrections by Cadence Adams. He was speaking very quickly. His face had adopted a ruddy color, and Wren couldn't tell if it was still raining, or if Monroe was spitting.

Wren kept his frown off his face and reflected his father's smile.

Yes, yes, there was never so tragic a romance, and all that, Vanity and Ellis trying to run away, mere days before the wedding, and all of that. Knowing they'd fail.

Wren looked over the sprawl of her broken body as the gloved staff picked through, termites skittering over wood. Threading the witches' fingers together. Turning her chin and opening her mouth, slightly, slightly, in horror or in awe. So that they would be facing each other, if Ellis still had a face, if the bomb in his neck had not blown it away. Some would titter, oh so cleverly, that she *was* kissing him—after all, the spray of him had tinted her whole face, her lips.

"But it's real," Wren said, when Monroe was done. *This isn't one of your black-and-white soaps,* he wanted to spit. *Can't you see what they mean to each other? That they would choose death, over this life for one another?*

The words frothed on his tongue like a chemical reaction, they would boil up and out of him—

His father raised a steel-gray eyebrow. "Real?" Monroe echoed, frowning slightly. "What do you mean?"

XXVIII

THE FRONT DOOR WAS OPEN. Clover stopped short on the second-floor landing, then took a few steps backward. Her reflection in the front mirror of the foyer retreating, too. It was ridiculous; everyone out in the yard could see her anyway. Still, the bright rectangle of light, the rush of fresh air through it, made Clover feel wholly exposed. Raw.

She pulled her sweater tighter around her, peeking out from around the corner of the upstairs hall. Down on the first floor, Lavender stood in the blank doorframe. Her bare, manicured feet toeing the bristles of the stoop mat.

"Mom," Clover hissed. "What are you doing?" They never opened the door during the day.

"There's no one here."

"What?"

"They're all over there. . . ."

Then Lavender stepped fully outside. Clover flinched. But her mother was only turning this way and that, the breeze fluttering her plaid skirt, so Clover could see flashes of the backs of her legs. It was quiet, Clover realized. She heard no shouting, no flashbulbs catching and burning.

So then she was downstairs and standing behind her mother. And they *were* all *over there*. The tourist crowd, pushing, puckering, past the gates. Away from her.

Clover knew what had happened immediately. She'd always been a smart girl.

Lavender was talking and talking and Clover's head was talking louder. Why had they tried to run from her? Why were they afraid of *her*? She should be the afraid one. Her fingers grappling the doorframe. Her heartbeat throbbing on the tip of her tongue. She wasn't jealous, she was furious. She wasn't *jealous*.

It hurt so much.

It was all backward. Vanity should be the one pulling them around, pulling them apart. Instead she'd just let everything happen to her. Let Clover and Ellis happen to her. Didn't she understand how much she could hurt them? Vanity, after all, was the one coming apart. . . . Yes. And when she came apart fully, that was it. Everyone run. Everyone hide.

🖋

"Open wide."

Vanity did without question. She was kneeling on the grass and Ellis was still dead. It could have been weeks ago or hours ago, separate instances indistinguishable, really, always the same thing every time. Clover put her hand on Vanity's jaw and peered.

"Well?"

"Nothing. As usual."

Vanity had closed her mouth, stared up with her usual expression, the one that made her a passable sleepwalker. Any wired energy only reared its terrifying head when Arrogance was around.

It had been months or days or hours of this, and Clover still wasn't entirely sure if Vanity believed her.

Clover also had never been sure, even all these weeks of checking its progress—and lying through her teeth about it—what exactly it was made of. The "hand."

She guessed it was incorporeal, since Vanity would've choked and died by now. Well, she did choke, sometimes, and claw at her throat, and cry, desperately pleading to Clover that it was real, she swore it was, could Clover just please check again?

A hand, anyway, was the best thing to call it—this seemed like the most consistent form it took. Of course, every time Clover told Vanity to open her mouth—her pupils blown from resurrection, tongue twisting, often covered in dirt from her habitual digging for creatures or else just to feel the coolness of the earth—there was no telling what she'd actually find. It had a tendency to change form. Or maybe it would be more accurate to say the space itself—Vanity's throat—had a tendency to change, to not look like a throat, not all the time. Imagine Clover's startlement the first time she glanced and saw a room, a white room, clumped with bodies that seemed unable to tangle. Another time it seemed Clover was standing in a front yard looking up at the glass face of one of the cottages, and occupying the first and second floors were faceless forms standing shoulder to shoulder, presumably staring out. Another time: a bird's-eye view of the Pockmarked Island, either years ago or a fantasy altogether, wiped of its metropolis. Another time: the churning sea. A body, half buried. A graveyard. A war. Clover herself, staring back. She saw Ellis, too. Her mother. His father. Other people she didn't recognize, maybe witches past, deceased relatives, or maybe those with their bodies prone and withering in the Sanatorium. The hand, again. Rising.

Of course none of it could be defined as real, barring the fact that Clover could see it, that the images followed her home and kept her up at night and made her lose her hair, literal clumps of hair that came away in her fingers that she twisted and twisted and broke. It was just something formless attempting to have form, something attempting to articulate itself that couldn't be articulated.

After all, how does the notion of being cosmically fucked present itself? Well. It seemed confused on the concept, too.

The closest way Clover believed she could describe it: nature was out of balance, and it had come to a head in Vanity. Death—admittedly, Ellis and Clover's deaths, primarily—and destruction swirled and shifted in her throat. Which wasn't a throat, but a cauldron. An incubator. Like how Vanity wasn't really a girl, not really, but death, leaked into the world through a gap in the shape of her body, her words and her mind.

Well, anyway. It was a good day when it was the hand. That felt the easiest to read. Clover knew she was getting close.

When was she done?

When Vanity wasn't just death incarnate—peace and quiet and, ultimately, a curable nothing—but something more total. Something they couldn't take back. Something like apocalypse.

XXIX

"OPEN WIDE."

Clover did without question. Her heart thudding fresh and hot in her chest. Down went Ro's fingers. Up came the death, for Clover returned with it lodged in the back of her throat. That strange mass, clogged with magic, removed from her like an organ she'd grown in moments.

This had happened before.

This happened every time.

All while Vanity watched distantly, the resurrections having blown her somewhere else, she'd watched from the grasses that tickled her ankles and she'd watched from the cold tile of her bathroom. Ellis had opened his mouth, too, willingly, neck drawn over the lip of the tub. They'd let Ro touch them and take from them, while all Vanity did was give herself and lose herself. They'd let Ro take their death and their magic and let her tilt her head and unhook her jaw, and feed.

✳

Vanity, death having purged the magic from her head, attempted to push herself up from the damp grass. Slow rain slicking the backs of her hands; she couldn't pull them from the ground. Vanity blinked away the water that had gathered in her eye, then saw that her fingers were threaded through Ellis's. Saw, following up his wrist and up his arm, that he had no head.

It had gone all hazy, after reading Clover's notebook. Had they really tried to run away from her?

Above Vanity, Cadence was hovering. Tipping forward and back on her feet. Her mother had on a thick sheen of red lipstick, split by the megawatt smile lighting up her face. The magic hitting her synapses making the expression all plasticky.

"Where's Ro?" Vanity murmured.

Cadence, hypnotically drawn to the remaining death, ignored her and leaned over Ellis. But Monroe shook his head. Cadence, drooling now, pulled back and waited.

Monroe was wanting Vanity's reaction, she'd react explosively over finding Ellis dead and all the people watching her would put their hands over their hearts and feel for her. Would come back the next day, purchase Party tickets. But Vanity had seen Ellis dead so many times already, so she only pulled her fingers from his and waited for him to get back with her hands in her lap. Wren, standing inside the plastic chain that kept the tourists at bay, frowned at her.

So then Cadence was getting a move on and Ellis was becoming alive again. As his head knit back together, as she blinked in the searing light of the flashbulbs, Vanity knew the reasons, for all of it would come back to her soon. Why she kept going back to them.

Here it went: Didn't Vanity not want to be Vanity, anyway? Hadn't she never wanted to be herself, didn't she just want to go away, didn't she just want everything that was horrible and happening to her and all of it endlessly? Didn't she want to get sicker? And wasn't it all because she'd always had that question in her head, that senseless, hysterical, desperate question—why why why don't I feel sick enough yet?

🖋

Perhaps it was winter, or spring.

"I don't feel good," murmured Ro from her bed. Her sister did not turn that dark head of tangled hair; her words pressed into the mattress. "Don't go."

Vanity didn't feel good either. Honestly it had all been going fine, before she had come back, clutching the truth that Ro was using her, too. "I know what you've been doing with them."

"What have I been doing with them?"

"Feeding on their deaths."

Out trickled Ro's airy chuckle. "Oh, but, haven't you been feeding on them, too? In a way . . ."

"Is it true?"

"Is *what* true? What are you even talking about? Do you even know what you're talking about? Describing such horrible things, dear sister, oh. You'd have to be out of your mind. . . ."

Downstairs in their kitchen, Cadence had taken everything out of the fridge and laid it out on the black-and-white countertop. Slabs of cheese and meat, slices of fruit. A large glass of red wine with chunks of the cork bobbing in it swirling in her left hand as she regarded the smorgasbord. "Vanity," she said again, now lifting her eyes to her daughter.

"Yes?"

"Where are you going?"

"I don't know. On a walk."

"You've been taking a lot of walks lately." Vanity thought her mother hadn't noticed. "Where do you go? When you go walking." Slicing up the last word, making it bleed suspicion. *Walk. Ing.*

"Around the estate," said Vanity. "The garden, mostly."

Her mother sniffed. "How pious."

Vanity didn't know what she meant by that, so she was quiet, waiting to be dismissed. Ro would just walk away, ignoring Cadence and the look on her face, pitiful at the same time it was poisonous. Cadence sipped her wine. Chewed the cork-bits absently.

"Did you eat today?" She was going to avoid all of it, wasn't she?

"Yes."

But then Cadence's eyes were on her stomach. Simply peering to catch the lie.

Such moments startled Vanity. That her mother, despite her strange states, possessed her full abilities. She reiterated, "Well, I don't remember—"

"Come sit with me." Cadence wasn't sitting. Vanity waited, hoped she would just forget about the request a moment later, but Cadence just spoke sharper. "What? You're too popular to associate with your old crow of a mother, is that it?"

Vanity's bare feet moved over the tiled floor, stopped a few paces away from where her mother braced her weight against the countertop.

"Yes?" Vanity murmured, gaze wandering over the food. Cheese just beginning to sweat in oily beads. Disgust churned in her; she looked back at Cadence.

Vanity, expecting her to be staring out into space as usual, went still at the focus her mother had pinned on her.

"There's something different about you."

"I don't know." Resisting tugging at her fingers. "I died."

That detail wasn't important. "Monroe says something's been digging in the garden. The gardener is in hysterics." Cadence laughed, hollow. She wasn't going to touch on this morning at all, resurrecting her disfigured daughter. She wasn't going to ask if Vanity had tried to run away, or if she was truly in love, or if any of it had hurt.

Vanity picked up a slice of orange, held it up as if inspecting its golden chambers against the single yellow bulb that shone out over the stove.

Dropped it back onto the cutting board. "Maybe something came up from the woods. Maybe Monroe's eating dirt. Maybe—"

"Your heartbeat is rising," said Cadence, peering at the wet, moving contents of Vanity's chest.

It was rare, this moment of clarity from her mother. Or maybe what was rare was Cadence paying attention to her at all. Ro was her favorite, Vanity had always suspected this. But that made sense. Vanity was her mother's heir, her competition. And this business with Ellis only made it worse.

Vanity didn't even know how long it had been going on, all the dates, the endless dinners and dances, the indistinguishable Parties marking indistinguishable weeks and months and seasons. Legitimately no fucking clue. She couldn't remember how it felt to not be entangled with him, with Clover. Couldn't remember how it felt to be scared of or hopeful about or disappointed in them. They had become her wallpaper. The skin of her hands. Wrong to peel away.

She was going to go tell Clover that she hadn't meant to run. Or maybe she was going to Clover to scream at her. Or maybe they'd just end up doing the same thing they always did.

Cadence picked up a slice of salami. Placed it on her tongue. Washed it down with a sip of wine-and-cork.

Vanity said, couldn't help it, "I wanted to ask—"

"Eat something, Vanity."

"I'm—not hungry."

"Eat something and I'll answer."

Vanity swallowed. "Fine." She selected a cube of white cheese. Fingers slipping against the oil. She exchanged it for the orange slice she'd dropped. Tore meat from rind, a dry and clinging sound. "I wanted to ask about the Machine. What you remember of it."

She realized after a moment that Cadence was waiting for her to eat. So she did. Chewed and swallowed. Sent the pulped mess down into the back depths of her body, where it would boil and corrode.

ZOE HANA MIKUTA

"Nothing," Cadence said.

"Nothing," Vanity breathed, trying to keep the disappointment from her face. The hope, even now, was to bring Clover something, anything. Her life and her mind weren't enough. Clover didn't care about them.

"Well. I don't know. I know it was a box."

Even at this, at the smallest of details, Vanity's skin went ice cold.

"A box," she whispered.

"Eat something else."

Vanity picked up a block of cheddar—less oily. Nausea still churned when it went soft and waxy against her teeth. But was it from the act of eating, or the look on Cadence's face?

"Ask."

"What was inside it?"

"I don't think it makes sense." Cadence laughed again. Less hollow, more shrill. She took three massive gulps of her wine. "It's blurry."

"But we don't make sense, anyway," Vanity pressed. "You taught me that."

"Did I, did I . . . ?"

"Mother."

"Me, over and over again." Cadence's eyes were fluttering closed.

"What?"

"I swear, it was me, inside the box, over and over and over again. . . ."

"In it? In the Machine?" Cadence shook her head in a twitching way. She seemed to gesture to something, which sloshed red wine against the countertop and the food. "Mother—"

Cadence grabbed Vanity's arm.

"Do you think you're the first, to pull a little charade, to play at being the favorite? Do you think you can get out?" Vanity jerked, not at the contact but at the sudden closeness of her mother's horrible, beautiful face. She looked so much like Ro. Like Vanity. "Your naivety disgusts me."

Vanity looked away from her. "I'm not playing any charades."

She'd wanted Ellis to love her; he did. She'd wanted Clover's attention;

280

she had it. She'd buried them, just like she wanted. What else was there to pretend at?

Cadence was still holding her. Vanity didn't struggle. She never did.

Vanity said, quieter, "And I don't think I can get out."

None of this had ever been about the cure. It had been about being needed.

"I wanted to leave too, you know." Cadence's expression was feverish, half-smiling. Tears sliding down into her mouth. Her words collapsed into a whisper. "But we don't get to go away. We don't get to stop. We're supposed to be here, like this. Especially you." Vanity shook her head; Cadence pulled her in even closer. "You're all wrong. I told Monroe to leave you all alone. You're a wicked and dangerous girl."

"I just wanted them to like me."

Cadence's eyes went wide, like it was the worst thing she could've said. Maybe it was the worst thing. And suddenly her mother was screaming.

"Why do you reek of death and magic?" Vanity's mouth opened, but she realized she had no lie prepared, nothing to cover with. Of course her mother had noticed, the slick of resurrection all over her. If she'd told Monroe— "Ever since you were little. I don't understand it. What's wrong with you. What's wrong with you! Why didn't the Machine peel it from you like it should have?"

Confusion hit Vanity first, then the frustrated blush in her cheeks. Cadence was confusing her with Ro again.

Vanity shook her off. It was easy; Cadence blinked once and slowly at her empty hand. All the tension bled out of the air like a body drained, leaving it cold and quiet. Cadence went for her cigarettes. The paper corner of the carton dyed with the wine.

"That's Arrogance," Vanity breathed irritably, even though there was no point, was never any point. "You're talking about Arrogance—"

"This again? Don't start." For a moment Cadence's unfocused eyes roamed Vanity's face. As she had many times before, Vanity watched her mother retreat further and further into herself, until what was left was only a body, mimicking presence. Cadence could've been talking to her daughter or to the wall. "Don't tell me what I'm talking about."

↙

"Clover. Are you up there? I didn't mean to. It was an accident."

But Vanity was standing under Clover's bedroom window and it was raining, she was shivering and alive again and a little livid. Every time she opened her mouth she swallowed water, and some part of her was able to watch it slip down her tongue down her throat down into the acid vat of her stomach. She watched how she took in the world and then destroyed it.

"Can I ask *you* some questions now? Like what you actually wanted me for, with all of this? You have all the answers, don't you? Are we stopping now? Do you know if we can even stop? I know you're up there. You give off so much heat, and you smell like you usually smell. Do you know how I know that? You built things in me I can't take out. I don't know why I keep coming back to you. I don't know why I'm hungry when I'm not with you. But you do. Don't you, Clover? Clover? It'll come out, what you're doing to me that I can't remember. It'll come up and out of me. And then I'll be better. I think my *cure* is finally knowing. Finally understanding what I mean to you. I'm excited. For something new. Am I making you different, too? Clover? Clover, why are you shaking? Why are you so scared of me? Why are you still there?"

XXX

HER FINGERS PULLING the black ribbon at her throat, into a knot and then into a bow.

A gorgeous white dress had been hung on their bedroom door that morning. What was the special occasion? Vanity didn't know, she just shut herself up in the bathroom that night to slip it on. Attached to the dress's protective plastic was a note to paint red circles on her cheeks, but Vanity thought it must be some kind of joke and ignored it. The dress glittered like champagne, skirts draping like sheets of water, but there was some kind of stiffer cropped coat attached to it that eluded her. The note also gave instructions on how to tie the coat shut, but once Vanity did this it hardly looked right, so she took scissors and snipped off the knot, and then also the silky tassel that hung from the skirt, and then a bit of the ends of her hair, and then the tip of her left pinkie finger.

She sucked on it until it grew back, then went on to don her usuals, black gloves and diamond earrings—sliding it through the fresh piercing on her left lobe—and went downstairs. Ro's footsteps silent on the carpet behind her, in some mood.

"Dear god, what did you do to your ~~wedding~~ dress?" Cadence murmured when Vanity stepped past her to open the door.

"Hm?" Vanity wanted to see Ellis. Ellis, in his suit. Ellis, breaking glasses and biting at people. She'd be staring at Clover, too. It was like daring her. Club was over now, Ellis had reset everything by leaving Clover behind, betraying the coven like that, and everything was going back to normal. It was like they were going back to the start. It would be like time had stood still, or skipped a beat, a season, like nothing had happened at all.

Cadence frowned at her. "Are you really so excited for tonight? ~~The other day I leaned over your body and brought you back from the black. I know you are up to something horrifying. You've always been so horrifying.~~"

"Yes, sure," said Vanity. Ro sat as a dark spot in the corner of her vision, glowering, so Vanity looked at her reflection in the foyer wall and whispered, "I know you were only trying to protect me. Now we can go back to normal, because the coven is broken." Heat shimmered in her eyes as she admitted it. "We can just rely on each other again."

Ro said, "Ellis hurt you so I'm going to hurt him."

Cadence squinted at her. Ro bounded forward. She was kissing Vanity on her cheeks, and Vanity was laughing, throwing her arms around her. She felt grounded again, no magic to cloud her, distract her, lie to her. That's when Cadence lurched forward.

Her mother's hand snapped out, her gloves fingers curling into Vanity's cheeks. Vanity immediately bit down, sealed her mouth like a tomb, but Cadence only made a small, contemplative noise that slid the tension out from her jaw. Eased the muscles just like that, and Cadence was peering down into her daughter's throat. "Yes, cavities," she breathed. "Rot, moving along..."

The small magic that had unwound her jaw had sent the foyer ceiling wavering above her, the chandelier tilting. Vanity wobbled in her heels. The panic rose and then eased away when it recognized how relaxed her body had become. Her mother holding her with one hand around her waist, the other reaching into her mouth.

"Mother," Vanity tried.

"You haven't been flossing."

Vanity jerked and gagged.

"You won't replace me. Not yet. It's not my time yet." Her voice was feverish. Pinching her daughter's rotting tooth. So. It was happening. Cadence took out one molar and then she took out two.

These pieces of Vanity went willingly into the tips of her mother's fingers; it barely hurt, her gums easing open in the wake of Cadence's coaxing. Vanity spasmed as the blood flecked the back of her throat. Cadence set her down gently, the rug tickling her limbs. Then Ro was standing over her, shaking her head, Vanity murmuring, "Her, too, her, too . . ." the world sliding away. . . .

🖋

Yes, she thought they were all done, but of course they weren't. Of course she was in the woods again. And all those extra people were here, again. Meaning Vanity had to pretend what was happening wasn't actually happening.

It was difficult, with her mother's magic still blotting her, for Vanity to focus on the Party. Well, no, she never really focused on the Party, did she—to focus on Ellis and Clover. The trickling of her blood from her raw gums down her throat down into the sack of her stomach distracted her, the bodies around her sloughing off their usual heat, the wet glide of their organs . . .

Ro, on the other hand, existed on the opposite end of Vanity's haziness. Vanity, in turn, gravitated toward her sister's vibrance and light. Holding the hem of her glove with her fingers, unspeaking, as Ro chattered and flirted and danced. Practically dragging Vanity behind her as they swept across the marble floor of the clearing. Marble floor? She stared at the shiny, shiny expanse beneath her heels. Where were Ellis and Clover? Had she already buried them? It would be hard to get them out from under the marble.

Gawkers giggling as they moved past, as Vanity's feet dragged and her terrible, terrible mood pushed blood into in her face. All of them stared from behind white lace that wrapped up their heads.

"Congratulations."

"Happy tidings!"

"To a long and happy marriage, Miss Adams! Or should I say . . ."

They were trying to trip her up but it wouldn't work it wouldn't.

"I'm hungry," Ro chattered, her arms promptly unhooking from around Vanity. She stumbled. Knocked into one of the caterers, a full tray of champagne tipping from his hold. The floor teemed with glass and bubbles. It looked like the marble itself was frothing; Vanity stood there in the midst of it and stared. Behind lace, eyeballs rolled in sockets and swiveled toward her.

Ro tugged at her. "Come on."

"I don't want to eat."

"I know."

Vanity only realized who was over by the banquet table after Ro had started to drag her. Clover had her hair tied in braids. She was wearing all black, like mourning colors.

"Sometimes white is a mourning color," whispered Ro in Vanity's ear. "Are you in mourning, dear sister?"

Vanity approached as Clover's eyes widened. "I'm here," she said breathlessly.

Clover leveled her with the usual hazel stare. So cold that Vanity shivered. "Where is here, Vanity?"

Out of her peripheral vision, Vanity watched Ro plucking things and placing them in the cup of her hand. A jelly tart. Red bean mochi. A skewer of meat. All of them touching and touching each other. Ro shrugged. "They'll mix in my stomach, anyway." And Vanity thought, Ro. Ro, so unbothered by everything, everyone. Vanity wanted to be unbothered like that.

"Don't," Ro said, eating out of her hand. But Vanity had already stumbled forward. Hanging herself on Clover's shoulders, even as the contact roiled her nausea. She smelled so sweet. The rush of her blood in her delicate, perfect veins filling up Vanity's ears.

"I don't want to stop," she said.

"Vanity—"

"I'm sorry if I hurt you."

"You didn't."

"I'd never leave you behind. I never wanted to hurt you."

Clover's voice was seething. "It's *impossible*."

"I can handle it. Everything you want to do with me." A lie. The truth was she didn't want to be able to handle it, any of it. There was something in her that desired to be crushed. To reach for a feeling she'd never felt before and have it destroy her. "Please, let's keep going. We can't possibly stop now."

Ro was laughing at her, maliciously. Food crumbling out of her mouth. Vanity was acting oh so embarrassing.

Now another presence slinked up, a daring one, peeled from the perimeter of the crowd that thickened around them like fluid on a fresh wound.

Wren, poised with his hair brushed back, a white flower blooming from his lapel. "Vanity," he said, "won't you come with me? I have something for you. We're about to begin." And Vanity was being pulled away. *About to begin?* No, no, that wasn't right. They were on a path that went round and round. Where was the starting point on a circle?

Ro, connected by interlaced fingers, whispered into the shell of Vanity's ear, "Life. Growth. Death. Rot. Life . . ."

One they're going to die two I'm going to bring them back three she's going to look in my throat four . . .

And Vanity looked at Clover and Clover was alive, not lying still in the grass, not on a plate. Wren pulling on her arm, the crowd parting for them like the thistles of the clearing...

"Clover? Clover?" Vanity called back, her neck twisting to see. "Are we going around again?"

Clover in black, Clover in mourning. Holding herself in the places where Vanity had touched her. And she gave the barest nod.

⚐

Wren brought Vanity into the velvet-draped back hall where the teeny rooms for tarot readings were clustered. He made her sit in a chair where she shook and shook, so much that her teeth rattled.

"Vanity?" Wren began gently. He knelt before her. He knew she didn't like to be touched, so he braced his hands against the wood rests of the chair. "Are you nervous?"

Vanity's hands wandered mechanically, as if on their own, knocking over the stack of tarot cards on the table. They tipped and spilled across the velvet.

"No, I'm not nervous," she murmured. "I've done this before."

She chose a card.

"Death." Wren smiled. But of course.

"It means transformation, too."

"Ah, I see."

Her fingers worried at the edge of the card. "I don't want all these people here," she whispered.

Wren reached into his pocket and produced a small blue box, placing it on top of Death. "This will help." Then, when she didn't move, "It's for you."

Vanity opened the box and drew out a bridal veil. Her expression remained blank. Her chin turned back toward the cards.

"Let me help you put it on. There we go. See, Vanity. It hides you. No one will be able to see you, so there's no reason to be nervous."

"No one will see me?"

Her large almond eyes peered up through the silver mesh of the veil. Wren smiled kindly. "You're completely safe. All you have to do is walk down the aisle."

She was quiet for a moment. Then: "I don't want them to see. Like you saw."

A flash of an image, of her in the woods. Her spine snapping straight. The shine of her skin, her mouth, in the moonlight.

Her fingers reached, flipping another card. The Lovers. Wren's stomach somersaulted at the sight of the two skeletons, their ribs threaded together.

"And what did I see, Vanity?" He could barely conjure enough breath to lift the words.

Her eyes, formless behind the veil, were past his shoulder. As if there were someone standing behind him. It was an expression he, and everyone else, had come to know well. She chose her last card.

"I don't know," she said. "Can you tell me?"

The Devil smiled up at him.

"I didn't do anything wrong," Vanity whispered. "It's just. That I'm all wrong."

*

In the ballroom, rows and rows of chairs had been laid out, and every corner and table had exploded into strange arrangements of flowers, curling purple lilies, black roses, blue-beaked birds-of-paradise. Colors that clashed and shrieked for attention. Ellis had been located and led up to the temporary stage, wreathed in wisteria; Monroe stood up there too, acting as minister, of course.

And what a big Party it was shaping to be, out there. Business had never been better.

And Wren knew everyone had never been worse.

They had all come to watch a soap opera. World dyeing their tongues, they had come to reap yet another spiritual experience, what would simply be a diluted photograph of their prior spiritual experience. They had come to do the same things they always did, to not look at each other and pretend to understand everything.

They thought this was love, *connection*?

Looking out at all the chatter between the velvet drapery of the back hall, Wren's arm looped around Vanity's.

"It's time to go now, sweetheart."

"Where are we going?"

"We're going to see Ellis."

Did he see her teeth flash then, beneath her veil?

"Good," she said, voice suddenly sharp. "We need to talk."

Wren could hear the casual obsession in her voice. And the anger, and the hurt. He saw the madness that swirled in her, and thought how much he wanted to feel anything that vividly for anyone. He wanted to tell her the truth, then. He'd seen the blankness on her face, outside the gates of the Museum, when she'd come alive again next to Ellis's corpse. It was only later that Wren understood she'd believed, likely hazy with her trauma, that Ellis had dragged her across the border.

"Ellis would never hurt you. You know that, right?" Monroe had staged the entire thing. Dragged them out of their homes and across the border. His father would never admit to it, but Wren knew. The fanfare began— Wren's cue to lead Vanity out into the ballroom. But first he needed to hear her say she wasn't heartbroken. That she wasn't scared. Wren didn't want her to be scared. She needed to know she was so loved. "Vanity?"

"I'm safe from him." The words crawled out of her, small and sure.

Heat broke in Wren's eyes, he was so relieved.

It was time.

Everything in the ballroom seemed to sparkle. The brass and silver of the musician's instruments crowded off to the side of the stage practically singing, everyone's jewelry and fine suits swallowing up the glow of the electric chandeliers above. And the flash of the camera bulbs, the flash of smiles, all their teeth and World-spun tears.

"The stars are so bright tonight," Vanity murmured as they drifted down the aisle, her gloved hand looped though his arm.

"Yes," Wren said. "It's quite lovely."

"The next part is the worst part. And then it gets better."

"Hm?"

Vanity said something else, and though Wren was looking at her, he didn't catch it. So transfixed was he by the obscured look on her face, as she gazed up at Ellis on the stage. As she turned her head slightly when they passed Clover by, the only one standing still, and Vanity's eyes filled with tears.

Wren had felt the world in its vicious, exhausting ends. Or at least to the ends of this blasted island. But Wren could not say that he'd ever felt a single significant thing for another person. He wanted to be peeled raw.

They reached the stage. Monroe nodded, and Wren let Vanity go to stand before Ellis. Ellis, whose expression was so open and tender that Wren, brushing himself quietly to the side, couldn't help but feel proud at how far the witch had come.

Vanity took a kitchen knife out from the waist of her skirt. Ellis smiled on, fondly. It all happened very quickly after that.

XXXI

ALWAYS SO DIFFICULT, to tell the sisters apart, but Clover was fairly positive it was Arrogance who was standing over Ellis, who was stabbing him over and over again.

And then, yes, now she was certain it was Vanity who was kneeling, simply because when one of them was dead she brought them back. Couldn't help but reach for them.

Too many people around, for her to linger, for her to slip dead things into his pockets, to bury him. People that swirled around Clover, scrambling for the exits, as she stood unmoving and watching.

Clover was considering, as she had considered time and time before, which sister it might be, when Ellis was coughing, all bloody, all alive, who went to open his mouth, pry out the residual clotted mass of death from his throat, and eat it.

Yes, always so difficult...

"Clover. *Clover!* What is she doing?" It was Wren, who had scrambled off the stage. His father was still up there, doubled over and vomiting.

"I told you," said Clover. "She eats when she's with us."

She could only look at Wren's horrified expression with an analytical appreciation. Yes, that was how someone was supposed to look, after all, if all of it was brand-new to them. Wren looked like that every time. She grabbed his arm before he could flee. World was frying his head, of course, and he was sluggish and always misunderstanding of the danger. Always reeling closer to her.

"Vanity," Clover called. "Come here."

Certainly Vanity, who neared. But one, of course, was never too far behind the other. Her eyes glazed and glittering with the high of her magic, the excitement of fear-fueled bodies. Her mouth, of course, opening.

"Nothing there," Clover lied. She pushed Wren so he stumbled backward over one of the wood foldout chairs. Vanity was on him before he could gasp.

Then came the other part, the part Clover never liked to watch. So she didn't. She looked at the ceiling. The other parts moved smoothly below her, such a practiced dance it all was, by now. By the time Clover looked back, Vanity was done, wiping her bloody mouth, and Wren's eyes were open again, his jaw already dropping to scream. But there was Ellis, the next part in their practiced dance, whispering his sweetened words, making Wren forget the horrible all of it, making Wren sleep.

Clover didn't want to go. Go to the altar of the world, the Machine, the place she'd feared her whole life. There had once been a part of her that would rather be lying bloated on the ocean floor. But throughout all the weeks and all the months of this, the truth had been revealed to her with miraculous, horrible urgency. With each death, Vanity had peeled away her sense of time, had sent Clover floating further and further above all of it. She saw past and present and future so clearly now.

How indistinguishable it all was, one age to the next. One life to the next. Party to Party, meeting to meeting, mother to daughter.

They couldn't keep doing the same thing. Something had to change. Change was the cure. Complete and undoable change.

Or else, someday, they were going to try to leave her behind again.

So, then. Clover went over her options, calmly, logically. Yes. Cadence was first. Only because she was walking up.

※

Vanity felt full, and like she was someone else. She was watching Clover killing her. Everyone, always with the kitchen knives. They should really stop giving them kitchen knives. They were quite dangerous.

And then Clover was drawing that thin line across her neck that spilled her away, like a milk jug emptying. It was only when the body dropped on top of her that Vanity realized it was not she whom Clover had killed but her mother.

Cadence's soul was around her wrist, curling, growing colder and colder by the moment. Vanity was on her knees. Holding Cadence's head. It was no act of affection; no such acts had ever passed between them. Vanity was smoothing her silky hair, dark like ink spilling against the marble floor. It was, really, like she was holding herself.

She looked up to find her friends. Perhaps to ask them a question. But both were gone, across the room. Clover, splattered in blood, was walking toward Lavender. And Ellis was trailing after her.

This she witnessed through a gap in the closing bodies. People drifting back, now that she was small on the ground. She was only able to pick Monroe out from the mass of teeming flesh that was the crowd because he was the only one who was daring to move closer, even as they chattered behind him.

"Oh, dead, then, is she—"

"The look on the girl's face, and wasn't that her mother? Heartless creatures."

"But isn't it the thing that—aren't they *not* supposed to remember how to—"

"Monroe. Mister Monroe, are tarot readings still booking after this? Is Vanity available—?"

"So will there be one less act for the Afterparty, then? Because what I paid for—"

"No, of course not," said Monroe. One of his hands drifted into his coat pocket, producing a small tin like the one Cadence carried around. He opened the pills to the light. "Vanity. Take these. You'll feel better. Oh, you poor child. The Machine will provide you stability."

Her heartbeat jumped. "I don't want to go. I'm not ready." Magic was too easy. It was a rain-slick hill and Monroe was lying to her. Remembering all of it wouldn't ease her. "Don't make me go. Please. I don't want it to be so loud. It's so loud all the time."

"I know," Monroe said, a few feet away now. The tin of pills rattling quietly in his hand. "I know."

"You don't," Vanity said. "You couldn't. You couldn't. You couldn't."

"Don't, Vanity," Ro snarled, but she'd already pulled Cadence closer. Her hair falling away from the shell of her ear, and Vanity pressed her lips to that exposed velvet curve.

"Rise."

Cadence jerked in her arms. Unwilling, her mother was, rising from the calm black, but Vanity pressed her soul into the sticky sap of her bodily form and held it there. Cadence opened her mouth on her own, the first noise that arose from it a cracked sob, and then she fixed her daughter with a gaze clearer than Vanity had ever witnessed in her life. Breath shook Cadence's lungs, slid against her vocal cords. "Let me—"

Blood sprayed Vanity's lips. She could feel the path the bullet ripped through Cadence's brain matter before she saw its entrance in her temple. The shot was so close, steaming from the barrel of Monroe's pistol, that for a moment she could hear nothing. Not Ro's laughter. Not the scrape of her own heels beneath her, moving on their own. Not the crowd as they screamed and scattered, more terrified of the manmade weapon than the arcane natural forces Vanity possessed; yes, why would they flee before nature babbling, nature on its knees. Cadence's head slid from her lap.

Through the parting of the crowd she finally saw Ellis. Standing like a pin in the middle of the chaos. She dodged Monroe's outstretched arm and she ran to him.

Vanity collided with him. Her arms wringing his torso. His rib bones arching toward her under his suit.

For a moment she believed he was going to push her away. But then Ellis's arms were around her, too. Holding her to him. Laughing a little; she knew it was at all of it. Knew he just couldn't help it.

"He wants me," Vanity said, choking on the words. "He's going to feed me to the Machine. D-don't let him take me—"

"I won't, Vanity, I swear I won't."

"Where's Ro?"

"Oh, Vanity . . ."

"What if they take her?"

"They won't. Love, they won't."

Vanity craned her neck up. Ellis was looking over her head; she followed his gaze across the room, back near one of the banquet tables

There stood Clover. Also unmoved in the scatter of people. Lavender was next to her. She took from the table a glass of wine and offered it to her daughter. Vanity watched, and in her high it was like the color had been bleached out of the image before her. Yes, she was watching a black-and-white soap. Watching Clover take the wineglass in one hand. Poised, taking a sip. Holding Vanity's gaze.

Ellis's arms slipped from her waist. He held her wrist.

On the screen, Clover tilted her head. The gesture was simple—Go.

Ellis began to move, towing her; Monroe was approaching them like a storm, but Vanity dragged her feet, neck twisted, watching Clover. It was happening again. Ellis was going to take her away and they'd leave Clover behind. "No," she mumbled, half laughing. "No . . ."

Ellis held her close. "There's no other way, Vanity."

Kitchen knife flashing in Clover's hand. The red of Cadence's blood across its blade the only thing in color. Through Lavender's usual glazed expression shone something like startlement. Her smile pleasant and plastic.

Ellis clutched Vanity's face in his hands before she could see the next part, but new death pooled coolly around her ankles, sudden stillness flooding across the room. . . .

"The woods," Ellis said. "Now. Stay there until we come for you. Vanity, Vanity. You're in the forest."

His magic sang through her head. It was a cool breeze, nudging all other thoughts away. Vanity stepped away from him. Stepped back.

She couldn't remember what else there was to do. She ran with no panic. And yes, good, then there were trees. They shivered above her head. Vanity sat to watch them, all alone. Someone. Someone would come and get her soon.

XXXII

FOR DAYS VANITY toiled in the lush growth of the Museumlands. Thinking, hands churning in the grasses, There is nowhere else to go. I am to stay right here.

There were people combing the woods for her, to take her to the Machine, but the thud of their hearts and the heat of their bodies made bold their approach. And when she slept, Ro kept sentinel. Whispering in her ear that people were close, Get up and run, Vanity, they're going to take you away.

Ro came and went as she pleased. She always found Vanity easily.

"Where did you go?" Vanity asked, the first time.

"Not far."

"Careful. They might mistake you for me. They might take you instead." It was hard to keep the bitterness out of her voice. There were twigs in her hair. She was still wearing the same strange dress from the

Party, and it was muddy, clotted with brambles. Ro was so clean. Vanity traced her unblemished arm with the tip of her finger.

"Oh, no, no." Ro smiled. "You scared them all, Vanity. They want you. Only you. Isn't that what you craved? Being adored?"

"Not like this."

"You dazzled them. You're a crowd favorite. A darling, uncontrollable."

"Ellis can." Tears flashed in her eyes. "Control me. Clover, too." They didn't even need magic. "There's so much wrong with my head."

Ro tapped her on the temple. "Maybe we should get high?" So they went looking for a dead thing.

It was night in the clearing. Stars bright and dusted overhead. Vanity tipped her head back and breathed in the cooled dark. All their deaths had changed the weight of the air here. Vanity dropped her focus from the sky to her feet, bare against the grasses. And against a tarot card. At least, she imagined it was a tarot card. Freeing it from the arch of her foot, and thinking, *Seven of Swords. Deception. Lack of conscience.* In her hand she held a leaf. She let it go.

"What if they send the dogs for me?"

"They won't. They need you alive." A moment of silence. Then a cricket chirped and Ro giggled at it, the cheery interruption, and then she said, "Why not go into the Machine?"

Vanity had only been doing magic for them. It didn't have any other purpose.

Ro said, "That's pathetic. Are you kidding me? They will send the dogs, actually, for you. I hope they do."

"You're such a bitch."

"I only treat you like you treat you." She tangled a hand in Vanity's hair, the dirty knots in it. Leaned in close and whispered, "Maybe you'll have a clearer view of the worth of your life when you're running for it."

Of course, soon, she would have to run.

She'd been missing for a time now. Enough to formally usher her out of Monroe's good graces and snuff out the grace period of his fascination; without the Museum, Vanity was no Spectacle. Just a witch without a leash. Feral.

📝

So back at the Museum, Wren Athalia, following his father's orders, ambled to the edge of the lawn before untethering the mutts at the black border of the forest. He would not move forward, why would he, with Vanity apparently knowing how to do god knew what. Better to let the beasts drag her back, Monroe had said.

But the beasts wouldn't come back, Wren knew. He'd given them their slick treats and patted their bellies and their heads, and told them they were going to die. The animals didn't understand this, of course. Perhaps if they had begged to stay . . . well, Wren would have chuckled, if that had happened. Then he would've given them more treats and more pats and said in a sterner voice, You stupid creatures, now go, you don't have any use if you're not doing what I tell you to.

Wren knew there were only two people who could bring Vanity back. Bring her home. He'd given them leave to do so. Because then, in a way, they'd all be home.

📝

The clearing thistles lashing against her ankles. Breath pounding up and out of her. Night sky and shadow-swallowed foliage wheeling, staccato flashes.

Vanity didn't know where Ro had gone until she tripped over a tree root and fell. Her teeth cut her tongue and her head spun with the taste of blood. Then there was the dog's lean smooth body on her, jaws clamping on the side of her neck and tearing, tearing, and Ro was beside her again. She slung a rock into the side of the dog's head and it went down. Another one not far behind, and Vanity, blood pushing from the marks at her throat with every frantic beat of her heart, pretended she had teeth

300

like that, too, teeth like knives, and when the dog descended she snapped back. It yelped and cowered and then Ro bludgeoned it. Red staining its gray coat. Then they had all the dead things they could want.

🖋

Tripping out. Whatever. Dragging along a dog by its neck. Up the hall. Though Vanity couldn't really be in the hall. The hall of the cottage. No, no. Cadence was saying, "No, no."

Her mother was on the couch, ivory limbs rippling under the glow of the TV, lovers adoring one another in black and white. Grasping each other, murmuring static murmurs: "I'd never leave you behind. I never wanted to hurt you. . . ."

"No . . . no!" Cadence kicked. She slipped from her seat, stumbling toward Vanity hovering in the doorway. Her hand clawing her daughter's. "Give it to me."

"No." Vanity closed her fist. She didn't know what it was but she didn't want it taken away. Her hand was small. She herself was dwarfed by Cadence. The kick of her heart told her she was afraid of the raised voice, the fury of her mother.

"Give. It. To. Me."

She pried open Vanity's hand easily. In her palm—a crumpled note.

"Who gave it to you?"

No one. Vanity had stolen it. She was still in her Party dress, too puffy and too glittery, her body growing and thus strange to her. Every angle and every thought awkward. Against her hip—the dog, growing cold. Her mouth stayed shut, knowing she'd cry if she spoke. *Why don't they give me notes, too? Why don't they like me, too?*

What's wrong with me?

Cadence unraveled the note. Vanity's neck craned. Before she could read it, Cadence's hand jerked forward. Paper scraping her mouth.

"Eat it."

Vanity clutched the dog tighter. Twisted away.

"If you want it, then *eat it*."

The TV crackled and sparked. It wasn't Cadence clutching Vanity, but Ro. And so Vanity was safe and so she did speak, "Why do they *ignore* me?"

She sniffed. Ro tutted, wiped her snot and tears away. Cadence was back on the couch, dozing. Her arms struck out this way and that. The note peeked out of her hand like a flower rising out of dead earth. Vanity had resisted her and won.

"Maybe one day I'll kill her," mused Ro. "I don't like how she talks to us."

"She likes you better."

"I'm not such a pushover."

Vanity bristled. "Maybe it'll be me who does it. Kills her."

Ro smiled at that. "You, me. Either-or. There's no difference." She plucked the note from Cadence's hand.

"What does it say?" asked Vanity. She had tried to read it but couldn't understand the words. When she tried to recall them now, they distorted like static. Tried to open her mouth to speak them and she couldn't.

Ro folded it smaller and smaller until it had vanished.

"Where did it go?"

"I hid it."

"Where?"

"With the others."

"You don't need to protect me. I want to know."

"No you don't. You don't. It's already out of your head, isn't it?" Vanity pulled the dog closer to her ribs and sniffed again, shuddered.

Ro said, "Don't cry, Vanity. Really. I know how to get them to notice you. I know how to make you feel better. Come on. Let's find something dead."

"Vanity. Vanity."

She opened her eyes. She hadn't traveled far from where the dogs fell upon her. The two of them with their spines against her ribs. Her arm around one of their necks. The morning light trickling through the branches above seemed to be sliding, globlike, against the foliage. She flinched a little, when the leaves shifted and pinpricks of sun broke in her eyes, briefly blinding.

"Arrogance?" she murmured, her mind clear but her vision still distorted, kaleidoscopic in beats. "Where did you go?"

"Get her up."

Her arm was being grabbed. The dogs sliding off of her, and Vanity was on her feet. She wobbled. She supposed she was weak from hunger. The body she tilted was warm and solid and Ellis's. She hugged him, breathed in the smell of his skin.

"You came for me."

"I said we would." His hand cradled the back of her head.

The noise that rose from Clover's throat was barbed, disbelieving. There's something different. Clover looks like Clover, except. Except her pulse . . .

"You're high." It hummed and pricked at Vanity's skin. "What did they give you?"

Clover licked the side of her mouth. "Only the good stuff."

"You killed Lavender." Her fingernails curled against Ellis's shirt.

"Yes. Yes."

"Was it to help me get away?" She could not keep the hopeful note from her voice. That someone she loved might do something horrible for her.

"Vanity. All of it. It was all for you."

Clover has said something like this before. The memory floating back, distorted and broken. Vanity thinks, strangely, did Ro do that? Always hiding truths away from her, the ones that would hurt . . .

"Why?"

"With Cadence dead, they were going to put you in. Put you in before me. Before I could go and remember. I. Yes. I remember. . . ." Clover trailed off. Her fingers swirled at her sides. And the tall grass that reached from the earth was set briefly aflame. Like sparklers. Clover smiled in the way she always had smiled, in the rare and few instances Vanity had witnessed. Satisfied, half-triumphant. "It worked, Vanity. Our club. Not like we thought it would, but wondrously. My magic didn't hit my brain and fry it; I'd already tasted it. The early highs are always the most potent. The other ones don't compare, do they? I remember. I do. The altar of the world."

Abandon it, rang Ro's voice in her ears. *Your sense, your self.*

Put it all on the altar of the world, for your cure.

Vanity's throat ran dry. "The Machine."

"What it is. Where it is."

"Where?"

"The Necropolis on the Pockmarked Island."

"We're going there, Vanity," Ellis murmured.

Somehow she had expected this. But she still didn't understand. "Why?"

"You're different from us," Clover said. She reached out a hand and Vanity, instinctively, shifted away. The hazel in Clover's eyes glinted black in the shadows fleeing from the rising sun. "You're special. They don't get to have you. They don't get to use you. You're going to save us. Don't you want that?"

And the fear hit her, and the first thought was that if she ran Clover would catch her, but—Vanity did. She breathed, and she remembered. Yes. This was all for them. "What are we going to do?"

"Break the Machine open. Break it open and purge you of your magic. Don't you see? It takes what is there. It gives back what isn't. This is the cure, Vanity."

"It works like that?" Vanity twisted her head up at Ellis.

"Yes, Vanity," he said. His eyes on her, then floating away. "Clover remembers. Just follow her lead. It's going to be fine."

There was some kind of tension curling in the air, causing shifting feet and sliding gazes, as if they were strangers to one another. Vanity couldn't tell if it was bleeding from herself or the other two, if it was their collective highs—chemical or magical—or something else.

"We have to bring Ro," Vanity said finally, briefly shutting her eyes. "She's always wanted to go back to the Necropolis."

She heard Clover let out a quick breath. Annoyance, or anticipation? "Yes. Of course. We'll bring Ro."

"Have you seen her?" Vanity asked.

"No. But she's always around here somewhere, isn't she?" Perhaps Clover was trying to be reassuring. Vanity only shivered. She let herself be led away.

*

Vanity didn't know how Clover had gotten the keys to the car. "Can you even drive?" she snapped, oddly irritable. It was cold and her head throbbed.

"Sure, sure," Clover responded. "I like driving. I know how to drive. I know how to do everything."

It wasn't exactly true. Clover put her foot on the gas and the car jolted forward and smashed into the bumper of the one in front of it. There were a lot of cars here, Vanity noted distantly. Was it another Party night already?

"Where's Ro?" Vanity was strapped into the front seat and Ellis acted sentinel in the back. She looked in the rearview mirror to find his eyes darting away. From hers? From Clover's? "Wait—we can't leave without Ro."

"Ro will come," said Clover. She was driving very slowly down the drive, getting the hang of it.

"What?"

Clover flashed that sharp smile. "She always shows up eventually!"

The shrill, sudden laugh that followed scared Vanity. She hardly sounded like Clover at all. She unbuckled her seat belt. "We can't—"

"Vanity! Why does she need to come? Doesn't she want to keep all of it? Doesn't she already know how to do magic? What does she need the Machine for?"

Vanity blanched. "She's— *I'm* the one—" Ellis let out a laugh, and she spat, "Don't *do* that—"

"Come here. Sit back here with me."

Then he was pulling her into the backseat, cradling her. Vanity shook, unable to help it, unable to look at him. "When did you know?"

"We figured it out eventually."

We we we. Tears sprang to her eyes. She lied, "I didn't mean to lie."

"Yes you did."

"I still brought you back. It was *me.*"

"Yes, Vanity. You did."

"Ro never wanted to bring you back."

"Why's that, love?" His arms were around her. She couldn't see his face, but could feel his eyes looking out right over her head. Looking at Clover in the mirror. Still with their secret looks. She boiled with it. Everything she had done she'd done for them.

"She thought you guys weren't good for me."

She waited for them to say something different even though she knew it wouldn't come.

"I'm sorry," Ellis said.

And then he held her tighter and said, "This part is going to hurt."

He told her that she wouldn't care about the pain. He told her to remain calm. But he didn't tell her not to look.

And so Vanity was looking down at her feet because she didn't want to look at either of them; her feet, practically black from her toiling days in the woods, yet still, through the skin of her left ankle there shone a red warning light.

Blinking slow at first, Vanity blinking slow too, tired, so, so tired, and then it was blinking faster and faster as they approached the perimeter, and then it was gone. Wetness patterning her lips. Yes. It did hurt. The heartbeat there, cradled in the raw, pushing the blood down in the foot space of the car, her toes wriggling in it. The ones she still had, anyway. Inclining her head, marveling at the sudden asymmetry: the jagged stump ending her left leg, the delicate path her right still took, supple ankle and its rounded node, the lacy network of veins.

She was too dead to notice it all last time. Too dead to observe that it hurt more than anything she'd ever felt before. Observing that Ellis's head was still on his neck and Clover was also still moving them, driving slow, intact. The both of them, always intact.

"It'll feel better soon," floated down Clover's voice. "You'll remember how to grow it back."

🪶

So Vanity knew it was going to end badly. She'd always known. From the very first time she'd brought him back. From the very first time he'd touched her. Above, the trees of the Necropolis stretched their limbs toward a shrouded sky.

She'd passed it before, the Machine, when she was little. The memory pulsing like a headache in her mind's eye. Ro clinging to the gates. *I don't want to go. I want to be* sacred.

You're not. And Cadence's cloying voice, disbelieving of her daughter's insistence. Reeling from what could only be described as a sense of piety. *You're broken.*

On either side they were holding her, tightly, and Ellis was saying, "Clover, Clover," and Clover was gritting her teeth, saying, "Hurry up, hurry up, she's fading. . . ."

She was being dragged toward a stone box that looked really just like any of the other stone boxes that stood around it, unlike a "machine" at all. Grass tickled the pad of her foot, and she felt all bodies under the earth in their little rooms, lying quietly, unaware she recognized them. Was something terrible happening? Ellis was letting her rest on the stone steps. He was wiping the sweat from her forehead and then he kissed it.

"Make me sleep, please," Vanity murmured. "I don't want to be awake."

"Keep your eyes open. Stay awake for us."

Above her, she was aware of something coming to loom over her. Tilting her head back made her dizzy, made her reel out of herself for a moment, view the scene from above. There were the three of them, surrounded by graveyard and greenery. There was Vanity, her leg a streak of red, red that also marked the path they'd taken up from the car; there was her pale, stricken face, looking up at Clover as she held open the lid of the Machine, casting its shadow over Vanity. How small they all looked, down there, yet there was a pulse that emitted from the three of them like a heartbeat. A vibration that wound around them and rang outward. And the trees leaned. And the clouds rushed. And the ground breathed. It reacted to them, everything fresh and organic and essential, reacted to their strange bodies capable of doing strange things, and it was all expecting something of them, begging something from them, begging, make it stop. Now Vanity was floating way, way above, there was this spot of green and the Museum and then there was the beep of cars and spewing exhaust and the ring of telephones and television static and all of it was nothing, make it all stop. Make it all right.

Vanity was crawling. Dragging her leg behind her. Like a soul dying of thirst drawn toward the sound of running water. Up the stone steps and then she was peering in.

"What is it?" she murmured. They were behind her, Ellis and Clover. Hovering. "What is this?"

At first, she thought it *was* water. Down there. Because she could see herself, in all of those pools. She reached a hand in, tentatively. Her hand did not break through a cold liquid surface. Instead, her fingers prodded cool glass.

"It's you, Vanity," said Clover.

Her heart thudded. Yes, certainly, there Vanity was. Over and over and over again.

The Machine wasn't a machine at all. It was a box full of mirrors. A magic trick.

"I don't want it," Vanity murmured. "I don't want her."

She looked back. There—Ellis and Clover exchanged a glance.

And then they were on her.

"Arrogance!" Vanity screamed and screamed. "Arrogance!"

Their hands were all over her, lifting her from the ground and forcing her flailing limbs into the Machine. "Please—" Her hands scrambled for purchase on the border, her legs kicking against the sky and then, horrifyingly, against the mirrors, because Ellis was pushing down her knees, he was pale and pleading with her. Clover was tight-lipped, focused and flushed in the face. Vanity couldn't help but look at their features, these people with all their attention on her, all hers, finally, yet still she was nothing to them, absolutely fucking nothing. Sob after sob bursting from her: "Ellis—Clover—please, I don't want to—" And then they were going away. The sky getting thinner and thinner, the light being swallowing up by darkness. "—don't leave me—" Their hands had moved to the cover, pulling it down. They were locking her in. "—no no no no—" The lid of stone and mirror smacking the top of her head; her world tilted. The fingers that Vanity would not move from the edge she simply lost. She shrieked and pulled them to her, what was left of them, crushed and torn lengths; everything hurt now and now she cared about it, all of it, she wasn't calm, and now she was alone. Just her and the ruins of her body.

"Let me out! Please! Please! I'll do anything you want. . . ."

But Vanity had done everything they wanted. Oh, god, she'd done all of it.

Curling in on herself, shivering, nauseous from hitting her head, from the blood loss, and she was cold, so so cold. Even now, the need to be held and kissed and comforted slammed down on her. It was all Vanity's fault. She'd allowed all of it to be done to her. She had never loved anyone with the expectation that they would do her no harm.

"Ro..." she sobbed. It was a waste of breath but it was the last person she had to call out for. The person who'd tried to protect her all along. And what had Vanity done to her? Threatened and hurt and hated. "Arrogance..."

"Vanity?"

Vanity startled. She scrambled onto her back, spine curling against one side of the Machine, chest and heartbeat heaving. Faint movement rippled at the edges of her vision—her reflection copying her movements. Either her eyes were adjusting or the Machine itself emitted a dull, otherworldly glow. It was just enough to see that she was alone.

"Ro?" Whispering now, her mouth dry. Her words carried and faded as if she were in a large room. "Where are you?"

Ro's voice came again. It sounded very close. "Vanity?"

Vanity looked behind her. Her nose brushing mirror. There was Ro's face, Vanity's face. The black eyes sunken in the dark. The sheen of blood and sweat accentuating the rise and fall of her collarbone. Vanity swallowed. Her broken fingers lifted to ghost her throat.

"Ro?" she said again.

Her mouth moved, and smiled. "Vanity."

Something jolted against her touch.

She screamed.

Her head knocked the lid again as her feet shifted under her to kick away—but kick away from what? At first her hand instinctively jumped from her neck, but then the something was pressing out, it was reaching for her, and she forced her palm back to her throat to shove it back, keep it in. The stalks of fingers prodded her, and then a startlingly intimate and precise pain in the shape of four crescents cutting the inside of her neck, and there were nails splitting the skin from the inside out, digging into her palm. Vanity now brought her other palm to her throat and pressed fast, choking the scream out of herself, squeezing, trying to break the hand that was attempting to rupture out of her, this thing she'd kept inside her for months, this thing she should've drowned in bleach or pried out but instead let fester and grow, because Ellis and Clover said it wasn't there, that there was no need to worry, she wasn't dying and she wasn't sick, she was fine, they were paying attention to her so she was fine. She was realer when the people she loved were looking at her; they were the ones who could better describe her, if they were looking at her now and said, You're not running out of air, you're fine, you're good, she'd nod with tears in her eyes and keep pressing, she'd be asking, Like this? Like this? if it were still possible to get the words out.

Black spots shot their way across her vision, and right when it seemed that her hands would slacken on their own, she felt the fingernails beneath pull back.

Vanity released her chokehold, falling back on her forearms as she retched and gasped for air.

She was afraid to look down at her body. It was still in her, it was in her torso, she knew because her dress was sweat-pasted to her skin and it was moving. The hand had retreated somewhere down inside her and was hiding and so Vanity wanted to leave. She wanted to leave she wanted to leave she wanted to leave. But there was nowhere else to go she was stuck here in her body and that's why she opened her mouth to scream, and when she did she felt the hand come skittering up from the inside of her stomach up her chest up her throat and it was prying open her mouth and when it emerged when it shot against the mirror so hard it fractured it wasn't just a hand it had a wrist and then an arm and then—more, she assumed, flipping inside out, more, another girl, another Vanity, an extraction, a cure.

XXXIII

A LONG TIME AGO

"WELL? WELL? WHAT IS IT?" Clover was impatient and she was anxious. She blamed it on the sudden proximity to Ellis—a natural response, she observed and then categorized and then filed away into the appropriate place in her head. To mark what arose in herself as in her control versus out of her control was beneficial organization.

Ellis Kim wasn't supposed to be here. Ellis Kim knew that. Walking here to the window of her and her mother's kitchen—that was not a natural response, it was in his control, to travel and knock at her window and break all the rules.

"I need to talk to you," Ellis finally managed. They were both ten years old. They knew what the rest of their lives would look like. A hazy growing up, back into the Machine for the reharvesting of their powers, rites, drugs, rites, drugs, babies, drugs, rites, suicide or Sanatorium or execution. The word rang in Clover's head. *Need. Need. Need.*

"Spit it out," she said, swaying slightly alongside the house.

"It's about Vanity."

"Vanity? Vanity. Vanity?" Images flashing through Clover's head. The depressed-looking little girl who looked like she was about to throw up all the time, hovering at the corners of the Parties. Staring at Clover, and Clover thinking, Please don't ever don't ever come up and talk to me. Please all of you just leave me alone. "What about Vanity?"

"Well, it's just." Ellis swallowed. She watched the laugh travel up and out of his throat, his fingers skittering across her windowsill. "Sometimes there's two of her."

✒

Clover wrote out instructions, one small letter per Party, for Ellis, dropping them in plant pots or underneath the dirty dish trays. Though sometimes he was looking through her rather than at her, and the letters would go uncollected, and Clover would have to circle back and discard them. Largely it would be reminders to not interact with Vanity. He was always glancing over at her. He never looked through Vanity.

Though really Clover never looked through Vanity, either. There was some quality about her that made her seem more vivid than other people. Before, Clover had figured it was because she was ludicrously gorgeous, always had been. But after Ellis's visit, it was clear it was because she was radiating magic, which should have been impossible. The Machine was supposed to have cleared it all out, purged those arcane instincts, like it had for Clover and Ellis, leaving them only the effects of auras, at whim to the strains of magic already present in the world. Which is why Ellis could see Vanity's hallucinations. Clover couldn't see any reason for him to lie. She also couldn't see how Vanity could have been affected by such deep psychosis without having magical ability—she had to be able to do *something*, even if she herself wasn't aware of it, to be so mentally afflicted like this.

Clover's curiosity was like a pet with a biting problem, one so dear to her she had difficulty muzzling it. Thus there came a point when, instead of instructions, she began to ask Ellis questions. *Why did you tell me about Vanity?* He'd taken that letter from where she'd tucked it into the ballroom curtains and put it into his suit pocket; she'd watched him do it. Then he'd looked at her from across the room and shrugged. The next week, at the next Party: *Be more specific.* The next week, a note back: *Be more specific about what?* A colossal waste of time. She'd tried again. *Be more specific about why you told me about Vanity.* He'd written back: *I'm not sure if everything I see is real, either.*

Well, there we go, Clover thought. Progress. She loved progress, cycles marching forward. Progress was one half of the nature of the world. The other half was taking that progress apart.

So then they were both paying close attention to Vanity. Watching her talk to herself. Watching her talk to *Arrogance.* The Partygoers chittering at the darling, sullen child, so pathetic and lonely that she spoke to the air. No one, of course, ever bothering to inform Vanity she was always completely alone.

As they all grew older and older, Clover would watch Vanity shift effortlessly. Sometimes she was bold and witty and grinning, and other times she was herself. Expressions changing like fast-moving clouds over her face. Ellis wrote notes to Clover that Arrogance would flicker in and out of the room. They never could quite figure out what Vanity was talking about. Often she'd say shut up or don't talk or don't do that. What secrets was the girl cradling within her, unbeknownst to even herself? It was impossible to know. And all of them were growing more and more restless as they grew up. Clover felt them approaching some apex, the edge of some cliff. She could feel change in the air. She kept every letter from Ellis, feeling the paper where he touched, tracing over Vanity's name. She could feel them all connected, and they were special, because of it. A bond outside of their control. A natural infatuation. She'd find what she was looking for, in Vanity. Salvation. A cure—

What *was* that?

These thoughts weren't Clover's. Her strings were being pulled by something in her that wasn't her, something arcane, and every night Clover tried to forget it, tried not to think about how it was already in her head, how it *was* her head, this force she feared she didn't stand a fucking chance against. So she tried to forget about it, forget about her.

As long as she left Vanity alone, she'd be okay.

She'd be rational about this. Would follow her gut feeling to protect her—the knowing that they were going to destroy one another.

So, said her brain quietly, *ask something else.*

How could they figure out a way not to hurt one another?

Or. Or...

Or hurt one another without it mattering.

XXXIV

NOW

VANITY LEFT ELLIS THERE, at some point, on the ballroom floor. It seems as if he blinked and she had vanished. Her panic has always been the sweetest, most blinding rush. Perhaps even more so than the rush of her pulling him back to the cold surface of life, like dragging him out of water.

Ellis scratches at the floor, unsure of what to do.

But really he always knows what to do. Look for her, and find her.

The candles have burned out and it is pitch-dark; luckily this doesn't matter. Vanity is thinking and thinking and thinking. Ellis follows her thoughts, written all over the dust on the walls, in indescribable, incomprehensible black. Outlining the world for him.

He has moved into the hall of small, curtained rooms. Being drawn back here himself to read tarot for the tourists is, of course, dozens of lifetimes ago, but truly it feels like that routine belonged to someone else entirely. The low light of the fabric-draped electric chandeliers burning a headache into his temples, the tourists' noises, either constituting excitement or disbelief—all from someone else's life. Everything he was before going into the Machine to retrieve his magic was obliterated; perhaps it is extremely lucky that he doesn't recall if this former self is worth missing. But he'll recall, for the rest of his life—and the next one, and the next—how it felt to miss her.

"Vanity?" he whispers, pulling aside the curtain of the room he knows she waits in.

She sits at the reading table, her back toward him. A single tealight candle dances on the table, sweating white wax.

"I just wanted to check," says Vanity, so quietly. She doesn't turn around. Her hands are moving, accompanied by the slow *shush shush shush* of shuffling cards. "I just needed to see...."

Wasn't it inevitable, that Ellis had fallen for her? What could he expect, really? When every time he died, she was the one who tugged him back. When he woke up and she was the one holding the other end of his soul, until it fit the palm of her hand better than it did his body.

"What do you see, Vanity?"

"Sit."

Ellis sits across from her. The light carves out her features, and when her bloodshot black eyes rise to meet him, Ellis realizes he is clear enough from death to be afraid.

"I used to think this was bullshit," Vanity says, tapping the cards. "But they didn't exactly ever tell us it was bullshit, did they? Whatever. What does it matter, anyway, knowing the future, if we can't change it?" *Tap. Tap. Tap.* "If we can't change."

Ellis attempts a laugh. "Just for kicks?"

Her little, cheerless smile drops cold through him. And then she draws a card.

Ellis goes very still. Vanity puts it face down on the table between them.

"Well. Mostly I was good with it, separating what was true from what I was making up in my head." *Tap. Tap. Tap.* "And for what I missed—there was you. You, and then Clover. You would check me. You would tell me what was real."

She turns the card over.

"Why didn't you tell me what was real?" she murmurs. The Tower rises to meet him. His vision spurs, vertigo pricking at him, its black, gold-outlined bricks blurring past him, as if he's mid-plummet. "Why didn't you tell me what was happening to me?"

For anyone else, the major arcana would signify some kind of upheaval, potentially an especially shitty day. For them—a reckoning. Apocalypse. The end of the world.

Ellis doesn't say *I didn't think anything bad would happen* because he had always known it would, and he doesn't say *I didn't think you would get hurt* because he had. So he says he is sorry and that she can do anything she wants with him now, he says it can be forever like that, he is on his knees before her now and he'd stay forever, like this, please, Vanity, grasping for her hands, struggling to draw breath for his words, and when he's sobbing, "I love you. I loved you then, too," she looks at him and says, "You didn't do it right."

↙

The first thing they see when they open the front doors is legs. Clover's legs, struck out on the drive. She lies there with her cheek turned to the weakening sunlight. A cigarette long burned to ash in her hand. She attempts to sit up, but it doesn't work. "Where are you going?" Then her nose wrinkles. "You died."

"We're going to see Ro, Clover," Ellis says. "Vanity's going to put an end to this."

"Don't go." Clover grabs the end of Vanity's pant leg. "Vanity."

"No, Clover," she says. "No."

"I've been alive for a year, please." Vanity tastes salt on her tongue before there's tears shining on Clover's cheeks. "Please, it's killing me."

"We're going, Clover," Ellis says, already stepping past her.

"She can't," Clover spits, with such finality that Vanity blinks, that Vanity believes it. *I can't, I can't.* But then she forces herself to relax—believing Clover is just a habit her body remembers. Because Clover was the clearest.

Well. Look at her now.

Ellis says, "You said if anyone could—"

"This never ends. Don't you see that? This never ends. We should all stay right here and wait."

"Wait for *what*?" Vanity asks, because she truly, truly wants to know—

"I don't know! I don't know, okay?" Clover rocks from side to side, wiping her face with an ash-smirched hand. "For it to be over. The end. We're waiting for the end—"

"We don't get an end," Vanity seethes. "None of us. You made it like that, didn't you? We're all immune to whatever is happening." Her lip curls, all on its own. Vanity revels in it, the cradling of her body, defending her like this. "You got your cure."

"I didn't think—"

"Didn't think what? That it would turn out this way? That you would feel so guilty, having me back? Just let it go, Clover. You won't find redemption in me." She cuts her gaze to Ellis. "Either of you. I'm not asking for your apologies. I just need a ride."

She brushes past both of them and heads for the car. Ellis trails after her. Then the weight of the air seems to shift. The hairs on the back of Vanity's neck prickling. When she turns her head, Clover is standing. Body half-obscured by one of the pillars. Hands folded in front of her.

"Don't leave," Clover calls. She looks rather steady, now. Completely still. "Don't leave me again, or I'll have to chase you."

Vanity pauses to look, but Ellis gives a tight shake of his head. His hand snaps out and opens the passenger door.

"Get in the car, Vanity." A sudden, slight franticness plucks at his voice.

"What? What is it?"

"Oh, it's nothing, nothing. Hurry up now." Vanity gets in, and Ellis rounds the hood quickly, sliding into the driver's seat. Vanity looks back again to find Clover is still shock-still, just staring at them, until Ellis starts the engine. Then she takes a step forward. The bricks at her feet blacken and soften. House and ground and sky seem to warp and curl around her; Vanity snaps her eyes back to the dashboard, blinking rapidly. "Uh-oh," Ellis chuckles, putting his foot to the gas. "Yeah. She's in a bad mood. Seat belts, please."

↙

They are speeding over the lick of road ribboning the past the Museum gates. The City glittering below them. All she can hear is her own breathing and the car engine. There's a crack in the windshield, blood smeared there. She dances her fingers across it, so clean from this side. "Did we hit someone?" she laughs.

Ellis doesn't answer her. Instead he says, eyes scanning the road, the flashing trunks of trees on their either side, "You know, there's usually more of a *teeming* going on here. Usually they're not standing so still. Do you know what they're waiting for?"

Vanity shrugs. She pretends the state of the world has nothing to do with her.

Clover is driving behind them, sentinel, her headlights lighting up the back of their heads.

"How did you guys learn to drive?"

"Slowly and horribly."

"Did that help pass the time?"

"Oh, sure."

He's in a sour mood. She thrills at that, the invitation to be horrible. "You were romanticizing me all year long, you forgot how much you hated me. I remind you about all the awful parts of yourself."

"I don't hate you, Vanity, don't say that."

320

It would've made more sense if you did, she thinks of saying, *given what you did to me*. But that wouldn't be so fair. Vanity had never expected him to make sense.

Closing her eyes, now. In the dark, she frames the windshield fracture and the bloodstain with her hands, feeling, in the palms of her hands, the warmth still breathing through it. "I did think we were making each other better, for a minute there, way back when. I used to think we all must feel the same way—why else would we keep going, otherwise? I wanted to be so happy, like that. But I knew somewhere in the back of my head that we were just hooked on the magic, too. How we built it up in each other. We were doing incredible things." She only opens her eyes when she covers them with her hands. "We were just making each other sicker and sicker. Always just making each other sicker and sicker. But you never thought otherwise, did you?"

Ellis is silent.

Vanity says, "I know you loved it. You loved making me crazy. You loved driving me off the fucking rails. That's why you followed me around. That's why you showed me Clover's journal. That's why you brought me back."

She wants him to admit it out loud so much that it throbs in her like fascination. Watching between her fingers as Ellis's throat works. That beautiful profile, so ethereal and perfect to her it was as if it'd been hewn from something immaterial—light, or the breath in her throat.

"Well, yes," Ellis says quietly. "I suppose I remember that."

Tears prick her eyes. "You don't even know if that's true."

Ellis tenses. His eyes flick to the rearview mirror.

"What. What is it?"

And Ellis goes, "Oh, well, Clover—"

Vanity feels it, then—the whipcrack of magic rushing up behind them. Goose bumps erupt up her spine, grin clattering to her face in their wake, just as Clover puts her foot flat to the gas.

The collision jolts them forward in their seats. Vanity almost bites off the tip of her tongue. Ellis lays on the horn; Clover only responds with a longer peal. "God damn it!" he shouts again, that shout spiked with laughter, and that laughter hysterical. "She's spiraling—"

And then they're making a curve of road, and Vanity looks out her window, and Clover is there, to the left of them, wild smile cracking her cheeks, her hands spinning on the wheel. Another jolt, and this time Vanity does taste blood. She knows so precisely how the inside of her mouth has opened up, with Clover running them off the cliff, that she could draw it out on paper. And then they are weightless, turning over. Vanity sees black sea and black sky and the sickle edge of the Pockmarked Island. Then the car hits a rock and her neck snaps. And that's it. Nothing. Finally.

V

DRY

VANITY. STANDING THERE IN THE DARK, her hands
holding her wrists. She was talking and Clover had been listening, as
always, trying not to flinch, trying not to grab her and shake her and
scream, *How could you not see it?* Trying not to run away. "Say you're sorry.
Excuse me? Say you're sorry. To both of them. *Arrogance.* Just *say it.* Even
if I don't mean it? I am going to throttle you, I really am. You'll have to
catch me first. You're insufferable. You're a pushover. Am not. Yes you
are. You'd totally let them push you over. They wouldn't. Yes they would."
Vanity's hand flew to her mouth. "Shut *up.* Why are you like this? Can't
you just be *nice* for once?"

When all the screaming stopped, Clover braced herself against the lid
and opened up the Machine. There was the delicate reek of magic that
curled her lips and churned sensation in the marrow of her bones, a

reaching, or a recoiling. Ellis, though of no help, sitting on the steps with his arms over his head, could feel it too. Clover thought it mad for him not to want to take a first look.

Within the Machine resided two girls, copies of each other, except one was naked and awake and smiling up at her.

"Hello, Arrogance," said Clover. "It's nice to finally meet you."

Though, perhaps they'd met before. It was quite difficult to discern whether Ro had existed as her own person inside Vanity's body, but Clover thought the more likely option was that Ro hadn't been real until this very moment.

Vanity, after all, was a chronically lonely creature, and delusion was a side effect of witchcraft, witchcraft that Vanity had never really been purged of. A malfunction of the Machine, or Vanity as a manifestation of especially pissed-off, lonely, and hurt nature?

Perhaps Ro had come to be in the back of her head as an unholy amalgamation of both. Had come to be, physically, by the coven, coaxed together by a spiritually implanted, senseless desire.

But did the *how* of it matter? Clover's hypotheses had been right. Vanity had performed magic, she'd eaten their deaths, she'd fallen for them, and the Machine took what was there, and the Machine took Ro—primed by carnage, incubated by flesh and obsession—out of Vanity. Clover could abandon what questions she had left, what mysteries of the universe she might never know. She had the complete synthesis of all of it breathing in front of her.

After all, what was more real than flesh and blood?

"You have no idea what's about to happen." Arrogance's first words, at least out of a mouth that was her own. A mouth that giggled, one she touched now, as if trying to catch the bright and pealing notes. Clover had never seen that look on Vanity's face before, no matter how far gone she'd been. "You have no idea."

"Well, generally?" Clover shrugged. "The end of the world."

There was no cure for magic, of course. That had never been Clover's intention. She knew it could never have been her intention. There couldn't be expected a remedy for nature. They couldn't be expected to fix Vanity. She'd been born to reach for the coven, and be fed by their closeness and by their deaths, and, eventually, to be used by them. To create a different kind of cure.

A cure for the Museum.

A cure for the set path of their lives.

A cure for other people, for this era of concrete and artificial highs and goddamn, godforsaken spectacle—a cure for the whole world.

An apocalypse.

And the apocalypse was staring at her, and, oh—Clover would admit it now—she really was so gorgeous.

"Just look at her, Ellis," Clover breathed. She took a step back, to allow Arrogance to rise. The beautiful girl's beautiful hands curling, then lifting, white limbs cutting air, pulling herself out of the Machine. All of her possessed of a quality that Clover could only describe as a *teeming*, the edges of her soaked in static like she was about to come apart. But she did not scatter into a million pieces. She was whole. She was standing now. "You won't believe it."

"I don't want to," Ellis moaned. He was still holding his head, struggling to draw breath. There seemed to be some kind of low fog rolling in from the surrounding Necropolis, gathering around him.

"Don't worry. I planned it all out, Ellis. We survive what comes next. We fed her our deaths, so we survive all of it. It's our apocalypse, too."

"You don't know what I feel. There's barely a mind there. There's just— oh, god, I see it. There's so much skin." His mouth popped open and he was screaming. "The growing. It's—everywhere—" He was writhing. His long legs jolting, lifting the fog. "You have no idea—"

"Everyone is always telling me I have no idea," said Clover, waving him off. "Like I'm like the rest of you. You think you could've pulled this off? You think you could've seen what I saw in her? In her throat? You just thought it was a hand, a freak growth—I *knew* it had to be something else, something spectacular, I knew it was Ro, living down there. Well, I know now. Ro was just as real as Vanity makes her, as we make her. Made her. *I* made her." Her head was spinning, the fog sickly sweet in her throat. Ellis had fallen over, his eyes and mouth half-opened. "I remembered the Machine, and I brought her here. I did all of this. I was always the one who was going to fix everything. Ellis? Are you listening to me?" This was important. This was essential. "I was always the clearest out of all of us."

⤲

Wren kicked the witches, just to be sure they'd all gone down properly, like dropped sacks of potatoes. His breath echoing in his gas mask, watching the shadowed figures of his men surge through the knockout mist they'd pumped into the graveyard.

It had taken them mere minutes to find them—the better question was, *what* had Wren found, here, exactly?

It was certainly a scene to behold—everyone in their evening attire, scattered around, painted with what Wren presumed was Vanity's blood. She was whole, though, her ankle and foot had regenerated—a sign that her magic had settled back correctly. The whole process must've been wildly traumatic.

His neck prickled and he spun. All he saw were misted graves.

Relax, he scolded himself brightly. Just nerves, then—it was a special day, after all. And besides. Everyone dangerous was accounted for.

He had, of course, been the one to request to Ellis and Clover go and coax Vanity from her hiding place in the forest and deliver her to the Machine. He, of course, had deactivated the bombs in their bodies for the task—he would with Vanity's, too, once they'd informed him of her collection, though they seemed to have forgotten to. Poor girl.

It was all a test, the last test.

Wren had, of course, expected them to find her and then run away—not that there was anywhere to run to; they'd be naturally repelled from the City metropolis, and the Pockmarked Island was the only other green spot they didn't have to swim across an ocean to reach. And the hopeful part of Wren had been vindicated.

They'd come to the Machine and placed dear, dirty Vanity within. They'd come to complete their coven.

They hadn't been able to help themselves.

Now Wren took out the remote he always kept on his person and selected the button that rearmed the bombs in Clover's leg and Ellis's neck. Another selection would cause them to go off, just in case they woke up on the way to the Sanatorium and decided to cause a fuss—Vanity would have to be gifted a new implant upon arrival—though that was highly unlikely with the high quality of the gas, as well as Wren's security prodding their mouths with pills, moving their jaws and throats for them for proper consumption. They would sleep deeply.

And wake to a new world.

It was hard not to reach out, as they were dragged past, loaded up into the cars. Touch Clover's gorgeous hand, the tip of Ellis's shoulder, brush the matted hair from Vanity's eyes. How tangled the witches were now, threaded together like the nerves of a body to the meat of its limbs. To rip away would be to kill. What ecstatic and essential intimacy.

Wren had a knot in his throat he could not swallow down, and he was glad for the gas mask hiding his features.

He owed it all to them. Everything he was going to feel.

XXXVI

"**ARROGANCE, YOU'RE SCARING ME. ARE WE** just
playing pretend, or is there no other way to act? I don't know how much
of me is just pretending to be like I am. I think I need to be someone else.
Why did you cut off your ear? Why did you have to hurt yourself? To show
me what? That I'll remember this forever? That I was so horrified? That
I could cross things out? Cross things out and make them unterrifying,
make them nothing, or gold. I could almost be someone else like that,
couldn't I? Arrogance? That's your name and not mine, right?"

XXXVII

"DO YOU FEEL NERVOUS AROUND OTHER people? Do you struggle to feel at home, with other people? It is important to feel at home."

The words pushed at Vanity. They'd been from a mouth, at some point. Not now. Now they trickled down on her from a series of plastic holes bordering the television on the opposite wall. To see this, Vanity peeled back skin delicately lined with hair, allowing in light for the viscous matter nestled in her sockets to translate, to inform her, This is the place around you, and her brain responded, An unknown place a bad place.

The TV droned on, "In today's highly modern, highly populated world, it is important not to have social anxiety."

"Where is she?" Vanity murmured. She knew it was Wren sitting beside her bed. It was inherent in the beating of his heart, which pulsed in her ears.

"Where's who?"

"Ro."

Wren laughed. "Who's Ro?"

"I saw her. They saw her."

"Sh." Wren was leaning forward, his elbows balancing on his knees. "Pay attention to this. This is a moment in history."

Her eyes struggled and strained to focus on the screen in front of her. It was all so bright.

"From the company that brought you WORLD now comes a brand-new over-the-counter pharmaceutical—don't just reconnect with nature! Reconnect with one another!"

"Isn't it amazing?" Wren was saying. "We didn't want you tripping over wires and getting suspicious. It's a new invention called *batteries* that allow cameras to run without being plugged into a socket. I had them set up all over the property. Don't worry, you still had privacy in your cottages. Well, except in the kitchens. And the living rooms. It's called a *living* room for a reason, after all . . ."

Vanity's vision was gradually knitting together, the motion on the screen was becoming limbs and faces she recognized. The clips were quick and smearing and completely silent, save for the faint buzz of static and the occasional voice-over.

Clover and Ellis in their Party attire, in the Museum hall, close-ups of their smiles and their frowns, paper notes ghosting in their hands, the twisting of rings and the movements of their throats. Another girl, a close-up of her mascaraed eyes, her teeth chewing on lipsticked lips. "Don't be nervous." Fingers playing on a black ribbon. Vanity stared at her own face, the naked longing set there. "Talk to them." Then a series of other clips—Vanity opening her door for Ellis, Ellis pouring out her tea at the kitchen counter, Clover turning in her garden as Vanity trailed behind her, the tip of Clover's shoulder against the tip of Vanity's as the TV flickered in front of them, Ellis holding Vanity's hand as they moved into the forest. All recorded from awkward angles, giving the sensation of intimacy and stolen private moments. "They could love you, too."

None of the images came from the clearing, or from Vanity's bathroom. Or from the dog shed. A giggle spilled up Vanity's throat. Wren had no idea what they'd actually been doing, the resurrections, the experiment, the cure—Arrogance. Arrogance. Vanity's eyes slid around the room, half expecting her to be crouched in some dark corner, waiting to be acknowledged. Ro was always near. All Vanity's life she'd always been near. When Vanity was down Ro encouraged her, and when the world was too much Ro got her high, and when people hurt Vanity Ro didn't hesitate to hurt them, too.

"Do you want to get out of your own way?" the television intoned.

But there was no Arrogance to protect Vanity now.

"Do you want to experience young love again? Do you want to form real connections with other people?" Then came Vanity, again. Vanity, lying in the same cottony hospital bed she was currently, hair splayed out neatly on either side of her pillow. Her hands laid out on her stomach, her skin clean and her breath even. The tube that fed into her arm dripped gently. The black-and-white screen couldn't capture the emerald-colored substance the bag over her head swelled with.

"Try COVEN," the TV blared joyfully. "Harvested from real lovesick flesh witches from a real coven! Available over the counter, tested one hundred percent magic-free to avoid psychological..."

Instead of Monroe standing in front of the Museum, opening his hand to reveal a small tab nestled into his palm, it was Wren. Bold type drawing itself under him: IT IS IMPORTANT TO FORM MEANINGFUL CONNECTIONS.

Wren stood to shut off the screen. He pressed a button next to the speakers; a tape ejected with a low whir.

"It hasn't aired yet," said Wren, practically thrumming with anticipation.

Vanity's eyes went around the room again. Checking. Her voice cracked out of a dry throat. "Why am I awake?"

She had all her magic now; she knew how to do everything. And how simple everything seemed. How much she wanted to pull all those threads, to touch everything, every part of the world she could. Of course she could feel the bomb now raising a lump in her sternum, and of course she knew Wren's hand in his pocket was not a casual posture, but his finger on the trigger of the detonator. Vanity rubbed the pads of her own fingers together. She could feel what he felt, if she focused. The sensation of the rubbery button. The hairs on his head moving with the slight flow of the air conditioner. The giddy thud of his heart.

"Oh, well," Wren said, "I just wanted you to see, that's all."

"Where are they?"

"Come on, Vanity, tell me what you think. I'm dying here."

Vanity looked again at the green bag swinging above her head. Was that all her love, in there? Was that all her affection, filling up that sac? How much more until it was gone from her?

"You have it in you," said Vanity. "Coven. I can feel it. Blowing apart your synapses."

"Yes," breathed Wren. His pupils were blown. "I feel quite connected to you. Maybe that's why I woke you up. It's really very nice."

"Then you got it wrong." Vanity didn't know what chemical processes her harvested materials would undergo, what would be added and taken away as it went along on its pharmaceutical lifespan, up the conveyor belt, onto a teeny paper tab, onto a tongue. "If you really felt what it was like to love like I do, you'd feel like you were going out of your mind."

"Well," Wren said, frowning, "but that doesn't sound very pleasant."

Clover's notebook scribblings, the stopwatch, her tarot cards and all her questions. To convince Vanity it was all some grand experiment. To convince Vanity she wasn't using her as an incubator, a cauldron. Brewing apocalypse in the hollow of her throat.

Clover hadn't needed to bother with any of it. Ellis needn't have bothered with the fits and starts of alleviating his guilt—begging her to stay away, telling her they weren't good for her, that Clover was dangerous—he still kept coming to her bathtub, to the forest clearing, and he still, in the end, put her into the Machine. She knew from the start that he came to her for the next hit, not for affection. They didn't need to lie to her. Vanity would've done anything for them.

"I used to think it was all going to be so romantic." Her voice came quietly, barely there. "Did you think this was going to be a love story, too?"

"It still is, Vanity." His eyes were earnest. He really believed it.

"No," she whispered. "I wanted to love them right, I did. But I wanted them so badly that it turned into hunger." Ro was gone from her, and she was all alone. "You mistake hunger for love and you end up eating them alive."

Wren gazed at her. His expression all dreamy. Nothing she said horrified him, he understood her so. The product tangling his synapses making her all lovely, all right. But Vanity wasn't right. She was all wrong. And she was still hungry.

"They're here," she said. "I feel them. Past the walls."

"Oh, yes, well, we're going to pump all we can out of you guys before sending you back."

"Back?"

"To the Museum." Wren chuckled. "You really thought the holes were your fate? You're all still the darlings. No doubt after the commercial, too, sales will be up. Nothing sells like young love, after all. Already your Spectacle performances are booked solid for the next *two years*. Even though Father feels like wringing my neck for all of this, he still can't deny—"

"Your father is going to die." Vanity wanted to roll over and go back to sleep, but an ache had seeped through her body that warned her not to move. Instead she closed her eyes. "Everyone is going to die."

"Wow," said Wren dryly. "You really do know everything now, don't you? Though I'm pretty sure mortality is already public knowledge."

He was deeply amused with her. With all of it. Everything had gone according to plan, panned out exactly. The sorry, despicable creatures had enjoyed their moment basking in the sun, the warmth of one another.

337

Wren continued to chatter about this as he wandered closer and pressed the little button next to Vanity's bed that would send her back to sleep, chattered about reverse engineering and synthetic copies and perhaps later spin-off drugs, sequel commercials, what vast number of options were available for all of them. The Museum wouldn't show such simple, fabricated Spectacles any longer—it'd show the stuff of real life, real witches in their natural habitats and moods. It would be the era of covens. Nothing would sell like love and reality!

And as Vanity observed the cold and foreign sap feeding into her bloodstream, as his droning became fainter and fainter, she thought, Well, sure, of course, how brilliant. After all, she'd bought into that same fantasy, a romance at odds with her brain, with everything she was. She'd done anything to see it through.

"You should run," she was murmuring to Wren. "She won't be able to help herself," and Wren was laughing, again, he was asking "Who? Who are you talking about, you silly creature?" and Vanity was thinking now, well, actually, nothing was able to help itself. Things just happened as they tended to, didn't they? Life. Growth. Death. Rot. Life. Growth. Death. Rot.

🖋

Perhaps the problem was, love truly did conquer all. It had made Vanity do anything to get and keep their attention, and it had killed any compassion for herself she might have possessed.

Well, Vanity supposed she must've had compassion at some point. But maybe that wasn't right. Maybe there had only been Arrogance.

🖋

There was a hand touching her face. A hand she knew. A hand she had truly believed she'd held before. She was pressed under layers and layers of cottony sleep serum. Her body purred with it.

"Vanity."

Go away, she thought, perhaps a force of habit. Once, that would've worked.

"Dear sister, awake."

Vanity didn't have a sister. She'd only ever had herself. Alone in that stuffy house with her mother, reaching for comfort. Making it up when she found only void.

"I woke them up too, for you. I've pulled the needles out of their veins and the sleep from their heads, and they're waiting for you. . . ."

"What do you want from me?" Her own voice was nearly unrecognizable. She had no idea how long it'd been since Wren had left.

"From you. Ha. I couldn't want anything, being from you. . . ."

Vanity's eyes blinked open, revealing the world behind a hazy film.

Arrogance was there. She was sitting on the bed. But also she was blurring, she was all over the room. This was only because she was not supposed to be here. She was arcane habits made physical, a smear between life and death, growth and stillness, so perhaps it made sense that she was corporeal—since a body usually occurred between such instances—but also it didn't make sense, she didn't make sense at all.

Vanity had, apparently, never made any sense, either.

"What now?" she asked, wholly finished with all of it. "Is it done?"

"It's done. Everyone is alive. Everyone is growing. Everyone is dead, and rotting, and getting up again. . . ."

"So what now?"

"It depends. All of this is for you."

And Arrogance smiled. It was a smile on her face but also one that shone on the backs of her hands and slid against Vanity's skin, she felt it pressed in the back of her throat and the bottoms of her feet. Vanity was held perpetually, and she was so adored. Now, she realized, tears breaking in the corners of her eyes, she was not alone.

"What do you want, Vanity?"

XXXVIII

HER FEET ON THE ROAD AND her feet on flesh. Clover stumbled. The skin was dripping out from a car that had smashed into the side of the bridge. Not the first one she'd seen, not the last. Her eyes watered in the smell of it, the smell of them, whoever was driving and whoever was just along for the ride, all exploded against the interior.

Although *exploded* wasn't the right word, their flesh hadn't broken after all, after all it was still gushing out, out of the gap of the shattered windshield, sprouting limbs and fingers and ribs.

Clover waved a hand, gave a passing thought to pull a thread of the world. Clover knew how to make things go away now of course now she knew how to make things smaller and smaller. She wasn't sure if the things—she could no longer call them *people*—were dangerous, but she knew they were perhaps alive and disgusting and honestly that was enough for her. She took her bare feet off the carpet of skin before it started to bubble.

Looking down she saw the fresh lumpy scar puckering her ankle. She'd woken up in her hospital bed with the needle removed from her arm and the bomb from her leg. There was only one person who could've pulled off such an extraction. Well, two, now. Clover didn't know which one she wanted to run into less.

On one hand there was Arrogance, who had started the apocalypse.

This was clear from Clover's discovery of the lumps in the hospital. Noting the garments peeking out from the various folds like tissues out of the box, Clover diagnosed these lumps as the doctors and the nurses and everyone else who was missing—not *missing*, of course, but now indiscernible, now just flesh growing, flesh collapsing. The apocalypse was brilliant, artful, even, a pantomime of the growth of metropolis, except when they eventually crumbled and died they might feed the earth.

Was it a contagion, that Ro had placed in the air? Or had her sudden existence simply flipped a switch in all forms? Yes, this is how it would happen, Clover was certain—how it was always going to happen anyway: People would grow. Then they would die and they would rot. The problem was—something Vanity had babbled about in one of her many black spots—there was a cycle at work here. Life. Growth. Death. Rot. Life, again. Would the people who died come back?

On the other hand, there was Vanity.

Vanity, who was also missing.

Vanity, whose room Clover had passed, drawn inside because she could smell her still on those rumpled sheets, the salt of her tears, and there were a few of her long, nearly black hairs on the pillow.

Vanity, ringing through Clover's head. *Vanity Vanity Vanity.*

Clover had stumbled out of the front doors of the Sanatorium and found a new world awaiting her. She couldn't see all the way downtown, but she could picture the plushy thrall of it. Outlines blurring and merging. It was hard to say when it all began—she'd missed the initial stages, unconscious and dripping out Wren's precious harvest in her hospital bed—but it was long enough ago that the screams had stopped. For once the rush of the ocean overpowered the din of the City.

The usual weather ambled on—a low haze that was already burning out in the morning sun. The sea breeze rippled the Necropolis trees that swallowed the north side of the Pockmarked Island; the pockmarks themselves, splitting apart the land behind the Sanatorium building, gaped with an aura of deathly stillness. Clover didn't know where the other witches were, if they were still all down there in their comas, bleeding their materials into IV bags that would never be changed, that would eventually pop. Clover could only hope the ones who weren't dead yet would be soon. Nature didn't need any more witches. Nature had won.

This was what Clover had wanted.

No no no that wasn't right. Clover had wanted to be free. The two had just happened to be one and the same, making the coven and destroying the Museum—it had been all Clover's plan. Hadn't it been? She'd always had it all under her control, and it had been her idea the entire time, no other outside influence, no other force whispering in her blood, no subconscious thought patterns, all her head was her own head the entire time, she was the clear one, the clearest out of all of them. The flesh spilled all over the bridge and the cold breeze snapping at her hospital gown and her head full of magic and her self, all alone, bare feet scraping asphalt, blissfully, distinctly alone, it had all been her plan, it was all because of her, it was all her fault.

Clover hiccupped, wrapping her arms around herself, looking around as she shivered. There were tears on her cheeks, but they were nonsensical, so she ignored them. New world! New world! What would she do with herself now? Clover could do anything she liked. She'd had plans, of course, but what were they? Where was she going? Across the bridge, currently, certainly. The Museum hill coming to loom above her head, and the City rising on her right. She had to go to the house, of course, pack her things. Then she would walk down to the docks and steal a boat. Then Clover would go away. That's what she'd wanted, right? To go away?

She stopped at the center of the bridge, turning in a slow circle. "Ellis?" she called into the blankness. "Vanity?" Rubbing at the wetness on her cheeks. Rubbing harder, but it wouldn't stop. Her voice came louder now, more frantic. "Ellis? Vanity?"

Why was she calling their names? Clover didn't care about them, she couldn't. She had to save herself. She had to save her own mind, and they weren't good for it. Didn't she know that? So why was she still screaming their names? Why was her heart beating so fast she tasted blood in her mouth? *Stop it right now, you don't mean it. It's not you. It's not you. Something else in your head. You didn't mean it. You didn't mean any of it—* "Stop it. Shut up! I did! I did—" Because hadn't she? Please? Didn't she?

🪶

Opening her front door, letting in a slice of gray light across the carpets. It had begun to rain at some point, Clover could tell because she was dripping wet.

The house was dark, save for a staticky flicker emitting from the living room. The television screen. Perhaps there had been an emergency broadcast, at some point. Or perhaps no one had gotten the chance to send one out.

Clover almost opened her mouth and did it. Almost called, "Mom?" But Lavender was dead. Clover had taken her life, and she wasn't even sure where the body had gone. Maybe Clover had unknowingly passed it in the Sanatorium, tidily butchered and properly stored in shiny jars, awaiting for transport back to the Museum for auctioning.

She made for the second floor. To get her things—because obviously she had so many physical possessions she was viciously attached to. To leave all of this behind—because clearly she knew exactly where to go.

Well. Maybe she'd just drink a lot and draw a bath, then.

"You knew."

Clover froze.

The voice had come from the living room.

From her position on the stairs, slowly, slowly looking over her shoulder, the mirror wall was visible through the living room doorway. There, standing in front of the television—the shadowed, still form of a girl. The twitching light of the screen cutting over the sides of her face, pretending to fray the skin. Her mouth moving again, and it was impossible to tell if there was a smile there, or a frown, or nothing at all, or more than there should be. Another teeming. Another girl, trying to crawl out.

"You knew I made her up in my head." Vanity's voice carried with an unearthly calm. She was really quite quiet. "I guess I made you up, too."

Clover's laughter rose, a scattering of notes. "I'm real." She didn't understand. Didn't understand why she was moving. Leaning her weight against the doorway. "I'm real."

It took everything to pull her eyes off the reflection, to look at the real thing. Distorted light clawed Vanity's edges. Now a full-blown witch, Vanity hummed with power. But she'd always done that. Shouldn't Clover be humming, too? Shouldn't she not be so terrified?

"We belong here, in places like this," Clover said. "They were right to keep us locked up."

"It worked for a while. Until me. Until you." Vanity's head tilted. Clover couldn't tell if her eyes were focused on her, or if they still resided in their usual haze. She'd hardly known Vanity when Vanity wasn't out of it. That had been perfect. Clover had needed her like that. "Is it everything like you pictured?"

A tightness cracked through Clover's chest, and impossibly, she was letting the words out of her mouth. "I didn't think it'd hurt so much."

"She asked me what I wanted. Ro." The line of her shoulders hitched—a sob? A laugh? "I've never wanted anything except the two of you. You, with your notes and your stopwatch and your experiment. But I would've done anything you asked."

"And didn't you ever think that was strange? We never deserved it. We only ever treated you badly, Vanity." Clover said it savagely, as if she was disgusted with all of it. She was. Vanity had never told her to stop.

She'd only clung to them and told them to keep going. Clover had been the worst person and still Vanity had hovered, Vanity had smiled, and what was Clover supposed to do with that? When you gave someone your worst possible self, and they still smiled at you *like that*, how were you supposed to feel?

"Oh, I don't know. It was fun, sometimes." The slice of a smile split Clover open, bled her out and made her cold. "Getting as bad as I could get."

"So," Clover managed. "What happens now?"

"Well, nothing's changed. I still can't get you off my mind." She was definitely laughing. It was definitely sending Clover's head spinning. "I guess it is strange. I know it might not all be me. I don't know how to separate the part of me that's me and the part of me that's something else. But I don't know how else to live. I don't know who I am when I'm feeling okay. I don't think I want to feel okay. I just. Want to feel like it again."

"Feel like what?"

"Alive." Vanity shrugged. Tears pooled in her eyes and trickled down her cheeks. She hugged her arms around herself, and that gesture was stabbing Clover in the chest over and over again, it was killing her.

"She asked me what I wanted. And I guess all I wanted was for it to be a love story. At least for it to seem like one." Vanity's head turned. "At least for a little while."

She was looking over her shoulder. Something in the gesture tugged at something loose in Clover, sent her last sense of grounding skittering away from her. Her vision twisted, and then things seemed to double. The room stretched, filled with twice the couches, twice the flickering televisions, twice the flowers papering the wall, twice the girls. No, no, it wasn't right, remember that wasn't right, this was right: Clover was clinging to the doorway, and her chin had turned toward the mirror, and there was someone standing behind Vanity.

Static murmured through Clover's head as Vanity whispered to Ro, "Let's try it again."

Over the next year, Clover would look back at what happened next multiple, deeply excruciating times, and solely because Ellis begged her to tell him. *Vanity died* didn't suffice; neither did the insistence that it was impossible to describe, and neither did the subsequent screaming: *She's dead, okay, Ellis, and she's not coming back*—because, of course, Clover knew that Vanity was in fact coming back. She'd known that entire year, watching Ellis drive himself nuts. Vanity was going to come back because they weren't allowed off this merry-go-round, they weren't allowed to be done. There would always be nature. There would always be the coven.

But really what happened next was so simple that it took Clover a beat to realize what had happened. Vanity collapsed. Her painless and instant death rocked through the air, through Clover, and collapsed her too. And as Clover's head knocked the doorway Ro was dragging Vanity past her, over her legs, and Clover's fingers combed through Vanity's hair. So soft. And then completely gone.

Later Clover would pretend this was an attempt to save Vanity. Yet another lie. It was Clover that Vanity was being saved from.

Then through the open front door she watched as Ro walked into the earth. The ground didn't open up for her so much as reach for her and cradle her; Clover saw Vanity's feet arch and lift from the ground and then she saw nothing at all.

Grass drifting in the breeze. The world was quiet, and empty.

Just like Clover wanted. All according to plan.

Just her, gripping her head and screaming.

It was such a waste of time, so it was fine. There was nothing to do but waste time.

HE KNOWS VANITY CAN'T BE JUDGED, chattering to people who aren't there. Because Ellis is chattering to Vanity, who is no longer here. She's broken her neck. Her body is all tangled up in her seat belt.

"—have to go." His own words knitting back together amid the ringing in his ears. He is crouched outside, grabbing at Vanity's shoulders through the small space of the window, its frame crushed from the point the car had turned over. Slanted cliffside under his feet, his head all fucked up. Blood drips into his eyes. The seat belt snaps. Ellis pulls most of Vanity's body out, then, but her ankle catches on something he can't see. And then a laugh he shouldn't be able to hear over the jackhammering of his heartbeat crests above them.

Ellis looks over his shoulder.

At the top of the cliff, framed by the two frayed ends of the torn railing, stands Clover.

He can see no whites of her eyes, only black. The air wavers around her, and the metal of the railing puckers and hisses, rust singeing, curling them away from her form.

Her voice floats down, airy and harrowing. Ellis watches one of her hands lift, twist through the air. "Things turning over..."

"God damn it, Clover! Snap out of it!"

Clover is coming slow down the hill, taking her time, murmuring to herself. He can't get Vanity free. If he had a knife and a little more time, he would hack off her foot, no problem. But Ellis has no knife. And now Clover is leaning over him. The ground and oil around her feet bubbling. Delirious—when is he ever not delirious—Ellis wonders at what point she'd taken off her shoes. He settles himself fully on his knees, Vanity half draped across his lap. Tilting his head back. It had been like this before, with the two of them and Clover, some pantomimed version of this, them staring up at her.

"Hey. Hey, Clover. Don't bring us back." Ellis tries to look her in the eyes, those dark pits, and she does not flinch away. "Don't. Just let us go. Let's be done."

"We can't be done." Words tumbling from her mouth. A flame spilling out from some realm known only to her, into the palm of her hand, its light filling up the black of her eyes. She is monstrous. At the same time, she doesn't look like anyone else. Same old Clover, about to wipe them off the face of the earth. What else could she be expected to do? "It's not in our nature."

⚡

All the death, making the air all sticky. Uncomfortable. Clover swallows, trying to clear her dry throat. When she grits her teeth, she finds Ellis and Vanity had worked their way there, too.

Really, she thinks, having collected what there was to collect and making her way back up the incline, cradling their dust in each palm of her hands, really, killing them hadn't been *that* ludicrous a whim. Yes, she should just tell them the truth, what was really going through her head, as much as she could remember.

Remember—it was all almost over, anyway. Of course I'd want to save you from that. We can try again in the next life. Controlled burn, things growing back fresher, stronger. Things turning over. I just wanted to make you safe. God damn it, aren't you sick of all of it? I'm tired of the highs. Tired of being wired like this. Tired of this cycle. Aren't you just exhausted? Let's just stop, okay. It'll feel better when we're not feeling anything anymore. You'll see. I'll drive you over the side of the cliff and you'll see.

Now, of course, because Clover is alive, and Vanity and Ellis are not alive, and have no heads, it's—Now I just want them back.

Clover climbs back into her car; she hadn't even closed the driver's door. This pleases her, because she is holding Vanity in one hand and Ellis in the other and it would've been awkward to maneuver that. Once she is settled in, she pours them out into the cupholders. Sorry, she considers saying, but doesn't. There is just ash, in the car, with her, and she is saner than Ellis and Vanity, always has been. Too sane to talk to people who aren't there. She buckles her seat belt. Safety first.

She starts the car. Feels the chemical reactions kick up in the engine crouched just past the bend of her knees, pantomiming signs of life. "I'm alive," she says, annoyed. She puts her foot to the gas.

Some might say that Ellis and Clover lost it a little after Ro killed Vanity. Him of a broken heart, or so he believed. But none of them actually possessed such metaphorical-metaphysical-whatever "heart," true enough to be broken. Clover had known the actuality of what they were experiencing: withdrawal. She had underestimated how it would feel, being cut off from Vanity's proximity, from her magic snapped out of the air. She'd glued herself to Ellis's side for months afterward, which she found embarrassing, but she wouldn't have survived otherwise. The lack of Vanity would kill her, she'd been sure of it. Time passed. It cauterized all wounds. In retrospect, she is sure, it hadn't been that big of a deal. Eventually she was able to leave Ellis without feeling like it was the end of the world, like her stomach had been lifted out of her torso. Ellis tutted at her. He suggested she was in mourning, the ridiculous boy. Mourning and withdrawal were interchangeable.

※

She stands at the edge of the gaping maw of the earth, her friends in her hands.

Clover is noting the off things. It's important to know what is off and what remains normal, that way she can... The color of the sky over the Island, for one, is off, blue and purple and silver like a cyanotic patient. And Clover herself, a little bit off, she is swaying on her feet—does she usually do that? Something is missing. No, someones. "Where are they, Ro?" Clover calls down, or. It is more like she shrieks. She sounds thrilled.

All the other witches in all the other cells, shoved down around them in the cold flesh of the earth, they had all gone missing. Clover has noted the claw marks on the cells' concrete sides, the footsteps dragged through the dead grass. Gray flesh stamped into the prints.

Clover's vision is swirling from being on the Pockmarked Island, and she's given up following the direction of the footprints. Or, at least, she's forgotten that's what she'd been trying to do. Now she wavers on the edge of Arrogance's cell. "Don't answer that. Wait, wait. I can figure this out," she snaps down to Ro. Clover is so brilliant; Vanity was always saying that.

Missing bodies. And the ones peppering the ground past the gates, standing still. Waiting. Waiting like Clover had been waiting around for Vanity to come back. And now that she is back—what?

Well, what is it always?

"Did I get it right, Arrogance? Ro? Did you hear me?" She breathes in a rattling breath, strained with laughter. "It's always about the coven, right?" She can't tell if the tears on her cheeks are from sheer exhaustion or ecstasy. Either way, it is delirium. It all feels so absolutely perfect. "There's always going to be a coven."

Does Ro look off? Or has she always looked like that? She is attached halfway up the throat of her cell, her smile split up to her earlobes. Has she always had that many teeth? Were they always that glossy, obsidian black? Ro has four arms. Maybe more—it is hard to count, they seem to blur as they twitch. The bottom sets spilling out from her torso, the points of emergence shining with erupted, puffed flesh, a smattering of fragmented rib bones.

Clover squints.

The length of Ro's hair, *that* certainly isn't normal. Or is it the color? It seems that it hangs quite long and glittering and youthful until Ro spasms or Clover blinks or the light shifts overhead, and then it changes. Now it is reedy and silver and thinning—no, glinting, healthy—no—is she aging or losing age? Wait, wait, wait. It doesn't matter. Stop wondering about it. Clover has come here for one thing. But she can't stop wondering, wondering about everything. She is such a curious, restless creature. Is Ro clinging or is she secreting something that allows her to stay stuck to the side of the cell, like glue? Her skin is waxy, keeps peeling off her face and arms and legs in strips, congealing when it slicks against the concrete. The exposed, raw bits healing, lifting, healing, lifting. She is a cosmos of movement. The air around her wavering, as if struck with heat. Clover is mesmerized. How long has she been standing here? What did she mean to ask?

It will all be over soon, and then everyone will be gone, and the world will be quiet and still.

Until the next time.

Ro will restart the cycle eventually. They must behave naturally, after all.

But who knows. Maybe they'll be free eventually. Maybe their magic will smear them, change them like it had done to Ro. They won't be all that human, but they're already a step over from humanity to begin with. They'll find some wall or valley or cave to stick to and not have to move, not think of moving. They'll stop talking to each other, at least out loud; there will be no need. They'll know what the others are thinking by how the clouds shift, how well the seasons settle. They'll speak this way for centuries, until they forget language, until they are completely natural like that. And maybe someday people will come back. Drifting in from across the sea. Won't know they're treading upon sacred ground. They'll find the witches petrified, morbid, permanent fixtures of the land. They'll call them gods, or arcane horrors. They won't be wrong.

Oh, god, oh, god. The images reel through Clover's mind. It will all become true. Oh, god, it all scares the shit out of her. They are better as dust. They are better locked up, shoved down into the ground. But, oh, how beautiful they are. Much too lovely to leave out of the light. Never a pity, when the vain ones drive themselves mad.

"I won't let you have them," Clover says. She cradles her palms to her chest, their ashes coating the front of her shirt. "We won't become like you."

Ro shudders. And, when she opens her mouth, small human forms seem to spill out of the corners of her mouth. Tumbling over each other into the open light, liquid.

What is Ro saying?

Difficult to tell, words muffled by bodies, or perhaps it is only a fault of Clover's ears, ringing, ringing.

Distantly, she notices she has fallen down on the grass. She'd tried to turn and flee, and had failed.

Will she find Ellis and Vanity on the other side?

No, no. Probably not.

It was only Vanity who could open one strange eye in all that darkness, who could pick them out of the black. What will she find, of Clover? What of Clover is so genuine and essential that it exists on the other side? She struggles to think. The grass is against her nostrils. It tickles. She laughs.

The ground slides under her; her body is moving on its own.

What of her would carry over . . . ?

Vanity had been wrong about her. So wrong about her, the ridiculous, fantastical girl, rendered shocked and dazed by her own romanticiza- tions. Answer the question, god damn it. What would carry over? What would Vanity feel of her, in all that oblivion? Clover is delirious with the question. Almost always delirious, upon every question that has ever drifted through her head. The part of Clover that is her body, that con- tains her human fear, is screaming for her attention.

This is because Ro has crawled partially out of the hole, limbs clat- tering over the edge. She has bitten down on Clover's ankle. This has partially severed Clover's foot. When Ro begins to skitter back it severs completely. Clover does nothing with her brief freedom. She is still trying to answer the question. Everything hurts so much. Stop thinking about it. Stop dwelling. Focus. What the fuck are you going to carry over? What the fuck did you do? Answer. The. Question.

But all that floats up into her mind's eye is a single image: Vanity.

"I just didn't want to be like this," Clover mumbles to her. Vanity has to know. "I was so scared of being like this."

Do magic and help me, her body shrieks, but no. Clover will not. Ro creeps forward once more, approaching with loping, swishing movements on six or eight or ten limbs. Teeth close over what broken mess remains of Clover's ankle.

Clover cannot unclench her hands to grab on to something, even as she is dragged back. She is holding the only other people who could understand. She will not let them go.

VI

RISE

"DO YOU KNOW HOW TO START an apocalypse?" Vanity asked as she stood in front of the bathroom mirror. She smiled to herself and said, "Yes, of course. Would you like me to tell you? You have a coven. They come to you to die. When they die you eat their deaths. You take it from their throats and you eat and you eat until it grows something inside of you. And when you're back they feed you, too. Be feeding. Be fed. Doesn't that feel like love, to you? What do they feed me? Why, are you going to tell them? I think I should. Why? Because I'm supposed to, aren't I? Isn't it supposed to happen like this? That's right. That's so good, Vanity, that's exactly right. Not even death can stop what's coming. Should I tell them that, too? Oh, if you remember. But we don't want to scare them too much, do we? I guess we don't. Well, wonderful, then. Then, here you go. You feed on them, and they feed you someone else."

VANITY, CHATTERING TO HERSELF and looking at her shoes. Ellis held a lock of her hair as she talked, trying to talk over the barking dogs, they were so loud and it pounded in her temples. They were upset, so upset. Vanity felt bad for them. Vanity hadn't been upset for a while now, but she remembered what it was like.

The image that should be, by all counts, singed into the forefront of Vanity's mind—after all, it had happened over and over again, and it would continue to happen, over and over and over again—of Clover emerging from the dog shed, covered in blood. Wren behind her, lying down, always with the glassy eyes, always on his back with his shirt unbuttoned, his chest ripped open. After, Vanity would simply push the blood back where it was supposed to be, out of clothes and out of skin and out of her teeth, and everything would be perfectly clean. Clover's expression was steely with her focus, but then it'd melt, when she saw Vanity, smiling at her, coaxing her. A heart weighing down her hand.

Here, Vanity.

This is for you.

Ellis would let go of her hair. Vanity would reach, and Clover would jerk her hand away. Nodding behind her. Him first, Vanity.

So Vanity would bring Wren back, bring him back whole, and then Clover would give her his heart, which was really Clover's own heart, if Vanity thought about it. Or didn't think about it. If she just made it up, but really, how much was she making up? All she was doing was taking the image at face value, because shouldn't she, because shouldn't she not miss the beauty of this moment, a daydream made flesh, Clover smiling, handing her heart over, still steaming, still beating, Vanity swore sometimes, pulsing against her teeth and her tongue before she bit down and it relaxed, before she ate it whole. And Clover looked so excited. Oh, god, that look on her face.

The memory never stuck around. Or, at least, it never got the chance to.

"Vanity and Wren, they won't remember?" Clover asked. She only bothered to the first time.

"No," said Ellis. "They won't."

"Well, that's good. It's only for this I want to be absolutely sure she doesn't. Just with all her things about eating. She wouldn't be able to cope if—you know. Okay." Clover was going down her list. Vanity knew that look on her face, when she was checking things off, nodding and nodding with her regulated giddiness at being so efficient, while Vanity wiped at her mouth with the back of her hand, panting in the deaths, all those deaths. And her throat twitching. And her voice asking. And Clover kneeling in front of her. Saying, Open wide. Okay. Not quite.

WREN IS WATCHING THE GREAT MASS come up the hill.

He'd been in Clover's house, he'd been going through her things. It'd been perfect timing really, finding the little baggie of Coven taped to the fridge, tab on his tongue good and dissolved by the time he opened up the front door to see it arrive.

It'd been so lovely of Clover to find the samples in the Sanatorium, to ration Coven over the course of this year for him. He should've thought from the get-go that love would be so addictive. Wren needn't feel so guilty about going into her house—his possessing guilt at all being proof the drug was working quite potently as always—and besides, Clover wasn't coming back, none of them were, he'd known that from the moment he'd seen their cars rush away.

God, did Wren miss them so harshly, and how miserably he staggered out onto the front stoop, wiping the tears from his eyes, so terrible it was, being so alone in the world now, and—oh. His tears came quicker now, out of relief. Thank god. Thank god. There was a mass.

A gorgeous, unspeakable mass, a body made of bodies and stacking several stories tall, crushing the front gates, muffling the groan of its iron under thousands and thousands of pounds of flesh. Wren hiccups over his elation, wiping his eyes, and past the veil of tears the sunlight sharpens, burns white and glorious through the cloudscape. Practically crashing through the white picket fence, nearly breaking his ankles tripping past the scatter of Ellis's dugouts, he sprints up the hill. He's gasping for air, for his own life, his wonderful, unbelievable life, to still be alive like this to witness it all, them all, everybody, every single person the world had to offer, coming up from the City and the Sanatorium and across the oceans, all of them coming here, arriving to stay, to stay with him forever.

SO: TO BE COMPLETELY honest now—might as well—Vanity hadn't been entirely truthful with them. It hadn't been just her normal self-deprecation, when she told herself all this was all her fault. Of course Ro knew—of course Vanity knew, deep, deep down—how to take the ankle bomb out, how to ease open the skin there so it barely hurt, or maybe Vanity had grown used to it at some point, its slick extraction. It was good for Ro to go and blow off some steam. Vanity wanted to say she'd trailed along—through the gap under the electric fence some animal had dug out and onto the road feeding toward the City—to keep an eye on Ro.

But honestly. Vanity was just along for the ride.

Shrugging. Leaning forward and taking whatever was offered to her at whatever club they were at. The lights and the bodies pulsing around them. Because the only time she didn't think about them, the only time she had her brain to herself, was when she was high. And so—blotting away the nights. Ro always got her home okay, anyway, waking up in her bed with her mouth dry and her headache pounding, but what was there to do in the day anyway but lie around in the dark of her room and wait for the tourists to disperse?

And so she could've asked Ro to take Ellis's and Clover's bombs out and shown them the gap in the fence and saved them from the beginning, but. If she did that? What then? Where would they go?

What if it was away from her?

YOU'RE A LIAR. I'M A LIAR.

You didn't want a fresh start, you never did. You never wanted anything but to come apart.

Oh, but, my love, you could never not be remaining.

So. How was it?

Was it everything you wanted?

What do you want, now that you know all of it?

I brought you something, it's here now, waiting for you. I hope it helps. I hope it doesn't hurt this time.

Vanity?

Ah, well.

Death has never stuck to you before....

RO—IF YOU COULD CALL HER RO, anymore, if you could call her anything at all, manage to open your mouth and describe her as something other than *something, something else*—is grafted to the ceiling. Limbs spread wide, her flesh churning in the crystals of the chandeliers; they chime slightly as she breathes.

Ro is growing. Growing all over the room. Either her body stretches or she has many, many bodies, fused together, many eyes that blink and many heads that roll and smile and age and rot, and sink upward into their necks, only to emerge again, fresh. . . . Well. It is difficult to tell, always, what Vanity is making up.

"They were waiting for you to come back."

Vanity's eyes, still blinking back her death, slide from looking above over to Wren. She is lying on the floor of the Museum's ballroom and he is hovering by the big west-facing window. Tugging and tugging at the curtains, rings fixed on the rod above his head to remain tastefully closed—concealing the glittering reach of the City skyline. Why look over there, anyway, when here is horrifying nature dressed in satin and silk, where it has a mouth that can smile at you and arms you can stroke, and you can look it in the eye and pretend it's just a girl, just fine, unterrifying. . . .

Vanity puts her hands on her stomach, and, knowing she'd been dust, before, breathes.

On either side of her, blinking awake—Ellis and Clover. Rousing. Fresh-eyed with their fresh deaths.

"What's happening?" Clover murmurs, pushing herself upright. Perhaps for the first time Vanity sees her clearly then. The dark patches under her hazel eyes, her patchy, shaved head, coated in dirt. The metal punched unevenly into her face, the sickly, wobbling tattoos. Ellis isn't that far off, blinking and blinking, tongue moving over his cracked, pierced mouth. This is who they are, without Vanity. Grasping, gasping for clarity.

They need her. Curling around her now, murmuring, "Vanity? Vanity . . ."

Vanity isn't sure what she needs.

She doesn't know how many years they've been dead. Wren is older, his hair graying, his face tilled with lines. Spots on the backs of his hands, those hands soft and veined. He looks so much like Monroe now. "Vanity, did you hear me?" he calls. He sounds nearly in hysterics. She can feel the longing thrumming through his body; wholly familiar to her is the clutch of need tightening his chest. "They were waiting for you!"

"Who, Wren?" Vanity murmurs, ignoring the unquiet flocking of the others.

"Everybody!" Wren screams, and finally the curtain rod breaks and falls, and the world comes in whole.

There is no sky. Past the glass—faces, and teeth, and hands, rippling skin and shadows of teeming bone. And Vanity knows it is everywhere, this amalgamation, crested over the entirety of the Museum, the hill, the road licking down to the City. She knows it is growing and will keep growing. Knows that Ro has kept them dead long enough to wait for all of them to arrive, from all over the world, that death has purged the magic from her head so that she can see everything for what it truly is— horrifying, and here for her.

She is on her knees now, wiping at her cheeks with the back of her hands. She cannot seem to stop crying.

"Vanity," says Ellis. "Stand up, we need to—"

"Need to what?" She laughs, startling him. *"Leave?"*

"Yes!" he insists. "Yes yes yes *leave*—"

Vanity looks past him. Clover is on her feet, glancing around the ballroom with frantic eyes. The teeming past the window does not faze her; she is only pale from whatever her attention has caught on at the back of the room. She shakes her head once, like she refuses to believe what she is seeing.

Vanity looks back. But it is not the Machine—its solemn lines still marked with her own blood, blackened, older than she is—that her focus lands on.

Ro is there. Beside it. Leaning her singular body against its cold granite.

Her hair spills as wildly as it does in Vanity's memory. Her fingernails curling, those fine, long hands cradling the Machine's edges. Heart-shaped face cut with the sharpest of smiles. Vanity always thought she was so beautiful.

Does Vanity really look like that?

She wipes the tears tracing her cheeks, hiccupping. And begins to move forward.

"Vanity," Clover says. "Stop."

What is Ro, really? Or, at least, what was she, before? Vanity's body healing itself over and over again. Forgiving her, for all the horribleness

367

she'd hosted in it, willingly, extravagantly, for all the hate she'd held for it. Over and over and over again.

"Ellis," Clover snaps. "Tell her to stop."

"Stop, Vanity," Ellis says, and his command slides past her. It is nothing. It doesn't matter. Ro's hands are already over Vanity's ears. Warm and more familiar than anything else in the world.

"I hurt you," Vanity whispers, grasping her wrists, her arms. The striations of scars, the patterned, lacy damage. "I'm sorry. I'm so sorry."

Ro isn't holding her; Vanity is holding herself. The person she sees before her is her. She is kneeling in front of the Machine; she'd opened it, she is peering within. Head bowed over the mirror pieces. Watching her own pretty lips move, forming words, murmuring . . .

She'd loved that, once, so *much*, talking to herself. . . .

But suddenly all her best words were reserved for other people and all her worst ones she cracked with her back teeth and swallowed and misunderstood that she was eating herself alive. You're nothing like I wanted you to be. You are not enough for the people you love. And I am going to hurt you for it.

"At the end, we circle around again. . . . What do you think will come out, now that you have lonely parts, too . . ." Her own words bleeding in and out of her ears, and they weren't hateful things, no, they were such pretty things. Clover has come up behind her now, Ellis slinking at her heels on hands and knees, her loyal dog. "Why didn't you ever go back?" murmurs Vanity without turning. "Yes, I'm talking to you. Why didn't you ever return to the Machine? Have it take everything back."

"We couldn't." Clover speaking, of course.

"Why not?" Vanity has always been, after all, so interested in hearing what Clover has to say. All of her brilliant thoughts.

And Clover explodes. "Because we can't take it back! We're supposed to be like this. We have magic and the coven and everything else is performance. It isn't fucking *real*. Our minds, shot. Our cultures fabricated—" Her voice comes quicker and quicker. "Our faces manufactured, our histories unraveled, our lives—*repeated*. Repeating. Always repeating. If we go in the Machine, how long could we stand it, before we return to it, wanting? No. I won't go back. We're this, or we're nothing."

"Stand still, then," says Vanity.

Clover quiets. Her eyes slide slowly off of Vanity, past Ellis, silent and kneeling at Clover's feet, and over to the opened window. Over to where everyone is. Cracking the glass now, delicately patterned destruction.

"We were dead for a long time, this time. It hasn't cleared your head?" says Vanity. Gesturing to the Machine. Which was to gesture to herself. "Can't you see? There's only room for one."

Clover looks at her hatefully.

"It isn't the altar of the world," Vanity says, so softly. "We are."

"So what?"

"So. You should've been kinder."

"Oh, yes, Vanity, because we are meant to be so *kind*! Hm, Ellis? Is that true? Are we capable of that?" Clover grabs the back of Ellis's shirt collar, shakes him. He lets her, but doesn't look at her. He's looking at Vanity.

"That night you buried us," he rasps. "Why did you dig us back up?"

Vanity looks at the boy and the girl she has loved over multiple lifetimes, and she shrugs.

"Oh, I don't know," she says. "I should have left you for the worms."

Clover barks a cold laugh at that. "You think anyone will look back on this and look at you *kindly*? Do you really seek *pity*? You're not such a sympathetic creature."

Vanity knows that.

They've all done egregious wrongs to each other, to themselves. Yet Ellis tugs on Clover's dirty sleeves and Clover does not pull away. And Vanity does not pull at their strings and hurt them as bad as she possibly can.

"Why did *you* bring us back, Clover?" asks Vanity.

"Because I was out of my mind."

"And now?"

"Now *what*, Vanity? Now! Years later, you mean? What does time matter, to a coven? It doesn't. It doesn't! How could we expect to be different, now? *Ever?*"

"It's different because I remember."

Tears instantly break in Ellis's eyes. They mean nothing to her. "Vanity—"

"Remember *what?*" Clover demands.

Vanity's eyes drift back to the ceiling. Where Ro hangs again, grafted, ever changing. Smiling at her? Perhaps . . .

"I was always wondering where I drew the line, with you both. At what point I would have enough, and I would leave. Now I know." They are altars of the world. Nature's coven. Vanity says, her throat host to apocalypse after apocalypse, "You made me fucking eat him."

Ellis covers his face with his hands. "I didn't mean to. I told you to run."

Clover's eyes burn. "Oh, you liked it. You never ran away."

Over by the window, Wren gives a sharp, elated sob. The glass rises, now completely frosted with fractures. Wren spins around, stumbles once, and moves toward the three of them. Always moving toward them. Seeking salvation.

"Please, please, don't cry," he gasps at them as the window gives. "All of this is for you!"

The flesh comes rushing in.

Across floorboards and up the walls. Consuming art. A wave of conjoined forms running on legs or crawling or dragging themselves forward. Vanity knows it is all reaching for her like she'd wanted them to reach for her, to need her, not for what she had to offer but for anything else. She laughs, at Clover, at Ellis, at everyone. "I hope you got it," she says, turning away from all of it, her hands bracing again on the Machine. "The apocalypse you wanted from me. I hope it was everything you sowed."

"Please, please, Vanity," Ellis says.

"Don't go," Clover says, furiously.

Vanity tips her head back, tears sliding down her cheeks. There she is, too, far above. And, oh. She looks so happy.

The others have crowded in now, rising from the floor, dripping from the walls. Great sheaths of flesh beginning to pull at Clover and Ellis and Wren's clothes with fingers and with teeth, tearing at them. They are still. They are waiting for her.

Vanity can feel all their warmth, vicious and certain, wholly there. Real things that would look at her and think of her and be like her and exist beyond her, unruinable... Well. Some things just can't be helped.

Vanity didn't feel real unless she was in love with someone. Unless she was talking to them, thinking of them. Unless they were hurting her, needing her... yes, there was nothing like that warmth. The possibility of going up in flames.

Her fingers trace upon the cold lines of the Machine.

All her selves within, copying her movements. They don't beckon her forward or urge her away. They wait, blinking and smiling, for her to decide what she wants.

What does she want?

"Goodbye," Vanity whispers. "I'll see you later."

ACKNOWLEDGMENTS

WHEN YOU'RE A TEENAGER, every feeling feels like the end of the world. For the characters in this book, their feelings *are* the end of the world. This was very cathartic to write, and I'm glad it all exists outside of me now.

I wrote this book for the girls who are people pleasers, including the one who resides in me. You can stop that immediately and still be a kind person. I would only consider this to be a romantic book to the extent that the habits of romanticizing and daydreaming are where I drew the story's horror elements from. I always found it very scary how people can convince themselves of anything.

I would like to extend thanks to the following wonderful people for making this horrible tale possible:

To Kiva and Mira, my loves, I am always missing you.

To Ty and Mom and Dad! Especially!

To Laura, my lovely agent, for always fighting so hard for me.

To Rebecca, my ultra-talented editor. Thank you, so much, for encouraging strangeness in my plots and my prose style. To have such an advocate for my individual voice as a writer means the absolute world.

To Roundtable, for stoking my love of the craft.

To D.A.C.U.: Christina, Chloe, Tashie, and Rocky. Distance does really make the heart grow fonder, and I'm so lucky to have you guys in my corner.

To Cafe Allegro, for having the best coffee in Seattle, and for letting me loiter.

To the cover artist, Jana Heidersdorf, and the designer, Zareen Johnson, for putting together the most delicious and unsettling final form. And my immense gratitude to the entire capable team at Hyperion, the champions behind this book. Thank you so, so much.